Winter, having a gift from God
is nothing to be ashamed of.
You have the gift of prophecy,
and according to the Bible, it's one of
the greatest gifts God could give.

Winter

KEVEN NEWSOME

Winter

Keven Newsome

3ⁿᵈ Edition

ISBN: 978-0-9989596-1-0

KevenNewsome.com

PRESS EPIC

To DeAnna.
Thank you for always believing.

Do not rejoice over me, O my enemy.
Though I fall, I will rise;
Though I dwell in darkness,
the Lord is a light for me.
Micah 7:8 (NAS)

1

Present Day

The stairs wandered to the right—old wooden stairs. With the first step they groaned, and she hesitated. Small candles sat on the steps, spread out—only one every four or five steps. They oozed lifeless blood that pooled at their base and coagulated into white scabs. She broke a candle free and continued her ascent, tilting it so it bled on the planks.

Darkness pressed in from beyond the candlelight. The shadows behind taunted her by name, while the shadows above beckoned with false hope. More than once, she thought she recognized a shape—a person or animal—in the shadows, only to have the light flicker and send the phantom away. Slotted windows perforated the outer wall every few feet, staring at her with cold, lidless eyes.

She passed a rough wooden door with an iron handle. It was not her destination, so she continued. On her journey she passed many doors the same as the first. The stairs dissolved into black eternity. Her feet hurt, her knees hurt, and her heart pounded with cold dread. Each footstep echoed in the empty stairwell, answered by moans from the wooden steps. She wanted to flee—to turn and go back. But she couldn't. She must continue. Sweat leaked from her body, matting her clothes to her skin. A bitter breeze drifted through a window and she shuddered.

Finally, the endless line of candles stopped before a door just like all the others she had passed. She reached out and brushed the handle with the tips of her fingers. It felt cold. Cold radiated from the door like heat from a furnace. Evil waited beyond this door…expecting her. She could feel it, and the instinct to flee seized her stronger than ever. Every hair on her body stood rigid, and she trembled with anticipation. Her arms and legs numbed, but she knew she must enter. Here lay her destiny—her calling. She grabbed the handle, took a deep, desperate breath, and pushed.

Inside was a round room. She hesitated before entering, heart pounding. Fear grabbed her and wouldn't let go, and her knees threatened to buckle. Never had she seen such a sight.

Blood flowed down the walls like cascading waterfalls. Blood rained down from the ceiling like a summer shower. Blood pooled over every inch of the floor like glassy oil. It was as if she had stepped into the very bowels of Hell itself.

In the center stood a man. No…not a man. A demon. The grotesque black creature reached out a scaly, bony hand to her. It smiled, revealing long, pointed teeth.

"Winterrrr," it hissed, calling her by name with a roll of the final R. "Winterrrr."

"Winter."

Winter sat up and stared out the rain-streaked window of her dad's Dodge Dakota. The windshield wipers squeaked in paused intervals as Randy Travis wailed in the background. The smell of pine tree air freshener mingled with that of motor oil. Winter closed her eyes and sighed, trying to shake away the hellish nightmare.

"Winter?"

This time she turned to face her dad, forcing her expression blank. Her jet-black hair brushed against her face.

"I think we're here." He hoisted his travel coffee mug to his lips.

They turned off the interstate and passed beneath the boughs covering Hoole Boulevard. Extra-large drops of water fell from the branches, striking the windshield with small splashes.

Winter leaned her elbow on the door and watched collegiate suburbia pass by. After a few miles, the arched gateway of Tishbe University loomed before them. Winter's dad stopped at the guardhouse.

"Moving in," he told the guard.

The guard smiled and greeted them, then passed them a map of the campus before turning his attention to the next vehicle.

Winter didn't even try to follow the twists and turns of the school roads. At one point she saw a large lawn between two buildings. A few people walked along pathways crisscrossing the well-manicured grass. Some held umbrellas or wore ponchos, some just slumped beneath the weight of their backpacks. Winter took it all in during the second before they passed behind the next building.

Eventually, they found their destination—a large dorm in the shape of a U. A parking lot lay between the arms, and small grassy knolls padded the ends of each. The grassy area to the right displayed a blue plaque reading "Carmichael Hall."

"Looks nice," her dad said. Winter grunted and shifted in her seat. He pulled into the parking lot across two spaces to allow for the trailer. "All right," he said, "are you ready?"

Winter gazed back to the covered entrance for a moment, then opened the door, being sure to take her time. She wore black carpenter pants and a baggy black Jack the Pumpkin King T-shirt. The chain dangling from her belt loops jingled as she walked. She kept her arms crossed and watched the pavement between her feet.

Pounding steps on wet pavement announced someone rushing to them. Winter cut her eyes up and saw a grinning girl with hair so rain-soaked it was impossible to tell whether she was blonde or brunette.

"Hello!" the girl said. "I'm Amber. Welcome to Carmichael Hall!"

"Hi, Amber. I'm Steve Maessen. This is my daughter, Winter."

Amber grinned. Winter scowled and Amber's grin melted away.

"Follow me," said Amber, as if robbed of her most favorite thing in the world. She led them through the double doors to a spacious lobby.

There was no line at the registration table, and check-in went by in less than twenty minutes. Winter signed the check-in form and accepted the room inspection form. Her dad paid the room deposit. Though urged to smile for her ID picture, Winter crossed her arms and tried to look bored. When all was done, Amber led them to Winter's room.

On the second floor, girls scurried everywhere. Parents and luggage crowded the hall, and loud music blared from an unknown location. From the end of the long hall, sunlight filtered in through a plate glass window. Everything smelled like carpet cleaner.

They followed Amber through the confusion almost to the end of the hall and stopped in front of a door with the number 211 painted near the top. A dry-erase board hanging on the door had "Summer's room" written in frilly pink letters. Winter huffed— figured they would get her name wrong.

"If you need help, just find someone with a nametag," Amber said.

"Thank you," said Winter's dad, with a bemused smile. Winter huffed at him. He chuckled as Amber bounded away.

Winter took out her ID card and inserted it into the lock. She pulled it free and the lock clicked, flashing a little green light. She paused as she began to turn the knob and took a deep breath. Horror stories of "institution white" walls, doorless closets, and cold laminate floors echoed in her mind. But as she opened the door, Winter saw the last thing she expected.

Pink.

Pink curtains hung from the window. The walls had been painted with pink daisies and decorated with Hello Kitty posters. A dark pink rug lay on the floor. The left side of the room held two twin beds: one closer to the door, another beneath the window. The nearer one wore frilly, flowery, froofy pink bedding. The other was bare. A microwave and a small refrigerator stood between the beds, flanked on both sides by dressers. One dresser sprouted with an assortment of skin care products and a flower-shaped makeup mirror. Sliding doors in the right wall hid two closets. Nooks on either side of the closets contained built-in study desks. The nearest desk sported a pink laptop computer.

Winter drifted down the center of the room.

"NO...WAY!"

"There's no pink in here," her dad said from one of the closets.

Winter spun to face him, and instead locked eyes with a girl in the doorway. Short white shorts. Pink tank top. The girl grinned and bounced into the room.

"Are you Winter?" she asked, tossing her bright blonde hair over her shoulder.

"How do you know my name?"

"Easy. I asked at the check-in desk who my roommate was." The blonde girl stepped closer, and Winter stepped back to avoid the swirling smell of roses.

"You are my roommate?" Winter asked.

"Of course, silly! My name is Summer." She extended her hand. Winter glowered at it. "Isn't it awesome?" she continued without noticing. "Summer and Winter in the same room! What are the chances?"

"You have got to be kidding."

Her dad smirked, and Winter shot him a nasty glare.

Summer tilted her head. "Kidding? What do you mean?"

"I mean, this is some kind of joke, right? Someone found out about my name and decided to have a little fun. Is that it?"

Summer tried to laugh. "Um…no. It's not a joke."

"Then your name is really Summer?"

"Yes. My name is Summer." The smile slid from her face.

"I don't believe you." Winter's eyes narrowed. "Show me your ID."

The blonde reached into her back pocket and pulled out a maroon card. It read, "Summer Reilly" beside her grinning picture.

Satisfied, Winter looked up. Summer put the card away.

"Did you decorate the room?" Winter asked.

Summer perked up and smiled again. "Yes! Do you li—"

"Dad, I'm leaving." Winter pushed past Summer, knocking her onto the bed, and stormed out of the room. She didn't slow until she reached the check-in table.

"I need a new roommate," she said to whomever would listen. An older lady, who seemed to be leading everything, stepped forward to answer. She looked like she had been carved from stone.

"That's something you'll have to talk to your RA about," she said.

"My what?"

"Your Resident Assistant—an upperclassman who supervises your floor. But regardless, you won't be allowed to change roommates for two weeks. I'm sorry."

"Two weeks?" Winter slammed her palms onto the table.

"That's the policy," said the lady. "Would you mind telling me the problem?"

"Yeah." Winter gestured to the stairs with her arm. "She decorated the room pink! Do I look like I like pink?" Winter tugged at her black T-shirt. "And she's…she's…BLONDE. And to top it all off she thinks it's 'awesome' that her name is Summer and mine is

Winter and that we're in the same room."

The lady grinned. "That is rather unusual," she said. "But I do have one suggestion for you."

"Great."

"Get to know her a little bit, and you might come to like her. If you still want to move after two weeks, then talk to your RA."

Winter's face burned. Her pulse raced and her arms twitched from the lack of a violent outlet. She spun and stalked outside, not knowing exactly where to go or what to do next. She would not go back to that room.

Gentle strong hands touched her shoulder. She jumped.

"Deep breaths, sweetheart." Her dad rubbed her shoulders and back. "Remember, God's ways are not our ways."

Winter nodded. She took a deep breath and said a silent prayer. She closed her eyes and cleared her mind, allowing her heartbeat to slow. Her dad continued to massage her back. After a few quiet moments, Winter allowed herself to recognize the humor in the situation.

"Okay, Dad. I'm ready." She turned to face him. "I'll try to make it work. I won't promise I'll like it, but I'll try."

"That's good enough," he said. "Shall we unload?"

"You go ahead…I need to do something first."

"I'll meet you at the side door, then."

As he walked away, Winter hurried back to her room.

She found Summer alone, sitting on her pink bed, holding a crumpled tissue. Tears had left streaks of makeup down the side of her face. When she saw Winter come in, she looked back down at her trembling hands. Winter grabbed Summer's desk chair, rolled it to the bed, and sat in front of her roommate.

"Listen," Winter said. "I don't know you and you don't know me. I'm sorry I hurt your feelings but coming here is a big step for me and the pink room was a little too much. And I tend to overreact—it's something I'm trying to work on. I'd really like to erase what happened earlier and start over." Winter grinned to relieve tension.

"I thought all girls liked pink." Summer sniffed. "At least all my friends back home do."

"No, Summer, all girls do not like pink."

Summer chuckle-sobbed and sniffed again. "It doesn't have to be so pink. We can change it however you want."

"Oh, really?" Winter asked. "Are you sure?" She tugged her black T-shirt.

"Well," Summer said with a shy smile, "to a point."

Winter laughed and shook her head, and Summer laughed with her.

"So what do you say? Can we start over?"

Summer nodded and scooted to the edge of her bed. "And at least our names are still pretty cool. I mean, don't you think it's neat that—"

Winter interrupted her with an upheld hand. "Too far."

While her dad finished unloading the last items from the trailer, Winter made her first order of business the carefully packed box containing her pictures. She unwrapped the first five-by-seven frame and looked at it for a long time.

Summer came closer. "Who's that?"

"My mom," Winter said.

"She's pretty."

"Yeah, she is."

"You look a lot like her," Summer said. Winter just smiled. "Why didn't she come with you to move in?"

Winter placed the picture on her dresser. "She died three years ago."

2

Four Years Ago

Winter climbed off the bus, giggling at her friends. The bus pulled away while her friends yelled at her from the windows. She waved, then turned and froze. Her dad's truck sat in the drive behind her mom's car. Winter's stomach lurched at the thought of what might be waiting for her inside. Pulling her books closer to her chest, Winter hurried up the sidewalk, her long golden-brown hair hanging limply on her back.

She eased the door open and crept inside. Her mom and dad sat together in the living room but did not seem to be arguing as she expected. Winter paused with the impulse to rush back out and hide. They stopped talking when they spotted her standing in the doorway. Their faces betrayed a sadness she couldn't understand, causing the pit of her stomach to sink even further.

Her mom smiled. "Hey, Winter," she said in almost a whisper. She brushed a strand of her own golden-brown hair behind her ear. "Come have a seat, sweetheart. We need to talk."

"What's going on?" Winter asked, her voice shaky and insecure.

She retreated to the love seat, which was nearest, dropped her things on the floor and wrapped her arms around herself. Her dad glanced at her mom, who took the cue.

"There's no easy way to say this, so I'm just going to tell you as quickly as I can. You know how I've been having really bad headaches lately?"

"Yeah." Winter started to shake and twisted in her seat to hide it.

"Well, two months ago I had one so bad, I passed out at work. They took me to the hospital and gave me some tests."

"And is everything okay?" Winter asked.

Her mom took a deep breath and looked at the floor. Winter cut her eyes to her dad, but he stared out the window. When her mom lifted her face back up, Winter noticed for the first time the redness and swelling of her eyes. When she spoke, her voice wavered.

"Winter, I have...cancer."

All the warmth in the room sucked away. "What do you mean?" Her own voice sounded like a stranger's.

"They found four tumors..."

Numbness replaced the shaking, and Winter held her breath. Her mom's voice came from a long tunnel.

"...one of them is in my—in my brain."

The newly formed knot in Winter's throat almost prevented her from speaking. "Wha—what does that mean?"

"Sweetheart, the tumor in my brain is inoperable and too deep for any treatments. I could do chemo, but it wouldn't help much— just give me a little longer."

"Mom, I don't understand," Winter said. "Did you get a second opinion?"

Her mom nodded. "I did. A second and a third. The last results came in just two days ago. That's when I called your dad."

"And what did the doctors say? What's going to happen?" Her cheeks warmed with wetness. Her mom cried too...so did her dad.

"I'm going to die, Winter, in less than a year. There's nothing they can do."

Cold. Pain. "No, you can't! Why are you telling me this?"

Her mom stood and rushed across the room to sit beside Winter. Her arms wrapped around Winter and clung to her while they both wept. Winter's body shook with each and every sob.

"I don't want you to die," Winter croaked after several minutes.

Her mom stroked Winter's hair and kissed the top of her head.

"I know...I know, sweetie."

"There's got to be something we can do."

"I wish there was."

They held each other for a long while more without anyone speaking. Eventually, her dad cleared his throat, and her mom sat up and looked at him. Winter noticed the cue and straightened in panic.

"What's going on? You haven't told me everything. Why is he here?"

"I won't be able to care for you much longer." Her mom fumbled with her own fingers.

Winter crossed her arms. "What does that mean?"

"The doctors say that within a couple of months the blackouts and headaches will be so bad that I won't be able to function properly. So we've decided to go ahead and move you in with Dad. I know how important your first year of high school is, and I want you to get settled in at your dad's as soon as possible."

"What? You're sending me away?"

"I'm not sending you away, I have no choice. Believe me, I want you here as long as possible, but this is for the best."

"I don't believe this! First you tell me you're going to die, and now you're getting rid of me!"

"Winter, don't. You know I'd never get rid of you, please don't say things like that. I love you."

"No, Mom, I won't go! All my friends are here. Don't make me leave. Please..."

Her dad said, "You'll have to move in with me, anyway. There's a good school there, and this way you'll be able to make new friends sooner. I think you'll like it there. I know it's tough right now, and you don't really understand what's happening, but you'll just have to trust that we both have your best interest in mind. We're going to let you finish the week out here and then I'll come back Saturday to help you move."

"But I don't want to go, I want to stay with you, Mom! Why didn't you tell me sooner? We could have gone away...just us. Please, Mom, don't do this!"

"I didn't want you to worry if it was nothing, sweetheart. I'm sorry. I wish I had told you sooner, and we could have had one last trip together."

"We can still go away, Mom!" Winter stood and planted her feet. "I'm not leaving!"

"No we can't...it's too late. The cancer's progressed too far. I'm sorry, Winter, but I don't want you here if something bad were to happen. You'll get to come and see me during holidays and as many weekends as possible. And you can call me on the phone every day. I want to spend as much time as I have left with you." She wrapped her arms back around Winter. "It's just going to take some effort to adjust to the idea."

Winter trembled and moaned into her mom's shoulder. "But why can't I just stay with you? I don't want to move, I can help."

"Sweetheart, I'm not staying here either. I've decided to move into a home for the terminally ill where nurses can help me if something bad happens."

"Then let me come, too."

"I can't. I'd love nothing more for you to come with me, but they won't allow it."

Winter clenched her fists and her eyes. "But what about our house?"

Her dad said, "Some of the money from selling the house will be put up for you to go to college."

"You're selling my house? But I grew up here!"

"I know this is a lot to accept in one day, Winter," said her mom.

"A lot? This is the worst day of my life!" Winter's voice almost failed as she pushed away and looked into her mom's eyes. "Why do you have to die? Why is this happening to me?"

Winter embraced herself this time, but her mom pulled her in again despite Winter's resistance. Winter's sobs returned, more loudly than before, and her body shuddered with each breath.

"It's okay, sweetie, I'm ready. You may not understand now, but there's a reason for this happening. This is the way God wants it to be."

Winter shoved out of her mom's arms. Her face burned. "No, Mom! This is NOT how God wants it! How can you say that?" she screamed. "How could God do this? Just because you've been all involved in church these past couple months doesn't make you an expert! If this is what God wants, then...I HATE HIM!" She turned to her dad. "This is all your fault! If you hadn't left us then I could stay here with my friends! I hate BOTH of you!"

She stormed out of the room and slammed her bedroom door so hard, the windows shook. Then she curled up on her bed and cried herself to sleep.

3

Present Day

After a long goodbye with her dad, Winter finally came to an agreement with Summer about the decoration of their dorm room. They divided the room in half, with the centerline stretching from between the closets on the right to the micro-fridge on the left. Summer laid out the pink rug on her side and Winter her black rug on the other. As for the walls, each only decorated her own side: Summer with pink, fuzzy, Hello Kitty, and other assorted "girly" things; Winter with The Nightmare Before Christmas, U2, Gothic fairies, and otherwise dark, ominous things. The only thing Winter disliked was having to cross the "pink zone" before reaching her own sanctuary. The dry-erase board on the door now read, "Summer and Winter's room" in frilly letters.

As they put the finishing touches on the room that evening, there came a loud banging on the door. Summer opened it, and a pretty girl with dark brown hair thrust a flyer into Summer's hands. "Welcome party at the CLC at six!" Then the girl pivoted to bang on the next door.

"What did Angie want?" Winter asked, after only a quick glance up.

Summer turned. "There's a party for freshmen tonight at six. Wait…do you know her?"

"No," said Winter. She stood and took the flyer from Summer's hands.

"Then how did you—"

"Are you going or not?" she asked with more force than she intended.

Summer blinked. "Y—yes, I suppose; that is, if you go. But how did you know her name?"

Winter shrugged and studied the flyer. "I don't know, maybe I heard it somewhere. We should probably get ready." She turned away to her closet before Summer had a chance to press the matter.

Winter laid out some clothes on the bed, then went down the hall to use the bathroom. A long, spotty mirror covered the wall above the rust-stained porcelain sinks.

"Perfect."

She sighed and crossed the slick tile floor to a row of drab green stalls. The place smelled of bleach and bad perfume.

Back in her room, Winter replaced her black T-shirt with a black tank and a black knit shawl. She pulled on black gaucho pants, and a pair of three-inch platform shoes. Winter left her black hair down, framing her petite face the way she preferred. Around her neck, she hung the only color in her wardrobe—a golden locket with her name inlaid in silver across the top. She added golden studs to several of her ear piercings and one in her nose. She also threaded a small hoop through her eyebrow.

Then she applied pale powder all over her face and black lipstick. Deep purple eyeshadow made her sky-blue eyes seem darker. About halfway through touching up her black fingernail polish, she noticed Summer staring at her.

"Do you have something to say?" Winter asked.

Summer seemed to deliberate whether to answer. Finally, resolve settled behind her eyes. She sat on her bed, her makeup pretty and perfect. It made Winter sick.

"Are you…are you," then she whispered, "a Goth?" She fluffed the skirt of her pretty blue sundress and tossed the curled ends of her blonde hair over her shoulder.

Winter chuckled to herself and went back to her black nails. "Let's just say I'm sorta in Goth rehab."

4

Four Years Ago

Winter walked as quickly as she could through the crowded hall of Trenton Hills High School. Orange and blue lockers striped the hall, and the ceiling stretched high enough to expose iron joists. Judging by the old and musty smell, Winter suspected the school building was at least older than her dad. She turned down a hall with no lockers, passing a long, monotonous line of old senior class composites instead. The oldest she saw was the Class of '52—handmade with yellowed pictures curling at the edges; only twenty-five graduates or so. Winter's freshman class had 392 members, or so she had heard. She missed her old school, which had less than a quarter of that number.

Somebody slammed into her shoulder, and she almost lost the books she used to guard her chest. Winter wondered if anyone in this mass of strangers could really see her or if she had recently become invisible. It had been a week now, and very few people had even spoken to her. Winter hated this new school and the town it was in. She hated just the sight of it. It was old and cold, not alive like her old home. She hated each and every one of those stupid three hundred and ninety-two students.

The hall began to clear. Winter increased her speed, fearing the wrath of the heartless teachers trained to torture new students. Didn't they understand her old school was much smaller? Did they have to give her two tardies in one week? Five minutes between classes was not enough. Winter tucked her chin and started jogging.

At lunchtime, she found a small, round table in a corner, where she could eat her meatloaf alone. She even hated the food. Her old school would never serve meatloaf made from yesterday's leftover hamburgers. The lunch trays here had faded and cracked from years of use. Her fork even had a layer of soap grime.

She occasionally watched the passing of the nameless drones, but mostly kept her eyes on her own safe table. At first, she didn't see the two boys who had detached from the drones as they came to her from the left. When she did notice them, Winter jumped.

"What do you want?" she asked, her voice timid from nonuse.

Standing tall and wiry, both had overworked muscles that were smaller than either probably would admit. Their long, shaggy hair hung in their eyes...the "in" style for guys here. To Winter it just looked sloppy. Not the type of people she would go out of her way to meet, even at her old school. Here at Trenton Hills she felt repulsed by their mere existence.

The boys grinned and took their hands from behind their backs. Each carried a half-eaten helping of meatloaf in bare hands. The sauce oozed between their fingers. Winter sat up straight, alarmed and disgusted.

"We just wanted to welcome you to our school, New Girl," the tallest one said. Then the boys rushed to either side of Winter and crammed the meatloaf into her hair.

Winter was so shocked, she couldn't even scream. The boys laughed and gave each other a high five. Someone else pointed at her. Soon the entire cafeteria full of drones craned their necks and laughed. Where were the teachers? Winter fled through the nearest door as fast as she could, leaving everything behind.

The door shut, blocking out the laughter, plunging her into sudden silence. Winter burst into the nearby restroom and locked herself in the first stall. She sat down, buried her face in her hands, and cried.

Footsteps came to the stall door. "Hey, are you okay?" a girl asked.

"Go away!" Winter shouted.

"Do you want me to get a teacher?"

"No! Just leave me alone!"

"Fine." Something heavy thumped onto the floor just outside the stall. Winter leaned over and looked beneath the door.

It was her books.

The girl walked away and exited the restroom without another word.

Alone again, Winter eased the door open and picked up her books. Then she dug into her pockets and pulled out the little prepaid flip-phone her dad had given her the day she moved in.

"Hello?" her dad answered after three rings. Saws and hammers filled her ear.

"Dad, it's me." She fought to suppress her sobs.

"Winter, what's wrong?"

Winter let a sob escape, and she thought she heard her dad swear. "I don't feel well," she said, sure that her cracking voice betrayed the lie.

"Did you go to the office?"

"No," she said. "Just come get me."

"Winter, I don't know if I can. I'm in the middle of something. I can't just leave my men and pick you up every time you claim to not feel well."

"Please, Dad. I need you to come get me. Mom would."

He hesitated. *"All right. It may be a few minutes. But as soon as I finish what I'm doing, I'll be right there."* He hung up without saying goodbye.

Twenty minutes later, the bell rang for the next period to begin. Winter could hear the noise diminishing through the walls. When all fell silent, she emerged from the stall like a frightened rabbit, and made her way to the sink and mirror.

Her eyes were red and puffy. Carefully, she took out her barrette and cleaned her hair with her fingers and water. When she finished, she ventured into the hall and tried to make it to the office undetected. There, she spent the next forty-five minutes waiting for her dad, while listening to the aging counselor's lecture about fitting in with others, even though she had given her the same lie she had given her dad.

5

Present Day

Winter walked beside Summer up the short sidewalk to the ivy-covered walls of the Christian Life Center. Winter hesitated a moment with her hand on the door handle before pulling it open, wondering what people seeing the two of them together would think. She grinned and went in.

After passing through a vacant room full of couches and armchairs, they followed the signs and descended a set of stairs into a wash of voices and music.

"Are we late?" asked Summer.

Winter checked her watch: three minutes to six. "Not quite."

They came to a large room supported by orderly white columns. At the far end of the room stood a temporary stage, where a band prepared to play. Speakers at either end of the stage blared Christian rock music. Rows of metal folding chairs covered over half the floor. In the unfurnished half of the room, several hundred students meandered and socialized.

"What do you think?" Summer asked.

Winter inspected her for a second. "I think you're overdressed."

Summer shook her head. "I mean, where do you want to sit?"

"In the back, of course." Winter led the way through the crowd to a couple of empty chairs on the next-to-last row.

A rousing introduction by the CLC student president, a tall guy with shaggy hair who introduced himself as Peter, gave way to loud rock music from the band. The crowd screamed as if at a concert. After a couple of songs, people began to ooze away from their seats, and a line formed at the refreshment table.

Suddenly, Summer thrust her arm into the air and waved at someone. She glanced at Winter and seemed reluctant to move.

"Go," Winter said. "Don't mind me. I'm fine."

"Okay, thanks!" Summer took off.

Winter wandered to an empty chair as far away from the crowds as she could, attracting stares and awkward looks along the way.

Over the next hour, the only person who did not give Winter a wide berth was Summer. Her roommate would occasionally sit with her and make an attempt to talk over the music for a couple of minutes, before rushing off for more mingling.

"Why do you keep coming over here?" Winter asked, after Summer returned for the sixth time.

"What do you mean?"

"You've been bouncing all over this room, but you always come back. Why?"

Summer considered it for a moment. "I don't know. I guess…well, I don't know. You're my roommate."

Winter shook her head. "I don't get you."

"I don't get you either." She laughed. "Why don't you come with me and talk to some people?"

"I don't do crowds."

Summer shrugged. "Well, suit yourself."

They sat for a second, listening to the band play yet another loud and energetic song.

"Do you think they'll run out of songs soon?" Winter asked.

"I don't know," Summer said. "Hey!" she shouted and bounced away, chasing someone else.

As Winter watched her go, she decided to get a drink and shuffled to the refreshment line.

"Hey, Winter!"

Winter turned from her spot in line to find the wayward Summer standing there with two guys.

"This is Davis and Jeffrey," Summer said, indicating Davis as the shorter one with glasses and Jeffrey the taller. Both looked at Winter with reservation.

Winter gave them a meek smile and said, "Hey."

"Jeffrey and I used to go to high school together. He's a sophomore now," Summer said with a wide grin. "Davis is his roommate."

"It's nice to meet both of you." Winter's geniality seemed to ease Davis somewhat, but not Jeffrey.

"Listen—" Jeffrey ruffled his dark brown hair. "We're going in a few minutes to find our classes. Would you two like to come with us?"

"I don't..." Winter said but stopped when she saw Summer's wide-eyed pleading look of excitement. "It's up to Summer."

"Yes!" Summer shouted before Winter had completely finished speaking. She bounced on her heels and pawed at Jeffrey's shoulder.

"Great," Jeffrey said. "Do you know your schedules?"

Summer's face fell. "No, they're in our room."

"No problem," he said. "You can go get them and we'll meet you in the lobby. Carmichael Hall, right?"

"Yes," said Summer.

Jeffrey glanced at his watch. "We'll meet you there about seven-thirty, that okay?"

"Sounds great!"

"See you then." Jeffrey and Davis walked away, Jeffrey

backpedaling and gazing at Summer.

"Bye!" Summer said. She waved until they disappeared into the crowd.

"Are you sure we should do this?" Winter asked.

"Oh, don't be such a killjoy," Summer said. "They're cool."

Winter frowned. Something about the arrangement made her feel uncomfortable—yet, it was not about the guys. She couldn't explain it. The line had moved enough for her to finally reach a soda. She took a long drink in order to buy herself more time to think. Why did she not want to go? No reasons came—just a strange, uncomfortable feeling.

"Come on, Winter. Please?"

Winter sighed in defeat. "Okay. I guess."

Summer bounced and clapped her hands with glee.

They left immediately, taking Summer's shiny lime-green VW Beetle back to the brightly lit student parking lot at their dorm. By then, it was seven-fifteen. They rushed inside to throw on jeans and comfortable shoes before searching for their schedules. Winter had to power up her laptop and plug in the printer to get hers. While she worked, Summer busied herself by reapplying her makeup. Winter sighed deeply with the realization that to Summer, this had turned into nothing more than a group date. It would be a long night.

At seven-thirty, they rushed downstairs to the lobby, where Jeffrey and Davis waited for them as promised. They had changed into jeans and T-shirts, too. Summer beamed when she saw Jeffrey, and he returned a warm smile.

"Ready?" Jeffrey asked and held out an arm to Summer.

She giggled and took his arm. "Sure!"

As they walked out of the front doors, Winter reluctantly fell in step with Davis. He didn't seem too happy either.

Jeffrey led them down the nearest sidewalk. He and Summer talked constantly. Davis, however, appeared content to walk in silence, for which Winter felt grateful. Soon, they approached the backside of a large building. The empty parking lot, dumpster, and central air modules made Winter feel like she was looking at its underwear. As they passed by the building, the huge lawn at the heart of campus stretched out before them.

Sidewalks crisscrossed the landscaped grass and pools of light collected from the many strategically placed lamp posts. The glow cast light into just about every dark corner of the lawn. Great shade trees stood guard over flowerbeds in rounded brick borders. A wooden bench sat beside each flower bed. The sweet smell of carefully tended grass and budding flowers wafted toward them on a warm breeze.

"Where are we?" Winter asked.

"This is the King's Meadow," Davis said. "But we just call it the Meadow."

Summer giggled at a joke Winter couldn't hear.

"It's nice," Winter said.

The group paused as they entered the Meadow. Jeffrey pointed out and named all the buildings, and Winter checked them with her schedule.

"Any questions?" he asked.

Winter looked up. "That covers all of my classes. Easy enough. What about you, Summer?"

"Oh," Summer said, "I'm a music major, so most of my classes are in the music buildings. I already know where they are. Hey! Would you like to see them?"

"You mean, you already know where your classes are?"

"Yup!"

"Then why…" She snapped her mouth shut. Winter made a mental note to seek revenge for being forced to come on Summer's "date."

"All right, we'll go there too," Jeffrey said. "But let's stop by the Union first and get something to drink."

Summer squealed. Winter and Davis simultaneously sighed. They looked at each other and snickered with the same unspoken frustration.

They resumed walking down the center pathway. In the middle of the Meadow stood the largest live oak tree Winter had ever seen. The pathway split and circled it, other paths branching off like spokes in a wheel. In one place, a large branch draped over the walkway, nearly touching the ground on the other side. Several benches and picnic tables surrounded the trunk of the tree on either side of the walkway. A concrete plaque covered with moss lay at the foot of the tree.

"What is this?" Winter asked as they approached.

"It's the Ancient," Davis said. "They say this tree was planted by the founders of the college back in 1876."

Jeffrey said, "People use it sort of like a central meeting place sometimes. And lots of students like to eat or study here."

They took the pathway that circled to the left of the Ancient, under the overhanging branches. About two-thirds of the way around the tree, they turned onto a path that headed toward the Union, at least a hundred yards away. As they approached, Winter could see the silhouettes of people through the brightly lit windows.

The doors of the Union opened into a large room filled with people eating and milling about. Scattered tables, chairs, and booths filled both the main floor and a railed balcony above. It looked like a mixture of cafeteria and restaurant—the smell was definitely that of a cafeteria. In the wall on the right, closed metal roll-up windows and turnstiles indicated the lunch lines. Neon lights glowed from the bare ceiling joists. In every corner, and hung strategically from the ceiling, TVs flickered various channels. Most of them had the volumes off and captions on, but a few blared—including one with music videos.

Past the balcony stairs, in an alcove, stood an open counter beneath a green neon sign that read "The Grill." Jeffrey used his ID card to buy four sodas, and they sat in a booth.

"So what do you girls want to do after the music buildings?" Jeffrey asked.

"I don't know," Winter said. "What time is it?"

Davis looked at his phone. "Almost eight."

"Let's go look around some more," Summer said. "I'm sure there's loads more we haven't seen."

"This is my second year here, and I haven't seen everything," Davis said.

"I don't know," Winter said. "Maybe we should…" The hairs on the back of her neck stood up and a cold chill swept over her, as if someone had blown frigid air down her shirt, but she felt no breeze.

"Maybe we should do what?" asked Jeffrey. Winter held up a hand to silence him. Jeffrey gave Summer a very puzzled look, but Summer just shrugged.

"What are you doing?" he asked.

"Shh!"

She scanned the Union for the source of her chill. Winter gravitated to the source by following the chills as they lessened or worsened, as if using a metal detector. When she located it, her entire body responded with rigid goosebumps.

A man in dark brown sat by himself in a booth across the room. His long, dark-blonde hair hung down his back in a ponytail. Winter felt drawn to him, but she didn't know why. It unnerved her—scared her. Something about the man brought fear into the pit of her stomach.

Evil. It was the only description she could think of. Not just bad or mischievous, but pure, unadulterated evil.

7

"Winter?" Summer asked. "What's wrong?"

"I—" She hesitated. "I'm not sure. Who is that?"

The other three followed her gaze and her quick flick with one finger to the guy in the booth.

"I don't know," Jeffrey said, his annoyance seething out. "There are nearly three thousand students here. I don't know everyone."

The guy suddenly stood. Winter faced the table and tried to look nonchalant. The others did the same. Winter watched him out of the corner of her eye as he threw away his trash and began walking to the doors leading to the Meadow.

"We have to follow him."

"What?" Jeffrey asked. "Are you insane?"

"You just have to trust me," Winter said, wishing she had more justification. "Something's not right."

"Winter, I don't understand," Summer said. "What's not right?"

"Listen, I don't have time to explain right now. I just know we have to follow him."

"Do whatever you want," Jeffrey said. "I'm not coming."

"Fine! I'll do it by myself!" She slammed her palms on the table and slid out of the booth.

"Wait!" Summer said. "I'll come with you."

Winter slowed, allowing Summer to catch up. Davis was beside them within a couple seconds, and by the time they reached the doors Jeffrey had arrived, mumbling beneath his breath.

She walked out the doors, trying to look casual, and down the steps of the Union while scanning the Meadow for any signs of the strange guy. A strong sense of urgency and confidence had replaced her initial fear.

"There he is," she said, indicating with a nod of her head. He traveled down the walkway that ran the outer perimeter of the Meadow, almost a hundred yards away now.

Without saying a word to her companions, she turned to follow. Winter tried to walk as fast as she could and still look casual, but the tension in her neck and shoulders made it awkward. The others followed several feet behind. She could almost feel their nervous silence against her back.

The man passed the administration building, the business building, and then the history building before anything happened. Then he turned down a path that ran between the history building and the religion building. As soon as he disappeared, Winter started to jog.

"Winter, what are you doing?" Jeffrey asked. She ignored him.

When she made the turn between the two buildings, the man was gone. She stopped. The others caught up seconds later.

Summer asked, "Now what?"

"We need to look for him," Winter said.

"I don't think this is a good idea," said Davis.

"Come on, let's go," said Jeffrey. "We've had enough crazy for one night."

But Winter started walking again. She watched the shadows for any movement, walking slowly so she wouldn't miss anything.

"You're kidding, right?" Jeffrey asked.

Winter turned to glare at him and found them already following. Summer and Davis were even being as cautious as she.

As they passed between the history and religion buildings, a grove of trees and flower bushes materialized within the twilight of shadows and lamp posts. The artificial lighting made the garden look plastic.

To her left, something resembling a large Gothic church emerged from the darkness. Attached to it, a round tower loomed into the night sky—its base as big as the church itself. The top of the tower, untouched by the feeble lamp posts below, could only be seen by the light of the full moon. Winter stopped and stared, her confidence displaced again by fear.

"What is this place?" she whispered, as the blood drained from her face and her knees weakened. The chills came back, too.

"The Chapel of Radiance," Davis said from behind her. "The students used to be required to attend chapel years ago. The bell tower is called Olamel. It was built several years later."

As if on cue, the bells began to ring. With the first strike, Winter screamed. She fell to the ground, covering her ears. The others rushed to her side, seemingly oblivious to the pain that now seared the inside of her skull.

The bells struck again. Images flashed through Winter's mind like strobe lights. Several faces appeared, most of which she didn't recognize. A little girl with dark hair…A black man…A silver and black mask…A man in a wheel-chair…Claire with red eyes and a twisted smile…A brown-eyed girl with a petite face and wavy brown hair…Herself on fire…

The bells struck three. Hate. Anger. Lust. She was running. Out of breath. They were chasing her. She tried to run faster. They were everywhere. Flying…running…swirling like mist. She couldn't get away. She couldn't get away. Claire…A train whistle…

The bells struck four. Someone screaming for help. She screamed for help. No help was coming. Alone. No, not alone. Someone in front of her. A gun to her head…Rain pounding…A girl with short, red hair…

The bells struck five. Pain ripping through her arms, legs, and face. Her whole body burned. Every nerve wailed in agony. Too much…she was going to die. Her skin was splitting. It was too much…

The bells struck six. Stairs…a demon…blood. Blood on the walls. Blood on the floor. Blood everywhere. A bloody body. The child…Save the child…

The bells struck seven. She couldn't breathe. A weight crushed her chest. Not just a weight, but a stabbing, painful presence. Faces grinned at her from above. She felt the life draining from her body. Fire…fire…fire…fire everywhere…

The bells struck eight. Every cell in her body screamed in pain, ravaged and shredded until nothing remained. It wouldn't stop…It wouldn't stop. Then everything went dark. Death.

As the last toll echoed into silence, Winter pushed herself partway off the ground. The visions vanished as quickly as they had started. She shook and cried, unable to process what had happened. The others crowded in all at once and tried to help her stand. She shoved them away and hid her face in her hands.

"Are you okay? Are you hurt? What's wrong?" Summer's voice trembled as she rested her unsteady hand on Winter's shoulder.

"What was that?" Jeffrey asked. "Do you have seizures or something?" He ran a hand through his hair.

Winter glanced back at the bell tower Davis had called Olamel. Her mind flashed again with the searing images, and she winced. Making an effort to suppress the tears and steady her voice, she said, "I need to go back to my room." She took Davis's outstretched hand and let him pull her up.

"But what happened?" Jeffrey asked. "Should we take you to a doctor? Something's terribly wrong with you! People just don't fall down screaming like that!"

"I don't need a doctor! And there's nothing wrong with me! I don't know what happened. I…I just need to go rest." Summer came to her side, and Winter wrapped an arm around her for support. Her knees still felt weak. Winter let her roommate lead her back toward the Meadow.

"But what about the guy?" Davis asked.

"Doesn't matter anymore," Winter said. She looked at Summer. "Please hurry."

Winter woke up sweating, heart pounding. She tried again to suppress the bloody room and the demon. But it was more real this time. She clenched her eyes and took slow, deep breaths. As she did, she could clearly see the flashing images of the night before. Her body surged with adrenaline and she sat up.

I have to get out of here, she thought.

She swung her feet to the floor and looked around her room, tinted in grays and blues from the early morning twilight. She put her elbows on her knees and leaned her face into her hands. That's when it hit her...when one small word engulfed her thoughts.

Tumor.

Could it be? Could she have a brain tumor just like her mom? Winter shuddered and tried to ignore the idea.

She grabbed her Bible and headed down to the lobby to do her reading without even bothering to brush her hair.

The time with God calmed her nerves. Once finished, Winter went back to her room. Summer snoozed, entwined in her bedding, and only dignified Winter's loud passage with a small grunt.

After Winter had showered and dressed, she passed the time by checking her e-mail and surfing the net.

Eight o'clock neared, and Summer was still not awake. Winter sighed in frustration and snapped the stereo on, full-blast.

Summer sat straight up in her bed with a wide, frightened expression. She clutched at a teddy bear and scanned the room with unblinking, unfocused eyes.

"Good morning," Winter said. Summer managed to focus on her long enough to glare before collapsing back onto the bed. Winter turned the stereo's volume down.

"It's Sunday. Are you planning on going to church?" she asked.

Summer grunted. "What time is it?"

"Almost eight."

Summer rolled over and looked at Winter with half-closed eyes.

"Church?" Winter asked again. "I don't have a car, so I can't go without you."

"But I'm not from here," Summer moaned. "I don't know where a church is."

Winter thought for a moment. "We could go find one. I'm sure there are several around. We just drive and stop at the first one we find."

"I don't even think I could find my way off campus."

"That's not true. Are you saying you don't want to go to church?"

Summer rolled over and pulled her blanket up to her chin. "No, I'm saying that I don't know where to go. Can't we just find out about churches at the CLC tomorrow night? I'm sure they'll let us know."

"But I really feel like we should go, Summer. Church is church, no matter where it is or if we know anybody there. We should go."

Summer pulled the pillow over her head. "Leave me alone. I want to go back to sleep. I've got eight o'clock classes every morning this week. I'd like to sleep past eight today."

"Are you going to do this every weekend?"

"No," came Summer's muffled voice. "But it's my first weekend away from home. I just want a break for one weekend. Okay?"

"Fine." Winter grabbed her Bible again and left, slamming the door.

Forcing her feet to move and her mind not to think, she took the quickest route back to the Chapel of Radiance and to the garden that stretched out before it. The cultivated beauty of the garden amazed Winter, and she wondered how many hours of careful manicuring it took to keep it that way. She found a secluded spot beneath a magnolia tree and sat on the ground with her back to the trunk. The flowers and ornamental trees swayed gently in the breeze, while the sweet smells teased her senses. Larger trees stood as stately sentinels over the holy scene.

The old church seemed smaller and less threatening in the daylight. The Tower of Olamel, easily the highest point on campus, spiraled to the sky. The top of the tower wore a square crown of tall arches facing all four sides, allowing bells and sunlight to be seen. Just below this section, a circle of iron Roman numerals and two iron hands clung to the brick wall. In the walls of the lower sections were small rectangular windows. Winter suspected there might be bells throughout the entire tower.

As she studied the tower, she forced herself to recall some of the images she had seen the night before. It was like remembering a horror movie. With calm, calculated breathing, she kept the fearful chills and strange sense of destiny at bay. She decided to read her Bible and pray until the bells rang at nine, hoping that perhaps the visions would return and she would have another chance to understand them.

She read of the Samaritan woman. One thing in particular caught Winter's attention as she studied: Jesus knew of the woman's past relationships... without being told. Winter had done the same thing. She knew Angie's name. She tried to comprehend that she had done something Jesus himself had done, but she couldn't come to any logical explanation.

Winter bowed her head and prayed. She thanked God for loving her even though she was as awful as the Samaritan woman in so many ways. She also prayed for forgiveness for showing frustration with Summer. She asked earnestly that God would help her understand the meaning of the images she had seen. Then she took a deep, reflective breath and stilled herself, listening with her heart for God to speak. She let the silence settle across her mind and body, and relaxed for several minutes...listening for God.

Then Winter remembered the bell tower. She checked her watch. Two minutes to nine. There remained a small section of Scripture to read, but she decided to save that for later. She closed her Bible and turned to watch the Tower of Olamel, steeling herself for another onslaught of horrific images.

A symphony of bells erupted from the tower, the notes blending and rising with alternating consonance and dissonance and pulsating to mark the number of the hour. The sharp resonance reverberated and echoed from the walls of nearby buildings, doubling and tripling the perception of the number of bells actually ringing.

It was the most beautiful sound she had ever heard.

But nothing happened to her. As the last bell echoed across the campus of Tishbe University, the sound returning muffled and inert, Winter sighed with disappointment that the images had not come back.

Her stomach awoke with a loud complaint. She stood, dusted herself off, and left the chapel garden to go to the Union.

When Winter returned to the dorm, she found Summer and Summer's shower caddy missing.

The moment Summer returned, Winter said, "I need to apologize for snapping at you."

"What?" Summer's hair hung wet and tangled across the shoulders of her pajamas. The lack of makeup did nothing to hinder her looks.

"I said I'm sorry. I shouldn't have gotten upset."

Summer grabbed her brush from her dresser and began pulling it through her hair. "I don't know what you're talking about."

"This morning? I wanted to go to church and you wanted to stay in bed. Remember?"

Summer shrugged. "Sorry, no…must have still been mostly asleep."

Winter rolled her eyes.

For the rest of the morning they finished decorating their room. Following a suggestion from their RA, Shanna, they swapped one poster each to make the room "flow" better. Winter selected a poster covered with purple daisies, and Summer chose one of a Gothic fairy. Winter laughed. The fairy had pink wings—probably the only pink she owned. At least the background was black.

After hanging the posters, they stood back and admired their handiwork.

Shanna stuck her head around the door. "Hey, girls…oh…"

Winter looked at Summer and they both laughed.

"What do you think?" Winter asked.

Shanna shuffled her feet. "Um…wow. It still looks awful. But better…I guess."

Winter and Summer laughed again.

"Must you brush your hair so much?" Winter asked. "It's almost seven, and I'm hungry."

Summer sighed. "It's the first day, I want to make a good impression. Besides, you could use a little extra brushing yourself."

Winter crossed her arms and turned back to the cartoons on TV. But when Summer left for the bathroom, she grabbed her brush and went over her hair again.

They spoke very little at breakfast. In fact, a nervous silence blanketed the entire cafeteria. The two girls parted ways at the foot of the Union steps, and Summer ran across the access road to the arts plaza. Winter went next door to Ingram Hall, the education department, and searched for Room 228.

She found her speech class near the end of a long hall with a freshly waxed wooden floor. Winter hated speaking in front of people, but the small, nine-student class helped her relax somewhat.

Algebra and biology followed. Then she returned to the Union, where she met Summer for lunch. They ate and discussed the overwhelming task of reviewing syllabi, which seemed to be the lesson plan for every professor that day. At one-thirty, Summer departed to her flute lesson, and Winter made her way to French class.

About halfway there, her toe caught the edge of an uneven section of walkway. Her backpack shifted down one arm, and she crashed to the ground. The cold pain of embarrassment washed over her from head to toe. Laughter floated through the air, and she felt her face redden. Some guy said, "Freshman," as Winter tried to gather what dignity she had left and stand. Without even dusting herself off, she rushed away.

9

Four Years Ago

"Hey Winter, wait up!" someone called from behind as she exited her fourth-period science class on the way to lunch. She slowed and turned. A girl with reddish-brown hair jogged up to her and smiled. She stood just a little taller than Winter.

"Hey," said the girl. "I saw what Randy and Scott did to you yesterday. They're jerks. Not everyone here is like that."

"Um, thanks." Winter turned to walk away. The girl fell into step beside her.

"Listen, if you want, you can come sit with me and my friends," she said. "I mean, there's no need to sit by yourself at lunch."

Winter half-smiled and furrowed her eyebrows. "I don't even know you."

"I'm Claire Parker. I brought your books to you in the bathroom, remember? And you're never going to get to know people if you don't talk to anyone."

Winter thought it over for a moment.

"Well?"

"Okay," Winter said, and Claire grinned.

Claire stayed with her all the way to the lunchroom and through the lunch line—talking constantly. Winter tried to listen but found the barrage of trivial conversation tiring. Still, Winter followed Claire to a table already occupied by two other girls and one guy. One girl had dark brown hair framing an Asian face. The other girl, a blonde, sat tantalizingly close to the sandy-blonde boy.

"Guys, this is Winter," Claire said. "Winter, this is Stacy Shu," she indicated the brunette, "and this is Alison Young and Phillip Adams, they kinda go together."

Winter tried to smile and returned waves to each of them. Then she sat and started forking through her potatoes.

"So," said Stacy, "where are you from?"

Winter looked up. All four of them stared. "South Waverly," she said quietly and went back to her potatoes.

"Wow," Stacy said.

"That's got to be, like, six hours away," said Alison.

"Five, actually," Winter said.

"So why did you move way down here to Trenton Hills?" Stacy asked.

Winter shoved a bite of potatoes in her mouth to avoid answering—maybe they were edible after all. Her jaw stiffened in the awkward silence, as they waited for her to swallow. She wished they would just let the question die, but they kept staring.

"I, um," Winter said. "I moved in with my dad." She took another quick bite.

"Parents divorced?" Stacy asked, with a crinkled nose. Winter nodded. "Well, you've come to the right table. My parents have been divorced since before I can remember. Ali lives with her grandparents because her mom dumped her off and disappeared, and Phillip's dad ran off with a stripper five years ago. Claire, here, wishes her parents were divorced."

"Yeah," Claire said, "They fight all the time. Maybe that's why they're still together—no one else will have them." Claire laughed and the others joined in. Winter felt some of her tension ease.

"So why did you move in with your dad?" Phillip asked.

Winter's little measure of confidence vanished, and she stared back down at her plate. She felt her cheeks quiver, as emotions rolled through her like shards of glass in a kaleidoscope. Her eyes started to water.

Ali punched Phillip in the shoulder.

"My mom's sick," Winter whispered.

"Is she going to get better?" Stacy asked.

Winter managed the meekest shake of her head. The whole table fell silent, and Winter began shuffling her fork in her food again. The din of the cafeteria somehow seemed rude and irreverent. She felt cold and empty. She dropped the fork and crossed her arms, willing herself not to cry. If only she could get them to change the subject, to stop looking at her.

"So what do you like to do for fun?" Claire asked.

Winter gazed at her for a moment, relief clawing at the new question. She could see apology in Claire's eyes. Winter took a deep breath and steered her mind to the new subject. The tightness in her chest lessened.

"I like to listen to music," she said. "And write poems. I like movies, too."

Claire's eyes widened. "Really? I love music. You've got to come over to my house sometime, and I'll put some stuff on your iPod."

"Okay," Winter said.

"Hey, you guys heard about the BLM concert coming to town?" asked Stacy.

"No! Really?" said Alison.

"Cool," said Phillip.

Winter looked at Stacy. "Who's BLM?"

"Bleed Like Me. They're an alternative, industrial, emo-type band," said Claire.

"We should all go," said Alison.

Winter resumed eating as the others made concert plans. She smiled as she listened, allowing a little warmth to spread through her chest.

Claire leaned over, squeezed her hand, and grinned. "See? Told you."

"Thank you," Winter said.

10

Present Day

That night, Winter and Summer went back to the Christian Life Center for freshman small groups. Winter didn't bother changing clothes, but Summer once again dressed as if for a date.

Winter didn't know what to expect, but what she saw at the CLC was much the same as Saturday night. She recognized the other freshmen easily—they were the ones standing around looking nervous. The sophomores, who would lead the groups, wandered around with name tags on their shirts, trying to greet each person individually. Instead of loud music, the soft rumble of people talking filled the room.

Before long, a petite, pretty sophomore with wavy brown hair came to them as if they were the targets of a sales pitch. She studied at them with intelligent brown eyes set in a round face, that seemed to penetrate any false pretenses. Winter felt simultaneously defensive and comforted. She couldn't shake the feeling she had seen this girl before.

"Hi, girls! My name is Kaci. You must be Summer and Winter."

Summer and Winter looked at each other. "How do you know that?" Summer asked.

"I'm the RA for the third floor in your dorm. You two are famous up there. Your names are easy to remember, and some of the girls say an angel and a demon are living together on the second floor. They've even snuck by your room to see if it's true. Maybe you should have an open house or something."

Winter rolled her eyes. "We had open house yesterday, and Summer is not a demon."

Kaci laughed.

"I don't get it," Summer said.

Kaci and Winter laughed again.

"Listen, girls," Kaci said, "the leaders will have about seven or eight in each group. When they tell everyone to divide up, why don't you two come with me?"

"Sure!" Summer said.

Winter shrugged.

"Great! Well, I'll see you two in a few minutes, then." Kaci walked away to her next target.

Winter led Summer to the back row of chairs where they'd sat Saturday night. Several other sophomores came to speak with them, but none as nice as Kaci—and none invited them to join their groups. Winter had trouble putting her finger on it, but there was something different about Kaci. A peace, or something, surrounded her…something unique. The only other time Winter felt that way was when she prayed.

A nervous-looking sophomore led a few praise songs with his acoustic guitar. Summer belted along, and Winter just listened. Then the CLC student president took the floor.

"Hello! My name is Peter Strong," he said. "Before we break into groups, I just wanted to take a moment and explain what these groups are about. These groups are not necessarily for Bible studies or devotions, but they are more like support groups. It's a time for you to get together and talk through your week, work out problems you may be facing spiritually or emotionally…even academically. Of course, academics can be a huge portion of everyone's emotional problems."

The room chuckled as one.

"In the course of your discussion, if Biblical insight is needed, so be it. Feel free to meet elsewhere or take field trips if you want, but remember The Raven can't seat all of us!"

The room chuckled again.

"What's the Raven?" Winter asked Summer.

"A deli-style restaurant off campus. Didn't you see it?"

"If you're a sophomore group leader, please stand," said Peter.

The freshmen sat up in their chairs, twisting their necks to see the dozen or so sophomores who had risen. Winter found Kaci and took careful note of where she stood.

"Thanks," said Peter. "These are your group leaders. They're here to answer your questions about college life, to help you make the transition without compromising your faith, and to facilitate orderly discussion in your groups. We want to keep these groups small, but we don't want to assign groups. If you've already gotten to know one of our leaders and want to be in that group, feel free. If not, come see me, and when the sorting has finished, I'll assign you to the smallest groups. All right, everybody stand." The room filled with the soft ruffling of clothing and metallic grunts of chairs being slid out of place. "Now find your groups!"

The room roiled with moving bodies. The group leaders maneuvered to different locations along the perimeter. Winter grabbed Summer's hand and pulled her in Kaci's direction. They found Kaci retreating to a far corner with two other girls already in tow.

Winter and Summer sat with them, creating a small circle. Winter looked around at the rest of the room. Within a few moments, most everybody had found a group, except for a few standing with Peter.

From inside her purse, Kaci produced a roll of toilet paper. "Pass this around," she said, "and take as much as you think you need."

This first girl took it and wrapped the paper around her hand once and tore it off. The next girl did likewise. Summer took it and wrapped it several times around her hand and passed the roll to Winter. Winter let the roll unravel in front of her, broke off a few sheets, and passed it back to Kaci.

"All right," Kaci said, "count the squares of paper you have and…" Before she could finish, Peter walked up leading another girl and a guy.

"These two haven't found a group yet," he told Kaci. "Do you have room?"

"Of course!" she said. "You guys make room for them."

The circle shifted to make places for the two new freshmen. Kaci handed them the toilet paper and gave them the same instructions.

"Now," she said after receiving the roll back, "count the squares of paper you have. For each square, you have to tell the group one fact about yourself. Your last fact must be something totally unique and interesting." A collective groan escaped from the group as they unraveled and counted their squares.

"Who wants to go first?" Kaci asked after a few moments.

"I will!" Summer said. "My name is Summer Reilly. I'm from New Port, South Carolina. I was a lifeguard in high school. I'm a music major and I play flute. I was in my All-State Band for two years. My dad's name is Mark, and my mom's name is Wanda. I live in Carmichael Hall, and I love my roommate! Oh, and I drive a green Bug!"

"Wow!" Kaci said. "Good job! Okay, who's next?"

The other three girls went in succession. Jamie, Sharon, Sophie—all lived in Carmichael. Winter thought she recognized one of them from Saturday but didn't recognize the name. The guy went last. His name was Jason, and he was dating the girl he came with, Sophie.

When they finished, Kaci looked at Winter. "Your turn."

"Must I?" she asked. Kaci gave her a firm look, and Winter sighed. "My name is Winter Maessen," she said in a low voice. "My mom died three years ago, and I live with my dad now. Summer is my roommate. And I've only been a Christian since May." She stopped, but the others still watched her.

"What's your something unique and interesting?" Kaci asked.

Winter hesitated, as she looked at all the staring faces. Most of them appeared uneasy or uninterested. Kaci's eyes brightened and she sat up a little straighter. Summer seemed eager for the answer.

Finally, Winter took a deep breath and closed her eyes. In that moment, she decided to tell the one thing she had longed to tell everyone but had only told her dad. It was an impulse, almost as if the decision were not fully her own. Though she faced complete strangers, she focused only on Kaci, as if the information belonged to her alone. She opened her mouth and hesitated only a moment. Then she rushed the words out before her mind could regain control and force her to keep quiet.

"God told me to come here."

"I'm sure God led us all to come here," Kaci said.

"You don't understand." It was all or nothing now. She was committed. "God spoke to me. He told me to come! I can't explain it, but it was the strangest experience in my life."

"Did God tell you the girl's name too?" Summer asked.

"What is she talking about?" asked Kaci.

"She knew Angie's name Saturday without anyone telling her," Summer said. The others turned from Summer to look at Winter, their expressions sliding from boredom to confusion.

Winter stared at the floor and lied. "No, I must have heard it somewhere."

"So...you're saying you actually heard God's voice?" asked Jason.

"She's lying!" said Sophie. "God doesn't talk to people like that."

"I'm not lying!"

"So God spoke to you?"

"Yes! I heard God! Now just shut up and leave me alone!"

One by one, the faces around the circle changed expressions from confusion to one Winter recognized well—they all thought she was crazy. She felt like crawling into a hole and hiding. She crossed her arms and hardened herself. Seconds ticked by. Still no one spoke.

"Say something," whispered Winter.

"We don't believe you," Sophie said. "You really are a freak."

"Sophie!" said Kaci.

Winter jumped up and fled toward the stairs.

"Winter, wait!" Kaci called.

Someone grabbed Winter's arm just before she put a foot on the bottom stair. She turned to see her roommate.

"Winter..."

Winter shook Summer off. "Leave me alone."

11

The next morning, Winter crossed the Meadow to the English building, admiring the beautiful flowerbeds. As she walked beneath the Ancient, she recognized a girl from her CLC small group sitting on a bench studying... Jamie, she thought. Winter tried to pass along a warm smile, but the girl seemed to purposefully avoid making eye contact. Story of her life. At least she hadn't tripped yet.

She suppressed the irritation and smiled, continuing to the English building. Easily one of the oldest on campus, it stood sentinel over the Meadow. She mounted the ancient concrete steps and checked her schedule to find the room number—315. The stairwell was easy to find, and she took the steps two at a time.

She'd always done well in English, but as she walked into the classroom something told her things were about to change. The old, drafty room smelled of mildew and dust. The waiting students watched as she crossed the room to the only available desk—on the front row, of course. It stuck out a little ahead of the other desks, as if the other students had moved theirs as far from the front as possible. She quickened her step and sat. Trying not to be obvious, she slid the chair even with the others. The heavy grating on the floor made her posture shrink and her confidence shrink even more. She checked her watch. She could not possibly be late. No, five minutes remained before the start of class. How was it possible that she was the last person to come in?

Many of the students continued to stare at her. Their looks displayed a curious mix of fear and judgment. Judgment she understood all too well…but fear? If they had directed it toward her, she could understand that, too. But it was more of an apologetic, we're-in-this-together fear. Winter fidgeted with her fingers. What was going on?

A woman in her sixties, with steel gray hair, a stiff burgundy suit dress, and a sour face, marched into the room. She set her briefcase on the desk and trained her narrowed eyes on Winter.

Winter looked at the scarred top of her desk, but she could still feel those glaring eyes. She slid down a little, wondering if it would be possible to hide, suddenly very aware of just how much black she wore.

"Young lady, we do not slouch in our seats," the professor said as she reached the lectern.

Winter bit her lip and obeyed.

The professor introduced herself as Mrs. Pritchett and immediately passed out a thick syllabus and course description. They spent most of the class time reviewing the numerous objectives. Winter's eyes widened at the vast amount of work. The syllabus contained things she had never heard of. A knot formed in the pit of her stomach.

After exhausting every detail of the course objectives, Mrs. Pritchett drew their attention to the first assignment—an informative essay about themselves, due the following week. Winter stifled a groan when she realized that the rest of the class had absorbed the assignment in total silence. Mrs. Pritchett explained the essay in great detail. Winter scrambled to take notes like everyone else. The scratching of pens on paper sounded like background static to Mrs. Pritchett's voice.

Finally, the excruciating class ended. Winter leapt to her feet, intending a quick escape. But the professor cleared her throat and motioned for Winter to approach. Winter sighed as she watched the rest of the class file through the door to freedom.

"I would appreciate it if you would try to conduct yourself like a young lady in my class," Mrs. Pritchett said. She glared at Winter over her reading glasses and tapped the edge of a stack of papers even.

Winter blinked. "What exactly do you mean?"

Mrs. Pritchett pursed her lips and looked Winter over from toes to head. "I believe you know exactly what I mean. This is a Christian university, young lady, and I expect students in my class to act and dress the way good Christian students should."

"You can't tell me how to dress," Winter said. "The way I dress has nothing to do with whether or not I'm a Christian!"

"I beg to differ."

"Then you're begging to be wrong!"

Mrs. Pritchett raised an eyebrow. "This is my class," she said. "My rules will be followed or your grade will reflect your actions. Do you understand?"

Winter stared at Mrs. Pritchett for several long seconds as she bit her tongue. A myriad of retorts revolved through her mind like cards in a Rolodex, searching for the best one.

"No standard curriculum guide protects you here," said Mrs. Pritchett. "Perhaps you should consider that, before you speak."

Winter clamped her mouth shut. She simply turned and walked away.

She stormed across the Meadow to the Union for lunch, never looking up. She let her anger take control and push aside all thoughts of faith and God. Vengeful plots flashed through her mind like an unholy parade. By the time she found herself in line for lunch, she could not remember having walked there.

She handed the lady her ID card and turned to eye the fried chicken and mashed potatoes on the trays of exiting students—skipping breakfast had caught up with her. Her stomach rumbled, and she turned back to await the return of her card. Her thoughts alternated between Mrs. Pritchett and fried chicken. The lady swiped the card again through the silver cash machine, her brow wrinkled.

"I'm sorry, honey," the lady said, "but your card doesn't seem to be working." She handed back the ID card.

"What does that mean?" Winter asked.

"It means the computer is not registering your account."

"And?"

The lady frowned. "And, I'm sorry, but you can't eat here today."

"But I have a meal plan," Winter said.

"Maybe so, dear, but if the computer doesn't register it, then I can't allow you through."

"You mean you're not going to let me eat my lunch? A lunch that's already paid for?" Winter's anger rose again.

"There's nothing I can do." The lady turned to take the next student in line.

Winter glared at the lady, trying to find something worthwhile to say or shout. She wanted to reach out and slap the glasses off her face. Heat radiated from her cheeks as if an internal furnace had blazed to life. Something that may have been God tugged at the back of her brain, but she willfully shut that door. She tried to intensify the anger she projected, as the lady allowed a third student to pass since handing back the card.

"You can pay in cash if you would like," the lady offered when she noticed that Winter still waited.

Winter slapped over a cup of pens and pencils. Before they hit the ground, she had already turned away. The brief clattering of the pens and pencils hitting the floor and rolling away faded into the feasting noise of the crowded Union.

Paranoia mingled with her anger, and she felt as if everyone stared at her—judging her like Pritchett, her entire English class, and even the lunch lady. She shoved the Union doors open so hard she nearly knocked someone over. The guy shouted, but she didn't care and didn't stop to apologize.

Winter charged across the Meadow, more angry now than after English class. She kept her face toward the ground, partly to avoid people she might recognize and partly to keep from crying. More than once she slammed her shoulders into someone walking the opposite direction. The crowded sidewalk forced her to step off and continue on grass.

The ID card was ready in her hand long before she came to the side door of Carmichael Hall. Winter swiped it through the card reader and pulled on the door. It wouldn't open. She looked at the card reader—the light glowed red. She swiped the card again and waited for the light to turn green, but it just flashed red.

Angry, frustrated tears erupted with a loud scream, like the bursting of a water pipe. Why should things here be any different than in high school?

She swiped the card again...red.

Winter kicked the door and beat on it with her fists. Her face burned, and she could barely see through the blur of tears. She was the same unlovable outcast—the same freak. No one would help her or be her friend.

She tried the card...red.

She shouldn't have come here—shouldn't have come to a Christian university full of judgmental hypocrites. Sophie, Jeffrey, the CLC group, the English class, Mrs. Pritchett, the lunch lady...all the same.

Her sobs neared the point of hyperventilation as she pounded on the card reader with the flat of her hand. Winter felt alone and abandoned. No friends. No place to go. Nothing to eat.

Again...red.

If only she could call her dad, he would come get her and take her home where she belonged. Winter fumbled in her backpack for her prepaid phone and realized she had left it in her room. She screamed again.

Red.

But she never really belonged with her dad either.

Red.

With one final barrage of poundings on the door and a guttural cry, Winter slid to the ground with her back against the glass, placed her head on her knees, and wept. As she inhaled, her voice raked. As she exhaled, her chest shuddered.

She didn't belong anywhere. She was unwanted…unloved…and her life was utterly useless.

Footsteps on the sidewalk…running. She didn't bother to look up and it was too late to hide. Let them come, she didn't care. They would judge her and pass by like all the others in her life.

The footsteps stopped. Someone knelt on the ground beside her.

"Oh, Winter, what's wrong?" the girl asked as she wrapped Winter in her arms. It was Kaci.

Winter couldn't stop her arms as they wrapped around Kaci. She lay her head on Kaci's shoulder and sobbed.

Kaci let her cry for several minutes, rocking Winter gently and stroking her hair. When Winter quieted, she asked again, "What happened?"

Winter sniffed and pulled away. "Everyone thinks I'm crazy. My teacher hates me, and my card doesn't work. I'm going to fail my class and they won't even let me eat. And now I can't get in." Her rational mind registered how silly her problems sounded, but it did nothing to lessen the hole in her chest.

Kaci's understanding smile disarmed Winter, and some of her anxiety ebbed away. Her heart lightened, and she almost smiled herself with the simple realization that Kaci was not judging her.

"It's okay, don't worry about it, we can fix this." Kaci stood and grabbed Winter's hand. "Come with me."

As Kaci swiped her own card and the light turned green, Winter glared at the card reader. "I hope that thing falls off."

Kaci chuckled.

Winter followed Kaci to the third floor. Kaci's RA room looked more like a real bedroom than any she had seen. Real carpet, not area rugs, blanketed the floor, and tall lamps lit the room from the corners. Kaci even had a small entertainment center. The deep-mauve paint caused the white curtains to pop out like a 3D movie. With only one bed, Kaci had plenty of room.

Kaci went to a small cabinet beside the micro-fridge and pulled out a pack of ramen noodles and a bowl, while Winter made herself comfortable on the futon couch opposite the TV.

"Thirsty?" she asked. Winter nodded, and Kaci handed her a generic cherry soda. "Maybe later I'll take you and Summer to the grocery store. Ramen noodles are really cheap and handy if you don't feel like walking all the way to the Union."

"Thanks," Winter whispered.

While the noodles cooked, Kaci turned on the TV and put it on the cartoon channel. By the time Kaci handed her the steaming bowl of noodles, Winter's mood had improved—though she now blushed with shame at her irrational outburst.

"I'm sorry," she said between bites.

Kaci smiled and sat down beside her. "For what?"

"For my stupid little moment outside…and for last night."

"Want to know a secret?" Kaci asked. "Every girl in this building will have a 'moment' before the end of the week. I think I had them every day for a month when I first moved in."

Winter grinned. "Yeah, but that was such a silly thing to get upset over."

"Not really," Kaci said as she brushed her hair off her shoulders. "Last year I cried myself to sleep because I had to take a cold shower, when really I just didn't know how to work the one-knob shower controls."

Winter could not help laughing. "You're joking, right?"

"No, I'm serious! Then another time I cried for two hours because my roommate ate the last Pop-Tart."

Winter almost spewed soda out her nose. She turned away laughing and coughing, wiping away the tears from the tingling in the back of her sinuses.

"It's not funny," Kaci objected playfully. "They were s'mores Pop-Tarts, and I needed chocolate."

Winter turned back. "You cried over chocolate?"

"You wouldn't?"

"No!"

"Well, it was all the chocolate we had." She feigned a pout.

Winter laughed again.

"You see?" Kaci said with a twinkle in her eyes. "You're not so silly. As for last night...I believe you."

Winter stopped laughing. "You do? You don't think I'm crazy?"

"Yes I believe you, and no, I don't think you're crazy. Not completely, at least."

Winter searched Kaci's face. "But why?"

"Because I can feel God in you."

"You what?"

Kaci laughed. "It's called discernment—it's a spiritual gift. Every Christian has at least one. With discernment I can usually tell if a person is doing something for Godly reasons or not."

"What's my spiritual gift?" Winter asked.

"You'll figure it out, when the time is right," Kaci said. "But if you've heard God speak, I bet it's going to be a good one."

12

Four Years Ago

During the first week, Winter found that she shared classes with Claire, Stacy, and Alison throughout the day. When possible, she moved seats to sit by them. She would give friend-making a try. But she had trouble believing Stacy and Alison were truly accepting her and not just being nice to "the new girl."

Claire was different. She went out of her way to do things with Winter and to get her involved. Claire always seemed to find her between classes and even walked with her to the buses each day. Being friends with Claire felt... natural.

One week after Winter's first day of school, they sat across from each other in the cafeteria, prattling about algebra, fashion, and boys. Stacy and Alison were having a conversation of their own—Phillip's class had already left. Soy burgers and tater tots sat before them on the faded trays.

"Hey," said Stacy. "I'm thinking about having a sleepover this Friday. What do you guys think?"

"That would be awesome!" Claire said with wide eyes, her

excitement almost unbelievable.

Stacy just smiled, and Winter thought she might be missing something. Maybe it was some inside joke. Doubtless there were many, and she really didn't expect to be included in any of them. Private jokes indicated real friendship.

"Sure, I'm in," said Alison with a flick of her hair.

"What about you, Winter?" Stacy asked.

She stopped chewing and stared at Stacy. "I—I don't know. I'd have to ask my dad." She needed time to think…to sort out the confusion in her head. Could she really have new friends? Did she even want new friends?

"Okay. Well, tell me tomorrow," said Stacy.

13

Present Day

Kaci took Winter to the Tishbe Card Services desk to get the card fixed. It was surprisingly easy. The desk attendant pulled up her account on the computer, reswiped her card through a card reader, and handed it back. Winter felt somewhat chagrined that she had forgotten about the Card Services desk.

By late afternoon, the crowd crossing the meadow had diminished, and the pathways were relatively empty as Kaci and Winter walked back to Carmichael. Winter looked between the two buildings toward the Chapel of Radiance as they passed.

"Do they ever use the chapel anymore?"

"Not really," Kaci said. "Sometimes the Religion Department will have a special speaker or something, and they use it for the extra room."

"Who works the bell tower?"

"It's probably electronic. I'm sure the controls are somewhere in the religion building." They turned a corner and came into sight of Carmichael Hall.

"That was fast," Winter said.

Kaci laughed. "You'll figure out lots of shortcuts—including cutting through buildings. Now let's test your card."

As they neared the side door, Winter spotted the card reader lying on the ground. The wires hanging naked from the brick wall looked like old, decayed spaghetti.

"That's weird," Kaci said with a frown. "These were new locks installed last year." She started toward the front entrance.

Winter stared at the amputated card reader, remembering how she had wished it would fall off.

Could I have...

She pushed the thought away and ran after Kaci.

Her feet slammed to the pavement in painful, methodic strides. All of her muscles protested the pace, but she had no choice. Heavier and faster feet pounded the ground behind. The man chasing her laughed. She turned to gauge the distance, but it was too dark. She tripped and smashed into the hard ground. Something snapped in her left arm. Before she could get back onto her feet the man was on her. She tried to scream, but the man slapped tape across her mouth. She kicked and hit her assailant, but he punched her in the face hard—pain exploded across the bridge of her nose, stunning her to immobility. He picked her up and slung her over his shoulders.

Winter sat up on her bed.

Cold sweat poured out of her body, and the sheet clung to her skin. Instinctively, she put a hand to her nose to check if it was broken. She took a deep breath and tried to shake the dream away. It was so...real. She put her head in her hands and trembled. The hellish dream during the car ride to school...the bell tower incident...the dream this morning...Should she see a doctor?

She shivered, not for the dream but for what a doctor might say.

Winter looked at Summer's empty bed, thankful her roommate was gone for the weekend. She lay back on her pillow and allowed herself to cry.

A commotion started in the hall. Someone pounded on the door. Winter rubbed her face dry and climbed out of bed to answer. It was Shanna.

"Turn on your TV, Channel 4. Hurry!" Shanna turned to the next door. Other girls rushed through the hall, talking with urgency.

Winter, puzzled and intrigued, brushed the hair from her face and crossed the room to pick up the TV remote. Curling up in her papasan chair, she aimed the remote and pushed the power button. Winter folded her arms and tried to rub away the cold sweat while the TV faded into focus from its perch on the topmost shelf over Winter's desk.

A special report was in progress. A well-groomed man in a shirt and tie stood in front of the Union. Winter turned up the volume.

"...further details have not been released yet, and we will get them to you as soon as possible. Back to you in the studio."

The scene changed to a man and woman behind a news desk with the Channel 4 logo in the background. "Thank you, Stan," the man said. "If you're just joining us, we have breaking news from Tishbe University. Early this morning federal agents raided the school's administrative offices, arresting President Charles Wissman as well as several members of his staff on federal charges of embezzlement, tax evasion, and fraud. Though details have not yet been released, a source informs us that the losses to the university could total in the millions. Tishbe's board of directors also wishes us to inform all students and parents not to panic, and that classes will continue as scheduled Monday morning."

Winter turned off the TV and sat in her silent room while students continued to wander in the halls and TVs blared the continuing news report from nearby open doors. She stared at the floor in thought, feeling a strong sense of importance about what she'd just seen—a strong sense of destiny, if such a thing existed. She couldn't explain it. Winter felt as if her dream and the news report were linked. Perhaps she could do something…but what? Shaking her head, she put the thought away as ludicrous. The politics of a university were beyond her, and no nightmare could make any difference.

At lunch, she braved going to the Union. It felt good to get out of the room, and she took her time walking across the Meadow. The sun beamed down through the clear blue sky, mocking her for spending all morning inside. Media vans, with satellite dishes pointed to the sky, parked all along the service road between the Union and the fine arts department. As Winter walked to the Union, she wondered where the reporters could be—perhaps in the administration building, camped outside the boardroom.

"Hey." Kaci waved from a booth near the entrance. "Want to join us?"

Winter inspected the other girls sitting at the table…all upperclassmen she didn't know. A flicker of jealousy sprang up inside her.

"No," she said. "I've…got plans. I'm getting my food to-go."

"Oh, okay," said Kaci, looking disappointed. "See you later."

"Yeah, later."

Winter took her food back to her room. For the rest of the day, she did nothing but berate herself for turning down Kaci.

The next morning, Kaci called. *"Get dressed, we're going to church."*

"Church?" asked Winter.

Kaci laughed. *"You do go to church, don't you?"*

"Yes, of course! I just thought…you want to take me?"

"Would you rather spend your entire weekend alone? You might fool everyone else, but you can't fool me. We leave in an hour. Meet me in the lobby."

"Are you sure?"

"I'm not asking, am I?" said Kaci.

"Okay. I'll be ready." Winter hung up the phone and rifled through her closet. She picked out the most normal outfit she could find—still black, of course, but more formal than Goth. She showered, dressed, and was waiting with her Bible in her lap with thirty minutes to spare.

14

By the end of the next week, Winter felt the fog of class overload begin to lift. Students no longer rushed frantically across the Meadow to find the shortest routes between buildings; the cafeteria served lunches at a steady pace that kept the line from becoming annoyingly long; and homework became a matter of habit, not an intruding inconvenience. Everything became routine—except English. Mrs. Pritchett seemed to think routine was a sin.

The next Monday, as Winter took notes in Biology, suddenly memory and perception aligned in a way that made her stop writing and look around in wonder. She scanned the room as the base of her skull tingled. It felt as if she had seen all of this before...as if she were living exact events and moments she had already lived. She could even recall with amazing clarity the very words the professor spoke...new words to her now, but yet somehow already part of her memory. She moved her head, her hand, and her feet in minute ways, not because she had to but because she was supposed to...it had already been done.

Pen, she thought, and turned to watch her neighbor drop a pen.

She was supposed to lean over and pick it up, so she did.

Danger. She turned to the door, expecting a gunman to crash through, but nothing happened. The strange intuition or déjà vu disappeared then, somehow leaving her feeling empty and blind.

It's just my imagination, she told herself. Just ordinary déjà vu. Right?

It happened again that evening. She knew beforehand when Kaci would knock on her door, and the exact number of steps Summer would take to open it.

"Are you coming?" Kaci asked.

Summer looked at Winter for an answer.

"Um...where?" To small group...

"To small group," Kaci said. "I won't take no for an answer."

"I don't know." That's what she was supposed to say. "Something's come up."

"What?"

"I, ah..." Were brain tumors genetic? Could I have one? That's what I thought...

"That's what I thought. Let's go, both of you," Kaci said. Summer turned for her purse and Winter stood.

"I guess." What's wrong with me? Can tumors cause déjà vu? Don't forget your Bible...

"Don't forget your Bible," Summer said.

Winter grabbed hers from the desk and followed Kaci out. As she passed through the door, the déjà vu ended. Chills ran down her body. The hall spun. She set a hand on the wall.

"Are you okay?" asked Summer.

"Yeah...I'm fine. I think I stood up too fast. Just a little disoriented, that's all. It's gone now, anyway."

Summer smiled and turned to catch up with Kaci. Winter sighed and followed.

"An F?!" she spat at Mrs. Pritchett after class later that week. "You gave me an F?"

"I did not give you an F," the old lady said, gazing over her round glasses. "You earned an F."

Winter scanned her paper again—it seemed to have been dipped in red ink. Blood dripping. Winter closed her eyes and tried to push away her most recent nightmare. "This is stupid, there's no way I deserved an F!" She slapped the paper against the lectern. "You can't do this!"

"Young lady," Pritchett said with only the slightest firming of her voice, "you are on dangerous ground. I suggest you change your attitude and give more effort for the next assignment."

"It wasn't my attitude or my effort that was the problem!" Winter felt her anger rising and her face flushing. "You just don't like me! Admit it!" Running…panting. Winter whimpered a little at the flash.

Mrs. Pritchett raised an eyebrow. "Admitted."

"But you don't even know me!" God, not again! Not now!

Pritchett looked Winter over from head to toe as she had done the week before. "I don't need to know you. Your dress tells me everything I need to know."

"The way I dress has nothing to do with who I am!" Déjà vu. Someone was coming. Winter's chest tightened with fear. She held her breath.

"On the contrary, the way a person dresses very often reflects that person's true nature. Your outward presentation is merely a mirror of your self-worth," said Mrs. Pritchett.

The déjà vu disappeared without anything happening. "I can't take it anymore!"

"Excuse me? By all means, drop the class if you feel so inclined."

Winter put her hands to the side of her head. "No, not the class.

I'm sorry."

Mrs. Pritchett's face softened. "Child, are you all right?"

"No, I'm not." Winter rushed out of the room, trying to hold back tears.

That night, she awoke screaming from yet another nightmare. This time, a little girl stood watching her while Kaci lay bleeding on the floor. For one fleeting moment, she thought she could still see the little girl watching from the corner of the room. She almost screamed again.

"What's wrong?" Summer moaned.

Winter took a deep breath and wiped the sweat from her forehead. "Nothing, sorry. Bad dream."

She lay back down and tried to clear her mind. Summer's breathing indicated she had fallen asleep again. Winter glanced at her clock—four forty-five. What was happening to her?

The next night was Friday, and Summer had her first official date with Jeffrey, leaving Winter alone.

Winter sat down to do a little Bible study and watch some TV at the same time. The barrage of disturbing nightmares and frightening déjà vus left her with many unanswered questions. Winter prayed for several minutes before beginning her study—asking for guidance and understanding. She found comfort in a passage from Psalm 24—a passage that she had flipped to randomly:

*"Such people may seek you and worship in your presence, O God of Jacob. Open up, **ancient** gates! Open up, **ancient** doors, and let the King of glory enter."*

Funny. Why was the word "ancient" in bold?

A phrase from the TV broke through her thoughts, the volume suddenly very loud.

"It's an ancient secret," said one of the cartoon characters. Winter eyed the TV with her head cocked sideways and one hand on the remote. Why had that phrase been louder than the rest?

Then a déjà vu and cold chill washed over her, like all the other times that week, but this time it disappeared after only a moment. When it faded away, she returned to her Bible.

The word "ancient" was no longer in bold.

Weird.

Someone walked by in the hall, talking on a cell phone. She could only distinguish a few words through the door as they passed by. "…later…sounds great…go to the Ancient…yeah…no way!"

The déjà vu returned—stronger than ever.

With it came the idea that all this might be from God. Perhaps these dreams and premonitions could lead to the reason God had told her to come to Tishbe University in the first place. Or did she really just have a tumor?

Winter shook her head and took a deep breath.

"Okay, God," she said. "I'm going. If this is you, please let me know. But if I'm sick, let me know that too. I'm tired of wondering." She closed her Bible and left to go to the Ancient.

A steady breeze blew from the north, and she wished she had brought a jacket. She folded her arms tight across her chest and walked down the dark sidewalk. Being alone at near midnight made her nervous. She quickened her pace.

It didn't take long to reach the Meadow using the shortcut Kaci had shown her. She saw only one other person walking that late at night, and as she made her way to the Ancient, that person left the Meadow, going between two buildings.

At the Ancient, she sat on one of the benches beside the trunk. Winter faced the way she had come, lost in her thoughts.

Could a person feel a brain tumor? Her scalp tingled at the thought, and she reached up to scratch her head. Was this how Mom felt? Perhaps she should tell her dad and go see a doctor—it would be the smart thing to do. If they could catch it early enough, the doctors might be able to help. But her mom never spoke about déjà vus or dreams. Of course, there was probably a lot she didn't tell Winter.

Her face drooped, and her heart felt heavy. She missed her mom…it had been a long three and a half years.

"This is crazy." She stood to leave.

"Winter?" a guy said from behind. Winter jumped and turned. It was Davis, Jeffery's roommate.

"Oh," she said, "hi. Don't sneak up on me."

"I didn't. What are you doing here this late?" He came to stand at her side.

"Just sitting and thinking." She sat back down.

"You shouldn't be out here alone."

She looked up at him. "Well, what about you? You're out here walking alone."

"I was in the Union working on a paper." He glanced around. "But that's beside the point. Before school was out in the spring, a couple of girls were attacked. It's not entirely safe for girls to be out alone."

"Attacked?"

"Yeah, and they never found out who was doing it."

"Were they okay?" she asked.

"I think one had a broken arm, but they both managed to get away," he said. "The whole school was pretty spooked over it. Has no one told you this?"

Winter thought about her uneasy premonitions and nightmares. Could there be a connection? Was God trying to warn her that the attacks would continue? And get worse? Did God send her out here just for this information? For the first time in two weeks, Winter let the idea creep in that she might not be crazy after all. She smiled and rubbed her head as it tingled again.

"What kind of paper were you working on?" she asked.

Davis took a seat beside her and set his backpack in front of his feet. "English Lit."

"You any good at it?"

"I guess. I mean, I usually get As."

Winter pursed her lips together. "I just got an F on my first paper."

Davis looked at her and adjusted his glasses. "Wow! Really? Who's your professor?"

"Pritchett."

"Pritchett's a prude." He chuckled. "I had her second term last year."

"I don't think she likes me," Winter said.

"No, I wouldn't imagine she does. She's sort of…old school."

Winter stared at the ground.

Davis took a deep breath. "Listen, I could help you if you'd like."

"No thanks, I'm good," she said. "It's not exactly my first F." Winter half-smiled. "Besides, I've got bigger things to worry about than a stupid F." She bit her lip.

"Okay, just let me know if you change your mind."

Winter heard footsteps. She looked to either side expecting someone else to come walking around the Ancient. But no one came and the footsteps continued. Cold chills came over her and she sat up straight. She had been here before…déjà vu. These footsteps meant something. This time Winter knew the danger was real.

Her time had come. All her premonitions and dreams of the past week had been leading to this moment. Now that it was happening, she had no doubt God had orchestrated everything. If only she could understand before it was too late. She stood. Adrenaline rushed through her body.

"What's wrong…" she whispered to herself…Davis was about

to say that.

"What's wrong?" Davis asked as soon as the very same words had escaped Winter's lips.

"Someone's coming, I hear footsteps." That's what she was supposed to reply.

"I don't hear anything," he said, his voice betraying his confusion. He stood and watched her.

Winter looked toward the history building, where the footsteps seemed to come from. But she saw no one walking to the Ancient. She moved and searched all around the tree, but no one came from any direction. Yet she could still hear the footsteps.

"You're freaking me..." she whispered.

"You're freaking me out," Davis said from right behind.

Winter looked again to the history building. Someone walked along the path on the far side of the Meadow. She studied the girl. It took only a moment to realize that the footsteps synchronized perfectly with the pace of the girl. Then the sound of the girl's footsteps faded, and she heard quicker and heavier footsteps. Winter's sense of urgency doubled, the adrenaline surging through her body again.

"What are you..."

"What are you doing?" Davis asked. He came alongside her.

She turned her head to the quicker steps, which seemed to be coming from the Union. A guy was walking very fast along the same path as the girl, his pace synchronized with the new footsteps.

"Will you please answer me?" Davis asked.

"Shhh!"

As Winter watched, the distance between the two shortened. The girl glanced back and then sped up. The guy began to run and so did the girl. Winter's legs were moving before her mind registered the need. It was impulse. She was supposed to run. She had done this before.

"Come on!" Winter shouted within the first two steps. Davis

sped past her toward the pursuing man.

"HEY!" Davis shouted. His voice cut through the cool air, echoing from the buildings.

The man saw Winter and Davis rushing across the Meadow and stopped. He looked around, then followed a path leading away and disappeared between two buildings.

The girl stopped and collapsed to the ground. When Winter reached her, she was shaking and crying with fear. Winter knelt and embraced her. Nearby, the bells of Olamel began tolling midnight.

"It's okay," she said. "It's okay. God was watching out for you."

15

Four Years Ago

"Since it's my house, I'll go first," said Stacy.

"Whatever you do," Claire said to Winter, "don't pick a dare from her."

Stacy grinned. "Okay, then…Claire, truth or dare?"

"Truth," said Claire without hesitation.

"Do you have a crush on someone?"

"Yes."

"Who?" Stacy asked.

"Unh unh…Only one question at a time," said Claire. "Winter…truth or dare?"

"Truth," Winter said softly.

"Why didn't your dad want you to come?"

Winter's mind raced for a viable answer. She had told the others that he argued with her for over an hour before relenting. She hated lying, but she didn't want them to think her reservations were her own.

"I guess he was afraid I would forget my old friends," she said.

"Your turn, Winter," said Claire.

"Um, okay. Alison?"

"Dare," said Alison.

Winter racked her brain but couldn't come up with anything good. "Uh, pick your nose?"

Alison grinned and shoved her finger up her nose. "Truth or dare, Claire?"

"Dare."

"Call Mark." She held her hand to Claire. Across her palm was written a phone number.

"But I didn't talk to him, you did," said Claire.

"Then pretend you're me."

"But I don't even know him! He's just some random boy we saw at the mall!"

"So?"

Claire bit her lip and grabbed the phone Stacy offered. She punched in the numbers and held the receiver gently to her ear.

"Hey," she said after a moment. "Is this Mark? This is…Alison." The other girls giggled. "I just wanted to know if you enjoyed the movie…Yeah, I'm glad you came with us too…What?" She put a hand over the mouthpiece and looked at Winter cautiously. "He wants to know why you ran out crying."

"Tell him," Stacy said. Winter bit her lip and looked away.

As Claire softly told Mark a little of Winter's story, Winter tuned her out and thought about the movie again. It mirrored her own life…a mother with cancer, a teenage daughter…In the movie, they had gone to a beach house to live out those last happy days together. Life was so unfair…nothing like a movie. She blinked back tears as she heard Claire hang up.

"Truth or dare, Stacy?" Claire asked, though she looked at Winter apologetically.

"Dare," said Stacy.

Claire narrowed her eyes. "Lick the bottom of one of your shoes."

Stacy hesitated, then stretched back to grab the nearest shoe. She licked it quickly and tossed it away.

"Alison," Stacy said, "truth or dare?" Stacy had a mischievous glint in her eyes, and, for a moment, Alison looked as if she might take the dare.

"Truth," Alison finally said.

"Are you still a virgin?"

Winter gasped...and she wasn't the only one. Suddenly, all four girls were sitting up straight and staring at each other with wide, shocked eyes.

Alison pursed her lips and didn't say anything.

"If you don't answer you'll be admitting that you're not," Stacy said with a grin. "So you might as well just say it." All eyes were on Alison.

"No," she said, as her face turned crimson.

"I knew it!"

"That question wasn't fair!" said Winter.

"All questions are fair! If you don't want the question, then pick the dare!"

"Still...you should leave personal stuff out of it!"

"Personal stuff is what makes this game fun! You have played truth or dare before, haven't you?" asked Stacy.

"I don't mind," Alison said. "Besides, you'd all find out Phillip and I were doing it anyway...he can't keep his mouth shut."

Winter's jaw dropped.

"Truth or dare, Winter?" asked Alison.

"What?" Winter's mind still reeled at Alison's and Stacy's callousness.

"Truth or dare? It's your turn now!" Alison also had a mischievous glint in her eyes.

Winter swallowed hard and ran through all the embarrassing things she'd done that she wasn't ready to tell her new friends.

"Dare," she croaked.

Alison jumped up and ran for the bathroom. She returned with a large jar of Vaseline.

"Smear this all over your face." She handed Winter the jar.

Forty-five minutes later, Winter had successfully dodged all of Stacy's and Alison's questions and only accepted Claire's more playful ones. The downside was that she had to endure all their horrendous dares. In addition to the Vaseline, Winter now had Cheerios plastered to her face and had been forced to eat a live daddy longlegs spider. At long last, the painful game ended.

"I need to call Phillip," said Alison.

"Oh, you remember him now, do you?" asked Claire. "I thought Mark was the new boy for you."

Alison stuck out her tongue and got up. As she walked out the room, she was already dialing the phone.

"How about drinks?" Stacy asked.

"Sure!" said Claire and the two girls stood and left.

Winter couldn't bring herself to move just yet. Her mind and body were in shock at what they had made her do and the things they had said. She had never realized how much of a sheltered life she had lived.

Once alone, Winter grabbed her bag and headed to the hall bathroom to clean her face and brush the spider remains out of her teeth.

The door rested against the frame unlatched, and Winter pushed it open without a sound. After a few inches, she stopped. Claire stood in front of the mirror in just her underwear, brushing her hair. She had assumed Claire had gone downstairs to help Stacy. Winter started to close the door and go back to Stacy's room, but something caught her eye.

Across Claire's back and shoulders were massive bruises. They were long and ugly in deep purples and blacks. There were more bruises on the backs of her legs. Claire turned to look at the door. Winter caught her breath and fled back to Stacy's room, hoping she had not been seen.

Present Day

When Summer came back to Carmichael after her date, Winter drifted away from the crowd to meet her near the entrance of the lobby.

"What's going on?" Summer asked.

Winter looked back to where a police officer spoke to Laurie. Kaci had her arms around the girl. Davis leaned against a wall nearby.

"That's Laurie Dunaway," Winter said. "She's on Kaci's floor. Someone tried to attack her tonight." She turned back to see Summer's face pale.

"What? Attack?"

Winter nodded and stepped to Summer's side. "Come on. Let's sit."

"I don't understand. What's Davis doing here?"

Winter glanced at Davis. "That, I think I can explain," she said. "What I can't explain is why he's been avoiding me since we got back."

"What? We? Winter, what happened?"

"Sit first." She led Summer to the nearest couch, where she gave a quick account of what happened in the Meadow, leaving out the unbelievable parts. She wasn't even sure she believed the full truth.

"Are you okay?" Summer asked. "I mean, you didn't get hurt or anything?"

The officer left, and the crowd began to disperse. Winter watched Kaci and Davis move away and whisper together in the far corner of the room.

"No, I'm fine," Winter said. Davis glanced at her, while Kaci spoke to him. They looked grim.

"You seem a little distracted."

"You think? Kaci's coming. Let's go." Winter grabbed Summer and pulled.

"Winter...stop."

"What's going on?" Winter asked Kaci.

"Um, we need to talk to you...to both of you," Kaci said. She turned and led them back to the table Davis had moved to. After they all sat, Kaci wrung her hands and eyed Davis.

"Say something." Winter folded her arms.

"I already told you some of it," Davis said. "But Summer needs to hear it too."

"Is this about the attacks last year?" Winter asked.

"Attacks? You mean this isn't the first time?" asked Summer with a high-pitched squeal.

Kaci nodded. "There were four attacks in all."

"Was anyone hurt?" Summer asked.

"Not really," said Kaci. "The first girl was just pushed to the ground and her purse was stolen, and the second was probably a stupid prank by one of the fraternities—someone in a mask jumped out from behind the Ancient and scared the crap out of a freshman. She lived on my floor too, by the way.

"But the third attack was more serious. The girl was struck on the head from behind and carried across the Meadow. She came to as they were walking between two buildings and managed to get away. But during the struggle, the attacker broke her arm with whatever it was he used to hit her head. Her screaming saved her. Some people nearby heard, and when they came rushing to see what was happening, he fled.

"The last attack was a near miss. The attacker was about to strike the girl from behind when a group of vigilante guys jumped up from some bushes and scared him away. That could have been a frat prank too."

"You don't think all of them could have been pranks?" Winter asked.

"The third attack was definitely not a prank," Kaci said.

"You mean, they never caught the attacker?" asked Summer.

Kaci shook her head. "The school beefed up security for a while, and claimed there was an investigation, but nobody was ever caught. The attacks did stop, though."

"Until now," said Davis.

"Until now." They looked at each other silently for a moment.

"What are we going to do?" Summer sounded as if she might cry.

"Well for one, don't ever go anywhere alone at night. That should be common sense anyway. And secondly, try not to be out late. Both of these, it seems, Winter decided not to do," Kaci said with a reprimanding glare.

"Hey, it was a good thing I was there, don't you think?" Winter asked.

"You were lucky…it could have been you getting attacked."

Davis sat up straighter. "By the way, why were you there? Did you know?"

Winter took a deep breath and tried to force a confused expression on her face. "Did I know what?"

"Did you know it was going to happen?" he asked.

Summer and Kaci exchanged a curious glance, then looked at Winter.

"I'm not sure I know what you mean," Winter said.

Davis leaned forward. "You were there waiting before I came along and you heard footsteps when I couldn't. How did you know what was going to happen?"

"You were waiting?" Summer asked.

Winter shrugged. "I was just sitting under the Ancient thinking."

Kaci leaned forward too, her eyes bright and engaged. "But why did you go to the Ancient so late at night?"

Winter shrugged again. "Just wanted to, I guess."

Davis shook his head. "I don't buy it. You're lying to us. You were waiting. Somehow you knew what was going to happen."

"Did you hear someone talking about the attack?" Kaci asked.

"Yeah, maybe I heard something." She crossed her arms. "I don't remember."

"Where?" asked Summer. "Did God tell you?"

"God?" Davis asked Summer. "What are you talking about?"

"She said she heard God speak to her last summer. And she knew Angie's name...I bet God told her that, too," said Summer.

"He did not!"

"So God told you what was going to happen?" asked Davis.

"No! I mean...I don't know. I—I don't remember!" said Winter.

"What do you mean, you don't remember?" Kaci asked.

"It means I don't remember! Just drop it!"

"Then how did you hear the footsteps?" asked Davis. "You said you heard footsteps, but I didn't hear a thing."

"Listen." Winter stood, her chair sliding back into the wall with a thud. "It's really late and I'm really tired. And I'd rather not be interrogated right now."

"Sorry," Davis said. "I was just wondering."

"Yeah, well, don't," she said. "Stay here and talk about me, I know you want to, but I'm going to bed." Winter turned and sped away.

17

In the second week of October, the weather cooled dramatically. Winter watched with longing as Summer readied herself for band rehearsal Wednesday afternoon. For what seemed like the millionth time, she almost called out to Summer as she left…almost called her back to tell her everything. Instead, Winter curled up in her papasan chair and stared at her third consecutive F in English comp. She sighed as the weight of depression spread through her chest again.

There was a knock on the door. Winter made no attempt to answer.

"Winter, I know you're there," came Kaci's voice, muffled by the door. "I saw you come in from class."

Winter still didn't speak.

"I want to talk to you," Kaci said. "And I'm not leaving until you let me in."

Winter rolled her eyes. "I'd rather have some privacy, if you don't mind."

"Not today," Kaci said with a little tartness. "I'm going to have a talk with you even if you make me use my master key."

Winter grunted. "Fine!" she shouted. "Use your key!"

There was a sound of a card sliding into the card reader and the click of the lock.

Winter stared out the open blinds, arms crossed. She didn't acknowledge Kaci's entrance. Kaci pulled one of the computer chairs over to sit beside her.

"Hey," Kaci said softly. "What's going on?"

"Nothing."

"That's not true. You haven't been the same since that night you saved Laurie," Kaci said. "Now tell me what's wrong."

"I don't want to talk about it."

"Winter, it's been weeks! You don't come to the CLC or church anymore. You barely speak one or two words to me or Summer. Summer thinks you hate her."

"Well, you seem to be getting along fine without me!"

"Is that what you want? Are you trying to push us away? I thought we were friends! Do you enjoy being miserable?"

Winter sat forward. "You think I enjoy this?" Her chin began to quiver. "I'm miserable because I don't know how to do anything different. That's what I do, Kaci. I push people away. It's the only thing I'm good at. I hate that about myself, do you understand? But I can't change! I don't..." She put a hand over her mouth and looked away. "I don't know how."

"Well, the first thing you can do is stop avoiding us."

"Kaci, I can't..."

"Why?"

Winter shifted in her seat.

"Why, Winter?"

Winter turned, her face burning. "Because you'll ask questions I don't want to answer. Just leave me alone!" She turned her head to the window and closed her eyes.

Kaci sat in silence for a few moments. "We've been doing a very interesting study at the CLC. I think you'll find the subject fascinating. And I think it might help you."

Winter heard her flipping pages.

"Romans 12:4-7 says: 'Just as our bodies have many parts and each part has a special function, so it is with Christ's body. We are many parts of one body, and we all belong to each other. In his grace, God has given us different gifts for doing certain things well. So if God has given you the ability to prophesy, speak out with as much faith as God has given you.'"

At this, Winter cut her eyes to Kaci and quickly cut them back. Kaci paused. Winter could feel Kaci's eyes boring into the side of her face.

Kaci went back to the Bible. "'If your gift is serving others, serve them well. If you are a teacher, teach well.' We each have different gifts given to us by God the moment he comes into our hearts."

Winter still did not reply. Again, she could feel Kaci watching her. She heard Kaci take a quick breath, and then the pages flipped again.

"Acts 2:17 says, 'In the last days, God says, I will pour out my Spirit upon all people. Your sons and daughters will prophesy. Your young men will see visions, and your old men will dream dreams.'"

This time Winter not only cut her eyes, but turned a little toward Kaci.

Kaci sighed and smiled. "Summer said you knew Angie's name without being told, and she told me about that night at the chapel. You also said that God told you to come here. But these aren't the only things that have happened, are they?"

Winter stared at the floor.

"Do you hear other things? Do you see things, Winter? Do you see visions or dream dreams like this verse says?"

Finally, Winter looked Kaci in the eyes, unable to stop the emotion from bursting out. "Yes," she croaked. "Am I going crazy? My mom had a brain tumor, do you think I could too? I'm scared, Kaci. I can't take this anymore."

"No, I don't think you're crazy at all or that anything's wrong with you. I think you have a gift—a very special and unique gift given by God."

"How can you be sure?"

"Because I recognize the signs. Winter, you don't realize how special you are. You really were sent here by God. Do you not believe that?"

"I don't know what to believe."

Kaci sat up. "Then just look around you. You've only been here a couple of months, and you've barely engaged anyone. But your mere presence has already changed lives. The only place Summer spends more time at than the music building or here is the CLC now. And I doubt she often went to church back home. Davis spends hours every night reading his Bible and studying somewhere in the Meadow, hoping he'll be the one to catch the attacker. He won't admit it, but you couldn't drag him out of the library last year, and he's not exactly the physical type. Every girl in this dorm knows your name, and you have no idea how encouraged and emboldened they are to be themselves and not be some plastic cutout of what the world expects a girl to be. All because of you! And Laurie…Laurie! I've never seen a person become so committed to God so quickly." Kaci spread her arms. "Imagine what you could accomplish if you actually cared enough to try. It's shameful that you have such a wonderful gift and you won't even use it!"

"I didn't ask for anything," Winter said. "I've seen the looks all those people give me. They think I'm crazy. Or evil."

"We don't ask for spiritual gifts, they're just given to us. And people don't think you're crazy or evil. It's hard to explain, but the best way to describe it is that they're awed by you."

"Maybe they don't think I'm crazy, but if they knew about what I see, they would. Please don't tell anyone. Being a freak is one thing, but this…this is too much. I can't be that again…I can't."

Kaci softened. "I won't tell anyone if you don't want me to. But, Winter, having a gift from God is nothing to be ashamed of. You have the gift of prophecy, and according to the Bible, it's one of the greatest gifts God could give."

"Yeah, but I doubt prophecy is a very common gift."

"No," Kaci said, "it's not common at all."

Winter looked away and wiped her eyes with her sleeve.

"How often do you see or hear things?" Kaci asked.

Winter shrugged. "It's been a while. Nothing's happened since Laurie. And I don't really see things…it's mostly like déjà vu. Sometimes I have dreams at night, too."

"So God did tell you what was about to happen. You were waiting, like Davis said."

Winter gazed out the window. She could just make out the tops of some of the buildings surrounding the Meadow. "No, not really. God just told me to go to the Ancient. I didn't know why, but I guess I should have. I had been having dreams about a girl being chased and attacked. When the attack started, it was as if I had already seen it and already knew what would happen." She turned back to Kaci, waiting for the impending judgment.

None came.

"Promise me this," Kaci said.

"What's that?"

"Promise me that if God shows you something again…anything…even if you don't understand it or you're not sure it's God, come tell me. You shouldn't have to do this alone."

Winter smiled and the heaviness in her chest lifted. Now she felt a surge of nervous energy. "Okay, I promise."

"And," Kaci said, "you should tell Summer."

Winter wrinkled her nose. "Summer wouldn't get it. It would probably freak her out, and she'd go tell everyone her roommate is crazy."

"Summer's not like that." Kaci grinned. "She might not be the brightest crayon in the box, but she's a good friend."

"I know," Winter said. "I just don't think I should tell her yet."

Kaci shrugged. "Sure, it's your call."

"So what's your gift?" Winter asked.

Kaci closed her Bible. "My gift? I told you already, did you forget? Discernment. And encouragement, I think. At least that's what everyone tells me I'm good at."

Winter nodded her approval. "Yeah, I can see that."

"So, you coming back to the CLC now?" asked Kaci. "And church?"

Winter considered it a moment. "Maybe. That is, if no one asks about the strange things I've done."

"Well, only a few of us know of them, and we're not telling," Kaci said with a smile.

"I guess so, then."

"Good," said Kaci. "There's an off-campus party Friday night at the CLC Director's house—sort of a celebration of the end of mid-terms."

"A party? Like, with beer and stuff?" asked Winter. "I...uh...I don't drink anymore."

Kaci looked insulted. "It's a party done by the CLC. There won't be anything like that there. Will you come?"

"I'll think about it."

Kaci nodded and stood to leave. "Okay then, maybe I'll see you there."

"Yeah, maybe."

Before Kaci reached the door she turned back. "By the way," she said, "do you know where Tishbe University gets its name?"

"No."

Kaci grinned again. "Ever hear of Elijah?"

"I think so," Winter said. "I mean, I haven't read much of the Bible yet, but I know the name."

"Elijah was the greatest prophet in the Bible—you can look him up in first Kings," Kaci said as she opened the door.

Winter furrowed her brow.

"He was from a little town called Tishbe." Kaci winked, and then she left.

Winter thought for a long time about what Kaci had said. Maybe there was something to this prophecy gift. Just having an alternative to the brain tumor theory was a huge relief. She looked again at the F on her paper and decided to call Davis.

Four Years Ago

Winter sat in history class taking notes from the projector. The hum of the projector fan and the warmth of the heater, being used for the first time that year, made her sleepy. Mr. Stevens, a middle-aged teacher with thinning hair, sat at his desk watching with his own set of drooping eyes.

Winter saw movement in her peripheral vision, and she turned to look out the rectangular window in the classroom door. Claire was walking by. Winter shot her hand into the air.

"Mr. Stevens?" she asked.

He looked at her.

"May I go to the restroom?"

At first it seemed as if he might object, but he relented and grabbed the hall pass from his desk. Winter dropped her pen, rushed to get the pass, and then hurried out the door. She scanned quickly up and down the empty hall, then darted for the restrooms. Her feet rapped like claves in the deserted corridor.

Winter eased open the door to the restroom and found Claire

standing in front of the mirror inspecting her make-up. Winter stepped in, let the door close, and then leaned back against it. She checked to make sure they were alone.

Claire looked at her, then back to the mirror. "Hey. What's up?"

"I saw the bruises."

Claire's eyes darted to her and then away. "I don't know what you're talking about."

"Last week at Stacy's house," Winter said. "You were changing in the bathroom, and I almost walked in on you. I saw the bruises on your back and legs."

Claire considered her for a moment. "I fell," she said unemotionally and then returned her compact to her purse.

"On your back?" asked Winter.

"Leave me alone," Claire said.

"Did someone do that to you?"

"I said, leave me alone!" Claire made a move to leave, but Winter refused to budge from in front of the door.

"Who was it? Was it your dad?"

Claire's face twisted in a mixture of anger, frustration, and fear. Her voice, low and calm, sounded emotionless. "Just stay out of it, okay, Winter?"

"I can't. Not if I'm going to be any kind of friend."

"If you want to be my friend, then forget what you saw and don't bring it up again," Claire whispered. She took a deep breath that shuddered her chest.

Claire's face filled with such anger, that Winter closed her eyes and held her hands over her face. Nothing happened. After a few seconds, she peaked through her fingers. Claire stared at the floor, tears on her cheek.

"He shouldn't do that to you, it's not right. You should call somebody—or, or I could. I'd do it anonymously or something."

Claire narrowed her eyes at the suggestion and drew her mouth tight. "Just...stay out of it and keep it to yourself." Then she shoved

Winter to the side and left.

Winter stayed in the restroom for a few minutes to give Claire time to get back to her class. Then she went back to class herself, wondering if she could do anything to help Claire. And if by doing so, would she completely destroy their friendship...if she hadn't destroyed it already.

19

Present Day

Davis and Winter sat at a table in the Union going over the finer points of grammar and punctuation to perfect Winter's mid-term essay, due the following day. Frustrated, she ran a hand through her hair and sighed. It was almost too overwhelming.

"I'm sorry…what's the prepositional phrase?"

"This," Davis said, pointing the tip of his mechanical pencil to her paper, "is your prepositional phrase, so you need to place a comma here."

"Okay, so I get the comma, but what is a preposition exactly?"

"You're kidding, right?" Davis let out his own frustrated sigh. "How do you expect to pass Pritchett's class if you don't even know elementary grammar?"

"Hey, I wasn't exactly concerned with this stuff in high school, all right? I did what I had to do to get a good grade, then I forgot it all," Winter said. "So drop the condescension."

"Condescension?"

"Just because I don't know proper grammar doesn't mean I'm

stupid."

"Okay, I get it." Davis closed his eyes.

"Now...prepositions?"

"Right, prepositions. A preposition is a word used before a noun or a pronoun to form a phrase—a prepositional phrase—that modifies..."

"Help me," someone whispered loudly in Winter's ear...a female voice. The hair by her ear swayed beneath the breath of the words. She jerked her head around...no one there.

"Winter? Are you listening?" Davis asked, eyeing her over the rim of his glasses.

"Huh? Oh yeah, prepositional phrase." Winter returned her attention to Davis. She rubbed the paranoid tingling from her ear.

"The phrase modifies," Davis pointed to an example on her paper, "a noun or verb. See?"

"I think so," Winter said. "And the comma?"

"Someone please help!" said the whispered voice again, more loudly and urgently this time. Winter jumped, as if pinched, and looked around. No one. She bit her lip. Her breath quickened. Was it happening again? She scanned the faces of as many people as she could. Nobody seemed to be paying attention to them, and nobody was close enough to have whispered in her ear.

"What's wrong?" Davis asked.

"Did you hear that?" Her voice trembled and she cleared her throat.

"I didn't hear anything, Winter," he said. He leaned back in his chair, folded his arms, and watched her.

"Someone's in trouble." She stood up and turned a complete circle.

Students milled about studying or eating—many doing both at the same time. She strained to hear the whispered voice, but the Union's din mocked her with smiling faces and laughter. Her stomach started to churn.

She heard no amplified footsteps, felt no premonition of danger or déjà vu. No one nearby appeared to be in trouble. She took a deep breath to slow her pulse.

"Winter, would you please explain to me what you're doing?" Davis asked. "Because unless you want to fail your mid-term, we need to keep working on this paper."

Winter frowned, not knowing what else to do. "You're right." She sat down. "I'm sorry, it must be the stress getting to me."

"No problem." He went back to explaining all the reasons why her paper would receive another F.

"God help me! I'm going to die!" the voice said, fainter and further away.

Winter darted her eyes around, trying not to let Davis notice. Nothing. No one. Anxiety gave way to nausea, but she went back to the paper and tried to concentrate on Davis. Perhaps this was simply God's way of warning her about something to come. Perhaps he would reveal more information when needed, and there was nothing immediate to do tonight. Her mind accepted the explanation, but her heart could not be entirely convinced. She felt sick, but what could she do?

By a quarter till midnight, Winter had a fully corrected paper. What's more, she mostly understood how Davis had made each correction.

But she never heard the strange voice again.

The next morning, Winter borrowed an outfit from Summer and tried her best to "pretty" herself, though she loathed every moment. Summer insisted on doing Winter's makeup and even handpicked a candy-striped scarf as an accessory to the white sweater Winter wore.

Winter had never felt so violated in her life. Pritchett better be worth it.

Pritchett seemed pleased at the change in Winter, who felt hopeful for a passing grade. It would be a long wait until her paper came back sometime next week.

After class, Winter skipped the cafeteria to have lunch in her room, in order to de-pretty-fy herself. Kaci lurked in the hallway waiting for her.

"Did you hear?" she asked as Winter walked to her door. "By the way, nice outfit."

Winter rolled her eyes in disgust. "Hear what?"

"Jennifer Hollingsworth, from fifth floor, didn't come home last night. Her roommate doesn't know where she is, and no one's heard from her."

"Okay," said Winter. "What's that mean?"

"I don't know," Kaci said. "But some of the girls think she may have been attacked. Just thought you should know."

Kaci watched her so knowingly that Winter felt her face pale. Winter put a hand to her churning stomach. "Thanks for telling me."

"Are you all right?"

Winter squinted her eyes. "Just feeling a little sick, that's all. Must have been lunch."

"Okay, well, if you hear anything please let me know."

Winter nodded. "I will." Kaci left and Winter fled into her room.

As soon as the door shut, she turned her back to it and sank to the floor. Pulling her knees in close, she hugged them and started to weep. Why was this happening to her? What had God expected her to do? She had no instructions of where to go or how to find the voice, so how could she have acted differently?

Winter simulated all the courses of action she could have chosen the night before—her distraught mind torturing her with images of heroic rescues. But the fact remained that when she heard the voice, she didn't know what to do or where to go.

It was easy to look back and see her mistakes now that she knew what had happened. Yet, if the same thing happened again tonight, would she react differently? Winter couldn't answer that question. That pained her all the more.

"I don't want this," she said to the empty room and to God. "Take it away...give it to someone else. Just let Jennifer be okay, please. I'm sorry I didn't listen. I'm sorry I didn't do anything. I can't have this gift...please, give it to someone else."

She felt the tears soaking through the knees of her pants. She looked up and blinked until she could see clearly. Her chest ached.

"This is all my fault. You can't use me...I'm broken, I'm worthless."

The air in the room stirred around her. A chill ran across her body, and a single beam of light pierced a crack in the blinds and landed on her hand.

She turned her hand over and held the light in her palm.

"What am I supposed to do? If you're not going to take this away, at least tell me what to do."

The beam widened. Winter watched the dust particles float through the air. She shifted and put her face in the light, letting the warmth play over her skin. Then she opened her eyes and stared into the beam.

Flash. A girl. Black hair.

Winter moved out of the light. "I can't do that! I don't know how!" She held the light in her hand a moment more, then plunged her face back in.

Flash. Running. Falling.

She moved away again. "Just tell me what to do! I don't know what you want!"

Again, she entered the light.

Flash. Kaci.

Winter sat back and held her breath. The light played nearby on the wall. A moment later, the beam was gone. "Of course! Kaci will know what to do!"

Winter stood and rushed into the hall. She took the stairs two at a time, and within a couple moments she knocked on Kaci's door.

"I think I may know what happened to Jennifer," Winter said the second the door opened.

Kaci swallowed hard, and her eyes widened. "You do?"

Winter nodded and stepped in.

Kaci closed the door. "Did you hear something?"

Winter nodded again. "Last night, when I was in the Union with Davis, I heard a voice."

"What kind of voice?"

"I think it was hers. She was calling for help."

Kaci thought for a few moments. "Did you do anything?"

Winter looked at the floor. "I didn't know what to do! It was like she was whispering in my ear, but she wasn't anywhere nearby. If I had known where she was, I might have done something, but I thought maybe it was just a warning...I didn't think it was actually happening!" Frustration constricted Winter's throat.

"It's okay, I understand. Don't get yourself upset."

"I can't handle this, Kaci! I don't want this gift!" It wasn't until Winter reached up and wiped the tears from her cheek that she realized she was crying again.

Kaci rubbed her arm. "You'll figure it out soon enough. Remember, God's never going to test you beyond what you can handle. If he had wanted you to help Jennifer, then he would have told you more."

"Yeah, maybe. What should we do now? I think she may have been hurt...or worse."

Kaci frowned and sat. "The only thing we can do, I guess...pray."

"That's it? Pray?"

"Yeah...that's it, Winter. What else are we supposed to do?"

Winter sighed. "I hate this," she mumbled.

"Maybe it's not so bad," said Kaci.

"I...I've got to go study." Winter left, and the tears started again as she walked down the stairs.

20

To make up for wearing Summer's girly clothes on Thursday, Winter dug out the best, blackest Goth outfit she could find for the CLC party Friday night: a black miniskirt with dark-purple striped tights underneath, a black corset with a leather shrug, and military-style boots. She painted on black eyeliner and lipstick, and powdered her face so her cheekbones looked hollow. Winter inserted a ring in all of her piercings for the first time that school year: three over her right eye, five in each ear, one in her nose, and one in her bellybutton.

Kaci and Summer waited for her in the lobby. When they first saw Winter, their eyes widened to the size of saucers.

"Do you like?" Winter asked.

"Winter, are you sure…" Kaci said.

"Is there a problem?"

Kaci and Summer shook their heads in unison, but their expressions didn't change. Perfect. Winter led them out the door.

When Winter entered the party, all heads turned to stare. Some wore expressions of alarm or concern, while others watched her with amusement. Winter suppressed a grin and carefully ignored their looks. It was an art she had perfected.

Kaci and Summer lurked behind, sulking on the porch. As she looked back at them, Winter could not help but smile at their horrified faces.

"Come on," she said.

They crept into the house and stood by her side. A few of the more immature guys in the CLC came loping through the Victorian foyer, but they stopped dead the moment they saw Winter. She almost laughed.

Loud music blared from somewhere. Kaci abandoned her to go speak to another friend, and Jeffrey showed up to rescue Summer. Winter made a mental note to get them back. A moment later, everyone returned to their conversations.

She walked into the next room, where she found a table full of refreshments. As she placed a cucumber sandwich on her plate, she saw Davis coming toward her.

"Hey," he said. "Nice outfit."

Winter smirked. "Thanks, I think."

"How did it go in English comp yesterday?"

"Okay, I hope. I won't know until Tuesday."

"I'm sure you'll pass this one—that is, since I practically rewrote the paper for you." He grinned.

Winter smiled. "We'll see."

Refreshments in hand, Winter and Davis made their way to the backyard, where two teams were engaged in a heated game of volleyball.

"You know, it's bad for your image to be seen with me." She sat down in a patio chair.

Davis shrugged and took the chair beside her. "I don't care about image. Most of these people are too wrapped up in themselves to get to know someone more than superficially anyway. I'd rather hang out with someone who's not afraid to be who they really are."

"Even if everyone thinks I'm a freak? You'll eventually turn into a freak by association."

"We're all freaks. It's just a matter of perspective."

"And what exactly is your perspective?" she asked.

"A freak is someone who denies who they are," Davis said. "Whether they pretend to be something they're not, or don't know who they are to begin with."

"So what does that make me?"

"You at least know who you are. In my book, that makes you one of the least freaky people here."

Winter laughed. "I don't think many people here would agree with you. You have a very strange perspective."

"Maybe so. I guess that's the thing that makes me a freak."

"Yeah, well…I think you'll find that I'm much more of a freak than you realize."

As dusk fell, spotlights were turned on to illuminate the game. Eventually, Kaci joined them, a soda in one hand and a small plate of snacks in the other.

After about an hour of listening to Davis and Kaci reminisce about freshman year, Winter leaned over to suggest to Kaci that they find Summer and go. Winter froze before the words could form on her lips. A guy walked by…someone she recognized but couldn't place the name.

Déjà vu washed over her as he passed. Her vision changed. Winter felt a twinge of fear at the new experience. Despite the feeble light from the floodlights, she could see through every shadow. Yet color no longer existed. Everything, from the manicured grass to the painted eaves, now appeared in shades of gray. Everything…but this one guy. His color shone brilliantly, as if he had absorbed all the pigment around him. All sounds but his diminished with the color. She could hear him breathing. When he spoke, his voice hurt her ears.

He walked past with a friend and entered the house. Winter's vision and hearing returned to normal. The déjà vu went away. The whole sensation had lasted just a few seconds.

Winter slapped Kaci on the arm.

"Oww! What?"

"Who was that?" Winter asked.

"Who?"

"The guy who just walked by. Tall, skinny, with shaggy brown hair?"

"Oh," Kaci said as she closed her eyes in thought. "I think you're talking about Peter Strong. He's this year's CLC president. Why do you ask?"

Winter gave her a knowing look. "We have to find him."

Kaci leaned toward her. "Did it happen again?" she whispered.

Winter widened her eyes with emphasis for an answer.

Kaci pursed her lips and nodded.

"What's going on?" Davis asked.

"Nothing," Winter said. "We're just about to leave, that's all." She and Kaci stood and started toward the door.

"Oh, okay." His voice lowered with disappointment. "Well, maybe I'll see you sometime this weekend."

"Yeah, maybe. Bye." Winter said as they entered the house.

After they were away from Davis and in the noisy confusion inside, Kaci grabbed Winter's arm and leaned close. "Okay, tell me what happened."

"Nothing, really," Winter said. "I just feel like something bad is going to happen to him. And it was weird…like something was wrong with my vision. Hey, there's Summer."

Winter grabbed Summer by the arm as they passed and pulled her away from Jeffrey. "We need to go," she said.

"But wait! What's wrong?"

Winter pulled harder and tried to convey urgency with her face.

Summer relented. "Call me!" she said. Jeffrey did not look happy.

Winter quickened her pace. By the time she reached the foyer she was almost running. She burst through the door and stopped short on the porch, scanning the cars parked along the street.

"There he is." Winter pointed to Peter as he climbed into his car. She rushed down the porch steps. "We have to hurry."

"What's going on?" Summer asked as they ran to Kaci's car. Peter was already pulling away.

"We'll explain on the way."

Summer took the back seat as Winter and Kaci jumped into the front. Kaci turned the ignition before the door closed and then spun the tires on the loose gravel. Summer fell sideways and scrambled for the seatbelt.

About half a mile up the street, Winter spotted the taillights she had been looking for.

"There," she said. "He's just ahead of us."

"Tell me what's happening!" said Summer. "You two are scaring me!"

Winter twisted in her seat. "Look…" She took a deep breath and tried not to shout. "God tells me things, okay? Don't ask me to explain it, and don't go telling everyone you know. You just have to trust me."

"What do you mean, God tells you things? He really speaks to you?"

Winter grunted. "No. It's not like that. Ever hear of prophecy?"

"Yeah."

"I do that!"

"You can see the future?"

Winter grunted again. "I'll explain it all later. Just trust me, okay? Peter's in trouble."

"Who's Peter?"

Winter threw her hands up and turned around to help Kaci follow Peter's taillights. Kaci had the pedal to the floor. He turned left onto a four-lane highway and they followed. Kaci fell in behind him and slowed.

"What do we do, Winter?" Kaci asked.

"I don't know," she said. "Just don't lose him. Maybe I'll get something else."

As they neared an intersection with a traffic light, fear surged through Winter as if it had been activated by remote.

"Kaci…" Winter said.

"What?"

"I'm having another déjà vu."

"What's that mean?"

"I don't know! It's from God…something's about to happen!"

"You're scaring me!" said Summer.

"What is it? Winter! What is it?" asked Kaci.

Time seemed to hesitate. Winter had already seen what would happen. Peter wouldn't stop at the upcoming red light. She knew without looking that a speeding eighteen-wheeler approached the intersection at the same time.

"STOP!" she shouted, clenching Kaci's arm. Kaci slammed on the brakes.

Peter continued through the traffic light.

The rushing truck plowed into the side of his car with a horrific screech of twisting metal. Shattered glass flew everywhere. Peter's car crumpled and folded. The bumper of the truck slid over the top and caught the roof, nearly ripping it off, twisting the tiny car onto its side. The truck's trailer jackknifed to the right and almost flipped the entire truck on top of Peter. Finally, the cab of the truck fell to the ground as the trailer rocked backward, leaving the car looking as if it had gone through a shredder. With a delayed shudder, the twisted remains fell back to its wheels.

It all happened in an instant but felt like slow motion.

Summer screamed.

"Go!" Winter said.

Kaci floored the gas. A few yards away from the ugly, smoldering wreck, Kaci slammed on her brakes again. Winter jumped out of the car. Summer and Kaci followed. Kaci already had her cell to her ear.

The truck driver stumbled out of the cab, cursing.

Winter reached the car first and grabbed the door handle, but it wouldn't budge. She planted one foot on the car and pulled as hard as she could. With a high-pitched scrape, the door bent open. Peter practically fell out of the car. Dark blood masked his head and face.

"What do we do?" Winter shouted. By this time Summer stood behind her, crying and squealing.

"SUMMER! What do we do?"

"I...I don't know! Why are you asking me?"

"You said you were a lifeguard, now THINK! What do we do?"

Summer took deep breaths as Winter dragged Peter away from the wreckage.

"Okay, okay," Summer said as she came to Peter's side. "Move." Winter moved out of the way. Summer tilted Peter's head back and put her ear to his bloody mouth.

"He's not breathing." Her voice trembled.

Kaci echoed Summer's words to the 911 operator.

"And go see if that truck has a first aid kit," Summer said.

"I'll get it," said the truck driver, who stood several feet away.

Summer pressed her fingers against Peter's neck, getting blood all over her hand. "He has no pulse!"

Kaci again echoed the information to the operator. She was crying now.

"Oh, God...I need to start CPR."

"Calm down, Summer," said Winter.

"I can't do this!" She started crying again, breathing too fast.

"Yes, you can!"

The truck driver huffed as he ran around the wreckage. "Here's the first aid kit."

Winter took the box and shoved it beneath Summer's nose. "You can do this!"

Summer hesitated a moment, then took it and flung open the top. She fumbled through the contents and brought out a little plastic square. It unfolded to make a large plastic sheet.

"What's that?" asked Winter.

"A face shield," Summer croaked. She laid the plastic over Peter's bloody face.

"I've never done this before."

"You're doing great." Winter said, voice shaking.

Summer took a hair band from around her wrist and pulled her hair back. Then she tentatively leaned over and put her mouth over Peter's. After giving him a couple of slow breaths, she placed her hands on his chest and began giving compressions.

"Winter," Kaci said. "The operator says we need to check the car for other victims."

The moment the words were out of Kaci's mouth, Winter felt the color drain from her face. It seemed again as if she had already lived this scene.

Winter stood up and rushed back to the car. There was no need to check the inside because she already knew where to look. Everything felt eerily familiar...she loathed this feeling now.

Winter went to the back of the car where the trunk had come unlatched during the crash and eased it open. Inside lay a girl with short black hair. Hundreds of knife slashes covered her naked body, some forming strange symbols on her skin. Beneath her bruised and broken face, a long, deep gash crossed her throat. Congealed blood looked like dead leeches on her pasty white flesh.

Winter put a hand to her mouth and took a queasy step back.

"What is it?" Kaci asked as she came to Winter's side.

"It's Jennifer." Winter fell to all fours and vomited.

21

Time blurred. Winter knelt beside Peter as Summer continued CPR through her tears. Winter couldn't tell how long they sat in the street. A crowd gathered. Paramedics took over. A policeman ushered Winter and the others out of the street and took their statements.

The intersection swarmed with rescue vehicles. An ambulance took Peter away. Another took Jennifer. Paramedics from a third inspected the truck driver. A tow truck hauled away the eighteen-wheeler.

"What do you think they're going to do?" Summer asked, after almost an hour of silent watching. Crime scene investigators crawled over Peter's car like maggots on rotting meat.

Kaci shrugged. "I don't know."

"There're so many of them."

"Don't you understand?" Winter asked. "They think Peter killed her."

They were silent for a moment.

"Maybe he did," said Summer.

"No way," said Winter. "He was set up."

"Maybe," Kaci said. "But can you prove that? For all we know, he just might have."

"I know he didn't do it."

"How?" Summer asked.

"I just do."

Summer took a deep breath. "Oh yeah, I forgot. So God really tells you things?"

"In a manner of speaking," Winter said.

Kaci shifted her weight. "Things are going to change after this. The school will probably go into lockdown."

"For how long?" asked Summer.

"Until they know for sure who killed Jennifer," Winter said.

"And if they say Peter did it?" Kaci asked.

Winter looked at Kaci with defiance. "Then we'll have to find the real killer for them."

Winter was half-way through her sloppy joe in the Union when Kaci walked over and tossed the school newspaper in front of her.

"Have you seen it yet?" Kaci's voice trembled.

Winter put down her sandwich and picked up the paper. "No."

"It's just like you said. They think Peter did it."

Winter read the front-page article. The police said Jennifer had been raped and tortured before being murdered, and the murder weapon was discovered with the body. Peter's fingerprints covered the knife. The only bright spot in the article, if it could be called a bright spot, was that Peter's injuries put him in a coma, so he couldn't go to jail until he fully recovered.

Winter's stomach flipped. She pushed the rest of her lunch away.

"How could they come to a conclusion so quickly?" Winter

scanned through the article again. "I don't understand it."

"I don't know," Kaci said. "I just can't believe this is happening. I mean, Peter's my friend."

"He's innocent, Kaci."

"How do you know?"

Winter frowned. "I'm not sure. But there's something missing here. I just don't know what it is."

22

The next week, a research project for world history consumed Winter's spare time. Though Summer was taking a different section of the course, they shared the same assignment. They skipped the CLC Tuesday night to do last-minute research in the library.

Winter sat beside Summer at the library terminals searching for books about their subjects.

"Okay...that makes three." Winter jotted down the last Library of Congress number. "I'm going to go find these."

Summer scribbled a number. "Me too. Let's go. We need to hurry, curfew's in thirty minutes."

"Oh, yeah. I forgot...lockdown."

They both walked toward the same area, but Winter's first book took her a few rows further to the religion section. The tall shelves of books were old and musty. Each book had its own unique layer of dust determined by the length of time since its last use. Human life and all sound had abandoned this part of the library. These books seemed sacred, and Winter felt as if she had discovered some forgotten secret. With the lightest of touches, she ran her finger across the leather spines, checking the numbers.

Some of the titles were old and faded, and Winter could not help reading every one. Ancient Eastern Religions. Monotheism in the Middle East. The Gods of Egypt. The Case for Global Flooding. Burning Rome.

Finally, she found the one she was looking for: Babylonian Gods and their Effect on Culture. Winter pulled the title from the shelf and, with an unexpected sense of loss, turned to walk out of the row in search of the next book.

Something caught her eye as she turned—the title of a book. She wasn't sure she was reading it right. She rubbed her eyes and leaned in closer.

Ancient Demonology.

For a moment, she clearly saw the demon from her dream reaching out to her. Her breath caught and her heart fluttered.

She grabbed the book and left.

Ten minutes later, she returned to the study table with four books in hand. "Hey Summer, look at this." Winter sat down and pushed the demonology book toward Summer.

"Creepy." Summer pushed it back. "Why do you want to read that?"

Winter shrugged. "I don't know. I think it's cool."

"I think you're a weirdo." Summer went back to her reading.

"I'll take that as a compliment."

As Summer proofread Winter's paper Wednesday night, Winter flipped through the demonology book, scanning some of the demon names.

"I wish you hadn't brought that here," Summer said.

"Did you finish?" Winter asked as she closed the book.

"Yeah, it's fine," Summer said.

"Are you sure?"

"I'm sure. I think Davis has really helped your writing."

"I hope so." Winter stood to stretch.

Summer handed Winter the paper. "It's almost midnight. I think I'm going to crash."

"Me too."

Summer crawled beneath her covers.

"Don't forget to pray about helping Peter," Winter said.

"Winter, it's late, and I've got an eight o'clock class."

Winter sighed and turned out the light. "I know. But we can't give up."

"Okay, I will," Summer said. "It may be a pretty short prayer, though."

"Thank you." Winter climbed into her bed. By the time she found a comfortable spot, Summer was already snoring.

She sat in the car following Peter. Kaci and Summer were there, but no one spoke. The intersection was before them, and Winter turned to see the eighteen-wheeler coming. Peter ran the red light again and was struck by the truck. It seemed faster. Her mind did not process the accident as it had before. She saw it not as premonition, but as memory…blurred and detached from time.

Yet, seeing the accident again was more horrifying than the first time. The screech of the metal and the squeal of the tires sliding across the pavement came louder and more vivid than before.

Just as Peter's car fell back to the ground, the scene restarted. But this time she was no longer in the car…she flew. Winter soared through the air mere feet away from the back of Peter's car. They approached the intersection, and Winter turned to watch in horror as the truck rushed to meet them. Her heart pounded at the impending collision, and she stiffened. But she was just far enough away that the truck did not touch her. The screech of metal dominated all sound, and the brake lights made the wreck look like a scene from Hell. Broken glass flew in all directions—some toward Winter. She shied away as the shards passed harmlessly through her to land on the road behind.

The scene rewound and she was forced to watch helplessly as Peter was struck a third time, closer now. This time she saw and heard his head hit the windshield. Blood splattered. She screamed.

The scene restarted a fourth time.

"What are you trying to show me?" she cried to the sky. She didn't want to watch the horrible wreck again and clenched her eyes…but the sounds of the twisting metal and shattering glass pierced her ears. She could still see it mentally.

Winter forced herself to look back at the car. Tears clouded her vision and the brake lights glistened like rubies through her watery eyes. Then they flickered and went out as the car fell back to its tires.

Brake lights.

Winter woke up. The faint glow of twilight filtered through the curtained window. She looked at the clock—four-thirty.

"Summer!" she shouted.

Summer sat straight up, wearing the half-asleep but scared-to-death expression Winter had seen several times. Static electricity from the dorm heaters made her hair float in all directions. She blinked and rubbed her eyes. "What is it?" she asked in groggy, slurred speech.

"Peter's brake lights. Do you remember them coming on?"

Summer collapsed on the bed. "What time is it?" she croaked.

"Think, Summer. Do you remember?"

Summer put a hand up to cover her eyes. "My mind is too fuzzy. I can't think about anything right now, Winter."

"I had a dream," Winter said. "I think Peter's brake lights came on just before the wreck."

"So?"

"So…he didn't stop, Summer. His brake lights came on, but he didn't stop."

Summer propped up on one elbow. "What's that mean?"

"It means someone sabotaged his brakes. Someone wanted him to have a wreck and wanted Jennifer's body found in his trunk."

"Why would anyone want to do that?"

"That's what we have to find out," said Winter. "Come on, get up. We have to wake Kaci."

"But," Summer said, "we followed him for several miles. He stopped at a stop sign and another red light. His brakes couldn't have been out."

Winter deflated. Did she get it wrong?

"Can I go back to sleep now?" Summer fell back onto the mattress, pulled her comforter up tight, and rolled onto her side.

Winter lowered herself back down and pulled up her own sheets to block out the early morning chill. Summer started breathing in the slow, methodic rhythm of deep sleep almost immediately. Winter replayed the dream in her mind over and over, but she could not find anything else unusual.

At five-thirty, enough light peeked through the metal blinds for Winter to move around the room safely without disturbing Summer. She climbed out of the bed, grabbed her toiletries and towel, and headed for the showers. The soothing hot water helped her relax.

Winter donned a dark-purple sweater and black jeans. She yanked a black stocking cap onto her head and climbed into her black trench coat. Then she snagged her Bible and books and headed for the Chapel Garden for some prayer and Bible study before classes. Maybe God would explain the dream to her there.

She went straight to her favorite reading spot, a secluded place where she could sit comfortably against the trunk of a tree, facing away from the chapel and toward an alcove wall of the history building.

After settling on the cold ground with the tail of her trench coat tucked beneath her, she opened her Bible to 1 Kings 17. Elijah the Prophet—the one Kaci had mentioned.

The chapter began with Elijah bringing King Ahab a message

from God that it would not rain until Elijah said it would. The King was obviously very angry, because God told Elijah to hide. That was the kind of thing she already knew about the prophets of the Bible…they delivered messages from God.

God provided for Elijah in the wilderness, then sent him to live with a widow. After several days, the widow's son became very sick and died. The distraught mother asked Elijah to help. Elijah prayed over the child, asking God to save him.

And the boy came back to life.

Winter stopped reading. This chapter raised more questions than it answered. If she really had the gift of prophecy, could she bring someone back to life? Surely not. There had to be a huge difference between having the gift of prophecy and actually being a prophet. And she was certain she was not a prophet…or prophetess. Kaci would probably know the difference.

But how did Elijah feel when God first spoke to him? What was it like the first time he had a vision? Had he always been a man of God, or was his past as fractured as her own? Maybe Kaci also knew of a prophet that freaked out the first time God spoke.

Winter started to read the passage a second time, but a premonition washed over her. The hairs on the back of her neck stood on end, like they did in the Union her first weekend of school. Ever so slowly, Winter leaned around the tree, though she already knew what she would see.

Several feet away, walking along the path, was the very same guy she had followed to the chapel before. He wore a long, dark-brown coat, and there was no mistaking his face and stride. Winter jerked her head back around the tree and pulled her legs in tight, praying she hadn't been seen. She held her breath and listened to his soft footsteps as the sound passed from one side of the tree to the other.

Winter looked around the opposite side. He stepped off the path and walked toward the Olamel bell tower. Winter closed her Bible and stood to get a better view. The man walked around the side of the tower and disappeared.

She followed. Among the trees and shrubs of the garden, she felt relatively concealed. But once she crossed the walkway, she sprinted on her toes and pressed against the front side of Olamel. Creeping to the corner of the tower's square base, she peered around. No one was there. Winter eased around and walked to the back corner where she would be able to see behind the chapel.

There he was. And he was not alone. At least four other guys and one girl, all dressed in black and looking close to her own age, stood with him.

There was also one man dressed in khaki pants and a polo shirt. He seemed nervous and out of place, a stark contrast to the Goths at his side.

The man she initially followed faced the guy in khaki and had his back to her. She felt from him a very strong presence that dominated everyone else.

The hairs on her arms and the back of her neck stood rigid again. He turned in her direction. Winter jerked back around the corner— her heart drumming against her ribs. She held her breath and strained to hear the approach of footsteps.

After several tense seconds, she heard a nervous voice say, "Let's get this over with. I don't like being out here in the open." It sounded like the guy in khaki speaking. She exhaled quietly and eased closer to the corner but refrained from peering around again.

"Relax, Taylor, no one will come here this early in the morning," said a gruff sneering voice.

The evil guy, Winter thought.

"I said not to use my name!"

"I just wanted to make sure you're still up to the task."

"Don't worry about my end. The board is under control, and they will approve your man," said Taylor. "What about you? I see the boy is still alive. We can't afford mistakes."

"I don't make mistakes."

"Really? Then why is the girl dead and not the boy? From what I understood, it was supposed to be the other way around."

"Fear. The campus is full of it now. And alive or not, the boy will be dealt with. These plans are much more complex than you can imagine."

"Looks like mistakes to me," said Taylor. "The police are going to figure it out. And if I go down, you're going down with me!"

"Do you think I'd have gotten this far if I didn't know how to deal with the police? They are fools. And if you threaten me again, I'll show just how dangerous I can be."

There was a brief, uncomfortable pause. "And what does the CLC have to do with this?" Taylor asked.

The CLC?

"Details. Wars are not won unless all the details have been accounted for. Once our man is in place, he'll take care of the CLC and everyone involved there. It would be best if you would worry only about your part and forget everything else you…"

DONNNNGGGGG.

The bells of Olamel began ringing. Winter couldn't hear anything and was almost tempted to peer around the corner again. The bells seemed to ring forever, each ring echoing multiple times from the walls of nearby buildings. Finally, the last bell died away.

Winter concentrated to hear more of the conversation.

What she heard instead were footsteps…close. A surge of adrenaline numbed her limbs. Her face flushed. She took off so quickly, she almost lost her balance and fell. She reached the walkway before hearing sounds of pursuit.

She glanced over her shoulder. The four Goth guys were less than twenty yards away. Winter tried to speed up, but her muscles burned. Still, she had enough lead and momentum that within just a few seconds, she passed the buildings and emerged into the Meadow. There were several people walking around, most going to breakfast. Winter never slowed.

"Help!" she shouted, as loud as her aching lungs would allow.

Everyone stopped and stared at her. Two security guards materialized, running to intercept. Winter chanced another look over her shoulder. The four pursuers stopped short of entering the Meadow and turned to run the other direction. A guard spotted them and altered his trajectory to give chase. He grabbed the mic on his shoulder and said something as he ran past Winter.

She kept running until she reached the Ancient, where she collapsed on a bench. Her numb legs quivered. Her chest heaved, her lungs aching in the thin, cold air.

The second security guard reached her. "What happened?"

"Four guys...chased...me," she said, huffing between phrases. "They were behind...the chapel...talking about...Jennifer Hollingsworth."

The guard nodded and turned to say something into his mic. He turned back. "Can you describe them?"

Her breathing slowed, and her mind cleared, but her heart still pounded. "Yeah, there were four of them. Two were really skinny. Behind the chapel there was one girl, too, who didn't chase me, and another guy with long, brown hair. Oh, and there was a man wearing normal clothes too. His name was Taylor."

The security guard wrote all this down on his notepad. "And what about the ones who did chase you? How were they dressed?"

"They were dressed all in black...you know...Goth."

24

Four Years Ago

Winter didn't question Claire any further about the bruises. She wanted desperately to respect her new friend by never mentioning the matter again. It didn't take long for Claire to realize that Winter wasn't going to blab this major secret to everyone, and within a couple of days they were back on good terms. There seemed to be an unspoken understanding between them.

Conversations in general became much darker. Apparently, Claire's little secret was not much of a secret within their group. It was as if Winter had passed some sort of test and had now been fully accepted into the personal lives of her new friends.

The barrier between the "new girl" and the others had lowered, and they dispensed with the friendly masks and laid their true selves out for Winter to see. Gone were the frilly girl topics everyone seemed to think meaningless and trivial, though just a few months ago they were all she ever thought about. Now they devoted the bulk of their conversation to the emptiness of life and to the hatred of parents. It was exactly how Winter felt inside since moving in with her dad.

Claire was the first to come to school wearing all black. It was the day before Halloween, and she showed up late for school. As she sat down at the lunch table, all eyes looked to the ugly bruise on the side of her face.

"I fell down," she said to the silent stares. Everyone nodded except Winter, whose mouth hung open.

"She fell down," Stacy told her. Winter took the hint and turned away.

"What's with the black?" Phillip asked.

Claire shrugged. "I don't know. Guess I was just in a black mood."

"Aren't we all," said Alison. The others nodded.

"I figured if I felt black on the inside, then I should dress black on the outside," Claire said. "I'm tired of pretending to be something I'm not."

"Tired of pretending to be something you're not...this on the eve of Halloween?" Stacy asked.

Claire shrugged. "I've been living Halloween all my life."

The next day, Claire wore all black again, and the day after that Stacy wore black too. The following week, all of them but Winter dressed in black every day. They started to get attention from their classmates—some positive and encouraging for not conforming to the norm, some negative and resentful for being so odd. Winter started to feel disconnected from her new friends.

"Why do you continue to dress so happy?" Claire asked her one day in class.

Winter shrugged. "This is just the way I've always dressed."

"It doesn't fit you anymore," Claire said. "It's not who you are.

You're one of us."

Winter considered it. Claire had made similar statements before, and they weren't entirely untrue. Winter had never really liked dark clothes, though.

When she didn't reply, Claire continued. "What have you got to be happy about? A new school, living with your stupid dad...your mom. I mean, stop kidding yourself."

Winter's spirits sunk and she sighed. "You're right, I guess."

Claire nodded. "Then don't pretend to be something you're not."

"But I..." Winter pursed her lips in defeat and looked away.

The next morning, Winter dug through her closet until she found a black shirt and a black pair of pants. After putting them on, she stared at herself in the mirror. Her earlier misgivings about fashion died away—she actually thought she still looked normal. She tugged the shirt straight and headed downstairs.

"What are you wearing?" her dad asked as she rounded the corner to the kitchen. He sat at the table drinking coffee and reading the morning paper. Winter gathered her books from the table.

"Nothing," she said.

"I'm not letting you leave the house like that. Go change."

Winter spun to confront her dad, her face twisted with confusion and anger. "What's wrong with what I'm wearing?"

He put down the paper and eyed her. "You look like one of those punks that hang out at the quarry. I won't have my daughter going out that way."

Winter groaned. "You're joking, right? It's just black, Dad! People wear black all the time. Dances, funerals, weddings..."

He stood. "It's not the same. People just don't wear black for the fun of it!"

"Well, maybe I do! Did you ever thank that I might like wearing black?"

"I don't know! I don't feel like I know you at all anymore."

"Perhaps if you hadn't left Mom, you would! It's your fault you don't know me…you were never there! And now you think you have the right to tell me what to wear? You gave up that right when you broke Mom's heart!"

Her dad's face flushed crimson and he stepped around the table toward her. "Leave your mom out of this. You have no idea what you're talking about. Now get upstairs and change!"

"NO! You can't tell me what to do, and you certainly can't tell me what to wear! I'll do whatever I want!"

"Go change or I'll…" Her dad balled his fist and half raised it.

"Or you'll what? Hit me?"

He dropped his hand. "Winter…" he said through clenched teeth. He took several deep breaths.

"That's what I thought!" she screamed, leaning into his face. "You're too much of a coward to hit me, just like you were too much of a coward to be my dad!"

Winter's face flew sideways with the force of his blow. The stinging of each finger burned her face. She turned back to her dad with her eyes wide and her mouth open.

Her dad sobered and his face fell. "Winter, I didn't mean…" He stepped forward and reached out to her.

Winter put a hand to her cheek and took a step back.

"I'm sorry," he whispered.

She took another step. Her eyes were watering. "You're just like Claire's dad," she said. Winter snatched up her book bag and fled to the door.

"Winter wait!" he called, but she didn't stop. "WINTER!"

She slammed the front door and never looked back.

Later, at school, Winter slipped Claire a note with only five words on it. "My dad hit me too."

Claire reached over and squeezed her hand.

25

Present Day

Winter burst into her dorm room.

"Get up, Summer!" she shouted at her still-slumbering roommate.

Summer sat straight up. "What time is it? Did I miss class?"

"Seven-thirty. You're not late, but I need to talk to you now!" Winter grabbed the telephone and punched in Kaci's number. "Hey, I need you to come down right away." She hung up without waiting for a reply.

"What's going on?" Summer asked. She climbed out of bed and pulled on a fuzzy pink bathrobe and matching slippers.

"I'll explain when Kaci gets here."

Summer sighed and rubbed her eyes. Then she sat back on her bed and slumped forward onto her knees. It didn't take long before there was a quick rapping on the door. Winter opened it and Kaci rushed in, fully awake and fully dressed.

"What's wrong?" she asked. "Are you okay?"

"Yeah, I'm fine." Winter paced the floor as Kaci crossed her arms. "I know who killed Jennifer," Winter said.

"What?"

"Huh?" asked Summer. She sat up.

"I was in the Chapel Garden, and he came by."

"Who came by?" Kaci asked.

"The guy Summer and I followed to the chapel the night of the CLC party."

"Oh," Summer said. "What about him?"

"He killed Jennifer."

Kaci asked, "And you know this how?"

"I saw him again this morning and I followed him to the backside of the chapel. He was all dressed in dark clothes and trench coat, and he met with a few Goth students and one normal looking guy. They were talking about Jennifer. He said he killed her. He also said that he'd make sure Peter died as well."

"Are you positive?"

"Yes."

Kaci crossed the room and sat in Winter's papasan.

"Did you recognize any of them?" she asked.

"No," Winter said. "Only the name Taylor. That's what he called the other normal guy."

"Great," said Kaci. "There could be hundreds of Taylors in Cherithville. We don't even know if it's a last name or first name."

Winter shrugged. "But we know Peter is innocent. That's a start."

"We should tell the police," said Summer.

"Tell them what?" Kaci asked. "All the proof points to Peter, and what Winter's saying would only be considered hearsay."

"Then we need to find proof that isn't hearsay," said Winter. "We'll start by finding Taylor."

"Are you sure we should do this?" Kaci asked.

Winter stopped pacing and looked from Kaci to Summer, then back to Kaci. "Yes."

The Monday afternoon before Thanksgiving, Winter hurried across the Meadow to meet Davis in the Union. She found him on the second floor eating a burger.

She rushed to the table and slapped down her latest English assignment. "C!"

"Good." He gave her a slight nod of approval. "And the history paper you did by yourself?"

"Also a C." She draped her black trench coat over the back of the chair and sat down.

"Now let's see if you can keep it up."

Winter pulled out her newest English assignment. "I've done three drafts." She removed the graded paper and replaced it with the new one. "I think it's pretty good."

"We'll see." Davis took the last bite of his hamburger and gathered his tray.

While Davis threw his trash away, Winter took out her pencil and English book. She placed everything in front of her, nice and neat, and waited for Davis to return.

"All right, let's get started." Davis sat down and adjusted his glasses. He reached across the table for Winter's paper.

The din of the Union grew much louder than normal, like a party had just started. Winter turned, and Davis looked up from the paper.

"What's going on?" he asked.

As if in response, someone rushed up the stairs and straight to one of the TVs. Soon all the TVs on the second level changed to the same channel.

The TV showed Langley Hall, the administration building. A reporter stood outside, but Winter still could not hear anything. Davis went to the nearest TV and increased the volume.

"In a rare move," the reporter said, "Tishbe University announced its new president this afternoon with a simple press release and not a formal press conference. When asked why the decision was made not to have a formal ceremony, board members said the new president wished the transition to be made discreetly. Dr. Louis Streffield declined interviews but expressed interest in getting to the job at hand: expediting the university's recovery from the recent scandal. Back to you in the studio."

A deep sense of dread settled in the pit of Winter's stomach like molten lead. Something was not right. She felt like this announcement and Jennifer's death were somehow linked.

"Um," she said to Davis, who still watched the TV, "I've got to go."

He looked at her. "What? But we haven't even started!"

Winter grabbed her things and shoved them back into her bag. "I know. I'm sorry…but something just came up."

"What just came up?"

Winter thrust her arms into her coat. "I need to talk with Kaci and Summer."

"Now?"

"Yes, now." Winter turned to leave, but a thought came to her. She immediately turned back, though she didn't understand why.

"You come too."

"Me? Why?" he asked.

Winter sighed. "I'll explain later."

Davis grunted and stood. "This better be good."

"Believe me, it is," she said.

"Now, would you please tell me what this is all about?" Davis asked twenty minutes later as the four of them sat on couches around a square coffee table in Carmichael.

"Before we get to that," Winter said, "there's something you need to know."

For the next fifteen minutes, Winter explained to Davis everything that had happened to her while she had been at school and all about her gift of prophecy.

"Davis?" Winter asked. "Are you okay?"

He stared at her and blinked rapidly.

"Davis?"

"So...you're saying you have the gift of prophecy?"

"Yes."

More staring.

"Are you sure? I mean, you've told me about your mom a little. How do you know that..."

"That I don't have a brain tumor?" Winter asked. "I don't. But the visions are real, and the dreams are real. I can't explain any better than that."

"She's telling the truth," Kaci said. "I've seen it myself. You've seen it too, Davis."

He looked at Kaci and his eyes narrowed.

"That night at the Ancient...she was waiting, just like you said. She was waiting because God told her to go there," said Kaci.

He turned back to Winter. "He told you?"

"In a manner of speaking."

Davis's face settled into an expression of complex calculation. "Why are you telling me this?"

Winter leaned forward. "Jennifer was killed, and Peter was set up. I know who really did it."

"Who?" Davis asked. Winter could see the wheels spinning behind his eyes.

"That's just it. I know who did it, but I don't know his name. If I saw him, I would recognize him, but finding him is the problem. And we need to find him soon."

"He's the guy we followed to the chapel the first week of school," Summer said.

Davis nodded. "And what does that have to do with us?"

"That's where the little prophecy thing comes in," Winter said. "I feel strongly that it's up to us to find Jennifer's real killer and help free Peter. I feel that's what God wants us to do. Or at least, that's what he wants me to do."

"But there's no way for us to do that," said Kaci.

"Why don't you just have a vision about how to prove Peter didn't do it?" Davis asked. "Or about how to find the real killer?"

Winter balled her hands into fists. "It doesn't work like that. God only gives me things I need to know at that moment, I guess."

"But that doesn't make sense," Davis said. "Why would God tell you to do something and withhold important information that would help you succeed? Maybe if you concentrated you could have more visions."

"I can't just have a vision whenever I want!"

"Why not? Does God give you each individual vision, or did he just give you the ability to have visions?"

"I—I don't know. I've never really thought about it."

"Well, there's a big difference. If he's given you the ability to have visions, then you should be able to have them whenever you want, and possibly about whatever you want."

"But there's no way for me to control it," she said.

"Are you sure?"

Winter didn't answer.

"When do you have these visions?" he asked.

"Usually when I'm asleep."

"Hmm. And the premonitions?" He tapped his fingers on the table.

"Those can happen at any moment."

Davis leaned back on the couch and sat in thought for a few seconds. "I wonder if we could find a common trigger between all the visions and premonitions you've had so far."

"There isn't one," Winter said. "And this is not what I wanted to talk about."

"But what if there were a way to control it?" Kaci asked. She scooted to the edge of her seat. "Wouldn't it be worth finding out how?"

Winter clenched her teeth. "I guess."

"I mean, maybe God gives you visions he wants you to have, but you may also have the ability to see things when you want. Like when you knew Angie's name. That didn't exactly have a divine purpose."

"Thank you, that's my point," said Davis.

"Okay, okay." Winter held her hands up in defeat. "I get what you two are saying. I'll try, all right? But I won't promise anything."

"Good enough," Davis said. "Start by trying to find some common trigger between these visions and premonitions."

Winter nodded.

"Whoa," said Summer who had been listening to the whole exchange with childish fascination. "This is kinda spooky. Like…" her voice dropped to a whisper, "like X-Files or something." Everyone turned to look at her. "What?"

"Now, about why I called you here," Winter said. "This new president has something to do with what's going on. I don't know how, but I know. There are things happening that we don't realize, and I think Peter and Jennifer were just the beginning...maybe even some sort of smoke screen hiding the real plan."

"So what do we do?" asked Kaci.

"First, we have to prove Peter's innocence, and do it soon. If he wakes up, he'll be put in prison. But once he's released from the hospital, he'll be killed. So we have to find that man. He's the real threat." The others nodded. "I'm staying here during Thanksgiving. It'll be the best time to do some snooping around. Are you guys going to stay too?"

"Yes," said Kaci.

"I was staying anyway," said Davis.

Summer looked a little crestfallen. "I've never missed a Thanksgiving before."

"I think Jeffrey's staying," said Davis.

Summer lit up. "Well, I guess it won't hurt to change my plans."

Winter rolled her eyes. "Okay, then. Where do we start?"

"How about the brake lights?" Summer said.

"What brake lights?" asked Kaci.

"Wow, I can't believe I forgot about that. I had a dream, and God showed me the wreck over and over until I noticed Peter's brake lights were on. He was pressing the brakes, but his car wouldn't stop."

"You know, I think you may be right!" Kaci said. "If that's true, then his brakes must have been tampered with!"

"But that doesn't make sense," said Winter. "Like Summer told me, he stopped several times before we came to that intersection."

"Oh, it still makes perfect sense," Davis said. "If there was a small hole in the brake line, then the brakes would have to be compressed several times before enough brake fluid escaped to make them fail."

All three girls sat up a little straighter.

Winter's adrenaline surged "That's it! We have to tell the police!"

"And what are you going to tell them?" asked Summer. "That

you had a dream that Peter's brakes were tampered with?"

"Well, we should still try," Winter said. "They might listen to us since we witnessed the wreck. And if they don't listen, maybe we could get into the impound and check the car ourselves."

"Do any of us know anything about cars?" asked Kaci.

"Davis seems to," said Winter.

"Oh, no. I just know basic engineering principles. I think Jeffrey can help, though."

"Good," Winter said. "Summer and Jeffrey can go to the impound if the police won't listen."

"But won't we get in trouble?"

"Only if you're caught," Davis said.

Summer huffed. "Great."

"Hey, I think someone should talk to Peter's parents, too," said Kaci. "Maybe there's some background info that could tell us why he was targeted."

"Good idea," Winter said. "You do that."

Kaci nodded.

Winter continued. "Behind the chapel, there was a guy named Taylor. Davis, can you go to the library and see if you can find out who he is? He said something about 'the board,' and I think he may be some big businessman around here. Check some of the board of directors listings for local businesses—like banks and stuff."

"Sure."

"What about you?" Summer asked.

"I'm going back to the chapel," she said. "I feel like there's something I'm missing there."

27

Four Years Ago

Winter leaned against the passenger door and stared out the window, brooding. All she could think about was her mom and what life would be like today had she not become sick. She wore all black again and didn't speak. Her dad didn't provoke her, for once. She suspected that he hoped a visit with her mom would remedy her wardrobe choices. What he didn't realize was that as long as she continued to live with him, she would never give him any such satisfaction. Why should she, when he resented her mere presence?

As they came into South Waverly, Winter sat up to watch, hoping to catch a glimpse of her old neighborhood. But the hospice was in a different part of the city. When she realized they wouldn't be going down any familiar streets, she slumped back in her seat.

Fifteen minutes later, they pulled into the parking lot of St. Benedict's Hospice. Winter followed several steps behind her dad up the short sidewalk, past the groomed flowerbeds filled with a rainbow of pansies, to the double glass doors. Inside, her dad spoke with the receptionist. She smiled at Winter and nodded.

"I'll wait," her dad said. He took a seat in the waiting room.

The receptionist walked around the counter. "This way." She led Winter down the sterile white hall and around a corner to Room 156.

Winter waited until the receptionist was gone before she knocked.

"Come in."

Winter eased open the door and peered in. The room was nicer than Winter expected. Hardwood floors created a rustic pattern accented by a beautiful oval rug. Lace curtains hung over the window from an ornate valance. A hospital bed, cleverly disguised to resemble a normal bed, stood beneath a homemade patchwork quilt hanging on an earth-tone wall. On the opposite wall, a TV was mounted near the ceiling.

Her mom waited in a wingback chair next to the window. She smiled at Winter and pushed her golden-brown hair behind her ears in that familiar way Winter had missed. She had lost a lot of weight in the past couple of months. Winter hardly recognized her.

The cold reality of impending death became visible. Winter's throat constricted. Her chest felt cold and hollow, and her lungs refused to work. The muscles in her face twisted, as she fought her emotions.

"Hey, Winter."

Winter rushed into her mom's arms and cried. Her mom stroked Winter's hair gently, crying too.

"I miss you," her mom said. "You should make your dad bring you more often."

Winter relaxed and looked into her mom's face. "I'll try. He doesn't exactly talk to me much. I don't think he wants me there."

"That's ridiculous. Of course he wants you there…he loves you."

Winter turned and wrung her fingers together.

"Maybe you should try talking to him more," her mom said. "You two are more alike than you think." She grinned. "You're both stubbornly independent."

"Maybe," Winter said. "But I'd rather be with you."

Abnormal silence passed between them, while her mom ran fingers through Winter's hair. Winter looked back and found her mom staring out the window.

"Mom?"

She turned back to Winter, her eyes distant. "What did you say?"

"I said, I'd rather be with you."

Her mom smiled, but the smile did not touch the emptiness of her eyes. "Of course you would." She turned and gazed back out the window.

Winter shuddered and stood. "Mom, what's wrong?"

"I'm sorry, dear. It's the pain medicine. It makes me think slow."

"But you seemed fine when I first came in," Winter said. She backed to the other chair and sat.

"I made them give me a dose just before you came. I didn't want you to see me..." Her mom turned away again.

"To see you what?"

"Cancer hurts, dear."

Winter eyed the floor and shuffled her feet. Her heart ached.

"Have you found a church yet?"

"No. It hasn't been exactly something I've felt like doing, Mom. It may be good for you, but it's not my thing." She looked back up.

"You really should. God is helping me through this, and he can help you too."

"Why doesn't God do something, then?" Winter asked. "If he loves you so much, why does he let you go through this kind of pain? Can't he just heal you?"

"I pray for that every day, sweetheart. But God may have other plans, and honestly, it's fine with me. I mean, I get to go to Heaven soon, and that won't be so bad at all."

Winter looked away and clenched her jaw.

"I see you've changed your wardrobe." Her mom chuckled.

Winter shrugged. "I've decided to dress the way I feel on the inside." She looked back at her mom through watery eyes.

"I'm not dead yet, Winter. Please don't punish yourself. We need to enjoy the time we do have."

"How can we when the only way you can spend time with me is on drugs?"

"I..." It was her mom's turn to stare at the floor. Winter waited, but it took almost a minute before her mom spoke again. "Tell me about your new friends."

Winter shrugged. "They're fine, I guess. I mean, they're not like my old friends."

"But you still keep in touch with your old friends, right?"

Winter shook her head. "They don't e-mail or call anymore. I guess they've forgotten about me."

"That's not true," her mom said. "They're probably just busy."

"Too busy to send a quick e-mail?"

"Well, yeah. Could be."

Winter crossed her arms and looked at her feet. "I don't think that's it at all, I think they're..."

There was sudden movement in Winter's peripheral vision and a crash beside her. Winter snapped her eyes to her mom...and screamed.

Her mom's arms stretched out to the sides and her body was rigid. Her eyes rolled back in their sockets, and she shook violently.

"HELP!" Winter stood and cast around the room. Then she ran to the door, flung it open, and shouted into the hall. "SOMEONE HELP!"

Two nurses jumped up from the nurses' station and rushed in. Winter, helpless, watched them grab her mom firmly and lower her to the floor. A third nurse came in and pulled Winter by the wrist.

"NO! Let me go!" She stretched her arm out to her mom. "MOM!"

Foam flecked from her mom's mouth.

"MOM!" Winter shouted again as the nurse finally dragged her through the door and shut her out.

Present Day

The campus was practically deserted the week of Thanksgiving. It seemed odd not to hear music blaring in the hallways or see students hunched beneath backpacks crossing the Meadow. The cafeteria only offered sandwiches and chips all week. For Thanksgiving Day, they promised a turkey sandwich.

"I called Peter's mom," Kaci said, during their Monday evening meeting.

"And?" Winter asked.

"And...it's not good." The others sank a little in their seats. "At first, she didn't want to talk to me, but I finally managed to explain who I was and that I knew Peter and everything, and she finally started listening.

"When I told her I thought he was innocent, she stopped me. She said, 'As much as I want to believe my son is innocent, I know he did it.'"

"What?" asked Summer. "His own mother thinks he did it?"

"When I asked why, she told me Peter and Jennifer dated over the summer, and that she dumped him for another guy just before school started."

"I wasn't aware they had dated," said Davis.

"Neither was I," said Kaci.

"Apparently," Winter said, "this guy who framed him did his homework."

"This doesn't look good at all. Everything points to Peter's guilt. We need more than just some dream that his brakes didn't work," said Davis.

Winter wrinkled her brow in thought and prayer. *What am I missing?*

"Okay, okay," she finally said. "There are still the guys behind the chapel that chased me. And the leader practically admitted to doing it."

"But we don't know who he is," said Summer.

"We know one of them." Winter looked at Davis.

Davis nodded. "I'm going to the library tonight. There will only be one or two people there working, and I can pretty much go anywhere I need without being seen. It was a good idea to wait for the break."

"What about you and Jeffrey?" she asked Summer.

"Well, he kinda doesn't want to do it."

"But we need him to. We need to know if my dream was right. We have to find out about those brakes!"

"I know, I'll keep trying. I'll see if I can get him to go tonight."

"All right then. We'll all meet back here at midnight tonight and see what you two found out."

"Can't," Kaci said. "Curfew."

"Fine…ten o'clock. Be here."

At eight-thirty that night, Winter left her room and walked as quickly as she could to the chapel. Despite the warnings of Tishbe security, Winter went alone and tried her best to walk in the darkest shadows away from direct light. Her black coat was especially helpful.

When she arrived, she hid within the shadows of the Chapel Garden, waiting for a good fifteen minutes for any signs of movement. Winter ran across the yard to the bell tower and eased to the corner. She peered around. Nothing. Her stomach fluttered as she crept around the corner and down the side of Olamel.

At the back corner, she hesitated before glancing around. She held her breath. But there was no one there. At least, no one she could see.

Winter took out a little penlight she had borrowed from Davis and clicked it on. She systematically searched all the dark corners until satisfied that she was alone. Then, starting at the wall of the building behind the chapel, she paced the length of the wall and scanned the ground with the light. She wasn't exactly sure what to look for, but Winter intuitively felt she needed to do this. Maybe intuition was part of the gift.

After pacing once, she turned and began pacing back, inching her way closer to the tower. Hidden in the shrubs she discovered a busted spotlight.

So that's why this place is so dark.

An hour later, Winter had only scanned half the area behind the chapel. She checked her watch and quickened her steps, hoping she wouldn't overlook anything.

Finally, after ten more minutes, something flashed in the light. A small white rectangle with a black stripe. Winter bent down and picked it up before she recognized it—a Tishbe ID card. She flipped it over.

Jennifer's ID.

She heard voices. Winter ran to the wall of the chapel and clicked off the light, listening. She slid to the corner of Olamel and peered around. The lamp posts revealed two students walking along the pathway from the Meadow. She waited until they were gone, then crept back around the bell tower and hurried to Carmichael.

Winter sat alone in her room looking at Jennifer's ID card, waiting for ten o'clock to come. Why was it behind the bell tower? Could one of those guys have dropped it when they were meeting? She prayed in silence for understanding, but none came.

A knock at the door made Winter nearly jump off her chair. She shoved the ID into her back pocket before easing open the door. It was just Kaci.

"Davis is back," she said and bounced on her heels. "He's waiting for us in the lobby. And he seems excited."

Winter didn't hesitate. "Okay."

Back in the lobby, Davis paced around the sofas. When the two girls approached, his eyes lit up, and he rushed to a nearby study table.

"What did you find out?" Winter asked as she and Kaci took seats. Winter leaned forward on her elbows.

"Well, I was in the archive section looking up newspaper articles and other periodicals I could find that might list the names of board members around Cherithville," he said.

"And?"

"And I found out very little. Short of actually visiting the businesses or calling them, I was beginning to think I wouldn't find the information I was looking for—at least not before curfew."

"Then what's the excitement about?" Kaci asked.

"As I was leaving, I noticed a wall of photos near the entrance of the library. The board of directors of Tishbe University. Third from the left: Matthew Taylor."

Winter's and Kaci's eyes doubled in size.

"Are you sure it's the right person?" Winter asked.

"I don't know, you tell me." Davis passed his cell phone to them, a photo pulled up on the screen.

"That's him!" Winter said. She showed the photo to Kaci.

"Well, one mystery solved," Kaci said. "But what do we do now?"

Winter sat for a moment, trying to recall the things Taylor had said that day. Then a thought came to her, and her heart sank.

"He told the other guy that the board was under control and would approve 'his man.'" She tried to organize her thoughts in an articulate manner. "That must mean the board he was referring to is the board of directors for the university."

"The university only approved one person this year," Davis said. "Which means that…"

"That 'his man' is the new president," Kaci said, finishing Winter's thought.

"Are you saying our new president and the people responsible for Jennifer's death and the other attacks are working together?" Davis asked.

Winter looked at him, the corners of her mouth tight, and nodded.

29

"Well," Winter asked Summer the next morning. "What did you and Jeffrey find out?"

Summer looked at the floor with a small grin. She twirled a finger in her hair and her cheeks reddened. "Well, we didn't exactly get to do that."

"Summer! This is important! We're the only ones who can keep Peter from getting killed, and instead of helping you go make out with your boyfriend?"

Summer collapsed on her bed looking penitent. "I know, I know." She sighed. "I'm sorry."

"So when are you going to go?" Winter asked.

"Jeffrey doesn't want to do it."

"What?"

"He's afraid we'll get caught and arrested," Summer said.

"But we need to know if the brakes were really cut!"

"I know." She fidgeted with her hands. "He says we're being silly, and he thinks Peter's guilty."

"Well, he's obviously no help," Winter said. She threw the book in her hand across the room.

Summer bit her lip. "Um…"

"What else?"

Summer glanced up nervously. "I'm sorry, Winter. But my dad wants me to come home. I stayed yesterday to help you, but I have to leave today. I was going to tell you, but I forgot."

Winter jumped to her feet and crossed the room to pick up the phone.

"What are you doing?" Summer asked, her eyes big and her voice unsteady.

"I'm calling the police and telling them what I know." She grabbed the phone.

"But I thought you said…"

"We've done all we can do, Summer." The silence of the receiver made her stop and wrinkle her brow.

"What's wrong?" Summer asked.

"There's no dial tone."

"Hello?" came a light tenor voice from the receiver.

Winter's eyes widened. "Hello?"

"Hello. This is Detective Fox from the Cherithville Police Department."

"Who is it?" Summer asked.

"It's the police," Winter whispered.

Summer took a sharp breath. "How did you do that??"

"Can I help you?" Winter asked.

"Yes, I'm trying to get in touch with—I hope I get these names right— Winter Maessen and Summer Reilly."

"Yes, you got the names right. This is Winter." She sat down in her computer chair.

"Great," Detective Fox said. *"I understand that you and your roommate witnessed the Peter Strong vehicle accident."*

"That's correct."

"Is it also correct that Summer Reilly performed CPR on Peter Strong, and that you were the one to discover the body of Jennifer Hollingsworth?" he asked.

"Yes, that's right."

"Okay, then. I'd like to arrange a face-to-face meeting with you two to go over some of the details."

"Great!" She flashed a grin to Summer. "But Summer will be leaving today to go home for Thanksgiving."

"Can you meet me in half an hour?"

Winter covered the transmitter of the phone with her hand. "When are you leaving?" she asked.

Summer shrugged. "I don't know, sometime before lunch."

Winter uncovered the phone. "That'll be fine."

"Great," he said. *"Is the Union okay with you?"*

"The Union is fine. How will we know who you are?" she asked.

"Well, maybe I'll just find you. What will you be wearing?"

"I have black hair and I'm wearing black. Summer is blonde and she's wearing light blue."

"Should be easy enough then. Thank you and see you in thirty minutes." He hung up, and Winter returned the handset to the cradle.

"What's going on?" Summer asked. "How did you do that?"

"That was the detective on Peter's case. He must have been calling when I picked up—the phone didn't have time to ring," she said. "He wants to meet with us."

"When?"

"Thirty minutes—in the Union."

"What's his name?"

"Detective Fox, I think," Winter said.

Summer's eyes widened a little more. "This is just like X-Files," she whispered.

Winter crinkled her nose. "Exactly how much old TV do you watch?"

Winter and Summer walked into the Student Union twenty minutes later. They looked around for a secluded table and to see if Detective Fox might already be waiting. Few people graced the Union that morning, and none matched their idea of how the detective might look. They were relieved to see Kaci waving at them from a table in the far corner.

"What are you two doing?" Kaci asked as they approached.

"We're supposed to meet with the detective on Peter's case," Winter said.

Kaci leaned across the table. "Me too." she said. "Sit down, I think he's expecting to talk to all three of us at the same time."

Summer took a seat beside Kaci, and Winter went to get sodas. When she returned, the other two were talking in hushed tones about the wreck and what they remembered.

Winter sat and divided up the drinks.

"Creepy old man alert." Summer shielded her eyes. A short, balding man with horn-rimmed glasses stood near the entrance. His button-front shirt and snug pants accentuated too much of his weight.

Winter rolled her eyes. "Not again. You'd think with all the new security, they'd keep creeps like that out of here."

"Yeah," Summer said. "He's probably a child molester or something." She looked up. "Ugh! He's ugly."

"Or worse," Winter said. "Maybe he's a professor."

Kaci snickered.

"He's coming this way!" Summer whispered. They went back to their drinks and tried to ignore the approaching man.

He walked right up to their table and stopped. "Hello girls," the man said with a light tenor voice. "Mind if I join you?"

Winter looked up and mustered her most hateful glare. "No, you can't join us. Go away before we call security."

The man smiled. "You must be Winter. Perhaps I should introduce myself properly." He reached for his back pocket and pulled out a wallet. Flipping it open to reveal a badge he said, "I am Detective Ted Fox."

All three girls gazed up that time. "I'm sorry...I..." Winter stuttered, but Fox just held up his hand.

"It's okay, I understand. College girls need to be careful when strange men come up to them, especially around here lately." He sat down in the empty chair.

"So you don't think Peter did it? I mean, you think the attacks may continue?" Winter asked.

"Now, I didn't say that," Fox said. "I do believe, however, based on the descriptions from the other girls who have been chased or attacked over the past few months, that Peter did not commit those. So...yes, the attacks may continue, because all the people involved have not yet been apprehended.

"I take it, by your question and the expressions on your faces, that none of you believe Peter is guilty?"

The three girls shook their heads in unison.

"Okay, then..." He looked across the table to Kaci. "Let's start with you, Kaci."

"How do you know who we are?" Kaci asked.

He smiled. "I'm a detective." Kaci narrowed her eyes, and he chuckled. "Winter told me she had black hair and that Summer was blonde. Seeing as you're the only one here with brown hair, I deduced that you were Kaci. Now, may I continue?"

Kaci nodded.

He took a pen and notepad from his shirt pocket. "How did you know Peter?"

"We were in a small group together last year at the CLC," she said. "He was the leader of it. He was also this year's CLC President."

Fox jotted it down. "And did you know Jennifer?"

Kaci shook her head a little. "Not really. She went to the CLC sometimes, but I didn't get to know her very well."

"I see." Fox wrote something else. "What about you, Summer?

Did you know Peter or Jennifer?" Summer shook her head. "Winter?" Winter shook her head as well. "Okay. So let's get to the accident. I understand you were all riding in the same car?"

"Why are you doing this?" Winter said. "We already gave our statements the night of the accident."

"You gave your statements to one of the officers at the scene—not me. Sometimes those officers don't ask the right questions and besides, I want to hear it straight from you three. Now, back to the car...all of you were riding together?"

"That's right," Kaci said, glaring at Winter.

"And who was driving?"

"Me."

Fox jotted something down. "Why exactly were you following him that night?" The three girls exchanged a knowing look, and Fox raised an eyebrow. "Well?"

"We just happened to leave the party at the same time," said Winter.

Fox nodded, his face showing his disbelief, and made another note. "What do you remember about the accident?"

Kaci told the details, while Winter and Summer interjected little things she forgot. They described pulling Peter from the car and giving him CPR, and how Kaci relayed information to the 911 operator.

When they came to the part about finding Jennifer's body, Winter told the gruesome details quickly while the others stared at their drinks.

Then Kaci finished the story, including how the truck driver directed traffic and how the ambulances seemed to take forever to get there.

Fox nodded and grunted throughout, asking unusual questions about minute details—like, "What color was the truck?" and "Did the back glass of Peter's car break?" He wrote for several seconds after Kaci had stopped talking.

He glanced up. "Is that everything?"

The three girls looked at each other. Winter decided to take a chance.

"Brake lights," she said. "His brake lights came on before he ran the red light."

Detective Fox raised his eyebrow again. "You remember this?"

Winter faltered. "Well, not exactly," she said. "I...I sort of remembered it during a dream."

"So, you had a dream in which you relived the accident, and in this dream Peter's brake lights came on? Is that it?"

"Yeah, that's about it." Winter felt silly and shuffled her straw through the ice in her drink. Kaci stared at her. Summer's face reddened.

He wrote something in his notepad. Probably that she was an idiot.

Fox stared at his paper for a moment. "Okay, I think that about covers everything involving you three. Thanks for your time." He stood. "Have a happy Thanksgiving."

"Wait!" Winter said. "There's something else."

"Winter, no!" Kaci hissed.

"What?" Fox watched Kaci and returned to his seat.

"I..." Winter looked to Kaci and Summer for support, but both of them were staring somewhere else. "I saw some guys back behind the chapel. They were talking about Jennifer."

"And what did you hear?"

"They said they killed her."

"Really?" Fox wrinkled his forehead and took out his pen again. "Do you know who they were?"

"No," Winter said. "One of them had long brown hair pulled back—I think he's the one that did it. He was obviously in charge. There were some guys and one girl dressed Goth. And..." She looked at Kaci, who sighed and nodded. "And there was a guy there they called Taylor."

"Taylor?" Fox stared at his notepad.

"Yeah," Kaci said. "We think it was Matthew Taylor, from the school's board of directors."

Detective Fox looked up. "Matthew Taylor? Are you sure?"

"Yeah, we think so," Winter said. "I recognized his picture."

Fox returned the pen and paper to his shirt pocket without writing the name down. "Who else knows about this?"

"Well," Winter said, "they saw me, I think. At least the Goth guys saw me and chased me into the Meadow. And our friend Davis found the picture."

"Listen." Fox lowered his voice. "Tell no one else what you just told me, do you understand?" The girls looked at each other and sat up.

"What do you mean?" Kaci asked.

"I mean, this investigation may be going someplace very dangerous, and I don't want anything happening to you, got it?"

"I don't understand," Winter said.

"Look." Fox sighed. "If what you said is true, then there are a lot of powerful people who would do anything to keep this information secret…anything. Now do you understand? I'm not even going to put it in my report for fear of my own safety."

The three girls stared at him, their faces going pale, as Fox stood up again. He leaned back over the table and whispered, "Keep your mouths shut and your noses in your own business. I don't want to come back to investigate your murders, too."

He turned and walked away.

Four Years Ago

"Are you ready?" Claire asked.

Winter scrunched her eyes. "Yes," she whispered.

"All right, here goes."

Winter felt a tug at her hair and heard a soft slicing sound.

"Look," said Claire. Winter opened her eyes to see a thick six-inch lock of her own golden-brown hair dangling before her. She opened her mouth in mixed emotion and reached back to feel at her neck.

"Oh my gosh! It's really gone. You really did it!"

"Look at yourself." Claire held up a mirror for her.

Winter stared for a long time. Most of her hair, except for a few strands, hung just below her ears. Her neck looked naked.

"I'm going to trim it up so it doesn't look so scraggly," Claire said.

Winter didn't say anything. She just ran her fingers through the bobbed hair.

"Well," asked Claire, "what do you think?"

"It's so short…"

"Yes, but we've talked about this already. You need a change and a new start. You can't hang on to the past. The hair is the first thing that needs to go. You said yourself that you look just like your mom. So we need to change the way you look."

"Yeah, I guess." Winter watched Claire toss her cut hair into the trash.

"Just let me do this," she said. "I promise you're going to like it."

Winter nodded.

Claire began cutting the loose strands, evening out the length. After several minutes, she handed Winter the mirror.

"Better?" she asked.

Winter again played with the ends of her short hair and tried to manage a smile. "Yeah, it's better. It's just so different."

"Different is good," Claire said. "We want different."

"Yeah," Winter said. "What will my dad think?"

"You mean he doesn't know you're doing this?"

"No."

"Oh well, he'll just have to deal. Now, for step two." Claire reached into a shopping bag and pulled out a box of black hair color. "And no more mirrors until I'm completely, one hundred percent done, okay?"

"Okay."

Claire applied the smelly hair coloring, and Winter settled down in front of the TV for thirty minutes while the dye set.

Just before Winter went to rinse the color out, Claire covered the mirror with a blanket. Blow-drying short hair took considerably less time than long hair.

Claire grinned when Winter came back in the bedroom. "Wow!

It looks great!"

"Can I have a mirror now?"

"No. We're not done. Put this on." Claire handed Winter a black bundle.

"What's this?"

"A present. Happy birthday!"

"It's not my birthday," Winter said.

"I know. I just don't know when your birthday is, and I saw this dress and thought it would be perfect for you. So, whether I missed it or I'm too early…Happy birthday!"

"You didn't miss it, it's next month," Winter said. "December 22—the first day of winter."

"So that explains your name," said Claire.

"Yeah. It was my mom's idea."

"Hmm, maybe we should start calling you by your middle name, then."

"No," Winter said. "I like my name."

Claire shrugged. "Okay, whatever."

"Thanks for the early present, by the way," Winter said.

"You're welcome. Now put it on!"

The dress had a scoop neckline, long lace sleeves, and deep-purple fringe at the seams. It was short, but didn't come too far above Winter's knees. After Winter donned it, Claire still would not let her look in a mirror. Instead, Claire made her sit down while she hauled out her make-up.

At last, Claire led her to the bathroom and stood at the side of the mirror, poised to remove the blanket for Winter's reveal.

"You ready?" she asked.

Winter tugged the skirt and shuffled her feet. "I guess so."

Claire smiled. "Don't worry. You look great!"

Winter tried to smile, but it didn't quite come out. "Okay," she said. "Do it."

Claire ripped the blanket from the mirror.

Winter didn't recognize herself. Claire had put sparkly makeup all over her face, with black eyeshadow and black lipstick. Short black hair framed her cheeks.

Winter almost started crying.

"No, no!" Claire rushed to Winter's side and rubbed her shoulder. "I think you look fantastic! Don't you?"

"I—I don't know what to think." Winter choked back the tears. "Is this really me?"

"With a name like Winter, I think this is perfectly you."

"But it's so different. I look…like a vampire."

"You're right. Maybe the makeup is a little ridiculous. You don't have to wear it. But different is what you want, remember? It's a new life and a new beginning…you need a new look. The dress is awesome, and your hair looks great!"

Winter stared at herself for several more moments. The makeup definitely had to go. But otherwise, it wasn't that bad. Claire was right. She needed a new beginning.

"My dad's going to hate it."

Claire chuckled. "Who cares what your dad thinks? Besides, you're hot! I think I'll dye my hair black too."

Winter laughed. "I'm not hot."

"One's things for certain," Claire said, "things are definitely going to change for you now. People are going to notice you, and you won't have to feel invisible anymore."

"I hope so," Winter said.

"I know so."

31

Present Day

On Thanksgiving Day, Winter grabbed the shopping bag from the floor by her closet and ventured into the hall like a frightened rabbit. The deserted corridor seemed to absorb excess sound. She was confident that no one on her floor had stayed for the holiday, but hurried anyway to the bathroom. She turned the deadbolt on the door after she entered.

She went to the counter of sinks and the long mirror across the wall. She grabbed a lock of her hair and leaned in close to inspect it. Her golden-brown roots gleamed at her—at least two inches' worth. Winter wrinkled her nose in disgust.

Winter took off her shirt and pulled out the box of black hair coloring from the bag. After mixing the color solution, she applied it to her roots first before emptying the bottle on her whole head. The ammonia fumes stung her nose. She pushed the sticky mess to a point at the top of her head and took off the latex gloves, then sat on the floor and set the timer on her watch.

While she waited, Winter pulled out Jennifer's ID card and gave it a thorough inspection, twirling it through her fingers a few times. Then she held it tight between both hands and closed her eyes.

Something flashed—her mind rejected the foreign sensation, and it vanished.

Winter opened her eyes in shock. Could it be? She looked back at Jennifer's picture, then closed her eyes and said a prayer. Trying to relax and stay calm, Winter cleared her mind of everything but Jennifer.

A colorful blob came into sight. Her conscious mind tried to reject it and pull Winter away, but she willed herself to concentrate on the floating blob. The blob became a person, and the person grew a face.

Jennifer. Other things came into focus…scenery and sounds. She was walking and it was dark. Someone came up from behind Jennifer and struck her on the head. She collapsed. "Help me…Someone please help me…" A man picked Jennifer up and slung her over his shoulder. "God help me, I'm going to die…" Then she lost consciousness.

The image, the voice, and the hauntingly familiar words overwhelmed Winter's mind. It grabbed her and pulled her away from the vision. Winter tried to stop it, but…

Back in the bathroom, she opened her eyes and inhaled. Her heart drummed. Her skin tingled as if her nerves had awoken for the first time.

Jennifer's picture stared back at her. Could she actually control her visions? Winter closed her eyes for a third attempt, but her watch beeped—time was up. She finished undressing and got into the shower to wash out her hair.

Afterwards, she blow-dried her hair and inspected it again in the mirror. The golden-brown roots were gone and her hair shone black. Winter smiled.

Early Friday morning, a banging on Winter's door woke her. She opened it, and Kaci thrust a newspaper toward her chest.

"Look!" said Kaci. Her face almost glowed red.

Winter took the paper as Kaci stormed into the room and crashed onto the papasan. The headline read: "Cutbacks at Tishbe Announced."

"Cutbacks?" Winter asked.

"Yes," Kaci snapped. "Remember when the president was arrested? The board said they were considering cutbacks, but they wanted to get a new president first and would let him handle it. Keep reading!"

Winter perused the article for a moment. When she found what had upset Kaci, she felt her own blood begin to boil.

"They're cutting the CLC?! This is what that guy was talking about behind the chapel!"

"I know! We have to do something." Kaci took a deep breath.

"But Detective Fox told us to keep out of it. I mean, we know Taylor and Streffield are somehow involved in Jennifer's death, and we've told Fox about Taylor—I'm sure he can handle it. So what do you expect us to do? We're only students."

Kaci crossed her arms. "I don't know, but I'm doing something." She stood and stomped across the room to take the newspaper back. "Look." She pointed to a line further down in the article. "One of the departments getting its funding partially cut is the Religion Department. It says their budget is being cut by over half! Don't you see what's happening, Winter?"

"Maybe."

Kaci sighed. "They're trying to take God out of the school. I mean, Tishbe is a Christian university, and they're trying to take God out!"

"That sounds a little extreme," Winter said. "They can't really do that, can they? As long as the students are faithful, then God will never be taken out, right?"

"Look," Kaci said, "this is just the first step, you'll see. You said Jennifer's death was to bring fear to the campus. Now they do this, and most of the students are probably too afraid to do anything now. The only person in this blasted place with enough guts to really stand up and do something was Peter!"

Winter tried to suppress the cold adrenaline coursing through her body. She took a deep breath. "You're right. No one else would dare stand up against this now. Whoever that guy is, he's manipulated everything perfectly."

Kaci sat and looked at the floor. "We have to do something, Winter. I know we're not supposed to get involved…but we have to do something."

"I know we do. But what?"

Later that week, Winter, Kaci, and Summer walked across campus to the CLC Christmas party. As they passed by the Ancient, a pair of Goth kids looked up from their books and scowled.

"Where'd they all come from?" asked Kaci when they were beyond hearing.

Winter shrugged. "I don't know."

"They're everywhere."

"We had this guy in world history today dressed like you…no offense," said Summer.

"None taken, go ahead."

"Anyway, in the middle of the lecture he raises his hand and starts talking about his First Amendment rights being violated and that he shouldn't be forced to listen to a Christian-biased view of history."

"What did the professor say?" Kaci asked.

"Nothing at first. We were all so shocked by the outburst that by the time the professor realized what was happening the guy had already finished his speech—honestly, it was as if he had rehearsed it. Then the professor told him to exercise his First Amendment rights by leaving, and the guy said he would rather do it by getting a lawyer."

"What did the professor say then?"

"Nothing. He just went back to teaching," said Summer. "But you could tell he was flustered. He even let the class out early. I think it's happening all over campus."

"Was he a student?" Winter asked. "Has he been in your class all year?"

"I guess," said Summer. "I mean, the professor won't allow non-students in the class, right? He probably used to dress normal."

"Strange." Kaci frowned at Winter. "I wonder what's going on?"

"Anyway," said Summer, "I can't believe it's almost Christmas break, can you?"

"I know," said Kaci. "Are you ready for finals next week?"

Summer laughed. "Not yet."

"Winter?" Kaci asked.

Winter rolled her eyes. "Maybe...if it wasn't for English."

Kaci led them to the back of the CLC building, where they could enter at ground level directly to the lower floor. Winter broke away and made for the refreshment table, losing Kaci and Summer to the party.

Someone shoved the back of her shoulder, and Winter spun around.

"Aren't you one of them?" Sophie asked.

Winter took a threatening step toward Sophie out of habit. "What are you doing here?"

"What am I doing here? You mean, what are you doing here?" Sophie crossed her arms and cocked her leg.

Winter blinked. "What do you mean?" Winter looked around and found everyone staring at them.

"I mean," Sophie said, "you waltz in here in your Goth outfit and expect us to just let you stay? You're a freak, and all your little Goth friends have been causing problems in class."

Winter glared at her. "Who do you think you are? I've been coming here all year! It's not my fault that they suddenly decided to dress the way I do."

Someone else shouted, "I bet it's your fault the CLC has to close!"

"No!"

But before the word was out of her mouth someone else shouted, "How can you be Goth and a Christian too?"

"Wait…NO!"

"She can't," Sophie said. "She's a Goth first, and her loyalty is with them."

Kaci shoved through the crowd gathered around Winter. "Hey, leave her alone! She's been a faithful member of the CLC all year! You all know that! How can you talk to her like this?"

"She was the first Goth here," Sophie said. "She's probably the leader of them all. I bet she's been spying on us all year, waiting for the right moment to shut us down!"

"NO! I'm not!" Winter's voice was absorbed by the wave of approval with Sophie. Kaci grabbed her arm and started pulling her toward the door.

"Get out of here, freak!" Sophie yelled. "This is our CLC, and you're not welcome!"

Kaci pulled Winter through the door and outside.

"What just happened?" Winter asked.

Kaci shook her head and pressed her lips in anger. "Isn't it obvious? All these Goth people running 'round causing problems…he's turning you into the enemy. And now the CLC is falling apart."

Summer stumbled out the door and rushed toward them crying,

followed by Sophie and several others. "We don't want you either!" Sophie shouted after Summer. Kaci grabbed Summer by the hand and pulled both down the sidewalk.

"She hasn't come here in months!" Winter said as they rounded the corner.

Summer trailed a few feet behind, still crying.

Kaci took a deep breath. "I know." She looked at Winter. "Maybe she was right about the spies."

"You don't mean…Could Sophie be one of them?"

Kaci shrugged. "It would make a lot of sense."

Winter gritted her teeth. "What are we going to do now?"

Kaci sighed. "There's nothing we can do, not before Christmas break anyway. The cutbacks don't start until after the break. We'll figure something out then."

The next week was finals week, and Winter spent a good deal of time in her room studying alone. Summer spent much of her time at the music building practicing for something she called "juries"— where she was supposed to perform alone in front of all the music professors for her final grade. Several times, Winter thought about cornering Sophie…but she was nowhere to be found.

That Thursday, when the time came for her to go to Mrs. Pritchett's class for her English Comp final, Winter's stomach twisted into knots. This final was an in-class essay, so she had no way to get help from Davis. For good measure, Winter decided to borrow some of Summer's clothes again and leave her nose ring on the dresser.

Winter agonized over the essay for the entire allotted time. The sound of pencils scratching across paper made each second absolute torture. The only other sounds were the ticking of the clock and the occasional awkward cough. During those two hours, she prayed for

God to help her remember everything Davis had taught her, and she reread each paragraph five times before moving on to the next. With only a few minutes left, Winter found herself alone in the room with Mrs. Pritchett.

Finally, she finished. The sudden noise of her movement in the deserted room resembled an elephant storming through a church. Mrs. Pritchett looked up from reading the completed papers of the other students. As Winter handed in the paper, she felt the gentle tug of the Holy Spirit prompting her to speak.

"Mrs. Pritchett," she said, in a clumsy half-whisper.

Mrs. Pritchett looked up at her in the condescending glare that Winter had become used to. "Yes?"

Winter fidgeted with her hands. "I just wanted to tell you…we may not have seen eye to eye on the way I dress, but it's what's inside that matters. What's in my heart is Jesus Christ and nothing can change that. I know I'm far from perfect, but I haven't been a Christian long, and God is changing me a little every day. For what it's worth, I'm a better person for having been in your class…so, thank you. You've taught me a lot."

"Much," Pritchett said. "Taught you much."

For the first time Winter could remember, Mrs. Pritchett smiled at her.

"I believe it is you who taught me, young lady. After thirty-five years of teaching English and Literature, you would think I'd have learned by now that you can't judge a book by its cover. You've shown me nothing but respect and hard work all semester."

Winter smiled and looked down at the floor. "Thank you."

By Friday afternoon, exams were complete. Winter and Summer walked back to their dorm from the Union, sipping hot chocolate from the Café. The cold December breeze burned Winter's face, and she pulled her black stocking cap down to cover her ears.

"I'm going to miss you," Summer said. She sniffled over the rim of her cocoa.

Winter rolled her eyes. "We're coming back in three weeks, Summer."

"I know, but it's going to be a long three weeks. I'm so glad we got to be friends. I mean, I wasn't sure you were going to like me for a while there."

"I wasn't sure either," Winter said.

"So, what are your plans for Christmas?"

"Nothing really," Winter said. "Hang out with my dad. Do the birthday and Christmas thing. Visit my mom."

"Visit your mom?"

"At the cemetery. I do it every Christmas."

"Oh."

"So what are your plans?"

"I think we're going to the mountains," Summer said. "I love Christmas in the mountains. We used to do it all the time."

"Sounds like fun. Wish I could be there."

"Maybe you could come next year! That is…if we go again next year."

"Maybe," said Winter.

Winter saw her dad's truck the second she reached the dorm, and she left Summer and ran to the lobby. Her dad waited for her just inside. Winter rushed to him and wrapped her arms around him.

33

Four Years Ago

Winter entered her mom's hospice room very cautiously this time. Her mom waited for her with a wide smile and distant eyes. She was thinner and paler than she had been at Thanksgiving, but Winter tried not to let her face betray the gnawing in her stomach.

"Happy birthday, sweetheart!" her mom said with passable enthusiasm.

"Thanks." Winter crossed the room and took a seat on the little couch.

"I'm sorry about last time." Her mom pronounced each word carefully.

Winter looked at the floor and shrugged. "It's okay."

Her mom handed her a small package. She moved as if in slow-motion. "Here, I know it's not much."

Winter took the little gift and unwrapped the silver paper. Inside was a rectangular black gift box etched in gold leafing. She opened it and found a beautiful golden locket inlaid with silver ivy. It was oval, with her name in silver overlay across the front.

Winter gazed up at her mom, her chest fluttering. "Mom…this is so expensive."

Her mom just smiled. "You're worth it, sweetie. Besides, I may not get to see you at Christmas. Your dad told me you two are going to see your grandparents."

"Yeah," Winter looked back at the locket. "I'd rather come here."

"There are lots of people who love you," her mom said. "I can't be selfish and neither should you."

"But still, Mom, one Christmas and birthday together don't warrant something like this."

"I was thinking ahead a little."

Winter's insides sunk.

"Open it."

Winter lifted the locket with the tips of her fingers and pried at the seams. The clasp was so tight, it took her a few seconds to get it open. Inside she found a picture taken one year ago on Winter's birthday. In the picture, Winter embraced her mom, their cheeks pressed together, as they both faced the camera. The happiness of that day mixed with her current sadness like oil and water. Winter's eyes began to tear. Opposite the picture were the engraved words "Never Forget."

"I wish we could go back to that day," Winter said weakly.

"Me too, but we can't dwell in the past. God has great things waiting for you, I know it."

"But I don't think I could ever be that happy again."

Her mom moved from her chair to the couch and put an arm across Winter's shoulders. "You will be, I promise. Do you see what I had engraved? Never Forget. Never forget me, never forget how to be happy, and never forget to live life."

"I just don't know if I can do that," Winter said, her throat thickening.

"Of course you can." Her mom ran fingers through Winter's hair. "I like your new look," she said.

Winter half chuckled, half groaned. "No you don't. You're just saying that to change the subject."

"No, I think it fits you. What does your dad think?"

"I don't know," she said. "He hasn't really said anything. Ever since the fight about me wearing black, he hasn't talked to me much."

"I'm sure he doesn't know what to think," her mom said. "On the one hand, this is pretty drastic, and he doesn't like change. But on the other, you don't exactly look like me anymore."

"That was part of the reason I did it," Winter said.

"So you wouldn't look like me? Then I agree. Things are changing, and if you need to make a change like this to help you adjust, then you need to do it."

They sat beside each other in silence for a few minutes while her mom played with Winter's hair. "Mmm...I can't believe you're fifteen today. I remember when you were born," she said. "The first day of winter."

Winter smiled.

"It snowed that day, did I tell you? The first official snow of winter on the first day of winter."

"No," Winter said. "You never told me that."

"The nurses said the first snowflake fell the moment of your first cry. You know, they say that when a child is born on the same day as the first snow that God will bless that child."

"That's not true." Winter tried to keep her voice emotionless and sterile.

Her mom smiled. "Well, we don't know yet, do we? Have you and your dad found a church?"

"Mom, stop it. I don't want to talk about that. I just want to spend my time with you."

"But Winter, I know it hurts that I'm dying. God is the only way you can get through this."

Winter stared at the floor.

"Don't be sad for me. I'm going to a much better place where there is no pain and no cancer."

"I don't want you to go," Winter whispered. Her voice trembled through quiet tears.

Her mom took the locket from Winter's hands and clasped it around Winter's neck. "Keep this with you, and I'll always be there."

Winter turned in her seat and wrapped her arms around her mom. "I love you," she said. She buried her face into her mom's shoulder.

"I love you too, sweetheart."

34

Present Day

Winter fidgeted with the locket around her neck as her dad went to the refrigerator and withdrew a store-bought birthday cake. He brought it over to the table where Winter waited and set it down. There was a big wax candle in the middle of it that read "19."

"Happy birthday." Her dad lit the candle.

Winter smiled and blew out the flame. A tendril of smoke curled upward. Her dad handed her a small wrapped box and a card as he sat down in the chair beside her. She opened the card first and smiled again at what she read. Enclosed was a prepaid MasterCard.

"I wasn't sure what to get you," he said. "You can use that card anywhere, so you can get whatever you want. There's a hundred dollars on the card."

"Thanks, Dad." She opened the box. Inside was a cell phone.

"That prepaid phone has outlived its usefulness. I know you've never asked for a real cell phone, but it's nice to know that I can call you anytime and anywhere you are without having to refinance the house. Besides, you're an adult now, and you and your friends probably drive all over the place. You'll need it to keep up with them."

Winter stood, as he was talking, and gave him a tight hug.

"It's got everything," he said.

"Thank you, really," Winter said. She kissed him on the check.

"You're welcome," he said and looked at the floor. "Now how about that cake?"

Christmas afternoon, her dad took her to the cemetery. As he walked over to his parents' graves, Winter went the other way with a dozen dark-red roses.

With her free arm, she hiked up the collar of her trench coat and pulled her stocking cap lower on her ears to block the harsh, cold wind. The thin layer of crystalline snow crunched beneath her boots as she strode across the undisturbed ground.

Winter knelt before her mom's tombstone, soaking her knees as the ice melted beneath her. Her mom's photo was lacquered to the granite face, just below her name. Beneath the picture was the Bible verse John 16:22, "So you have sorrow now, but I will see you again; then you will rejoice, and no one can rob you of that joy." A small statuette of an angel stood guard to one side.

Winter pulled the crumbling remains of last year's roses from the stone vase and replaced them with the new roses.

"Hi, Mom," she said. "Merry Christmas. I could really use you now—so much has happened. I made a lot of mistakes last year— things I really regret and wish I could undo." Winter smiled. "But I got saved. Mom, I got saved! And I never knew I could feel like this, I never knew I could feel so loved, you know? I wish I had listened to you from the very beginning. Then maybe I wouldn't have made so many bad choices.

"Dad got saved too, and he's been wonderful ever since. I mean,

I actually have a dad who cares for me now. You'd be proud of him, Mom, he's changed a lot—we both have. This is our first Christmas together as Christians, and it's been amazing.

"And you were right—God does have something planned for me. It's kinda strange and scary, and I don't know why he picked me. But he did. I think he spoke to me. I heard a voice last summer. I don't know if it was him for sure, but he definitely sent the message. And now I've had these visions and dreams, and sometimes I know things I'm not supposed to. It's a little overwhelming, and I wish I could get your advice. You were always good at things like this. Kaci says I have the gift of prophecy, but I don't know…I'm nothing like the prophets in the Bible, that's for sure."

The wind stirred. Winter pulled her coat tighter.

"By the way, I went to Tishbe University like you, Mom. I even think I'm staying in the same dorm you did, it's old enough. Strange things are happening there, and I think I'm supposed to help fix things. At least…I feel like…if I don't do it then no one will…and then things would get really bad. I've met some cool Christian friends. They really are great; I think you'd like them. There's Kaci, she's an RA in my dorm, and we've become pretty good friends. And Davis…he's been helping me with my English. Oh, and my roommate. Her name is Summer. You wouldn't believe the things people say about our names.

"What am I doing?" she said with a laugh. "You can't hear me, and you probably haven't even thought about me yet. I'm sure you're still dancing and singing in front of Jesus…can't blame you. I guess it just feels good to think I can talk to you."

Then she closed her eyes and bowed her head. "God, thank you for giving me such a wonderful mother while she was here. And thank you for not giving up on me or my dad, and for saving us. Listen, I know my mom is probably there in front of you somewhere, so if you could, please tell her I love her, and I miss her, and update her on what's going on down here. At least please tell her that Dad and I got saved. She'd want to know that. Thanks—Amen."

Winter stood and, with one last look at her mother's picture, she pulled the collar of her coat tight and walked back to the truck where her dad waited.

35

As they drove onto the campus of Tishbe University after the New Year, Winter felt a thrill within her where she'd felt dread in the fall. The campus looked quiet and peaceful with the thin crust of snow clinging to the shadows. She thought about the storm brewing beneath the surface and wondered if she had the courage to really face it.

Kaci found her later that day. After a brief hug and a quick summary of their vacations, they went to Winter's room to plan.

"I was thinking about the CLC over Christmas," Kaci said, "and I figured the first thing we can do to save it is to make sure the CLC doesn't stop completely."

"How are we going to do that?" Winter asked.

"What if we held small groups in the dorms and maybe the larger gatherings in the Union? Just because we don't have a building doesn't mean we have to stop doing everything the CLC does, right? I mean…it's like a church—the CLC isn't a building, it's the people in it."

"I like it. What do we do?"

"Well, we need to wait until everybody gets here. Then I'll start calling all the small group leaders."

"Hey guys!" Summer walked into the room carrying a duffel bag over one shoulder and pulling a very large suitcase.

"Hey!" said Kaci and Winter in unison. They both got up and gave Summer tight hugs before she could put down her stuff.

"I know you took more home than that." Winter looked at the bags Summer brought in and shook her head.

"The rest is in the car."

"I'll help," said Winter. She grinned and rolled her eyes for Kaci.

"Sorry, Summer," Kaci said. "But I need to get back upstairs to check-in the girls."

"That's okay," Summer said as Kaci left.

Winter and Summer went out into the hall, then headed for the stairs.

"Are we going to look for classes tonight?" Summer asked.

"Sure," Winter said. "But can we do it alone?" She pushed open the door to the stairwell.

Summer giggled. "Yeah, you don't have to worry about that. I broke up with Jeffrey over Christmas."

Winter blinked and stared at her. "Why?"

"I met James." She narrowed her eyes and grinned.

"Who's James?"

Summer laughed as they left the stairs. "Don't even try to keep up. I have a bad habit of jumping from one boy to another."

Winter shrugged. "Sounds kind of depressing."

"What do you mean?"

"I mean, relationships were meant to be more serious than that. Why are you wasting your time with stupid boys? Your future husband could be right under your nose and you wouldn't even notice because you're too busy having fun."

"But I..."

"Would you want him jumping from girl to girl?" Winter asked.

"Doing the kind of things you do? What if he were with a girl like you right now? Do you even realize what kind of person that makes you? Sounds like a great way to prepare for a future marriage. If you don't get over yourself and get serious about the life God has for you, he's going to take it all away. You need to stop playing, Summer, and start listening to God. You know he doesn't like the way you're acting. If you can't be the woman your future husband deserves, then God's going to find someone else for him. And you'll be miserable for the rest of your life, wondering where it all went wrong."

Summer stopped and sagged against the wall. She pressed her knuckles into her eyes and started shaking.

Winter turned back. "I'm...I'm sorry. I don't know why I said that. It just came out." What just happened? "Summer, I'm sorry." She eased beside her and hesitantly put an arm around Summer's shoulders. Winter bit her lip. Where did that come from?

After a couple of minutes Summer looked up. Redness circled her eyes, but her face tightened with an effort to control her emotions. Her cheeks were wet and her makeup smeared. "How did you...I've been..." She studied Winter with a mixture of awe and confusion.

"I'm sorry?" Winter offered again.

"No," said Summer. "It was exactly what I needed to hear." She sniffed. "I've been thinking about that kind of stuff lately. I just thought that if I ignored it, the guilt would go away."

"It wasn't just guilt."

Summer shook her head. "No. I guess it wasn't."

"For what it's worth, I really don't know where that came from. It just kind of spilled out."

"Well, now I believe Kaci was right about you."

"What do you mean?"

"Prophets deliver messages, don't they?" She attempted a laugh.

"I'm not a prophet. There's a difference."

"Is there?"

Winter gritted her teeth and grabbed Summer's hand. "Come on. Let's go get your things."

The night before classes started, the head resident of Carmichael Hall, a senior named Georgia Velasquez, called a meeting in the lobby for all three-hundred-plus dorm residents. Georgia stood in front of the muted TV while all the girls gathered. Furniture from the other side of the lobby was brought over, but more than half the girls still had to sit on the floor.

Winter couldn't help but notice that most of them gave her a wide berth. They had avoided her at the beginning of the year, but eventually became tolerant of her presence. But the new bad rep, thanks to the uprising of Goths, infuriated her.

It took Georgia several minutes to get everyone to quiet down. The grave seriousness written on her face quickened the process.

"Earlier today," she said after the room had silenced, "all the head residents, department heads, and organization sponsors were given a memo from the president. We were told to read it, make copies of it, and give it to everyone we oversee. Before I read this, though, please know that I have nothing to do with it, and that I am simply doing what I am told to do. The copies are on the lobby desk, and you can take one if you'd like."

She paused as she looked at the paper in her hands and shook her head. She took a deep breath. "To the students, faculty, and staff of Tishbe University," she said with a slight tremor in her voice. "The recent publicity over the arrest of our former president and over the monetary cutbacks we were forced to impose has brought our school to the forefront of our country's media. Among the organizations who have taken an interest in us is the American Foundation for the Rights of Citizens, better known as the AFRC. Citing the First

Amendment, this organization feels that Tishbe University, a formerly private institution that went public ten years ago, is in direct violation of the rights of its students, by forcing them to take religion-based classes and by emphasizing a Christian worldview in every subject taken.

"On December 17, the AFRC brought this grievance in the form of a legal suit before a federal court, and we have now been issued with a cease and desist order. A court date has been set for May. Until then, under federal court mandate, we regretfully make the following temporary changes.

"One…faculty are instructed not to include Christian teaching, doctrine, or viewpoints within the context of classroom curriculum, with the exception of specific religious courses.

"Two…students who have registered for any religion classes based on core curriculum requirements may change their schedule and register for another class without penalty."

Winter sat stunned. She looked around the silent room at other stunned faces. It was Kaci who finally spoke up.

"They can't do this!" she said. "This is a private university, and they can teach us whatever they want!"

"There's nothing we can do, this comes from a federal court," Georgia said. Her voice deflated. "And it's not a private university. It hasn't been for ten years."

Kaci clenched her teeth. "There's always something we can do."

"What?" asked Georgia.

Kaci stood. "In class, we fight for our own First Amendment rights. And we have CLC activities anyway. We continue to meet in dorm rooms, lobbies, the Union, or any other place we can find. We don't give up! Just because we don't have a building, it doesn't mean the CLC is dead. We keep it alive, regardless. We're more powerful than they are, and it's time we stood up for ourselves. This has gone too far!"

A smile crept across Georgia's face, and a murmur of excitement spread through the room.

Monday came and classes started. It didn't take long for Winter to realize that eight o'clock classes every day was a bad idea. The only bright spot of her week was the fact she shared World History with Kaci.

By Friday, she decided that one of the eight o'clock classes had to go. Even though she liked her new English Comp professor, she dropped the morning section of the class and registered for a later one.

The other eight o'clock class, geography, she dropped altogether. To make up for the missing class, she took Old Testament in the same time slot as her old English class. With only one eight o'clock class now, Winter was happier.

Kaci came by just as Winter finished making her class changes through the online server. "Where's Summer?" Kaci asked.

"At a recital."

Kaci frowned. "Well, we're about to start our Bible study in a few minutes. You coming?"

Winter nodded. "I'll be there."

As Winter and Summer walked to the cafeteria Saturday morning for breakfast, they noticed a man with a baseball cap and a wind jacket sitting beneath the Ancient. When the man saw them approach, he motioned for them to come closer. Winter and Summer stopped. Winter grabbed Summer's arm and took a step back.

"It's me," he said. "Detective Fox—keep walking." The girls started again, but slowly. As they passed by Detective Fox he said, "Meet me in the parking lot on the far side of the Union in thirty minutes. Keep walking."

"What do you think he wants?" Summer asked when they were halfway to the Union. Her voice trembled.

"I don't know."

Thirty minutes later, they exited the Union on the far side and walked to the adjacent parking lot. Not knowing what to do, they stood on the sidewalk and waited.

A black sedan pulled up to them after only a few moments, and the driver's window rolled down. "Get in," said Detective Fox. The two girls jumped into the back seat. Before the door had completely shut, Fox pulled away.

"What's going on? Where are you taking us?" Winter asked. Fox looped through the parking lot on the way back to the street. Winter's hand rested on the door handle, her muscles poised to yank it open and jump.

"This is the only way I could be sure we talked in private, and now that I think about it I'm not so sure my car is secure," he said.

"What are you talking about?"

Fox looked at them in his rear-view mirror. "You really have no idea what's going on here, do you?"

Winter ground her teeth. "We know Taylor and Streffield are working together. They've managed to close the CLC and stop the teachers from teaching about God. And that somehow it's all linked back to Peter and Jennifer through some mysterious guy who employs Goths, or rather random people he has dress like Goths, to do his dirty work."

"Hmm, I hadn't made those connections. You're too observant for your own good." Fox sighed as he pulled out onto the street and started driving slowly through campus. "You were right."

"About?" Winter asked.

"About the brakes," he said. "I went to the impound and checked for myself. There was a small cut in his brake line."

Winter and Summer both sat up straight. "So Peter's innocent?" Summer asked.

"I'm not sure," Fox said. "But someone tried to kill him that night. And there's another thing…Jennifer was dead at least a whole day before her body was found. The blood on the knife was fresh."

"What's that mean?" Winter asked.

"It means someone went to great lengths to set him up. Whoever killed Jennifer kept some of her blood refrigerated and, I think, applied it to the knife that night. Then they somehow put her body and the knife in his trunk during the party."

"Then, if you know he's innocent, why can't you do anything?"

Winter said.

"Because if they went that far to set him up, imagine how far they'll go to protect themselves. I don't think they meant for him to survive the crash. The best place for him right now is where he already is—the secure wing of the hospital under constant police supervision." Fox made a left onto another street.

"But you have your evidence!"

"I have it…but officially the police do not. If I report what I know, then either the evidence will disappear—or I will. And even if it doesn't disappear, it's only evidence to help release Peter, not to convict the real killer."

"Is it Taylor? Or that other guy?" Winter asked.

Fox sighed again. "Those are dangerous questions."

"Tell us! You're the one who freakin' told us to get in the car!"

Detective Fox took a deep breath. "Matthew Taylor is as crooked as they come…you know, like the 'godfather' of Cherithville. He's weaseled his way into some of the most politically powerful positions in town."

"So why don't you just arrest him?" she asked.

"For starters, we can't prove anything. It's all just speculation and chatter from real criminals. Secondly, the last person who tried to dig dirt on Taylor got himself and his entire family murdered. I'm not about to risk the lives of my family."

"But we have to do something to help Peter," Summer said. "We can't let Jennifer's real killer get away!"

"I know, I know—I'm working on it. This is a very delicate situation. And about the Goths. We've always had a pretty extensive Goth and emo scene in Cherithville, but they're quiet. Save for the occasional suicide. Not now. I hear they're causing quite a stir on campus. And those kids are by nature loners and pacifists, so it doesn't make sense."

"It's not the Goth kids," Winter said. "Real Goths wouldn't act like this. They're just dressing Goth."

Fox looked at her in the mirror, his eyes showing skepticism. "Crime in town has spiked too, and the rumors are that some big-time Satanic priest is in town, uniting these...whatever you want to call them...to a common purpose."

Summer's eyes widened. "A Satanic priest?"

Fox made a left.

"Do you know who he is?" Winter asked.

"No, I'm not sure. But I thought your mysterious man might be a good candidate."

"So that's why you wanted to talk to us. Behind the chapel, he had Goths with him when he was talking with Taylor, but he wasn't Goth. I had the distinct impression that he was the leader. He definitely had Taylor under control."

"Sounds like our guy," Fox said. "If he's controlling Taylor, then he's very dangerous."

"Wait," Summer said. "Weren't they talking about the president?"

"Yeah," Winter said. "Taylor told the creepy guy they would 'approve his man.' That's how I know Taylor and Streffield are working together."

"Hmm...I've just had a disturbing idea," said Fox.

"What?" Summer asked.

"Well, we've either got a Satanic priest with a lot of political power on our hands, or..."

"Or what?" asked Winter.

"Or the new president is the Satanic priest."

They all sat in silence as Fox made another right and began driving back towards the Union.

Finally, Winter spoke. "What are we going to do?"

"You two are going to forget we ever had this conversation and don't cause any trouble on campus. As for me...I'm going to call the Feds. They set up a new field office here about a year and a half ago. Heck, this is probably why they came. I'd bet they already know twice as much as I do."

Fox pulled back into the parking lot behind the Union. As Winter opened the door, he turned in the seat and said, "Remember, don't get involved."

37

After breakfast Monday morning, Winter walked to the nearby English building and found room 152. As she entered the room, Summer waved to her frantically and motioned for her to sit next to her on the front row—not the desk she would have chosen on her own, but she didn't want to let Summer down.

The newly renovated room felt more inviting than the room she had taken English Comp in last semester. The modern desks gleamed with graffiti-free surfaces, and a dry-erase board hung where the usual dusty chalkboard would.

Then Mrs. Pritchett walked through the door.

When she came in, her eyes locked onto Winter. Winter was suddenly aware of just how much black she wore and how many body piercings she had exposed. Black makeup and nail polish decorated her face and fingers. She slouched down in her chair in a futile effort to hide, and thought, *Even my underwear is black*.

Mrs. Pritchett placed her bag on the table and pulled out a manila folder. "Please turn in your papers at this time." She glared in Winter's direction.

Winter sat up straight with wide eyes as the rest of the class stood to bring Mrs. Pritchett their assignment. She shot up her hand.

Mrs. Pritchett took out a stapled packet of papers and handed it to the guy who was the last to turn in his paper. "Would you please give this to our new student?"

The guy walked over to Winter's desk and dropped the syllabus packet.

"Miss Maessen, you'll find the instructions for your first assignment on page five. You have until Wednesday to complete it."

Winter lowered her hand. "Thank you." She scanned through the thick bundle of papers.

The next morning, Winter arrived early for her first day in Old Testament class, having forgone her usual black attire in favor of something more conservative...just in case.

The classroom smelled musty and old, and the wooden desks stood in crooked rows. She wasn't entirely certain she was in the right place. Winter chose a seat near the back and read her Bible to pass the time.

About five minutes till eight, a group of students came in. She recognized a couple of them from the CLC. They stopped laughing with each other and stared at her with half-suspicious faces. Winter tried not to make eye contact but could still feel their glares as they sat down. Several more students trickled in just before eight, but the class remained small. A few of the students whispered. She wanted to jump up and scream that she was not one of them, but then the professor came in.

A short man in his late thirties, he had black hair and a well-trimmed goatee. He wore a suit and tie, and he carried a briefcase and a Bible under his arm. When he saw Winter he didn't even pause, but just smiled with bemusement and continued to the teacher's desk at the front of the room.

"May I see your schedule, please?" he asked. Winter brought him her new class schedule, feeling the eyes of everyone on her back. He checked it then smiled. "I'm Dr. Cook. Welcome to Old Testament class."

Winter tried to smile back. "Thank you."

"Here is a syllabus and course schedule." He handed her a single piece of paper, a far cry from Mrs. Pritchett's novella. "You'll need to catch up on your reading assignments, and we have our first test next week. See me in my office after class, and I'll get you copies of my notes from last week."

Winter nodded and said, "Thank you." Then she fled to her seat.

"Class," said Dr. Cook. "We have a new student with us this morning. Her name is Winter Maessen. Winter, the students who take this class are usually Religion majors. Would you mind sharing with us your major?"

Winter looked up from perusing the syllabus. Her heart fluttered. She could feel everyone staring again. She tried to clear her throat, but when she spoke her voice still cracked. "Um...undecided."

Dr. Cook nodded. "Well, Winter, last week I asked every student in the class to answer a question out loud. Though you are late coming, I'm still going to ask you the same question."

Winter looked around for help, but the other students just grinned.

"Are you ready?"

Winter looked at him and widened her eyes.

"Who is God?"

Winter's mind began to race. How was she supposed to answer that? What did he expect? A Sunday school answer? Winter tried to think of good "churchy" answers to the question, but she hadn't been going church long enough to know them. She wanted to quote the Bible, but she couldn't—she hadn't studied it enough. Then she thought about giving the obvious answers—like creator, savior, master...but felt those answers would cause her to fail the test. All she knew was what God had done for her, and what he was still doing to change her. She might not know much, but to Winter those things defined God. Gaining boldness as her mind and soul settled on an answer, she sat up straight and looked Dr. Cook in the eyes.

"He is the one who loved me when I was unlovable and saved me when I was beyond saving. I ran from him, hated him, and blamed him for my miserable life, but he never gave up on me. He took me, the lowest and most disgusting being in all of creation, and gave me a brand new life. When all hope was gone and the last step I could take was death, he was there to catch me and show me that there really was such a thing as hope.

"Most of you in this room have probably grown up knowing who God was and how to define him, but I didn't. All I know is what I've seen and learned in the nine months or so since I became a Christian. In that short time he has shown me what love and forgiveness are and is re-teaching me what life is meant to be. Every day I learn something more, and I look forward to the next day and what God will teach me then. I may not be able to 'define' God in churchy or religious terms, but I know who he is in my life and that's the best answer I can give."

Dr. Cook smiled and made a soft chuckle. "It is a good answer, Winter…a very good answer." He scanned the rest of the class. "And some of you could learn a thing or two from what she just said."

Winter chanced a look around the class. No one stared anymore, and most of the coldness in the room disappeared. Finally, she could relax.

38

Four Years Ago

Winter sat with her class watching the daily news program during homeroom. Among the stories was a report on the abuse and excessive killing of animals in shelters.

"I can't believe they treat those poor animals that way!" Stacy said later that day during lunch.

"I know," said Claire. "There are plenty of people out there who could take care of them."

"Or we could just send them to China to feed the hungry," Phillip said. Ali promptly punched him. The other girls shot him dirty looks. "What? I'm just kidding!"

"They can't help it if they're not wanted," Alison said.

Winter looked down at her plate. "I know how they feel."

"We all do. That's why we should do something," Claire said.

"Do something?" Winter asked as she looked up.

"So what exactly do you suggest?" Phillip asked.

Claire thought for a moment and then smiled. "How about a protest?"

Stacy, Ali, and Phillip all exchanged looks.

"You mean, like we protested the cutting down of that forest last year?" Ali asked.

Claire nodded. "Exactly."

"I'm in," said Phillip, leaning forward.

"Me too," said Ali.

"Me too," said Stacy.

They all turned to look at Winter.

"Well, you want to do it?" Claire asked.

"What are we doing?"

Claire laughed. "You'll just have to trust me."

A pit formed in her stomach. "I don't know."

"Please? It'll be fun, I promise."

Winter panned everyone else's eager faces. She sighed. "Yeah, I guess."

"Good." Claire turned to the others. "We'll meet at Stacy's house Friday night. Since Phillip just got his license, he can drive us. Winter...Tell your dad it's another sleep-over."

Friday afternoon, Winter and Claire rode the bus with Stacy. At six-thirty, Stacy's mom left on a date. At seven, Phillip and Ali showed up.

"You ready?" Claire asked Winter.

"I just wish you would tell me what we're going to do," Winter said.

Claire smiled. "You'll see. It's going to be awesome!"

Claire, Stacy, and Winter squeezed into the back seat of Phillip's little car, and he began driving before Winter could buckle her seatbelt.

"Move over a little," she said to Claire while looking for the buckle.

"Don't worry about that. Phillip's a good driver."

"But I was always told…"

"Do you always do everything you're told?" Claire asked. Stacy laughed.

Winter hesitated for a moment, then let the belt go. It slapped against the seat.

"So, when do you want to do this?" Ali asked Claire.

"Not until midnight," she said. "I figured we'd eat first and burn the rest of the time at the mall."

At eleven-thirty they finally left the mall and drove to a nearby animal shelter. Phillip parked a block away.

"What are we doing?" Winter asked. She scrambled out of the car after the others.

"You'll see," Ali said and laughed.

"I'm really getting tired of hearing that," Winter said.

Phillip opened his trunk and reached in. "Here," he said. He began passing things to the others. When one of them came to Winter's hand, she saw that it was spray paint.

"We can't do this! It's illegal!"

"Shh!" Claire said. "And yes we can."

Two more cans were loaded into Winter's arms. "But what if we get caught," she whispered.

"Oh, come on!" Stacy said with a groan. "Live a little! We won't get caught, I promise!"

The others started jogging to the animal shelter, leaving Winter momentarily alone. With a grimace, she turned and jogged after them. By the time she caught up, they were already spraying obscene words along an unlighted side of the building.

"Come on!" Claire said.

Winter found a spot on the wall and opened one of the cans of paint. She tried to think of something good to write but couldn't, so she drew a smiley face instead. Then she added pointy cat ears and some whiskers.

Winter smiled. This was fun.

Next she tried to draw a sad puppy face, but it wound up looking more like a rabbit. She peered at the others but couldn't quite see exactly what they were drawing. Winter thought of something to write beneath her drawings and painted, "Save the kitties and the puppies." She stood back and admired her handiwork. She looked back to the others, but they were not there.

Winter walked to the corner to join her friends on the other side. As she did, a bright light shone in her face. She stopped dead still, her heart leaping in her chest.

"Stop right there!" a man yelled.

Winter didn't know what to do. Her arms felt like cold jelly as she dropped the cans and raised her hands. Chancing a look down the street, she saw Phillip's taillights and heard the screech of tires as her friends sped away.

"Put your hands on your head and get down on your knees! Now!"

39

Present Day

Winter's cell phone rang as she walked across the Meadow the next Friday on her way to Carmichael Hall after lunch.

"Hello?"

"Winter! Where are you?" It was Kaci.

"Um, headed back to the dorm. Why?"

Kaci spoke very fast. *"Stop right where you are. I need you to do something."*

"What's going on?" Winter asked.

"The AFRC is meeting with Dr. Streffield right now in Langley Hall," Kaci said.

Winter turned. She stood beside Langley Hall now. "What do you want me to do?" she asked.

"Call everyone you can think of and have them meet us on the front steps of Langley."

"Okay...why?"

"We're going to have a silent protest," Kaci said.

"A protest? Are you sure we should do that?" Winter's mind

wandered to her first experience at a "protest." For a moment, she felt the stab of betrayal all over again.

"Of course. Can you make some calls or not?"

"Sure, I guess."

"Good. I gotta go make some more calls myself. See you in a few minutes." Kaci hung up before Winter could say anything else.

She didn't have many numbers saved in her new phone, but she called the ones she had. Kaci or someone else had already contacted most of them, and several already waited at Langley Hall. Winter started around to the front of the building as she dialed the last number.

Kaci showed up not long after Winter, bringing about twenty other students—most Winter recognized from either Carmichael or the CLC. There were at least ten others already waiting, and over the next few minutes about thirty more came. Some even thought to bring their Bibles. Everyone sat scattered on the steps. Kaci and Winter sat at the top next to a large marble column.

After only five minutes, a woman with graying hair in a bun, came out the front door. "You need to leave now, or I'm going to call security!"

Kaci stood. "This is a public building and we're not causing any kind of disturbance."

"If you don't leave, security will make you!"

"We have a constitutional right to be here. You can't legally make us go anywhere."

The lady turned and stormed back inside. A growing crowd began to gather to watch.

"So what exactly are we trying to prove?" Winter asked.

"That we care…that's all."

"But what if we get in trouble?"

"Winter," Kaci said, "there's nothing they can do to us. We have a legal right to be here."

"Yeah, but still…"

A concentration of black color drew her attention to a small group of Goth students accumulating to one side of the crowd. A premonition came over Winter.

Something was going to go wrong.

"Security's here," she said, relaying information from the premonition. Kaci nodded, and a few moments later the crowd confirmed it with a unified murmur.

"It's okay, they can't do anything," said Kaci.

After making their way through the onlookers, the security guards stood at the bottom of the stairs, talking to themselves. The lady came out again, looking frustrated, and went back inside.

The arrival of the security guards brought with it a generous swelling of the crowd. A few minutes later, Winter heard police sirens in the distance. Winter kept an eye on the growing conglomeration of black-clothed students. Her premonition grew stronger as their numbers increased.

"Um, Kaci?" she said.

"Yeah?"

"I've got a bad feeling about this."

Kaci frowned. "Like what?"

"I don't know. Like…" but she couldn't finish. The Cherithville Police arrived. An officer jogged up the stairs.

"He's going to ask who's in charge," she said to Kaci as she watched the Goth students disperse and mix into the crowd.

"Who's in charge here?" the officer asked a group of students near the top. One of them turned and pointed to Kaci, and the officer approached.

"What exactly is going on?" he asked.

Kaci stood. "We are peacefully protesting on the steps of a public building."

Winter stood beside her, her eyes flickering around the crowd, trying to keep track of the Goths.

The lady came out again. "Good!" she said. "Officer, please

remove these students!"

"I'm sorry, ma'am," the officer said. His brow furrowed. "But they're doing nothing illegal."

"What do we pay you for? Can't you do anything useful?"

The officer took the last step to the top of the landing—towering over the smaller lady. He crossed his arms. "We cannot make them leave, ma'am, but we will stay to ensure this protest remains a peaceful one."

"Too late," Winter said. "It's happening now."

Just then, a half-empty soft drink cup flew through the air and hit the officer in the back, sloshing to the ground. As the officer spun around, a partially eaten hamburger landed against his chest.

"See," the lady said, "they're starting trouble. Do something!"

Winter's eyes darted from one Goth student to the next, watching, trying to catch each movement. She thought some were preparing to throw more stuff at the officers and protesters, but she was certain she saw them "accidentally" pushing others in the crowd. Within moments, the crowd turned into a mob, hurling insults and trash.

The officer turned to Kaci. "That's it," he said. "This protest is over." He reached down to grab Kaci by the arm.

"No!" she said. "You can't do this. We're staying!"

"This is no longer a peaceful protest!" the officer shouted over the roar of the crowd. "Leave now, or you will be arrested!"

"Kaci, it's over. Come on!" said Winter.

With the suddenness of a rogue wave, the crowd surged toward the steps. Fueled by the malice and incitement of the Goths, one student rushed toward the protesters with a fist raised. A police officer pepper-sprayed him. He fell down the steps, clutching his eyes, screaming in pain. That only angered the crowd more, and they all rushed up the steps.

The officer beside Winter and Kaci cursed and said something into his shoulder mic. Then he pulled out his baton and joined the rest of his officers in deterring the crowd. Most of the other protestors had already fled.

Winter grabbed Kaci's arm and pulled. Kaci nodded, and the two of them ran to the right of the steps, where the crowd was less violent. As they left, Winter noticed someone across the street watching with folded arms. It was the man with brown hair.

Their eyes connected, and he smiled.

40

Sunday morning, Winter went again to the Chapel Garden to do her Bible study. She read the story of Elijah challenging all the prophets of Baal at once. It was to be a final showdown between God and Baal.

Even though he was alone, Elijah taunted and made fun of the other prophets. And then God sent fire from heaven at Elijah's request…fire that definitively proved God's power. Then Elijah had all the other prophets executed.

Winter thought about what it must have been like to witness God prove himself in such a dramatic way. Elijah had a faith that was bold and attuned to everything God wanted him to do. Even though he was just one man, he was not afraid to stand up to the king for what he believed. He could have been overwhelmed and killed at any time.

If only she could be that brave and confident in God. Why wasn't she? She knew what God wanted her to do, so why didn't she just do it?

Winter clenched her teeth. If God wanted it done, then she could do anything. God had already given her the tools she needed. She was just too afraid to use them.

"Please, God, help me control this ability and help me understand the full reason you've given me this strange gift. Peter's life depends on me, and I must find Jennifer's real killer before it's too late. Please, give me your help, your strength, and your courage. Amen."

She took out Jennifer's ID and stared unblinking at the picture until her sight darkened around the edges of Jennifer's face. She closed her eyes and let her mind slip away. Like before, the foreign sensation fought her rational mind, but Winter made an effort to relax and distance herself, as if she were simply a bystander watching. Moments later, images came into focus.

She saw Jennifer again, but this time she lay unconscious. The blurred surroundings yielded no clues about the location. A man wearing a hooded red cloak appeared over Jennifer with a knife. Chanting something Winter could not understand, he lifted the knife high above his head and then...

The bells of Olamel began to ring, and her mind started to pull away from the scene.

"No, not yet!" she shouted in frustration. She struggled to refocus the evaporating images.

The man in the red cloak threw back his hood and fixed his eyes on Winter...it was the man with the brown hair. Winter caught her breath and her heart started to pound. Had he heard her? Her mind pulled harder from the scene as the man tilted his head and cackled. When he looked back at her, his face had changed. Pure hatred and evil had twisted and contorted his face beyond human recognition. He reached out to her eagerly with an emaciated hand and, with one final lurch, her mind jerked her away to safety back in the garden.

Adrenaline surged down her arms and legs, numbing them. What just happened? It couldn't have been real, could it?

Winter noticed that the bells had stopped ringing. She checked her watch—eight twenty-one.

She turned sharply and looked at the silent bell tower. If the bells were a part of the vision, then there must be something else there...some clue to help her find this man. Twice now she had seen him around the chapel. He left the ID the last time...perhaps he left something the time before.

She needed to go inside.

Then a thought occurred to her: What if she were being set up? What if somehow this man had invaded her vision and led her to the wrong conclusion? Jennifer's ID was far too condemning to have been casually tossed aside. Detective Fox's warning to not get involved replayed over and over in her mind. There were too many risks, too many dangers.

But then again, it was broad daylight, and the chapel was supposed to be deserted. She had been sitting here for nearly an hour, and not one person had walked by. And God gave her the vision for a reason. He gave her the gift of prophecy to make a difference, not sit around twiddling her thumbs.

Be brave like Elijah, she told herself.

Whatever clue might be waiting in the chapel, it could only be found by her. Setting her jaw, she laid her Bible by the tree and began walking to the chapel.

As she ascended the stone steps to the Gothic wooden doors, a chill trickled down her spine. It turned into a premonition, as if she had done this before. She reached for the first door, but knew it was locked before her hand touched the handle. She looked at the other front doors, knowing they were all locked.

These were not the doors she was supposed to enter. The premonition revealed another. She looked around the side of the building and spotted it near the back. Locked or not, somehow she knew this door would open for her.

She reached the door and turned the knob. The creaking echoed in the darkness beyond as the door swung inside. Winter hesitated. A blast of stale air hit her. A moment later, her pupils adjusted to the lower light levels, and she blinked. Putting aside her fears, she stepped in.

The door opened into a hallway that went right and left. Following the premonition, she turned right, knowing she would find the sanctuary.

She pushed open the sanctuary door. Dark wooden pews lined the chapel floor in four neat sections. Exquisite stained-glass windows wearing crowns of intricately sculpted marble adorned both exterior walls. Giant wooden beams ribbed the cathedral ceiling, hung with boldly colored tapestries and crystal chandeliers. Sunlight streamed in through a large round stained-glass window on the high wall above the front doors, sending prismed light throughout the room. Winter could see dust glimmering in the rays. A long rail and kneeling bench lined the altar, and on the dais a wooden pulpit stood sentinel. It looked like it had been carved from a single piece of wood. On the wall behind the pulpit, enormous brass pipes stood in orderly rows. The organ waited a little to the side of the choir loft. A giant wooden cross hung from the ceiling in front of the pipes.

Winter stood in awe as she took in the magnificent chapel. She walked in front of the altar and dragged her finger through the thick dust on the rail. She wondered how long it had been since anyone had used the place.

What a waste. Perhaps there would be a way to get the CLC here.

Looking up, she discovered that a small balcony formed a semicircle around the two sides and the back of the sanctuary. Stairs descended from the balcony near the front doors and on either side near the altar. At the top of the stairs facing her stood a nondescript door.

Looking at that door brought the premonition back. It was a door to the bell tower, and she was supposed to go there. There she would find her answers. She started walking toward the stairs.

But before she had taken two steps, she heard voices coming from deeper in the chapel. The premonition vanished, and she almost panicked. She looked left and right, wondering where to go. The courage she found in the garden evaporated.

She spun around and ran back the way she had come. As she rounded the altar and came to the hallway door, the door opened. Two guys dressed in solid black walked in. Winter slid to a stop. Behind them stood the man with long brown hair.

He smiled at her. "Hello, Winter. I was hoping you would come today."

Winter turned and fled. She could hear the heavy footsteps of the two guys rushing down the aisle to catch her. Faster...she had to get away. Winter never slowed as she slammed her shoulder into the front door. Her hand grabbed the deadbolt and gave it a quick twist.

Pressure on the back of her head. She crumpled to the floor.

Blackness.

41

Four Years Ago

Winter tried to sit as alone as possible in the far corner of the cell. A stainless-steel toilet sat naked against one wall, and the cell reeked of stale urine. She pulled her coat tight in a futile attempt to make herself less visible. Her chest ached that her friends had abandoned her. Her stomach churned like sour milk that her dad might leave her there.

Two young women wearing trashy clothes shared her cell. They stood together chatting and smoking. Winter thought they might be prostitutes. In the neighboring cell, there were four men. Two of them looked homeless and drunk. A big black man sat alone on one of the beds, and a crazy skinny man stared at her through the bars.

"So what are you in for?" one of the prostitutes asked her.

Winter hugged herself tighter and looked away. The second prostitute started giggling.

"Probably a druggie. Look at that nappy hair!"

"Nah…she's too pretty to be a druggie," said the first. "She's a runaway."

"Yeah, that's it. One of those Goth types too. Look at the way she's dressed! I bet her parents hate her." They laughed, and Winter tried to shrink more.

"Hey, did I ever tell you what my parents did to me when I turned sixteen?"

"No, what?"

The conversation between them strayed away from Winter, and they seemed to forget she was there. She sighed with relief.

Two hours later, she heard the steel door slam down the hall, followed by several sets of footsteps. Everyone in the two cells looked to see who approached. It was the desk officer followed by her dad. Her dad looked at Winter with such ferocity it scared her.

He does hate me.

"Winter Maessen," the officer said. Winter nervously rose and walked to the cell door. A buzzing sound echoed through the hall. The cell door slid open with a loud rattle.

"See you later, honey!" one of the prostitutes said. Winter lowered her eyes to the floor and exited the cell. She didn't dare look up at her dad.

The men walked away to the cell block door, leaving Winter to trail behind. The officer led them to the front desk and handed her dad a clipboard and a pen. He silently signed the release form and handed it back.

"Thank you," he said, his voice strained and controlled.

The officer looked at Winter and said, "I hope we never have to see you again."

"Don't worry, you won't," her dad said. The officer nodded and walked away.

He didn't speak to her until they were already traveling down the highway. The dash clock read three in the morning.

"What's gotten into you?" he asked. "I don't understand, so why don't you tell me what the problem is?"

Winter took a deep breath and said nothing.

"ANSWER ME!"

She started crying. "I don't know, okay? I'm sorry!"

"That's all you have to say? I'm sorry?" he asked. "Do you have any idea what went through my mind when I got a call at one in the morning, and a police officer informs me that you've been arrested?"

"I'm sorry! It wasn't supposed to happen like that."

"And what was supposed to happen? Huh? Were you forced to do this?"

"No."

"Is it those friends of yours? Were they there too?"

Winter didn't answer.

"They were, weren't they? Those friends are a bad influence on you."

"No they're not!"

"Since you met them, you've changed your wardrobe and dyed your hair. You're not the same person anymore!"

"My friends have nothing to do with the way I'm acting."

"Then what is the problem? Why are you acting like this?"

Winter shot him a hateful glare before looking away.

"You're blaming me for this? That's it...I don't want you seeing those friends anymore, do you understand me?"

"But they're the only friends I have, Dad!"

"Then I suggest you find some more!"

Winter screamed. "Why don't you listen to me! You never listen! You don't care about me, so stop trying to control my life!"

"Don't start, young lady. You will do what I tell you to do."

"Mom never talked to me like that! Why don't you treat me more like Mom did?"

"Leave your mom out of this. This has nothing to do with her and everything to do with the fact that you were ARRESTED FOR VANDALISM!"

Winter crossed her arms and stared out of the window. The sudden silence left a vacuum. "I hate you," she whispered.

"What did you say?"

"I HATE YOU!"

Her dad cursed. "Winter, I swear if you don't stop I'll…"

"You'll hit me again?" Winter asked. "Just admit it! You hate me too!"

"That's not true!"

"You hate me and you probably wish I'd never been born!"

"Shut up! Just SHUT UP!"

Winter sniffed away the angry tears and turned back to the cold window. They sat in silence. The tension thickened with each second. Her dad exited the highway and turned down another street.

"What is it going to take for you to stop acting like this?" he asked, his voice controlled again.

"You trading places with Mom," she whispered.

"What did you say?"

"Nothing."

"Well, consider yourself grounded…from everything."

Winter closed her eyes and withdrew inside herself. She felt like her heart had been ripped from her chest and replaced with ice. She embraced herself, but it didn't help. Silent tears rolled down her cheeks, and her ribs shook when she breathed.

"Whatever."

42

Present Day

An assault of flashing images struggled to escape the solitude of her mind. Everything prophetic that had happened since her salvation experience now replayed, beating at her brain like a hammer. Blood...demons...stairs... Jennifer...a little girl. Winter tried to find a pattern, but it kept slipping from her grasp like a bar of wet soap.

Sounds and smells came.

Consciousness crept in. Her thoughts swayed between the flashing images and the real sensations of the world around her. Somehow disconnected, she realized the images were fading and her senses were beginning to awaken.

Her head throbbed in time to the flashes of the last vestiges of images. The air smelled musty and rotten. Water dripped nearby. The chapel. She had been in the chapel. Someone had chased her. Her head hurt.

Then she remembered everything.

Winter cracked open her eyes. She lay on the dirt floor of a small round room, alone, cheek pressed against the cold ground. A door nearby stood ajar, and the light beyond came from a source above, illuminating wooden steps. She heard voices in that direction.

She scanned her surroundings but couldn't see much more without getting up. She tried to move her hands but couldn't. Shifting her feet, she found they, at least, were not tied. The voices stopped, and the creaking of floorboards accompanied footsteps above.

She twisted until she lay on her back and tried to pull her feet through the inside of her bound hands. After struggling for several moments, she managed to pull her hands in front and could stand. Then she went to work gnawing at the tape around her wrist.

Winter stopped when a flashlight blinded her face. She recoiled, squinting. A rat skittered away with an indignant squeak.

"Sit down," a voice said. Winter didn't move. "I said sit down!" A gun clicked. Winter obeyed.

"What do you want with me?" she asked.

The man laughed as he struck a match and lit a lantern. He extinguished the flashlight, and Winter could now see the whole room. The walls were made of dark earth and lined with open shelves. Most of the shelves stood empty except for the occasional bottle or dusty box.

The man with brown hair stood before her, a gun in his hand and a smile on his face.

"Who said I wanted you?" he asked. He lowered himself to the last step before the door and set the lantern down. The gun hung loose in his hand.

"Then why am I here?" she asked, a tremor in her voice.

The man seemed to study her. "I wanted to talk."

"To talk?"

"Yes. I wanted to meet the new prophet face to face. You intrigue me, Winter."

"What are you talking about?"

"How quaint." He chuckled. "You don't even know who you are, do you?"

Winter clenched her teeth. Her mind raced to find an answer, but none came. Something about this man frightened her, but his words frightened her more. Who was she? She didn't really know anymore. She had the gift of prophecy, but did that make her a prophet? She didn't want to be a prophet and definitely didn't feel like one. Dreams and premonitions were one thing, but being a prophet was something else entirely.

"All the others," the man said, "were older religious types—pious and devout. But you..." He furrowed his brow. "You could be one of us."

"I could never be like you," she said, forcing boldness into her voice.

The man smiled. "Oh, but you already were, I think, not so long ago. This is an interesting tactic by your God...different, to say the least." Cold radiated from his eyes and evil seemed to ooze from him like invisible oil.

"Who are you?"

"Oh, I apologize. I neglected to introduce myself. Your face just now was a study in body language. You may call me Xaphan."

"Why are you attacking students?" She winced at her own question.

Xaphan just laughed again. "My dear Winter, you really don't have any idea what is happening, do you? Do you honestly think that is the extent of my plans? Allow me to explain how things work here. You see, there's this little game we play. I have an agenda given to me by my god and your god sends someone to stop me...the prophet, if you will. That's you now, unfortunately. You're just a stupid pawn put in my way by your so-called god, so take this as a warning. It's been over ten years of work getting to this point, and no child like you is going to stand in my way, understand? Your god has already sent several much more powerful and confident prophets to stop me. A few realized the futility of their efforts, but most had to be dealt with. I don't want to have to deal with you too."

Winter held her breath and didn't blink. What was he talking about? "I...I'm not a prophet."

Xaphan tilted his head to the ceiling. "Is this all you have left to send? A stupid kid?" When he looked back, he wore a triumphant smile.

Winter bit her lip. "Are you going to kill me?" she asked, her voice trembling.

"Not today, little prophet. But you and your friends are beginning to buzz around me like gnats and, contrary to my reputation, I don't actually kill people without a purpose. Consider this conversation as your warning to not create a purpose. Take this message to your friends Kaci, Summer, Davis, and even Detective Fox." He said each name slowly and deliberately. His eyes glinted—the same evil glint she had seen in her vision moments before his face transformed into a monster.

Winter swallowed hard. "How do you..."

"I know everything, Winter. I even know where your dad, Steve, lives and works. If you make this personal, I'll make this personal. You should take Detective Fox's advice and keep your nose in your own business. This is too big for you. You're getting in over your head. I don't want to see you, or someone you love, get hurt." His nose wrinkled on the word "love."

Xaphan's arrogant attempt at intimidation infuriated her. Heat rose through her body, and with it came the premonition. She could see the scene clearly now and knew exactly what to say next.

For a moment Xaphan's presumptuous smile wavered. Recognition flashed across his face.

She pushed forward and played out the scene exactly how she saw it in her mind. Stand up...two steps forward...narrow her eyes.

Xaphan blinked but didn't move.

"If you're so confident, why do you need local help? Why rely on someone like Taylor? Why not get the job done yourself?"

Xaphan curled his lip. "Taylor is lucky to be alive. He's a fool and an imbecile. It was a mistake to enlist him."

Winter straightened her back and pushed further. "And Streffield?"

Xaphan's face twisted in an unrecognizable emotion. He opened his mouth as if to speak, but stopped just as his lips began to move in formation of the first word. Winter held her breath for an agonizing second. Then Xaphan's face softened and he smiled.

"Clever girl." He stood. "You almost had me saying too much. There may be more to you than I anticipated. No matter. If my previous warning was not sufficient, then perhaps I can persuade you a different way."

He clapped his hands and heavy footsteps began to descend the stairs. Two Goth guys stepped past Xaphan and sneered. One of them cracked his knuckles.

Just before going up, Xaphan turned and said, "Please think more carefully before prying further into my affairs, won't you?" Then he left.

Winter tried to turn and run, but there was nowhere to go. The two guys rushed in and she covered her face. The first guy slammed his fist into her stomach, and she fell back to the ground. Then they started kicking and hitting her all over. Winter felt something crack in her side, sending fire to her brain. She screamed and tried to curl into a fetal position, her hands guarding the injury. A booted foot came into view and she covered her face again. The first kick to the head numbed her entire body. Her limp arms fell to the floor.

There was no blocking the second kick.

43

Winter awoke sluggish and dazed. Her face hurt. Her head throbbed. She tried to shift her weight where she lay, but her side objected with a blinding flash of pain. She was cold and lying face down, but something had changed. Winter held her breath and listened—crickets. A cool breeze blew across her body, chilling her bruised skin. Something prickly touched her face—grass.

Winter tried to open her eyes, but her left eye would not move. She twisted her head to look around and found that she was alone— thank God. She slowly pushed herself up onto one elbow and rolled to her left side. Pain. She whimpered. Rolling instead to her right, she sat on the grass and took heavy breaths.

The cold air made the darkness seem thin. The only light came from the stars, a sliver of moon, and a streetlamp two hundred yards away. Winter gingerly pulled the left side of her shirt up and felt along the side of her body. She winced when she pushed on one of her ribs and fought the urge to curse.

Cracked again. Probably the same one as before.

Then she felt her face and found swelling around her left eye. She probed at the swelling with her finger until her left eye sparkled with stars, unable to feel her own touch.

Last time a broken nose, now a black eye.

Methodically she inspected the rest of her body and found little more than bruises. There were two huge lumps on her head, one from being hit in the chapel and the other from being kicked. The stickiness of congealed blood matted the back of her hair.

"Well, not as bad as last year," she said aloud, as a test for her own voice. It sounded strained and foreign in the still night air.

She looked around and saw that she sat in a field on the edge of a dark forest. The streetlight ahead stood in a small parking lot in front of a building. Winter couldn't tell what the building was, just that there was a door, a lighted sign several feet from the door, and some fencing to one side. The darkness masked everything else from the forest to beyond the building. She strained her good eye for any other recognizable landmarks. After a few minutes she saw headlights in the distance. They came nearer and passed in front of the building.

A road.

She realized that she was looking at the back of the building—with that new orientation came the recognition of the lighted sign. It was a drive-through menu, and the building was a fast food restaurant. But which one? She scanned it for any recognizable logos. Painted on the back wall she found a little yellow hat with two green ovals on either side. Though too far away to see clearly, she recognized the sombrero and maracas. Taco Sam.

Winter felt her pockets for her phone and sighed with relief when she found it hadn't been taken. But as she pulled the phone from her front pocket, a sudden impulse of panic gripped her. She twisted despite her body's painful protesting and shoved a hand into her back pocket.

Jennifer's ID was gone.

She felt all along the ground where she had lain but knew it was useless before she started. Without out it, she couldn't save Peter.

Without it she couldn't have any visions. And without the visions she couldn't catch Xaphan.

Did she really want to catch him now?

And then she noticed a missing presence on her chest. "No...no!" She grabbed her neck, but there was nothing there. Her locket was gone. Despite the pain, Winter sobbed.

She eased back to the ground and stared at the blurry sky through her one open eye. As the stars whirled overhead she heaved a deep breath of helplessness. She should have never gotten involved...should have never let Kaci convince her to follow her strange visions and premonitions. This was beyond her control. What could have ever made her think that God would choose to use her? Xaphan was right—she used to be one of them, and she still wasn't much different. God needed someone stronger and more dedicated... more knowledgeable of the Bible. She was none of those things, just a stupid kid who had mistaken a brain tumor for a prophetic ability.

An emptiness she had not felt for nearly a year hollowed out her chest. She took a deep breath, but it exhaled as a whimper. So many things she thought had changed in her life now revealed themselves as stupid illusions. She thought she had purpose and meaning, but it was all nothing.

Xaphan could have killed her tonight. She knew it, he knew it...and God knew it. There were too many things in her screwed up life for God to ever overlook, much less call her to some great purpose. He had forgiven her and saved her...but that was the extent of his grace. The gift of prophecy? More like a delusion of grandeur. The cancer growing in her brain was the real gift and less than she deserved.

Her head throbbed from the tumor's pressure. Her solitude pressed on all sides, as her life slipped away. She wept. The hot tears warmed her cold cheeks. Her sinuses clogged, causing her head to pound even more. She closed her eyes and tried to take deep, calming, painful breaths, and let the tumor take control. Then…blackness.

Winter woke with a start and a sharp inhale of air, surprised to be alive. She had dreamed. There had been a man—no, an angel. And a voice like honey and roses. It whispered her name, and the hollowness in her chest filled with light. She tried to sit up, but a flash of pain reminded her why she lay on the ground in the first place.

No, she was not dead…yet. Now that the pain in her head had subsided, and she could think more clearly, Winter decided she didn't want to die anytime soon.

She remembered the phone in her hand. She eased up and flipped it open. Her fingers trembled as she pushed the buttons to scroll through the phonebook.

Finally, Winter found Kaci's number and pushed the dial button. Pain shot through her side again as she tried to bring the phone to her ear, so she switched hands and eased back down onto the grass.

The phone rang three times before Kaci answered. *"Hello?"*

"Kaci." Her voice sounded weak and haggard, worse than her last attempt to speak. It surprised her, and she tried to clear her throat, only to send more pain through her side. She gasped. Something caught in her throat and she coughed, which led to more pain and groaning.

"Winter? Is that you?"

"Yes," she said, struggling to make her voice clear.

"Thank God! We've been looking all over for you! Summer found your stuff in the garden and we thought the worst! Are you okay?"

"I'm not sure. I'm hurt."

"Hurt?"

"I think I have a broken rib. But other than that I'm okay, I think.

They let me live."

Kaci started to whimper. *"Someone took you! You were right, we shouldn't have gotten involved."*

"We?" Winter asked.

Silence. Winter thought she heard sniffling on the other end. *"This is all my fault. I'm sorry. I am so sorry."*

Winter huffed. "Just come get me, please."

"Where are you?" Kaci asked.

"I don't really know," Winter said. "I was unconscious when they left me here. I'm behind a Taco Sam, I think."

"There are three Taco Sams in Cherithville," Kaci said. *"Which one?"*

"Um…three?"

"Just tell me what everything looks like around you."

"There's no other buildings I can see. And I'm by a forest."

Kaci was silent for a moment. *"Okay. I think I know where that is. You really should call 911."*

"No."

Silence. *"Okay. I'm coming."*

"Thank you."

After only a few minutes, impatience set in. The cold night air burned with each shallow breath she took. The frigid temperature saturated her coat so it no longer helped. She constantly wiggled her fingers and toes to work out the numbness. Where was Kaci?

She glanced at her phone for the time…one thirty in the morning. She flipped through the menu to the call log…ten minutes since calling Kaci. Winter groaned and decided to walk to Taco Sam and wait there. Perhaps the movement would keep her warm.

As she climbed to her feet, the world around her began to spin. Winter extended her arms for balance. It took several moments for the sensation to pass. When it did, she set her face to Taco Sam and started walking—very slowly.

It took her longer than expected to make the short walk. As she neared the parking lot, Kaci flew in, scraping the bottom of the car on the curb. She screeched to a halt and jumped out, leaving the car idling.

"Oh no, Winter! What did they do to you? Who did this? Thank God you're not dead!" She flung her arms around Winter and squeezed. Winter yelped in pain.

"I'm sorry! I'm sorry!" Kaci backed away, covering her mouth with both hands. Winter hobbled forward a few more steps. "You need to go to the hospital!"

"No! No hospitals! I'll be fine."

"No you won't!" Kaci said. "Okay, how about this. My house is only a couple hours away, and my mom is a nurse. I'll take you to her."

"I don't think…"

"Don't argue! You need help. If you won't go to the hospital, then you're going to my mom."

Winter pursed her lips and fought the urge to snap back. Then she nodded with reluctance, and Kaci helped her to the passenger side of the car.

"What day is it?" Winter asked once they were inside. Kaci slammed the car back into gear and floored the accelerator.

"Monday."

"What about classes?"

"Forget classes," she said. "Now tell me what happened—tell me everything."

Winter started with the Bible reading Sunday morning, running through the events of the past day as best as she could remember. Kaci listened in silence.

When she finished, Kaci looked at her and asked, "Is that it?"

Winter sighed. "There's one other thing. I found Jennifer's ID several months ago."

"What?"

"I found it outside the bell tower. I've been using it to try to learn to control my visions."

"Why didn't you say anything? It might have had fingerprints on it or something!"

"I...I didn't think about that..."

"And if the police knew where you'd found it, they would have investigated the bell tower and maybe found more evidence. Winter...do you realize what you did by not telling anyone? You may have ruined everything!"

Winter felt her blood pressure rising. It made her head throb more, and her eye pulsed to the beat of her heart.

"Don't tell me what I should have done! I did what I thought was best and what I thought you wanted me to do. Besides, they have enough evidence to give Peter the chair, and no little ID is going to change that. Leave me ALONE!"

Kaci was silent.

"And for someone who wants me to go by the rules, you sure have a fantastic habit of ignoring them. I'm not the one stirring the pot here—you are. You can't just let things be, can you? Can't listen to Detective Fox or anyone else. You've got to get involved. Not me. I'm through. Hear me? Through. And if anyone is going to get killed over this it's you." She huffed, and dizziness washed over her. It reached her stomach, and she fought back nausea.

Kaci spoke low and trembling. "I'm sorry. You're right, this is all my fault." She started crying. "I should just leave things alone before someone else gets hurt."

Winter's chin quivered. "Someone already has. He took my locket, Kaci." She gazed out the window and let the tears caress her cheeks.

Kaci kept silent and cried. Winter tilted the seat back and tried to relax. Her head and face pounded like a sledgehammer until she fell asleep.

44

Four Years Ago

Winter avoided the others. She hated them. She hated her dad. She hated her life. The growing pain inside her began to numb her emotions. But she could still hate.

Claire finally cornered her in the cafeteria several days later. Winter's face flushed, and her heart hardened when Claire plopped into the chair across from her. Winter grabbed her tray and stood.

"Don't you dare get up!"

Winter gritted her teeth but sat. She slammed her tray down and stared daggers at Claire.

"I know you blame me for getting you in trouble and everything," Claire said, "but you should at least give me the opportunity to defend myself!"

"I'd rather not talk, if you don't mind." Winter's cheeks burned. Everything burned.

"Well, you're going to. Right now. If you have something to say to me, then SAY IT! I'm sick of being avoided!" Claire's face hardened to match Winter's. Neither of them blinked.

"You left me!" Winter said. "You left me, and I got arrested! They put me in this smelly cell with awful people, and I had to wait for hours before my dad came. And when he did, I got grounded from everything! It's all your fault, so thank you very much. I hope you're happy and thanks for being such a great friend."

Claire didn't flinch. "Is that it? Are you done?"

Winter narrowed her eyes more.

"Well, for your information, we did not leave you. Phillip saw the guy coming and ran around to get us. We thought you heard the warning too. I would never have left if I knew you hadn't heard him."

"I don't believe you," Winter said. "Why didn't you just grab my arm or something?"

"Because I was right beside you. I thought you saw me leave. I'm sorry you didn't, but it wasn't our fault."

"Are you saying it was my fault?"

"No! I'm saying it happened, and it was nobody's fault. Just a fluke." Claire's eyes softened.

"And whose idea was it in the first place? Who got me involved without explaining exactly what we were doing?"

Claire looked at the table. "That was my fault. I'm sorry, I really am. I should have told you what we were doing, but I was afraid that if I did, then you wouldn't come."

"I probably wouldn't have."

"It was stupid. None of us should have done it. I promise, no more stupid stunts. Just please stop avoiding me." Claire looked up with large pleading eyes. "I think you're the only one here who really gets me. I mean…the others like to pretend things are tough in their lives, but it's really just show."

"Really?"

"Yeah. Stacy's parents are divorced, but they still get along fine. Ali's grandparents are cooler than most real parents. And Phillip's mom remarried several years ago. So they all practically have normal lives. You're the only one who understands me."

Winter heaved a big sigh. She could see truth and real regret on Claire's face.

"Still friends?" Claire asked.

"Okay, I guess." Winter couldn't stop the smile that crept onto her face.

"If it's any consolation," said Claire, her voice wavering, "I got in trouble with my dad when I got home, too." She gave Winter a weak, knowing grin.

What lingering anger Winter had toward Claire instantly dissolved.

45

Present Day

"We're here," Kaci said, her voice tight and hoarse. Winter inclined her seat, already awake. The pain had only allowed her to doze intermittently.

Kaci turned her Honda Accord up the gently sloping drive of a cookie-cutter house at the end of a cul-de-sac. Identical streetlights and mailboxes decorated the end of each driveway.

"Where exactly are we?" Winter asked.

"Welcome to Grady. This is where I grew up, mostly."

Lights shone out the windows like glowing eyes. As Kaci shifted the car into park, a woman came rushing out of the carport door. She looked like an older version of Kaci, with shorter graying hair and a wrinkled forehead.

"That's my mom," Kaci said. "I called her while you were sleeping."

Without hesitation, Kaci's mom rushed to Winter's side and pulled open the door. Her face was soft and comforting. Motherly.

"Hi Winter, I'm Beverly," she said. "Let's get you inside."

"Thank you, Mrs. Beverly."

She helped Winter out of the car and to the door. Winter's side and head still pounded, but the pain had diminished to an annoying murmur. By the time they reached the door, Winter was glad for the help. Once inside, Beverly ushered Winter to a dining room chair.

Beverly retrieved an ice pack from the freezer and shoved it into Winter's hands. "Here. Put it on your eye."

Winter obeyed. As Beverly went to work inspecting the back of Winter's head, Kaci started doing something in the kitchen.

"I think it's just a small cut," she said. "Head cuts bleed really bad. It makes them look worse than they are. You'll need to shower to get the blood out, though. Now take off your shirt."

"Huh?"

"I need to see this broken rib Kaci told me about."

"Mom, let her eat something first. She hasn't eaten in a day."

Beverly tsked and left the room. A moment later, Kaci presented Winter with a plate of toast and a glass of juice.

"Thanks," Winter said.

Beverly returned from the other room with a large first aid kit. "Now take that shirt off. You can eat without it." She grabbed the tail of Winter's shirt and began tugging it up.

"What about Dad?" Kaci asked.

Winter looked around in alarm.

"He won't come out unless I call for him," she said, then hesitated. "He's on the phone."

"On the phone?" Kaci asked.

"Not the police," said Winter. "And please not my dad!"

"No, not the police or your dad, don't worry about it. Your shirt, please."

Winter set down her toast and complied. Kaci left the room to give Winter more privacy. As Beverly prodded the blackened bruise at her side, Winter hissed in pain.

"Yeah," Beverly said, "it's probably fractured. You should go to a hospital."

"No!" Winter said.

"But there could be some internal injuries, you really should go."

"I said no. No hospitals."

Beverly frowned. "Fine. It doesn't look too bad or appear to be out of place. But if you start getting sick or run a fever, I'm taking you anyway. Anything else?"

Winter shook her head. "Just some bruises on my arms and legs."

"Show me."

Winter stuck out her arms and Beverly looked them over. "Now your legs."

"Um…"

"Hurry, now. Take 'em off." She stepped to the hall entrance. "Kaci… bring a robe."

Winter stood and, even more self-consciously, peeled off her pants. As Beverly inspected the dark bruises on her legs, she paused over the purple tattoo of a rose on Winter's hip. Winter held her breath and tried to think of some sort of an explanation, but Beverly said nothing. Finally, she stood up and looked Winter in the eyes, all professional at this point—all nurse. Kaci came in and laid a fluffy robe over the back of the chair. Then she left again.

"Give me the ice."

Winter handed it over, and Beverly looked closely at the swollen eye.

She tsked again. "The swelling should go down soon, but you'll have a nice shiner for several days."

Winter sighed.

"Now, the bathroom is down the hall, first door on the right. Finish your toast and go shower. Kaci will bring you some clothes, so leave the door unlocked. Let me know when you're done, and I'll wrap that rib before you dress. Okay? It doesn't really help, but the bandage will remind you to take it easy."

Winter nodded. She put on the robe and sat back down. The cold chair gave her chills despite the thick cotton robe. She ate quickly.

When she finished, Winter walked to the bathroom as fast as her bruises would allow.

An hour later, Winter was showered, wrapped, and dressed warmly in a pair of Kaci's pajamas. The pants came above her ankles, but were comfortable otherwise, so she didn't mind. Kaci had prepared the guest bedroom. Winter settled into the freshly-made bed, took the painkiller Beverly had given her, and crashed.

She dreamed of a room. A large polished mahogany desk sat in the center, with a giant plate-glass window directly behind. To the left and right, bookshelves lined the walls, holding hundreds of books each. Rich amber walls crowned with an exquisite white molding could be seen in the places void of shelves. A modest chandelier hung from the ceiling, and floor lamps in each corner emitted a soft glow. The hardwood floor wore an oval maroon rug. Everything smelled new and freshly painted. The grandfather clock beside the window ticked like a giant metronome.

Her body began to move of its own will, like she was looking through someone else's eyes. She moved to the center of the room and paused before the desk. Then she turned and approached the bookshelf on the right. She stared at a group of green books sitting on the third shelf, each labeled with ascending volume numbers. She reached for them, and as the hand came into view she was relieved to find it her own hand. She grabbed the middle of the three books and pulled. All three came down as one unit.

The fake books revealed a small silver door with a black dial and handle. A safe. Winter reached for the dial and turned it. The ticking of the clock disappeared, replaced by the loud methodical clicks of the dial. She turned it slowly and deliberately.

Right 3. Left 22. Right 9. Then she reached for the handle.

Winter woke up, the dream lingering in active memory. She repeated the numbers. 3-22-9. She had to remember them. She didn't know why, just that she needed to. After repeating the numbers several times, Winter opened her eyes.

When she tried to roll over, the previous day came back in a shock of pain from her side. The chapel...Xaphan...her locket...Kaci's house...her tirade at Kaci in the car. Winter winced with regret.

She eased to one elbow. The throbbing in her head was nearly gone. She could also see out of both eyes. Winter slid out of bed and into a pair of Kaci's slippers. When she opened the door, something warm and delicious wafted through the hall. Her stomach rumbled with approval.

In the kitchen she found the Williams family and the source of the smell—breakfast. Kaci, still in her pajamas, leaned over a cup of hot chocolate at the bar. Her dad, a kind-looking man with glasses and thinning hair—a preacher, Kaci had said—propped against the counter drinking coffee. Beverly worked a spatula in a skillet.

"Good afternoon!" Kaci's dad said.

"Afternoon? What time is it?" Winter asked.

"Almost one," said Beverly.

Almost one! Winter took a stool beside Kaci.

"Kaci insisted on breakfast, not lunch," Beverly said. "She just got up herself."

Kaci grinned. "I like my mom's breakfast. Oh, and this is my dad, Chris."

"Nice to meet you, um, Reverend Chris."

Kaci's dad smiled. "No need to be so formal. Just plain Chris is fine."

"Winter, are you feeling sick or feverish?" asked Beverly without looking up from the stove.

"No, I'm feeling much better."

"Good. You need to call your dad. I'll have your food ready by the time you're done."

Winter sighed and went back to the bedroom to find her cell phone.

When she returned to the kitchen after phoning her dad, a steaming plate of scrambled eggs, sausage, and biscuits waited. Kaci was already eating.

"Wow. I haven't eaten like this since I lived with my mom."

Beverly smiled.

"Are these biscuits homemade?"

"Yup. Dig in."

As the first mouthful plunged downward, her stomach roared its approval, and she moaned despite herself.

"Well? What did your dad say?" Beverly asked.

It took a few moments for Winter to swallow the second oversized bite. "He was upset that I didn't call him last night, and he wanted to come to Grady."

"That's fine."

"I told him not to."

"Why?"

"He's got this big meeting today. And besides, I'm fine. I promised to let him come next weekend."

Beverly frowned. "Well, if he changes his mind, he's more than welcome to stay."

"I had a dream last night," Winter said, to change the subject. She stuffed her face with more eggs. Beverly and Chris looked at her and she hesitated.

Kaci bit her lip. "I told them everything, sorry."

"No, it's okay," Winter said, shaking her head. "Anyway, I was in this fancy office. And there were these fake books on a shelf. Behind the books was a safe." She took a generous bite of biscuit.

"What was in the safe?" asked Kaci.

"I don't know. But I know the combination."

"Tell me, I'll help you remember it in case you find that room."

"3-22-9."

"3-22-9," Kaci said.

"And, by the way, I'm really sorry about the way I acted last night. I didn't mean to snap at you like that. I was tired and hungry and in pain…I just wasn't thinking."

"No, you were right," Kaci said. "It was my fault you were hurt. I shouldn't stick my nose where it doesn't belong. I've been warned about doing that sort of thing before."

"I can get into plenty of trouble on my own, trust me," Winter said. "I'm the stupid one who went to the chapel, remember?"

Kaci grinned. "Yeah, well, let's not get involved anymore. It's too dangerous."

Winter nodded. "Besides…I'm really thinking there may be something wrong with me. Maybe I'm getting a tumor like my mom. I should go see a doctor."

"It's not a tumor," Beverly said.

Winter paused in the middle of chewing. "How do you know?" she asked, through a mouth full of food.

"Any seizures? Blackouts? Dizziness? Headaches that last for days?"

Winter shook her head.

"Unexplained nausea, mood swings, memory loss, or problems concentrating?"

She shook her head again.

"Then it's not a tumor."

Winter took a deep breath and sighed. "I guess that's a relief. Regardless though, fighting for the CLC just isn't worth it."

"Now girls," Chris said. "I don't think God would like either of you giving up. I mean, if you believe in something, and you believe it's what God wants you to do, then you need to do it."

"I know, Dad," Kaci said. "But this is getting out of control. These guys are killers. They've killed Jennifer already, and they could have killed Winter. Besides, I've been told to stay out of it, remember?"

"And how are you going to do that, Kaci? Quit school? Run away? Do you think hiding works? I think you're old enough to make your own decisions now."

"Are you serious?" Winter looked at Kaci for support, but Kaci just stared at her plate. "This guy has killed someone and he could have killed me. You're acting like that's no big deal."

"Of course it's a big deal," said Chris. "It scares me to death. But do you really think this will go away? He knows who you are, and he won't stop until you're dead. Who says being a Christian is never dangerous? When someone decides to fight for God, then Satan fights back. But if you don't fight for God, then Satan has already won." He paused and closed his eyes for a second. "There's no easy way out of this, whether you, I, or anyone else likes it. You have to fight, or just roll over and..." He lowered his face toward the floor and took a deep breath. When he looked up he wiped moisture from his eyes. "But we need to trust that God has given you these gifts for a reason, Winter. You may be the only one that can stop him."

"But we don't even know what to do anymore," Winter said. "It's all gotten so complicated. What can we do to make a difference? The school is like this huge machine, and we're just insignificant students. Does it really matter what we try to do?"

"Sure it matters. Some of the greatest things in this world happened because one person got involved. Winter, you have an unusual gift from God, and I doubt he gave it to you without having a great purpose in mind."

Winter shuffled her eggs with the fork.

"You already know what that purpose is, don't you?" Chris asked.

"I'm not certain," Winter said. "It's just something Xaphan said."

"What did he say?"

"He said God had sent others to stop him, and I was just the next in line."

"So you think God has sent you to stop this Xaphan guy?"

Winter thought it over. Everything that had happened this year centered on Xaphan. Every vision, premonition, or dream pointed to him in some way. Now that she thought about it, the answer seemed obvious.

"Yes. I don't think I have a choice."

"Kaci?" Chris asked.

"I…" She hesitated. "I'm supposed to help Winter."

Winter turned, but Kaci avoided her eyes.

"So what exactly is Xaphan doing?" asked Beverly.

"We know he killed Jennifer and framed Peter for it," Kaci said.

"Okay, what else?"

"He's organized and recruited students, maybe occultists, to dress Goth, and to disrupt classes and cause general chaos on campus," Winter said. "They could have been plants from the very beginning."

"Occultists?" asked Kaci.

"Must be. People who are just Goth are only trying to express themselves. And you even said these people may be dressing that way only to discredit me. If they've organized and are acting out violently under Xaphan's leadership, then something more than just dressing Goth is involved. Fox said a Satanic priest was in Cherithville. Connect that to these Goths, and you've got something very occult happening. These Goths are not just attention seekers. They are defined by some belief system."

"You mean like witchcraft or Satanism?" asked Kaci.

"Most likely Satanism, especially with the possibility of a priest in town. And Wiccans wouldn't associate with them."

"I'm impressed, Winter," said Chris. "I think I'm beginning to understand why God chose you for this."

"All the publicity attracted the AFRC," said Kaci. "And between them and the Goths, the court order to stop all religious teaching in non-religion classes was no accident. Xaphan was behind that, too."

"Maybe," said Winter.

"And the board of directors shut down the CLC," said Kaci.

"I thought that was because the other president stole funds from the college," Chris said.

"It was. Which means that the old president might have been linked to Xaphan too."

"We already know Taylor is," said Winter.

"Well, that's a start," Chris said. "Assuming all things are connected, you have two presidents and a board member working for Xaphan. The first president steals funds and loses his job…funding Xaphan, maybe? Then the board member uses the opportunity to raise a more influential president in his place. Then Xaphan uses him and local troublemakers to stop religious teaching and close the CLC."

"But where do Peter and Jennifer fit in?" asked Winter.

"Well, the goal is to stop Xaphan, right?" said Chris. "So you need to understand his goal. What is the purpose of him doing all these things?"

Winter felt like he already knew the answer and dangled it in front of them like a worm on a hook. Her pulse beat with—was this excitement or fear?

"He's trying to muscle out all things Christian," said Kaci. "He's trying to take God out of Tishbe."

Chris crossed his arms and narrowed his eyes at his daughter. Kaci looked down. "But why? What good does that do him? There are plenty of colleges out there that are secular. Why this one little Christian school? What is the threat? Of course, there has to be a threat to him, you know that, right? What is it? What makes him so scared that he would spend time and effort just to secularize one school?"

"Ten years," said Winter. "He said he's been working on this for ten years."

"Then the obvious answer, Kaci, does not justify the means. There's more to this, girls. Think. What's Xaphan's real purpose?"

Kaci stared at her plate, and Winter slowly chewed her food...the eggs were cold now. The question made her head spin. "Do you know why?" she asked after a few moments.

Chris shook his head. "I can't say, but that's the question someone's going to need to answer soon."

"But even that won't tell us what we should do," Kaci said.

"Well," Beverly said. She walked to the bar with a plate full of fresh scrambled eggs. Winter and Kaci started raking them onto their plates. "If he's trying to muscle out God, you should do the opposite."

"The opposite?"

"If these kids are disrupting class and challenging God, then challenge them. They brought in the AFRC, bring in a Christian organization like the Christian Legal Rights Association. They closed the CLC—you open it up again."

Winter's pulse quickened even more. It was definitely excitement. "But how? We're already having small groups, but what else can we do?"

"I don't know. That would be where your gift comes in," Chris said.

"What about the president? I mean, couldn't he just have us expelled?" Kaci asked.

Winter's eyes grew wide. "Kaci! I just remembered something else Xaphan said."

They all looked at her.

"He let it slip that Taylor had failed, and he stopped talking to me when I brought up Streffield. What if Streffield isn't the guy Xaphan wanted as president? What if that's the failure? The board didn't approve the right person!"

"I don't know, Winter," Kaci said. "Taylor could have been involved in other things."

"But why would a guy like Xaphan need someone like Taylor? Sure, Taylor's got political and underground power, but Xaphan doesn't need it—unless he needs to influence a decision by the board of directors. The board has only done two things: cut back the budget, which closed the CLC; and hired a new president. It makes perfect sense."

"I agree," Chris said.

"But how are we going to know for sure?" Kaci asked.

"Go talk to him," Beverly said.

"Just like that—go talk to him?" asked Winter.

"Why not?" Beverly shrugged.

"Well, for starters," Kaci said, "if he really is involved, he could kick us out of school."

"And if he's not, then you'll have a powerful ally."

"So," Winter said, "when we get back, we go talk to the president and start doing the opposite of the things Xaphan is trying to do."

"Sounds like a start," Chris said.

"But that won't stop Xaphan," Winter said.

"I'm sure God will tell you how to stop him when the time comes for that. But for now all you can do is nullify his actions."

"And if he goes through with his threat?" asked Winter. "What if he hurts or kills someone else?"

"You just do the things God tells you to do. Let him worry about the details."

47

Winter walked barefoot through the Chapel Garden. The premonition controlled her, ordaining each footstep. All the lamp posts were out, and a suffocating shroud of darkness pressed in from all sides. She took another tentative step toward the chapel.

A storm approached…she could smell the moisture in the air. The wind howled between the buildings, bringing with it a blast of cold. Lightning flashed, illuminating each brick of Olamel. She stopped and held her breath, but no thunder came.

"What do you see?" a small voice whispered to her in the stillness.

Winter spun around, but saw no one. "Hello? Who's there?" She felt the urge to run, but the premonition told her to stay.

"What do you see?"

The voice seemed to come from all directions at once. The darkness lightened when it spoke, and it brought a quickening of her heart.

"Who are you?" she asked with a little more confidence.

The voice laughed, but the laugh became the sound of rushing wind. Lightning flashed again. "What do you see?"

Now she recognized the whispering voice…she had heard it before—last summer. "I see the bell tower," Winter said, with a little more humility.

"Listen," the voice said, and the bells began to ring.

Winter listened, not sure what she was supposed to hear. The bells sounded like all the other times she had heard them. Except now they rang slowly, as if punctuating the end of individual sentences. Each bell rang alone instead of the customary harmonizing.

Five bells rang, and then there was silence.

"Listen," said the voice. The bells started to ring again. They rang three times.

"I don't understand. What does this mean?" she said.

"You must remember," said the voice. "Listen."

The bells rang five more times and then stopped. Then the voice again instructed her to listen and more bells followed. Winter tried to keep count, but there seemed to be no end. The sequence of events continued for at least half an hour—the voice telling her to listen, followed by the ringing of bells. Finally, after the twentieth time, the voice and the bells were silent, and Winter felt alone again in the darkness.

She grunted in frustration "What am I supposed to do?" she shouted.

Lightning flashed and lit up the sky.

"You must remember," said the voice, still and small.

"Remember what? The bells? I can't remember that! There were too many! Show them to someone else who can. Why not Kaci?"

The voice laughed and the laughing turned into rolling thunder. "You speak like Moses, yet he became one of my greatest prophets! Even now you ask me for your Aaron!" More laughter…more thunder. "You have been chosen, Winter. I, the Lord, believe in you! You will be, and you will remember all you have seen and heard!"

Lightning flashed again, and she no longer stood outside the chapel. Now she was in a small room. It was dark and smelled like sewage. She turned in a circle and found that the room was round. Small slits perforated the walls and served for windows. Chains hung from the ceiling, rattling in the draftiness of the room.

Lightning flashed outside, sending white light through the room. That's when she saw the blood. Blood covered everything. The walls were smeared with it, and the blood pooled on the floor. A pentagram was drawn on the wall in blood. Lightning flashed again. Winter looked down and saw that she stood in the center of a second pentagram. She screamed.

"REMEMBER!" God said in the rolling thunder.

Then she remembered. She remembered ascending old wooden stairs lined with candles and coming to a door. She remembered opening the door and coming to this very room. She remembered the blood that rained from the ceiling and ran down the walls like a cascading waterfall. And she remembered the demon that stood in the very place she now stood…the demon that reached out to her and called her by name. She remembered…and she recognized the hate-filled eyes and the evil smile.

Xaphan.

Winter awoke sweating. She looked at the calendar. February first…"D-Day" for her and Kaci. She had to get ready.

Dr. Greg Denmark led a lecture on the Protestant Reformation in World History 2. His stiff movements and hesitant speech revealed how painfully aware he was of the three students sitting in the back wearing all black.

Kaci raised her hand from the third row.

"Yes?" Dr. Denmark said.

Winter sat beside her friend, butterflies tickling her insides. She closed her eyes and took a deep, prayerful breath.

"Was Martin Luther wrong to post his ninety-five theses?" Kaci asked.

Dr. Denmark looked stunned and then glanced up at the three students in the back. Winter could see each thought cross his face, and for a moment she thought she would start reading his mind. Was that part of her gift?

The professor seemed to agonize over how to answer Kaci. To give any kind of opinionated answer would be to take a religious stance and thus violate the federal court order. He could lose his job. But he wanted to answer—he really did...Winter could see it in his eyes.

"Um. I'm afraid that question has no bearing on our lesson today," he said and turned to the board to write more notes.

"What do you mean it has no bearing?" Kaci asked.

Dr. Denmark turned back. "I mean, that in order to answer your question I would have to make a personal moral judgment. This is an academic class, not a philosophy class, and personal moral judgments do not belong in academics."

"So you think he was wrong to post his theses?"

"I didn't say that!"

"Are you saying he was right?"

Winter smiled. Kaci had baited him just as planned. Winter could tell that Dr. Denmark almost wanted Kaci to continue just so he would be justified in violating the court order. He seemed to hurt at having to keep silent.

"My opinion on the matter is not content for this class!" he said. But there was no anger on his face. Winter could see fear and excitement instead.

"Yet the opinions of Martin Luther are?"

"Yes. His opinions have become a matter of history."

"So if opinions can be a matter of history, why can't opinions be expressed when studying history?" Kaci asked.

"Because our opinions have not resulted in history-changing events."

"Not yet," Kaci said. "But would you agree that indirectly Martin Luther and the Protestant Reformation brought about the founding of Tishbe University?"

"I fail to see how."

Every head in the class watched the exchange like a ping-pong match. Some watched in horror, while others gave approving smiles and nods. Winter watched the three students in the back stand with their arms crossed. Dr. Denmark wiped sweat from his forehead. His face had turned a brilliant shade of red. Winter slouched in her seat, clenching her teeth.

"Is Tishbe University a Catholic school?"

Denmark didn't answer. But someone else shouted out, "No!"

"Then the founding of Tishbe University was an indirect result of the Protestant Reformation and an indirect result of the opinions of Martin Luther, even though he didn't intend to split the church. Would you agree, Dr. Denmark?"

Denmark placed his hands on the lectern and leaned. "Yes, I agree."

"And since I am paying tuition to a university that has its roots and owes its existence to the Protestant Reformation, which at its core is based on moral opinions, then I feel like my rights are being violated if you don't honor the core moral principles of this school and teach in a manner that is spiritually and morally accepting."

"Spirituality and morality are two completely different things." He looked ready to flee, fear and defeat trumping his previous excitement.

"By definition spirituality cannot exist without morality," Kaci said. "To speak of a religious event such as the Protestant Reformation is to speak of spirituality. And to speak of spirituality, you must by definition speak of morality. Are you saying the Protestant Reformation was neither spiritual nor moral? By doing so you are saying that Tishbe University wasn't spiritually or morally founded. I think you'll find many spiritual edicts engraved in this university's constitution and mission statement. And if the university is spiritual, then the sum of its classes must be spiritual. In turn, if you don't teach spiritually then you are violating the foundation of this school's heritage and the rights of the students who willingly attend such a school. You don't want to violate our rights, do you? I believe that would be immoral."

Denmark sighed in defeat. A couple of students shouted their agreements and applauded. Winter held her breath and waited. Several tense seconds clicked by and in that time, the room grew silent.

There was a loud bang as the door slammed shut. Winter turned to see that the three Goth students were gone.

Dr. Denmark's shoulders relaxed, and he stood a little straighter. "No," he said.

"Then tell us," Kaci said, "was Luther wrong to post his ninety-five theses?"

Denmark set his jaw and looked Kaci straight in the eyes. It was the old Dr. Denmark, the one Winter knew to be a no-nonsense Christian teacher of World History.

"No, he wasn't," he said. "And here's why." He turned to the board and began writing.

The class erupted with cheers.

"I can't believe we pulled it off!" Kaci said. "I didn't think two weeks would be enough to coordinate everybody."

"I know," said Davis. "When that Goth kid stood up and tried to argue with me, the entire class started booing him. It was great! And the professor just stood there and smiled!"

Everyone laughed but Winter. She only listened half-heartedly.

"What's the matter, Winter?" Summer asked.

Winter shrugged. "Just nervous I guess." She checked her watch.

Kaci reached across the table and grabbed her hand. "It'll be okay. We've rehearsed every possible response Streffield could have. You're more than prepared."

"But what if we're wrong? What if he is working with Xaphan?"

"Then I can't think of anyone better to confront him," Kaci said. "We must find out whose side he's on or else our whole plan may fail."

"But you could do this much better, Kaci. You think faster, and you're smarter."

"Maybe, but you're the one with the gift."

Winter took a deep breath and nodded. She checked her watch again.

"Well, here goes." She stood.

"We'll stay here and pray," Summer said. The others nodded.

"In fact, let's pray right now before you go," said Kaci.

She grabbed Winter's hand and bowed her head. Winter closed her eyes.

"Dear Father," Kaci said, "we have no idea what you have planned for us, or what the big picture is. But we do know that you have placed us here today, and we pray that you would give us the strength to follow your will in everything we do. You've given Winter an awesome gift, and I pray that you would place your hand on her and give her strength and confidence as she goes to the 'lion's den.' You are the same yesterday, today, and tomorrow, and regardless of today's outcome you already know what will happen and what will become of it. Thank you and we love you. Amen."

"Amen," the others said.

Winter took another deep breath and smiled at everyone. Then she left through the door that exited into the administrative parking lot between the Union and Langley Hall.

Streffield's charcoal Cadillac ticked in his reserved parking space. She made her way to the front of the building and ascended the steps where they had held their protest just a few weeks ago. Beyond the double doors was a reception desk where the lady who had instructed them to leave the protest sat watching.

Winter angled left and went straight to the stairs.

Her footsteps echoed in the bright laminate stairwell. Winter rehearsed her prepared responses in her head again. The image of Xaphan in demon form floated to the forefront of her mind. She shuddered and hurried up the rest of the stairs.

On the third floor, pictures of past presidents hung on paneled walls along a wide, carpeted hall. She walked past a set of mahogany doors that opened to a conference room where a lectern stood against a backdrop of the school emblem. Passing this, she entered a large room with chairs arranged in neat rows. In front of this waiting area, a faceted plate-glass window looked out to the front steps of the building. Winter approached the ornate chestnut desk at the back of the room and tried not to make eye contact with the secretary sitting there.

"I need to speak with the president," she said. Her words came fast and jumbled. *Calm down.*

"Do you have an appointment?"

"No."

The secretary looked at her computer monitor and typed something. "What's your name?" she asked.

"Winter Maessen."

"Okay. Have a seat, please." The secretary picked up the phone handset.

Winter found a seat not too far away and waited while the woman spoke on the phone. She strained to hear what was being said but couldn't. After only a few moments, the secretary hung up.

"I'm sorry, Miss Maessen, but you'll need to make an appointment."

"No," Winter said. "I need to speak with him now. This cannot wait."

"I'm sorry, but it will have to wait. The president is very busy right now."

Winter stood and walked to the desk. She clenched her jaw and thought about punching the pretty little secretary. At the last moment, Winter changed her mind and veered aside to the president's door.

"Wait! You can't do that!"

Winter reached the door and threw it open before the secretary could stop her. President Streffield, an older man with thin gray hair and a square chin, looked up from an array of papers on his desk. Winter stormed in several feet and stopped.

What she felt transcended déjà vu—she had physically seen this place before.

The secretary, shrieking with indignity, rushed in after Winter.

"I'm sorry, sir," the secretary said. "I tried to stop her."

Streffield held up his hand and patted the air. "It's okay, Nicole. I'll speak to her if it's that important."

Streffield sat behind a large cherry desk. Behind him was a giant plate-glass window that overlooked the Meadow…Winter could even see the top of the Ancient.

"Young lady, what is it you want?" he asked.

Bookshelves lined both walls, and an oval maroon carpet lay atop a hardwood floor. A simple chandelier hung from the ceiling….just like her dream, every detail exact and vivid.

"Young lady?"

Winter snapped herself out of it and remembered her rehearsed speech. She took several quick steps forward.

"I want to know why you insist on destroying everything that Tishbe University stands for. First you closed the CLC, and you conspired with the AFRC to get a court order for teachers to stop teaching the things they believe in. This school was founded on those beliefs, and you are undermining them. Why?"

"Please have a seat, Miss…?"

"Maessen."

"And do you have a first name, Miss Maessen?"

"Winter."

Streffield stiffened. "Winter," he whispered. His eyes widened at the admission of her name. His face turned a sickly shade of white.

"How do you know my name?" She eased forward and sat.

Streffield's face morphed from white to red. "I…I don't. It's just an unusual name."

Winter didn't know how to take this unexpected reaction. It was not one she had prepared for. Somehow, it made her angry. She sat forward with her hands on her knees and started to repeat her first statement…with more force this time.

"Why do you insist on destroying…"

"Miss Winter, you must first realize that my position as president of the university does not include the final decision on financial matters. You'll have the board to thank for that. My role is mainly to advise the board on financial matters and to oversee the educational quality of the school." He leaned back in his chair.

"That's not good enough! Please spare me the political answers and tell me the truth!"

Streffield clenched his teeth. He looked as if he were being pulled between two conflicting influences…strained almost to the point of breaking.

Winter decided to push harder. Maybe she could break him. "If you refuse to give me a satisfactory answer, then I will be forced to enlist the aid of the Christian Legal Rights Association. You owe your paying students an answer as to why you're taking God out of the school."

"I have not done anything of the kind," Streffield said with a tight voice. "And, I assure you, contacting the Christian Legal Rights Association will not be necessary."

He pulled open a desk drawer and retrieved a blank piece of paper. Then he leaned forward and grabbed a pen from his desk organizer.

Winter hesitated. What was he doing? "So you deny that it was your decision to stop the teachers from teaching Christian values?" she asked slower, her eyes on the paper.

He began to write as he spoke. "That was not my decision at all."

"What are you…" Winter started to ask, but Streffield held up a warning finger to his lips. Winter narrowed her eyes.

"I was given a federal court order, and I had no choice but to comply," he said, as if he had not been interrupted. Then he slid the paper across the desk and nodded at it.

The room is bugged, it read.

Winter's heart jolted, and she looked up. Bugged? She opened her mouth to say something, but Streffield held his finger to his lips again. Her mind raced, trying to incorporate this into her list of contingencies. If the office was bugged, could Streffield be...be what? He could be anything. For that matter, who was listening? Police, FBI, the board of directors, or Taylor? Xaphan?

Whoever it was, Streffield obviously felt the need to be very careful with his words and seemed to suggest that she do likewise. But she needed more information. She pushed the paper back.

"Does that mean that if you had your way the CLC would be open and the teachers could teach what they want?" she asked.

Streffield took a deep breath and Winter considered that her question may have been too direct. But he composed himself and wrote one word on the paper.

"My only concern is that our students receive the highest quality education no matter what the means." He pushed the paper across the desk. The smooth tone of his voice contrasted with the strain in his face and the sweat on his forehead.

Yes, the paper said. Winter wanted to celebrate inside. She knew it! He was on their side! She pushed it back and tried desperately to think of a less obvious way to phrase her next question.

"Then how exactly can you justify a decision that prevents teachers from teaching the very thing this university was founded on? I mean, isn't this a Christian university?"

She bit her lip and hoped he could read between the lines. He put the pen to the paper and wrote.

"Traditionally this may be a Christian university, but what you may not know is that the school went public ten years ago. We are now considered a secular school, you might say."

I have no choice. They've threatened my family.

"Who," she emphasized the word, "has the power to change that? Most students here want a Christian education—they should have it."

"Only the board of directors has the power to change anything. But I think you'll find that the school is too dependent on state funds for the board to reverse the decision."

Taylor.

Winter nodded, a little disappointed. Not Xaphan…It took her a moment to formulate a new coded question.

"Will you approve of me trying to help the situation?" she asked and slid the paper back. She almost felt dizzy trying to carry on two separate conversations.

Streffield nodded and wrote. Then he said, "It wouldn't do any good. The board would still be unanimous."

You're being watched, too.

She knew Xaphan watched her already, but Taylor? The idea of Cherithville's local crime lord having her followed sent shivers down her back.

"I'm not afraid to get my hands dirty."

"Then good luck to you," Streffield said. "Is there anything else I can help you with?"

Winter looked to her right and scanned the shelves. There they were, just like in her dream—three green books side by side. She eased out of her chair. Streffield sat up with a look of confusion on his face.

"I think I need something from you." She crossed to the green books.

Streffield stood but stayed behind his desk. "Something from me? And what exactly would that be?"

Winter reached for the green books. Fake—just like in her dream. She pulled them aside to reveal a small rectangular safe. Winter glanced back at Streffield. He took two steps closer, eyes wide and mouth open.

Winter smiled and reached for the dial. The numbers came easily from her memory and she spun…3…22…9…The safe door opened smoothly and quietly. The document safe was big enough to hold about a six-inch stack of file folders. It held only one file.

"I need some assurance." She reached in and pulled out the folder. "If I take the information you've given me to the right people, will you support our efforts to change the school's direction?"

"Yes, of course," he said. Winter held the unmarked folder against her chest. Streffield hadn't taken his eyes from it.

"That is," he said, gaining control of his excitement, "if what you have in mind is legal. I'll only support action that is in the best interest of the school and which can be ratified by the board of directors."

"Of course."

He reached out a shaky hand to the folder and then withdrew it. "What exactly is your plan?"

"I will take what I know," she indicated the folder, "to someone who can help. Perhaps they can find a way to do this in a manner that will be in the best interest of the students, faculty, and their families."

Streffield nodded. "I understand. I hope things work out as you have planned."

"With God's help, they will," she said. "Thank you for your time, Dr. Streffield. I'll keep you informed of our progress."

"Yes, by all means," he said, still wide-eyed. He stepped to the shelf and inspected the safe.

Winter turned and almost ran for the door. The room seemed larger than before and the long walk felt awkward—she could feel Streffield watching. As she reached for the doorknob, she chanced a quick glance back. Streffield had closed the safe and was shredding the paper he had written on, his eyes still on her. Winter hurried out—her mind spinning.

50

Winter, Summer, Kaci, and Davis all retreated to the library and sat around a secluded desk in one of the more private study rooms. Davis pored over the pages in the folder with a blank expression. The girls leaned forward on the table with their elbows and watched like little children. Davis never spoke as he flipped through the green and white papers, only pursed his lips. The noise of the turning pages sounded too loud in the vacant room. Finally, Winter could take the suspense no longer.

"Well," she whispered. "What is it?"

"I'm not sure," he said, flipping another page without looking up. "It's a financial ledger, that's for sure. But there are no names or descriptions—just a bunch of numbers."

"Can you tell if the numbers mean anything?" Kaci asked.

Davis finally looked up and pushed the folder to the middle of the table. "Well," he said as he pointed to a row of numbers, "these appear to be transaction amounts. And these," he pointed to another row, "are transaction numbers...a code for each item so names would not have to be written. And I think these," he pointed to some numbers at the top of the paper, "may be account numbers."

"But what does this have to do with the president?" Summer asked.

"I'm not sure it has anything to do with Streffield," Davis said. "But it could have a lot to do with Dr. Wissman."

"You mean, the president who got arrested at the beginning of the term?" Winter asked. "I had forgotten his name."

"Yeah, that's him," Davis said.

"But I thought they seized all his records," Kaci said. "And they've got all the evidence they need to convict him. What good is another financial ledger?"

"Unless," Winter said, "this folder implicates someone else."

"What are you saying?" Davis asked.

"I'm saying that this Dr. Wiseman…"

"Dr. Wissman," Davis said.

"Whatever. Maybe he wasn't a complete idiot. Maybe he hid some insurance so that he wouldn't go down alone. What if he intended for this folder to be found in the event that he was arrested, but wanted to keep it hidden so his partner wouldn't know?"

They sat thoughtfully for a moment.

"Well, there's only one thing for us to do then," Kaci said. "Call Detective Fox. And in the meantime, don't breathe a word of this to anyone. If Winter's right and Wissman concealed this to bring down his silent partner, then whoever this partner is may be dangerous."

"It's Taylor," Winter said before she realized she was speaking. Why did she say that? She certainly wasn't thinking it.

The others turned to her.

"Why do you think that?" Summer asked.

"I…" What should she say? "I don't, really. It just sort of came out of my mouth. I don't know why."

"She may be right," Kaci said. "It's the most obvious answer. If that's the case, we need to be very careful."

"How do you do that?" Summer asked Winter.

Winter just shrugged.

"Do you think Wissman was connected with Xaphan?" Davis asked.

"Probably not," Kaci said. "It seems that Xaphan's original plan was to replace Wissman with his own guy. I think he used Taylor to help bring Wissman down."

"At any rate," Davis said, "this ledger could probably get us all killed. So who's going to keep this until we give it the cops?"

Everyone stared at the table. Nobody wanted to volunteer, but Winter felt the gentle prodding of the Holy Spirit telling her this was her responsibility. She rolled her eyes and took a deep breath.

"I'll do it."

The others relaxed and looked up. Davis slid the folder to her.

As Winter took it, Kaci and Davis started to stand.

"Wait," Winter said. "There's something else."

"What is it?" Kaci asked as she and Davis sat back down.

"I had a dream last night."

"What kind of dream?" Summer asked. The others gave her a you-should-know-by-now look. "What?"

"So tell us about it," Kaci said.

"I saw the bell tower, and God spoke to me."

"God himself?" Summer asked.

"He told me to listen to the bells ring, and I counted them. Then he said I needed to remember them."

"So how many times did they ring?" asked Davis.

"That's just it," Winter said, "it was a whole bunch. They rang for like twenty minutes—stopping and starting again. Each time they rang it was a different amount and I counted each one separately...at least that's what I thought I was supposed to do. It turned into a whole string of numbers—I couldn't possibly remember them all."

"Can't you remember any of them?" Kaci asked.

"I don't think so."

"But you remembered that combination from the other dream."

"Kaci, that was only three numbers."

"Maybe you'll only remember them when you need them," Summer said.

"Maybe," said Kaci. "But you might remember more than you think. Why don't you try?"

"I remember the first one was five and I think the second one may have been three."

"That's a start," Kaci said. "Relax and see if you can remember more."

Winter heaved a big sigh. "Okay."

"Wait. Let me get something to write them down." Kaci dug into her purse and pulled out a scrap of paper and a pen. "Okay, go."

Winter closed her eyes. God's words came back to her and it was as if he were speaking again in her head. You will be, and you will remember all you have seen and heard!

Please, God, help me remember. Winter cleared her mind and tried to concentrate on the dream. She took a deep breath and then…

"53569314122217684244," she spat out faster than her brain could comprehend what was happening. Her eyes popped open in surprise.

"Whoa! Slow down!"

"I thought you said you couldn't remember them," Davis said.

Summer's mouth hung open.

"I…I don't know. I don't remember them. I don't think…" How could she repeat numbers she couldn't remember? She tried to recall the numbers into the forefront of her thoughts.

And they came—like a picture in her mind. She could see each individual digit clearly, and she could even hear the bells ringing. If she needed to, she could count them again.

"Can you repeat that?" Kaci asked. "Slowly this time?"

Winter did so without hesitation.

When Kaci had finished writing the numbers, she looked at them thoughtfully.

"What are they?" Summer asked.

"There are twenty of them."

"No standard number has twenty digits," Davis said. He leaned over to Kaci and studied them for a moment. "Added together they make 79."

"Hmm," Kaci said. "These first three…535."

"That's an area code upstate," Davis said.

"Right," Kaci said. "Could these first ten digits be a phone number?"

Winter looked at the number in her mind, still amazed that she could see it so clearly. "535-693-1412?"

"What about the other numbers?" Summer asked.

"Well, it's another ten digits, maybe it's another phone number," Kaci said.

Winter repeated the last ten digits—from memory—as if they were a phone number. "221-768-4244."

"Maybe," Davis said. "It could be another account number, or two account numbers, to go along with the folder. Maybe a Swiss account."

Kaci nodded. "Do any of these numbers match the ones in the folder?"

Winter opened the file and scanned the numbers across the top. "Most of these are seven digit numbers. Nothing matches that I can see."

"We should tell these numbers to Detective Fox too, just in case," Kaci said.

"No!" said Winter. "The numbers were for me. God told me to remember, not to tell them to the cops."

"But they might help."

"If God wants me to give the numbers up, then he'll tell me to," Winter said. "Until then, the numbers stay between us. Got it?"

"Okay, Winter. Your call," Kaci said.

"And there's something else."

"More?" asked Davis.

"After I heard the bells, I think God took me to the room where Jennifer was killed."

"What?" Summer asked.

"It was small, and the walls were covered in blood. And there was a pentagram on the floor."

"Why a pentagram, I wonder?" Kaci asked.

Winter stared at the table, memories flooding her mind. "Pentagrams like that are used as a point of power."

"Power?"

"Yeah, like for spells and stuff."

"Spells aren't real," Davis said.

Winter looked him in the eyes. "Yes, they are."

51

Four Years Ago

The bell rang for school to let out. Winter snatched up her books and hit the door before anyone else. Doors from other classes flew open, and a deluge of students flooded the hall. Winter pushed through to her locker.

She threw in her history and algebra books, and shoved her English and biology books into her backpack. When she slammed the locker closed, Claire leaned against the neighboring locker, waiting. Claire held her own backpack close to her chest and grinned.

"What are you doing?" Winter asked.

Claire's grin widened. "I have an idea!" she said and took a step closer.

"What is it?"

"I went to a bookstore the other day, and I found a book that might be able to help us!"

"What do you mean help us?"

"You know…" Claire motioned her head. "Help us—with your mom and my dad."

"How is a book supposed to help?"

Claire opened her backpack and slid out a thick, rust-colored hardback book. A pentagram was engraved on its cover. Everyday Wiccan Spells. Claire turned to face the lockers and held the book so no one else could see it.

"You want to cast a spell? That's insane." Winter shuffled her feet and cast around to make sure no one was watching.

"Let me show you something." Claire eased the book open and balanced it on her arm. She flipped to the table of contents and slid her finger down the listings.

"Here, 'Protection from an enemy.' That one's for me." Before Winter could respond, Claire scanned the contents again and pointed to another one. "'Healing for a loved one.' That's for you."

A knot formed in the pit of Winter's stomach. "How do you know these spells are real? I mean, couldn't this just be some fiction book? Performing some spell from a book you found in the bookstore is not exactly…well, it's not exactly normal."

Claire turned to the back of the book and pointed to the author's bio. "It says it was written by a real Wiccan priestess. Besides, what's it going to hurt to try? If it doesn't work, it doesn't work. At least we tried, right? If there was anything you could do to have your mother healed, wouldn't you do it?"

The knot tightened. "I'd do anything to save my mom," Winter said, "but this is crazy, Claire. A spell? Come on!"

"Don't be so closed-minded! How do you know it won't work? Lots of people all over this world believe in crazier things than magic."

"Like what?"

"Like God. Do you know how many people actually believe in him? They think he's so loving and kind. But people like us know better, don't we? If there really is a god, then why do bad things happen?"

"That has nothing to do with magic," Winter said.

"Really? All those things people claim God did in the Bible sure sound like magic to me. If that's real, then magic must be real."

"I understand what you're saying," Winter said, "but I'm just not ready to try some silly spell to heal my mom, okay?"

"Fine, but when you change your mind, let me know."

52

Present Day

A week after confronting the president, Winter sat in her room doing economics homework. Summer was at a recital and, when someone knocked on the door, Winter jumped up to welcome the interruption. It was Kaci.

"Thanks, I needed a break," Winter said. "I hate economics."

Kaci chuckled. "I should think your new photographic memory would help."

Winter grunted. "A little. But it doesn't seem to work for everything, so it's not a photographic memory. I wish you'd stop saying that."

"Do you still remember the numbers?" Kaci asked.

"535693141222217684244."

Kaci laughed.

"It's not funny!" Winter crossed her arms, sat back, and harrumphed.

"Have you called Detective Fox yet?" Kaci asked.

"No." Winter rolled her eyes.

"Well, I'm going to keep asking until you tell me God has lifted this gag order of yours."

"It's not a gag order. I just haven't felt the time was right."

"And how do you feel about it now?" Kaci asked.

She sighed. "I feel fine about it now."

Kaci's face stretched. "Then call! Do it now!"

"I'm in the middle of homework."

Kaci put her hands on her hips and shook her head. "I'll help you if you call."

Winter closed her eyes and took a deep breath. "All right."

She pulled out Fox's business card as she crossed back to her desk, and then picked up the dorm phone. She punched in the number while Kaci made herself comfortable on Winter's papasan.

The phone rang at least six times. *"What?"* he answered.

"Detective Fox? This is Winter."

"Winter, you shouldn't be calling me. What do you want?"

"I, uh, have something for you." Winter turned to give Kaci a concerned look, but Kaci returned a hearty thumbs-up.

"Listen, and listen carefully." Fox lowered his voice. *"This is out of my hands. I'm not calling the shots anymore—been pulled off the case."*

"But how do I…"

"My phone may be tapped, so stop talking and listen. Things are getting very dangerous for you."

"What's that mean?" Ice settled in her stomach. The premonition not to call returned, but it was too late. She shouldn't have done this.

"It means that you are not to call me anymore, and that you should not leave campus or travel anywhere alone. Got it? And for Christ's sake, you and your friends need to keep to yourselves and disappear. I don't know what exactly you've been up to, but people know who you are now…the wrong people. Understand?"

"Then what about…"

But Detective Fox had hung up.

"Well?" Kaci asked.

Winter set the phone down slowly. "Um…he says that he's been pulled off the case and for us not to call him anymore."

"What? How can that happen?"

"He also said things are getting too dangerous for us, and that the wrong people know who we are." She shuddered as she remembered Xaphan reciting everyone's names.

Kaci's shoulders drooped. "Now what do we do?"

Winter shrugged. "I don't know. I guess we need to hide this folder."

"Maybe we should burn it," Kaci said.

Winter sagged into her desk chair.

"My dad did say doing this might be dangerous," Kaci said.

"I know," said Winter. "But hearing it and experiencing it are different things. I never told you, but Xaphan knew all of our names. That night he took me was meant to be a warning. I don't think he would let any of us go a second time."

They sat in silence for several minutes.

"You know," said Winter, "all that planning and then restarting the CLC last night, even if it was in the parking lot, really made me think we were winning. I thought we were beating him. I guess it's just easy to forget the real danger is still hiding out there."

"I know," said Kaci. "But we can't give up. We need to keep pushing, regardless of how dangerous it is. We can't forget about Peter and Jennifer."

Winter nodded. "Maybe we should just..." The phone rang. Winter nearly jumped out of her chair. Kaci squealed.

Heart fluttering, Winter reached over and picked it up. "Hello?" Her voice trembled, and she grabbed the receiver with both hands.

"Miss Maessen?"

"Yes," she said.

"This is Agent Gains, with the FBI," said a voice with a slightly midwestern accent. *"I understand you have something for us."*

"Maybe," Winter said. "How did you get my number?" She covered the receiver and whispered to Kaci, "It's the FBI!"

Kaci sat up and leaned forward.

"A few minutes ago we received an urgent call from Detective Fox of the Cherithville Police Department. We've been working this case for some time. He's told us all about you, and your unfortunate habit of getting too involved. He seems to think you've come into some information that may put you in danger."

Winter looked at the folder sitting innocently on her desk.

"Yeah," she said. "I think I might. I'd like to get rid of it."

"Great. I'll meet you in your lobby in twenty minutes. I think you should come with me to our office."

Winter hesitated. "Is that really necessary? Couldn't I just give it to you when you get here?"

"No, I'm afraid you must come with us. We have some questions for you, and our office is the only secure location that we trust."

"All right, I guess," Winter said.

"See you in twenty minutes then." He hung up.

"Well?" Kaci asked.

Winter frowned at her. "I have to go meet with the FBI in twenty minutes."

Kaci grinned. "About time."

The premonition screamed at her. "I guess," she said.

A few minutes later, Winter unloaded her backpack except for two books. Then she very carefully slid the folder between the books and zipped the backpack closed. She shouldered it and went down to the lobby early.

He was already there, standing near the door with his hands in the pockets of his black trench coat. His dark sunglasses blended seamlessly into his short hair.

"Agent Gains?" she asked.

The man snapped his head toward her as she approached. "Yes.

You must be Winter."

The premonition came...a warning only, but no guidance. Winter took an unsteady step backward...something about the way he talked—something had changed.

"What's wrong?" she asked.

He looked out the window again. "I think I was followed. We have to hurry."

"Followed?"

"Yes! Now come on!" He took a quick step forward and grabbed her arm.

"Let go!" She jerked her arm away. The lobby desk attendant looked up, and Gains relaxed. He put his hand down and backed away.

"I'm sorry," he said. "But you have no idea what kind of people we are dealing with. If I was followed, things could turn very bad. We need to leave before they show themselves."

"I don't know..." The premonition throbbed.

"We may not have much time. Come on, we have to leave now. Or would you rather them come into your dorm looking for you?"

Winter pursed her lips. "Okay."

"This way." He led her out the door and rushed to a blue sedan, eyes scanning the parking lot constantly. Winter followed from several feet behind.

"In the back, quickly." Gains opened the rear passenger door for her, and she climbed in.

A brown sedan with tinted windows pulled up to the front of the dorm. At its appearance, Agent Gains slammed her door and ran to the other side.

"Who is that?" she asked.

Gains jumped behind the wheel and turned the ignition. "Someone who wants you as bad as I do." Gains slammed the car into gear and spun the tires.

Winter slid sideways as he made the first turn, then she reached for the seatbelt. She twisted around to look out the back window. The brown sedan followed. Gains turned on the far side of the Union, speeding through campus. She wanted to ask him to slow down, but her jaw locked.

The premonition berated her, stronger now than ever. What was wrong? What was happening? She felt trapped and out of control.

"Why do they want me?" she asked.

"It's not you, it's what you have." He turned onto Hoole Boulevard and floored the gas.

"They want the folder?"

"Yes! The folder! Do you have it?"

Chills spread along her arms. It was Gains. He was the problem. She had to get out, but Hoole Boulevard sped by in a blur as they headed toward Cherithville. She twisted again to look at the brown sedan and found it keeping up. Two shadowed figures sat behind the windshield. No premonition there…danger here. Winter held her breath.

She was in the wrong car.

"No. I didn't bring it." She turned back around. What am I going to do? She eyed the door and tried to quietly undo her seatbelt.

Gains slammed the steering wheel with both palms. "You were supposed to bring it!" He cussed and cut left onto another street. The car fishtailed before catching traction.

Winter slid across the seat and slammed into the door. She looked back and saw the brown sedan as it skittered behind them.

"I forgot it!"

"LIAR!" He half turned to look at her. His face had darkened to a deep shade of red, and his eyes glinted with hate. "Give it to me. Quickly! Before they catch us. I can't outrun them forever."

"No!" Winter reached for the door handle. Locked!

"GIVE IT TO ME!"

"Let me out!"

A gun clicked from the front seat. Gains reached over with one arm and pointed it at her.

"NOW! GET THE FOLDER!"

There was a loud thump from behind, and the car twisted. Winter's head whip-lashed into the door panel. The gun fired. Stuffing flew out of the seat inches from her shoulder. The concussion of sound made her ears ring.

"Unlock the door!" Winter said, as Gains hit the brakes and put both hands back on the wheel to regain control.

The door unlocked. Just her door, no other.

Gains looked at her in the rearview mirror with a mixture of anger and alarm. Just before she jumped out, the gun swung back over the seat.

Her foot planted, but the momentum swept it out from under her. She tucked her body and tried to make her shoulder absorb most of the impact. The unforgiving pavement knocked the air from her body and sent a pain through her injured rib. As she rolled, she held her breath and clenched her teeth, waiting for more pain. Finally, she crashed through some garbage cans and slammed into the curb. Her cracked rib erupted with fire. She screamed.

She opened her eyes in time to see Gains turn down an alley and accelerate. The open door shut itself as the car sped away.

At the same time, she heard a loud squeal to her right. The brown sedan slid to a halt. Winter tried to scramble to her feet, but the passengers were out of the sedan and rushing toward her before the car had fully stopped. One man was white, and the other was black and bald. They held their guns in outstretched arms, and their brown coats flapped as they ran.

Winter fell back to the ground in defeat. She pulled the backpack closer as if she could protect it.

But the guns didn't point at her; they pointed at the blue sedan speeding away. The white man followed the blue car for a few feet, aimed his gun, and fired two shots that echoed in the alley.

The black man holstered his weapon and ran to her. He reached into his back pocket and pulled out a wallet. Flipping it open to reveal his ID with one hand and reaching out to her with the other, he said, "I'm Agent Markus Gains with the FBI. Are you all right?"

Winter looked at the ID and felt like an idiot.

"Please, have a seat," said Agent Gains in his mid-western accent. Winter sat in the chair indicated for her at a plain dining table. Agent Gains sat on the other side.

"Soda?" he asked.

"Sure," she said.

"What do you have for us?"

Winter reached into her backpack and retrieved the folder. She pushed it across the table.

"I found this in Dr. Streffield's office. My friend thinks the numbers are account numbers and that they are linked to Matthew Taylor."

Agent Erickson, Gains's partner, handed her the soda already open.

"That's a pretty dangerous accusation." Gains took the folder and opened it.

"I'm not scared of danger," she said.

"So I've heard." He started thumbing through the folder. Agent Erickson retreated to another room.

Winter took a slow sip of her soda and looked around. The simple apartment was drab and sparsely decorated. The only furniture other than the table was another table loaded with papers, and one couch. A small TV sat on a very simple stand, but it didn't look like it was used much. The contractor-beige walls had absolutely no decorations.

"I like your apartment," Winter said.

"Thanks," Agent Gains said without looking up.

"It's...cozy."

Agent Gains smiled, but still didn't look up. "It's our office. It's sufficient, and it's close to the campus."

Winter bounced her legs and heaved a deep impatient sigh. "Well, what is it?"

"I'm not sure what this is," he said, "but we'll find out soon enough. I think your friend may be right, though. These do look like account numbers. Whether or not Taylor is connected like you seem to think...well, that's another matter. Needless to say, if he is we'll be very pleased."

Winter smiled. Agent Erickson emerged from the other room and took a seat with them. Gains slid the folder to him, and Erickson began reviewing it for himself.

"Now, if you don't mind, I'd like to ask you a few questions," Gains said, turning back to her.

"Okay."

"Fox told us you had gotten yourself dangerously involved, but until today I didn't really believe him. You're a freshman, right?"

"Yes."

"And what's your connection to all of this?"

"I, um...I stopped an attack on one girl, and I was first on the scene when Peter had the wreck. I also discovered Jennifer's body."

Gains nodded his head. "Yes, I know all of that. But why are you getting involved? Most people, under those circumstances, would stay out of it as much as possible."

"I guess it's something I feel I have to do. I mean, after Xaphan took me…"

"He took you?" Gains asked. Erickson looked up from the folder.

"Yeah. He took me and warned me not to get involved anymore. To someone like me, that's a challenge. I wasn't trying to get involved before, but now…now I'm going to stop Xaphan from hurting anyone else regardless of what it takes."

"How exactly did you get away?" asked Erickson.

"He let me go. But not before a good beating."

Gains pursed his lips. "You were lucky, then…very lucky."

"Who is he, anyway?" Winter asked.

"Xaphan—a.k.a. Rob Olsen. He's a very dangerous man that has cut a swath of death across the country. We've been following him for quite some time. We've arrested many of his followers, but can never seem to find enough evidence to arrest the man himself. And when we do happen upon evidence, Rob disappears. Anytime we even get close, he manages to slip through our fingers. Honestly, it's as if we've been chasing a ghost…no, worse than a ghost —a demon. We had a tip that Rob might be coming here long before Fox contacted us."

"So what can you do?" Winter asked.

"Nothing," he said. "Not without positive evidence and a lucky break that puts him in our hands."

"What about Peter's car?"

"Someone tampered with Peter's brakes, but that doesn't mean we can prove who did it. It doesn't even mean Peter's innocent, much less implicate Xaphan," Gains said.

Winter's shoulders drooped.

"It's not that we don't believe Peter may be innocent," Gains said. "It's just that Xaphan is very good at what he does. Besides, the evidence is so overwhelming that, short of a confession, I don't see any way the boy can go free."

Winter sat up. "What if I can get a confession out of him?"

Gains narrowed his eyes. He took a long time to answer, seeming to calculate his words. "If you get close enough to Xaphan and get him to confess to a murder, then you'll quickly be dead yourself. He may even kill you twice."

"But I have been that close to him," Winter said.

Gains crossed his arms. "And like I said, you were lucky to live. A confession is impossible."

"Nothing is impossible."

"I don't think you understand what you're getting into here." Gains frowned. "Xaphan is a dangerous man. He's already gotten to you once, hasn't he? And either he or Taylor almost got to you again today."

"I don't care," she said with her teeth clenched. "This is something I'm going to do with or without your help."

"What's it going to take to get you to understand? You're in over your head, Winter. Stay out of it."

"Stay out of it? Regardless of what you may think, Xaphan for some reason has picked me to be his rival."

"Oh, well, now it makes sense," Gains said and leaned back in his chair. "You must be the new prophet."

"How do you know that?"

"He always picks a prophet—it makes him feel powerful to outsmart another human being. And he always kills the prophet. It's a game, Winter. Don't be fooled. Xaphan is a madman, and he'll kill you if you continue to involve yourself."

"Even if I wanted to stay out of it, he'll make sure I'm involved, right? Like you said, he's crazy." She crossed her arms like Gains. "Maybe with my help, you can finally get close enough to catch him. He may have picked his own prophets in the past, but this time he didn't pick me…God did."

Gains looked at his partner. They exchanged expressions Winter couldn't interpret. But she was sure there was some secret she wasn't being told. Erickson's face firmed, and Gains nodded. He turned back to Winter.

"Okay, but give us some time to work the system. This little folder may contain all the evidence we need," Gains said.

"That still doesn't bring him to you," she said.

"But that's no reason to willingly put yourself in danger. Let us do our job. Yours is to concentrate on keeping you and your friends safe. Got it?"

"I'll give you till the end of the semester," she said. "Then I'm going to find Xaphan myself."

Agent Gains sighed and reached into his shirt pocket. "Before you do anything stupid, call us." He handed her a business card.

54

Four Years Ago

Winter reached out and took the report card from her homeroom teacher. She glanced down the list of grades—two Bs and three Cs. Her Dad would not be happy. She grimaced and started to walk away, but her teacher stopped her.

"Winter, I'm concerned about those grades," Mrs. Bradley said. "You used to make straight As at your other school, and you've been doing so well all year. I don't know about your other classes, but you've failed the last three of my English tests. What's happening?"

"It's nothing." Winter looked at her feet.

"That's not true," Mrs. Bradley said. "You don't have to talk to me if you don't want to—I just want you to know that you can."

Winter turned away.

"I'll be praying for you," Mrs. Bradley said to her back.

Winter paused, wrinkled her nose in disgust, and rushed back to her desk.

"Let me see!" whispered Claire as Winter sat down. Winter pushed the dreaded report card over to her friend. Claire studied it and shook her head. "That's nothing. I've got two Ds."

"So what?"

"What's wrong?" Claire asked.

Winter took a deep breath. "It's my mom. For the past few weeks she's been so doped up, she hardly recognizes who I am. And I've heard my dad whispering about her on the phone with someone. I think…" Her throat constricted and wouldn't allow any more words.

Claire pushed the report card back over. "Sorry."

"Yesterday," Winter said, her chin starting to quiver, "I called her, and when she picked up she didn't even recognize my voice. When I told her who I was, she said she didn't have a daughter and hung up." She couldn't stop the tears any longer.

Claire reached over and put a reassuring hand on Winter's back. Winter saw Mrs. Bradley watching, so she laid her head down on the desk to compose herself.

After a few moments, she lifted her head and looked directly into Claire's eyes. Her face burned and her eyes felt swollen. But the sadness had turned into resignation.

"Let's do it," she said.

"Do what?"

"The spell. I'll do anything to have my mom back. Let's do it—tonight."

"We can't just do it tonight," Claire said.

"Why not?"

"Well, we have to prepare and get ingredients."

"Then let's go get them," Winter said.

"And we need to do a test spell."

"A test? Why?"

"To make sure this book works like it says it does, and that it isn't just a bunch of bull, remember? It was basically your idea," Claire said. "Something easy too, so we'll know we didn't screw it up."

"What kind of test did you have in mind?"

"I'm not sure. I haven't looked through the whole book yet. But

I'll look tonight and let you know if I see anything good. Do you have any ideas?"

Winter shook her head. "I just want to save my mom."

Claire nodded. "Okay, then the last thing to talk about is...do we want to do this at my house or yours?"

The bell rang and everybody jumped out of their seats and rushed for the door. Winter looked around and saw Mrs. Bradley coming toward them.

"We'll finish talking about this later." Winter stood and grabbed her books. "You find a spell tonight, and we'll do it this weekend."

"Okay, this weekend," Claire said.

55

Present Day

Winter glided into the silent and empty room. She had been here before, but when? Something was different. The walls...No blood...She tiptoed through the round room, careful not to step in the strange piles of foul-smelling mush. She stopped. Something else lay on the floor.

A person...A girl...

The girl lay facedown, hair splayed.

"Hello?" Winter asked. The girl didn't move. Winter eased toward her. How did they get here? She didn't remember anything before she entered the room. Strange. Maybe she had been drugged. Xaphan was behind this—she knew it.

Something shuffled behind her. Winter spun around.

Nothing.

She felt her pockets for her cell phone, and almost panicked when she found it missing. Every hair on her body stood rigid. She should leave now. Agent Gains was right, things were too dangerous. Xaphan had gotten to her again.

But she couldn't leave the girl. She turned again and rushed to the girl's side.

"Get up!" She knelt beside the girl, grabbed her shoulder and shook. The girl didn't respond. She shoved at the girl's shoulders and rolled her over. Clasping a hand to her mouth, Winter fell backward on her haunches.

It was Kaci.

Her mouth hung frozen in a silent scream, her skin chalky. A long, jagged gash ran across her throat.

Winter stifled a cry. "No...no...no..." She darted her eyes into the shadows, expecting to see Xaphan.

Instead she saw the blood. Blood oozed down the walls. It dripped from somewhere and landed on her face. She blinked and tried to slap it away, only to smear it across her cheek. She looked down. The blood spread across the floor like a water leak, soaking into her jeans.

Then she noticed the lines on the floor. She was sitting in a pentagram.

Winter awoke with a gasp, as if she had been holding her breath underwater and had just burst through the surface. Her clothes stuck to her clammy skin. The dream felt so real...

She took quick, deep breaths for several minutes, as the horror replayed in her mind. She could still feel the drops of blood running down her face. She put a hand to her cheek and rubbed. Just sweat.

Only a dream, she told herself. Only a dream.

When her pounding heart slowed to a normal rate, she swung her feet out of bed...her own bed at home. Midterms had come and gone, and her dad had picked her up last Friday for spring break.

As she sat on her bed trying to chase away the images of her nightmare, a smell wafted into her room. Bacon. Her stomach rumbled.

Winter donned a robe and slippers, and went to the bathroom to splash cold water over her face. She grabbed her hairbrush and turned to the mirror.

Kaci's dead face stared at her.

Winter dropped the brush and blinked. When she looked back, it was her own face. Her whole body shook. Winter closed her eyes and tried to calm the sudden adrenaline surge. After a few minutes, she took a deep breath and went downstairs.

"Good morning!" her dad said, as she came into the kitchen. He stood by the stove working a spatula and a skillet.

She took a seat at the bar and pulled her robe tight.

Could any of it be real? What did Kaci have to do with it? Was she in danger? Where was the round room?

"Is something wrong?"

"Oh, um. Bad dream."

"Well, maybe a good breakfast will chase it away." He presented her with a plate of scrambled eggs, bacon, and toast. "Juice?"

"Sure."

Just then the phone rang.

"Now, remember, I should be back from my meeting around three this afternoon. I'm looking forward to our little date tonight." He set a glass of orange juice in front of her.

The phone rang again.

Winter smiled. "I can't wait either."

The phone rang a third time.

"Are you going to get that?" she asked.

Her dad furrowed his brow as he took a bite of toast. "What are you talking about?"

The phone rang again.

"The phone, Dad. Are you going to answer it?"

"Uh, Winter…the phone's not ringing."

Winter sat up. She stared at the black cordless phone hanging on the wall near the refrigerator, daring it to ring again.

The phone didn't ring.

Winter put a hand to her head.

"Are you okay?"

Winter felt her face flush. "I, um, must have been hearing things." So many strange things had happened to her this year, she expected almost anything now…even a phone call from God. The idea made a smile tug at the corners of her mouth.

Her dad shoved another giant bite in. Winter checked the clock.

"Dad, you're going to be late," she said.

"It'll be okay. I'm usually there early anyway."

After another two mouthfuls, he grabbed his bag, coat, and cell phone, gave her a quick peck on the cheek, and rushed out the door.

Winter eyed the phone while gnawing on a piece of toast. *I'm not going crazy. I did hear it. RING!*

The phone began to ring.

Winter jumped out of her seat and snatched the phone off the wall.

"Hello?"

Dial tone.

She returned to her breakfast and set the phone beside her plate. Just as she took a drink of orange juice, the phone rang. She grabbed it and shoved it against her ear.

"Hello?"

"If you need to make a call, please check your number and try dialing carefully," said the automated operator.

Winter narrowed her eyes. *That's wrong. The operator says something different.*

She set the phone down, and it immediately rang.

"HELLO?!"

Dial tone.

Winter felt like screaming, but grunted instead. She slammed the phone down on the counter and glared at the cream-colored number pad.

But it didn't ring this time.

As she thought about the operator's words, her eyes flicked across the numbers, retracing phone numbers she had memorized through the years. As if of their own will, the long number from her dream presented itself in her mind...she could even hear the bells ringing. Her eyes started tracing the twenty digits across the number pad.

Could these first ten digits be a phone number? said Kaci's voice in her memory.

The phone rang. Winter grabbed it. She knew there would be nothing but a dial tone on the other end and didn't even bother saying "Hello." This time, instead of slamming the phone back to the counter, she studied it.

Please check your number and try dialing carefully.

Without thinking, Winter dialed.

535-693-1412...the first ten digits from her dream. The phone rang three times, and then someone answered.

"Hello?" said a man with a deep voice.

What do I say? This is insane! Think! "Um, hi. My name is Winter. I go to Tishbe University."

"How did you get this number?" the man said. *"This number is private."*

"I can't explain it," she said. She bit her bottom lip and then pushed forward. "God gave me your number in a dream."

"A dream?"

"And I don't know why, but I think he wants me to tell you what's been happening at the school," she said.

Silence on the other end. Had he hung up?

Winter continued. "I believe there is a satanic priest named Xaphan on campus who has been trying to organize attacks on students. He's also had people challenging the Christian teachings of the professors, which resulted in a court order for the teachers to stop."

"A court order?"

Winter's heart pounded. "And the new president is being threatened by a guy on the board of directors named Taylor. They've shut down the CLC, and God only knows what else they have planned. I think Taylor and Xaphan are working together. Oh, and a girl died. Xaphan killed her and framed someone else for it."

She stopped. Her mind flickered through the past few months. Was that it? Was that everything?

"Young lady," the man said. *"I don't know how you got this number, but thank you. I'll check into what you've said and see what I can do."*

Winter's stomach lurched. Deep in her soul, she felt a shift in the balance of power away from Xaphan.

"Thank you, sir!" she said. "Thank you!"

"Um, you're welcome," he said. Then he hung up.

She trembled with excitement. Without one second's lapse she dialed the last ten digits.

221-768-4200. A lady with a voice full of confidence answered after only the second ring.

"Yes?"

"Hi!" Winter said. She winced at the burst of enthusiasm. "My name is Winter and I'm from Tishbe University."

"Oh, I've already donated this year, thank you," the woman said. *"And please remove this number from your list, it's a private cell phone."*

"No, wait!" Winter said. "I don't want money. I have some information about the school that you need to know—something you won't read in the papers."

Silence for a few moments. *"And what's that? You've got just two minutes, so be quick. I'm on my way to an early meeting."*

Winter launched into the same speech she had given the man. Except this time, she forgot to breathe in the middle. When she finished, her lungs burned and she made a loud sound of sucking in air.

"Is this true?" the woman asked.

"I swear," Winter said. "If you don't believe me, come see for yourself."

"I just might do that. Thank you for calling me."

"You're welcome, and thank you for listening!"

The woman hung up.

Winter set the phone on the bar and looked at it with wide eyes. Her heart drummed against her ribs, and she took quick breaths. What had she done? Who were those people?

She may have just started an avalanche. Winter grabbed the phone again and punched in Kaci's number.

Spring break ended before Winter knew it. And the next three weeks of school flew by faster than ever. She saw no sign of Xaphan, had no word from the feds or Detective Fox, and the Goth students seemed to have disappeared or assimilated into the student body, invisible again. Nothing happened except for classes.

Winter scheduled a meeting during the week before finals with Dr. Cook, her Old Testament professor, who also happened to be dean of the Religion Department.

"Come in," came his voice from the other side of the door. He looked up with a kind smile as she entered.

She wore her most unassuming dark clothing, hoping to appear more normal. "I was surprised to get your call. Please, have a seat. What can I do for you?"

Winter sat in the leather chair across the desk from Dr. Cook. The chair sat lower than she expected, and she tried to sit up on the edge of the seat. It took an effort not to fidget with her hands. A wall clock ticked nearby, and Dr. Cook watched her with a wry grin.

"I wanted to tell you how much I've enjoyed your class this

semester," she said.

"Well, your class participation and flawless grades are evidence of that," he said with a chuckle. "But I don't think that's why you wanted to talk to me, is it?"

"No," she said. "I've finally decided on a major."

"And?" he asked with an eyebrow raised.

"And I want to major in religion."

Dr. Cook leaned back in his chair and touched his fingers together in front of him. "Really? And why's that?"

She cleared her throat. "Because it's what I enjoy the most. And I was always told that you should major in what you enjoy. Besides, it's the only major that fits with what God is calling me to do."

"And what is he calling you to do?"

Winter's mind raced for an adequate answer, something truthful but not too revealing. "I, um…God is calling me to…" Be a prophetess? "to…well, I'm not entirely sure. I just know he wants me to do something in religion." Winter grimaced. That was a stupid answer.

Dr. Cook laughed. "I'm sorry, that question wasn't entirely fair. I find that students, especially freshmen, who think they know God's calling on their lives are usually fooling themselves. I know grown men who feel called by God, but still do not know exactly what he's called them to do. They simply live day-to-day doing what God leads them to do. Perhaps that is a calling in itself. Personally, I didn't fully realize my calling until after I was already doing it." He waved his hands and indicated his office.

"So, are you going to let me be a religion major?"

Dr. Cook smiled. "Of course. It's always good to get another student, especially one so eager as you. I must say though, you had Mary quite worried. She'll be pleased with this change of events. She asks me about you all the time."

"Mary?"

"Mary Pritchett, your English teacher. She goes to my church."

"Oh, really?"

Suddenly Mrs. Pritchett's change in attitude the past few weeks made a lot more sense.

Dr. Cook laughed again. "You'll need to sign up for an advisory meeting next week. We'll discuss your schedule and get you preregistered for classes next fall."

"And what do I need to do to change my major?" she asked.

"Go to the registrar, they have a form for you to fill out. The rest is up to me," he said.

57

Four Years Ago

They agreed to meet at Winter's house. Winter's dad relented on her punishment and let Claire come over on a Saturday night.

"Did you get the poster board like I wanted?" Claire asked when they rushed into Winter's room.

"Yeah, it's in my closet. I told my dad I needed it for a science project."

"Well, this is a science project," Claire said. "Let's get this over with before your dad comes to investigate."

Winter looked out of her door toward the stairs for a moment and then shut it. She hurried to the closet and retrieved the poster board.

"Okay, what should I do with it?"

"Just put it here in front of me," Claire said. She sat down with her legs crossed in the middle of Winter's bedroom floor. "And crack your window."

After Winter opened the window a little bit, Claire rummaged through a duffel bag and retrieved the spell book, five candles, a marker, and a bowl. Winter sat down opposite the poster board from Claire.

Claire pulled the cap off the marker, releasing the stinging smell of ammonia. "First, we need to draw the symbol of power." She drew a five-pointed star with a circle around it.

"Next, the candles." Claire placed one candle at each point of the star. She pulled out a lighter and lit each one. Winter looked at the door and wondered if the window would be enough to keep her dad from smelling the smoke.

"Now, turn out the lights," Claire said.

Winter jumped up and rushed to the door. With one hand she flipped the switch and with the other she twisted the lock on the doorknob. She paused and put her ear close to the door. All she could hear was muted voices from the TV downstairs.

She walked back to Claire. "So, what kind of spell are we doing?"

"A love spell," Claire said with a mischievous grin. She set the bowl in the center of the pentagram and began pulling more things out of her duffle bag.

"Why a love spell?" Winter asked.

"Because it's simple to do," Claire said. "If it works, then we can go on to the more complicated spells."

Claire opened the book to a page titled "Love Spell" and examined it. Winter tried to read it upside down.

"Okay. Now we need a picture of the person the spell is intended for." Claire pulled a wallet-sized picture from her purse.

"Hey! That's Phillip!"

"Yeah, I know."

"Do you like Phillip?"

"Well, not really. I mean, if he were available maybe."

"So you're hoping this spell will cause Ali and Phillip to break up and for him to come chasing you? Is that it?"

"Well," Claire said, "nothing can separate those two. So I figured this would be a pretty good way to test the spell book, don't you think?"

"A pretty dirty way to test it."

"Do you want me to stop, then? I could find another spell."

"No," Winter said. "Might as well keep going. My dad may not let me have you over again, and I don't want to wait."

"Good." Claire placed the picture face up in the bottom of the bowl. Then she reached into her duffle bag and pulled out a couple of Ziploc bags.

"What are those?" Winter asked.

"Ingredients."

She opened the first bag. "Rose petals." Claire sprinkled them over Phillip's picture. Then she opened the second bag. "Next, ginger—the spice of love." She winked at Winter and sprinkled the powder over the rose petals. Then Claire reached into the duffle bag and pulled out a box-cutting knife.

Winter held her breath. "What's that for?"

"The last ingredient—blood."

"Are you going to cut yourself?"

"You can do it if you want, but then Phillip may come after you instead."

"Um, no thanks. Are you sure about this?"

Claire smiled. "Relax. I've cut myself before with one of these. There's nothing to it."

"Why did you cut yourself?"

Claire hesitated. "Accident."

Winter raised her eyebrows, but Claire wouldn't look at her. Winter glanced at the door again. "Whatever. Just hurry up, okay?"

Claire took the box cutter and made a small incision across her forefinger. Winter cringed. Claire dangled her finger over the bowl, and the blood poured onto the mixture of rose petals and ginger.

"Get me something to stop the bleeding," Claire asked after a few tense seconds. Her voice shook.

Winter ran out of her room and paused at the top of the stairs to listen. Then she went down as quickly as she could without making too much noise. She skirted the living room and went into the kitchen.

"What are you doing?" her dad asked from the living room when Winter started banging around.

"Um, nothing," she called back.

"Doesn't sound like nothing."

Winter found the first aid kit and opened it. She grabbed a couple of bandages and shoved them into her pockets.

"Just getting some chips," she said.

"That's a lot of noise just for chips."

Winter heard him get up. She slammed the first aid kit closed and shoved it back into the cabinet. As the cabinet banged shut, her dad came around the corner.

"Well, the chips aren't in there," he said. She jumped and spun around.

"Where are they? I can't find them."

Her dad walked across the kitchen to one of the far cabinets. He reached in and pulled out a bag.

"Thanks, Dad." Winter snatched the chips from his hand and fled.

At the top of the stairs, she paused and waited to see if he was going to follow. She saw him cross in front of the stairs as he went back to his recliner. Winter rushed into her room and locked the door again.

It took Winter a moment for her eyes to readjust to the dim candlelight. Claire was sucking on her finger and leaning close to the spell book, reading.

"Thanks," she said, as Winter handed her a bandage. Winter tossed the chips onto the bed.

"Now," Claire said, after she had carefully wrapped her finger, "we need to hold hands and recite the spell."

Present Day

It was Thursday afternoon, the last week of school. Winter pored over her grammar handbook, trying to perfect her English Comp paper that was due the following day. Summer came in and sagged onto her bed.

"You still haven't finished that?" Summer asked.

"No," Winter said with almost a snarl.

"I finished mine two days ago. Is your new memory not helping this time?"

Winter gritted her teeth. "Stop gloating, Summer. It isn't funny."

"I think it is," she said with a smile. "It's only fair that you have problems like the rest of us."

"I've told you, it's not a photographic memory, okay? Drop it."

Summer laughed and turned on the TV. "I still think it's funny."

Winter groaned. "I need more sources. I'm going to the library." She closed out her word processor program and shut down her laptop.

"Do you need my help?"

"No." Winter shoved her computer into its bag. Summer chuckled again, and Winter walked out.

After retrieving several more references from the shelves, she added them to the stack of books she had brought from her room. Winter retreated to a remote corner of the third floor study room, where she placed the pile of books to her left and her computer in front. The silence weighed heavier than she expected.

After an hour, her fingers throbbed from typing, and her pointer finger ached from using the touchpad.

Her cell phone beeped and buzzed on the desk—a text message from Kaci.

Whr R U, it read.

Winter responded with Lbry and went back to her books. In the process, her elbow knocked one book to the floor. She bent over to retrieve it and stopped. It was the book on demonology.

"How did this get here?" Her voice sounded strange in the empty room. She picked the book up and set it on top of the book she was working with. "I thought I returned this last semester."

Winter pulled back the cover and scanned the contents. Her finger traced the lines of entries. She stopped at one near the bottom and caught her breath.

Xaphan.

Winter quickly flipped to the page number. She read:

"Xaphan was one of the fallen angels. He rebelled with Satan, and is a demon of the second rank. He is said to have an inventive mind and came up with the idea to set fire to heaven before he and the other fallen were cast out. He has a bellows as an emblem, but must fan the flames of the abyss with his mouth and hands."

Winter stared at the entry in disbelief. Was Xaphan really a demon? She thought about her dreams and the grotesque face that called out to her. Cold chills swept down her spine. She read the entry again. God had been trying to warn her this whole time, and she had been too blind to see it. What had she gotten herself into? She felt adrenaline flush her face. Her heart raced. Did she really want to find him?

She heard the sound of rushing feet and almost screamed. She slammed the book shut and turned to defend herself, but it was just Kaci.

Kaci's face glowed with excitement, and she hurried over and pulled up a chair.

"Did you hear?"

"Hear what?" Winter asked. She casually placed the book on the floor and tried to steady her shaking arms. Kaci didn't seem to notice. *God, what do I do now? Should I tell her?*

Kaci took a deep breath. "Peter's awake!"

"What?"

"He woke up last night sometime. I just got the word."

"Can we see him?"

"No." Kaci's shoulders drooped. "They've actually increased the security at his room. What's worse is that as soon as the hospital clears him, they're going to take him to jail to await his trial. Apparently, most of his injuries healed during the coma. All they have to do is a final psych evaluation, and then the cops are going to take him."

"They can't...he's innocent!"

"I know, but unfortunately we can't prove that, remember? We need to find Xaphan and get him to confess."

"No..." Winter's voice wavered.

Kaci furrowed her eyebrows. "You've been talking about it for weeks. What's wrong?"

"I just...everything's quieted down. I think he's gone. If he shows back up, then we'll find him." *A demon?*

"What about Peter? We have to do something. At the very least, I think we need to find the room in your dreams—the one you said

Jennifer was killed in. Maybe there's more evidence there."

Winter remembered Kaci lying dead in a pool of blood. "No, not a good idea either."

Kaci huffed. "Why not?"

"I just don't feel good about it, okay?"

"Well, that's not enough for me," Kaci said. "We have to help Peter any way we can. They're going to send him to prison if we don't."

"But if we try to find the room, then we may run into someone who will hurt us."

"You mean like Xaphan?" Kaci asked. Winter looked away. "Well, then we'll both get what we want. We'll find the room, and you might get that confession you were talking about. Either way, at least we're helping Peter, right?"

"But...let me do it alone."

"No. You're not doing anything alone again. Remember what happened last time? This is beyond you or us—it's about saving the life of an innocent person. You do know they enforce the death penalty in this state, don't you? Peter's sure to get it if we don't do this."

Winter took a deep heaving sigh. "Fine, when?"

Kaci grinned and scooted to the edge of her seat. "Tomorrow evening, before the big CLC farewell party."

"Okay," Winter said.

Kaci clapped her hands and stood. "I'll go start making plans."

Winter turned back to her computer as Kaci left. She clenched her eyes. Silent tears rolled down her cheeks.

59

The next morning, Winter tried to sleep in and enjoy the pleasant dreams for once, but at eight-thirty the room phone interrupted with a loud screech. She sat up wide-eyed and breathless. The phone screeched again, and Summer groaned in protest. Winter staggered to the desk and picked it up.

"Hello?" she croaked.

"Hi, is this Winter Maessen?" said a soft female voice. Winter thought she recognized it, but too much fuzz floated in her brain.

"Yes, it is."

"This is Nicole Warner, Dr. Streffield's assistant. Dr. Streffield would like you to attend a meeting this afternoon at one o'clock, in the boardroom."

Winter felt a knot form in her stomach and sat down. "Um, why?"

"I've not been told," Nicole said, *"but he's very insistent that you attend. Should I tell him you'll be there?"*

Winter took a deep breath and the knot loosened. A calmness came over her, and she knew that God's hand covered this situation—for better or worse. "Yes, I'll be there."

"Great, I'll let him know." Nicole hung up, and Winter crashed back on her bed.

Later that morning, she dressed in her favorite black peasant top and a pair of dark-colored jeans. It was casual enough that she didn't feel uncomfortable, but formal enough for the meeting that afternoon. She and Summer had a small brunch in their room and Winter left to do some last-minute editing in the library.

After putting her agonizing research paper in the drop box outside Mrs. Pritchett's office that afternoon, Winter found herself in the stairwell of Langley Hall on her way to the boardroom. She stopped at the halfway landing and leaned against the wall. With her eyes closed, she prayed for strength and guidance, but above all some sort of premonition to let her know what was going on. Nothing came.

When she exited the stairwell onto the executive floor, she turned to the double doors immediately to the left. The right door was propped open, and she could see a room full of people beyond. The board of directors sat around the long table, talking and drinking coffee. Chairs three rows deep lined the walls, filled with reporters and other various people.

Dr. Streffield smiled as she entered and indicated an empty chair on the front row near his right. Winter checked her step for a moment when she recognized the two FBI agents seated beside her own reserved chair. Her heart fluttered, and she hurried to her seat.

Agent Gains winked at her. "Relax."

Nicole Warner came in with a legal pad. She closed the door and took a seat near Dr. Streffield. When Streffield saw her, he stood and walked to the lectern at the head of the table. The room quieted at his approach, and he surveyed them with a warm smile.

"It seems we are ready to begin. I thank all of you for coming to this specially called board meeting. Our regularly scheduled end-of-term meeting will still be held next week, but we have several guests here who have requested to bring time-sensitive presentations. After speaking to each one in private, I determined that the urgency of these presentations warranted this full meeting. So with that in mind, I will now officially call us to order."

Streffield paused for a moment. Notepads opened and pens clicked to the ready. The reporters turned on their voice recorders. Winter sat with her legs crossed and twiddled with her fingers. Why was she here?

"First, we have Special Agent Markus Gains and Special Agent Greg Erickson with an update concerning the case against Dr. Wissman. Agent Gains?"

Streffield stepped aside and returned to his seat in the middle of the table. Meanwhile, the room turned as one to watch Agent Gains walk to the lectern. Winter, however, watched Agent Erickson, who moved toward the exit.

"Thank you, Dr. Streffield," Gains said. Every eye in the room focused on him now. "A little over a month ago, we came into possession of more financial evidence against Dr. Wissman. Whereas we have ample evidence of this sort, this particular piece brought to us some new information that greatly expanded our investigation. What we received is a financial ledger containing transaction amounts from Dr. Wissman's seized accounts. These transactions were made to a third party account—a party that, until the uncovering of this ledger, had not yet been discovered. In other words, ladies and gentlemen, Dr. Wissman had a silent partner in his scheme."

The silence in the room hung like a shroud. No sound was made save the whirring of the air vents.

"More than one account number received transactions from Wissman, according to this ledger, and the sum of these transactions totaled more than two million dollars. Though these accounts have long been closed, we were able to trace each of the numbers to the same party. Therefore we are indicting another suspect in this case. The charges will be corporate espionage, fraud, tax evasion, and grand theft."

Agent Gains paused and looked around at each board member. "This third party is one of your very own."

A collective gasp sliced through the tension. Gains looked at his partner and nodded. Agent Erickson reached into his coat and rested a hand on his gun. Winter held her breath. The premonition filled her. She knew where this was going.

"Mr. Taylor," Gains said. All eyes turned to the far end of the table. Matthew Taylor paused, halfway through standing. Sweat dripped from his round face, and his square jaw clenched in anger. "Would you care to come with us quietly or shall we make a scene?"

Everyone started talking at once. Reporters retrieved cameras and snapped pictures. Taylor shot Winter a brief, hate-filled glare before turning back to Gains.

"You can't do this!"

Agent Gains walked around the table toward Taylor. Agent Erickson went around the other side. Taylor backed away until he almost fell into the laps of the people sitting along the back wall.

"You have the right to remain silent…" Agent Gains applied handcuffs to Taylor's wrists. Cameras clicked like a drum roll as they led him down the length of the room, and he tried to cover his face with his elbow. His lips clenched and unclenched, but he didn't say a word.

Dr. Streffield stood when they passed by, and Gains paused to shake Streffield's hand…more pictures. Then the FBI agents led Taylor out.

The doors thundered when they closed, and the buzz in the room grew to a matching rumble. Streffield returned to the podium and held up a hand for several seconds, as if to push back the roar of the ocean. Slowly, the room quieted.

Streffield smiled. "Now, I'm sure we can all breathe a sigh of relief."

To Winter's surprise, most everyone chuckled together. She wondered how many people here had been blackmailed or threatened by Taylor.

"I apologize for the somewhat inappropriate manner of Agent Gains's presentation," said Streffield, "but I feel confident that arresting Mr. Taylor in a very public way would be best for us all."

Several people nodded agreement.

"I assure you the remaining three presentations will be much more enjoyable," Streffield said. "Now, I would like to yield the floor to Judge Joe Baxter, of the U.S. Circuit Court."

The room gave polite applause as a large African American man stood and walked to the podium. He wore a shiny black suit.

"Thank you," Judge Baxter said in a deep voice. "As you are all aware, last fall the District Court ordered an injunction banning all religious points of view from being expressed in the classrooms of this university. This ruling was immediately appealed and had been scheduled to go before the U.S. Circuit Court of Appeals. Unfortunately, due to a clerical error at the district level, the case was never brought to the Court of Appeals. In fact, if it hadn't been for a call from a university student..."

Winter's eyes widened. Could it be? Did she call a federal judge?

"...I might not have heard of the case for several years. I assure you, the persons responsible for this clerical error have been dealt with appropriately.

"Once the case was processed properly, I made sure the review was scheduled as soon as possible. We reviewed the case this morning, and by a vote of five to two, found the District Court ruling unconstitutional."

Applause broke out almost before he had finished. A few people cheered. Judge Joe Baxter smiled and nodded until they finished.

"Please accept my apology, as an alumnus of Tishbe University, for the inappropriate behavior of some of our court officials. In the future, if any legal action like this again threatens the school, please do not hesitate to call me personally for legal advice and assistance. Thank you."

The room applauded again, and Judge Baxter nodded in acknowledgment before leaving the podium. Dr. Streffield stood to shake his hand, and the cameras flashed like strobe lights.

"Thank you, Judge Baxter," Streffield said, returning to the podium. "Though it may be too late for this year, I'm sure our faculty will be excited about providing a quality Christian education to our students next term. Now, in conjunction with what we've heard thus far, let me now give the floor to Congresswoman Belinda Garrison, who has something else encouraging she would like to share."

An older woman, with steel gray hair and firm features, stood and walked to the podium. Once again the gathering gave her polite applause. She wore a dark red power suit and smiled as she measured the room with her eyes. Streffield returned to his seat, grinning like a schoolboy.

"Thank you very much," said Congresswoman Garrison. "I didn't realize, Joe, that you had received a call from a student a month ago, but it seems we both did. I even wrote down her name so I could find her and thank her in person. Perhaps you'll join me?"

"I would be delighted, Belinda," Judge Baxter said from his seat.

Winter couldn't believe what she heard. A judge and a congresswoman? She felt dizzy and excited at the same time. God had done something, all right, and Winter couldn't wait to hear what this woman had to say.

Belinda Garrison turned to address the room. "When I was a student here at Tishbe University, there was one organization on campus that meant more to me than any other—the Christian Life Center."

The CLC!

"In fact, it was during a small group session in my sophomore year that I gave my life to Christ. The CLC changed my life in ways nothing else on this Earth ever has. That's why, when I was called and told the CLC had closed because of the budget shortfall associated with Dr. Wissman's indictment, I was very distraught. The thought of the hundreds of students whose lives could be potentially changed forever, and who would never have the opportunity that I had, was too much for me. Could the next Billy Graham be in our student body? The next Adrian Rogers? Perhaps a missionary to the Far East? What if God had placed students here so they could be told about the love of Christ for the first time in their lives? And what about the trickle-down effect? Could we even imagine the impact these students may have on our world? Maybe the seed of the last great revival before the second coming of Christ is actually here in our midst. With the Christian Life Center closed, none of these things might ever happen.

"That is why I have contacted many business owners throughout our great state who are also alumni of this university. Together we have organized the Tishbe Missions Foundation. This foundation is privately funded, and its goal is to provide the financial means to further the gospel here on the campus of Tishbe University. Therefore, all funding for the operations of the Christian Life Center will come directly from this foundation and will no longer be dependent on funds from the university. Let the CLC reopen to a new chapter in its history, and may God bless each student who enters its doors! Thank you!"

Again, the room filled with enthusiastic applause as Congresswoman Belinda Garrison left the podium. Streffield stood and shook her hand beneath the flutter of the cameras. Then as she took her seat, Streffield stepped behind the podium and raised his hand for the room's attention.

"It's a comfort to know that Tishbe University alumni can be found in such powerful positions in our government. Thank you again, Judge Baxter and Congresswoman Garrison, for your support of and love for this university." More polite applause.

"There is just one more presentation to make. Without this student, nothing we have seen and heard today would have been possible. She is not only responsible for placing the calls to Judge

Baxter and Congresswoman Garrison, but is also the person who provided the FBI with the information necessary to arrest Matthew Taylor."

Streffield looked at Winter, and she suddenly wanted to hide. This was why they asked her to be here? She slouched in her chair.

"Winter Maessen, please come stand beside me."

Winter reluctantly stood and walked to Streffield's side. All eyes in the room watched every step. Streffield put a fatherly hand on her shoulder—he stood at least a head taller than she. Winter wrung her hands together and stared at her feet.

"Please accept this plaque for special services to Tishbe University, above and beyond expectations. We also extend thanks from the board of directors, the staff, faculty, and students, and also from me personally."

Winter looked up, and Streffield grabbed her right hand in his and shoved a plaque into her left.

"This is just a small token of our appreciation, but it comes sincerely from us all. If there is anything you need, please come see me. My door will always be open to you. Thank you and God bless."

The room erupted with applause and cheers. The cameras sounded like tap dancers, sending blinding flashes into her eyes. Winter squinted at the eager faces of the board members and ravenous reporters, and looked back at the floor. She tried to scuttle to her seat, but it seemed some unspoken gesture had rendered the meeting adjourned. Before she could get two steps away, people descended on her like flies.

Winter went straight to Kaci's room after finally escaping. Kaci smiled when she opened the door, but it immediately disappeared.

"Winter, what happened?"

Winter showed her the plaque, and Kaci looked at it without much understanding.

"Where did you get this?"

"From Dr. Streffield at the board meeting."

"A board meeting? Why were you there?"

"That folder had account numbers for Matthew Taylor, and they arrested him in front of everybody. Then, remember during spring break when I made those two phone calls?"

"Yeah."

"Well, apparently I called a federal judge and a congresswoman." Winter crossed the room and collapsed into a seat.

"No way!"

"Yeah. The judge had the court order against the school repealed, and the congresswoman found funding for the CLC." Winter sighed. "I need a nap."

Kaci's eyes blinked and her lips moved, as if she couldn't decide which point to address first. "So, Taylor was arrested at the meeting?"

"Yeah. I guess they wanted it to be as public as possible."

"And the CLC building can reopen?" Her voice grew with excitement. "This is going to make tonight's party better than ever! And the school! They can really go back to teaching the way they want?"

Winter managed a smile. "Yeah, it looks like we did it. We actually beat Xaphan."

Kaci beamed. "Now all we have to do is save Peter. This is the perfect time to do it too! Are you just about ready?"

"I want to go back to my room and change," she said.

"Okay. Well, call me when you're ready."

"Yeah, okay."

Winter drifted through the halls. Once in the room, she couldn't remember walking there. She started to change, but only managed to remove her shoes. All she could think about was sleep. She set her alarm clock for five and crashed onto her bed to nap.

She saw stairs and candles. A door with an old brass handle stood before her, and she opened the door. People dressed in black. Blood everywhere. It smelled like a dead animal. Xaphan stood in the middle of a pool of blood and smiled at her. He held a bloody knife in his hand. Kaci lay dead at his feet.

The phone rang.

Winter sat up and wiped the sweat from her face. The phone rang again and she got up to answer.

"Winter?" It was Kaci.

"Yeah?"

"Sorry, but you never called, and I was getting impatient. Are you ready?"

"Yeah, I was just napping a little."

"Oh. Sorry. Didn't mean to wake you. Are you all right?"

"I'm fine…just a little drained. I was going to get up at five anyway."

"Okay, so you ready to go then?"

"Sure."

"Good. I'll wait for you in the lobby."

Winter hung up the phone and tried to rub away the sleep. She went to the bathroom and splashed her face with cold water. She couldn't shake the nightmare or the premonition that had been throbbing since she woke up. She felt like she was living in a horror movie that neared its end. The worst still to come, yet she could do nothing to avoid it. Even more unnerving, the premonition only gave her a bad feeling, but told her nothing else. She felt helpless and trapped…like a crash test dummy speeding toward the barrier.

She stared at her white face in the mirror and took deep breaths. Her knees shook, and her muscles trembled. Caught in an unavoidable destiny, she ached with fear. Knowing that today had been a massive blow to Xaphan's plans scared her more than anything. If he was possessed by a real demon, then his retaliation would be inevitable. Winter swallowed hard and left for the lobby, hoping she could gain some measure of courage before facing Kaci.

Kaci waited for her near the door, her eyes bright and engaging. Winter considered backing out and telling Kaci she didn't feel well. But she also knew that Kaci would go with or without her help.

Kaci bounced on the balls of her feet. "I thought you were going to change?"

"I forgot."

Kaci frowned. "Do you want to? I'll wait."

"No, I'm fine. Kaci, I'm not so sure this is such a good idea. Maybe we should just lie low for a while to make sure nothing bad will happen. I mean, Xaphan must be pretty mad right now."

"Don't be silly! We're both going home tomorrow, and this may be our last chance to help Peter. By the time we get back to school, the trial may be over. We have to do this tonight. We have no choice."

Winter sighed. There would be no avoiding this—the

premonition told her so. This had to happen. "Okay. Let's go, but please can we try to do this fast?"

"Well, that depends on you. How quickly can we find this room?"

"What do you mean?"

"I mean, if you can have the right vision, then we might find the room quickly and be done," Kaci said.

"I don't know if I can. The only time I've had visions that I could control was when I had Jennifer's ID. That's gone now."

"But haven't you seen the room lately?"

"Yeah, but only in dreams. Dreams and visions are completely different." The bloody walls and Kaci lying dead filled her mind. She had no desire anymore to find that room.

"Then maybe we'll come across something that will spark a vision. And you might even be able to have a vision without anything."

"I don't know. Seems unlikely."

Kaci frowned. "Well, it's worth a try anyway. Let's go."

Kaci held the door open for Winter, and the two girls walked across the parking lot to Kaci's Honda Accord. She cranked the car, and they fastened their seatbelts.

"Now would be a good time to try...before we leave," Kaci said.

Winter shook her head and closed her eyes. God, give me a vision, she prayed and cleared her mind. The seconds ticked by.

"Sorry," Winter said when she looked up.

"That's okay." Kaci put the car into gear. "You can try again later."

"Where are we going?"

"I had a great idea, and I don't know why I didn't think of it before," Kaci said.

"What?"

"There's this old farm just outside of campus. It used to be the president's house back when the college was small. It's been condemned for several years."

"So?"

"So, I asked around and it's the only place anyone knows around here with a cellar."

"Do you think Xaphan took me to this farm?"

"I think it's a really good possibility. There's another thing too."

"What?"

"There's an old grain silo there. Grain silos are round."

Winter nodded. "The round room."

"Maybe. At any rate, it's the best idea we've had all year," said Kaci as she turned onto another road. "And if it's the right place, there's a chance we may find your locket."

"Fine," Winter said. "Let's just hurry."

As they left campus, Kaci turned down a country road bordered by a field on one side and a forest on the other.

"It's not far," said Kaci. "Look. There's the CLC party."

They rounded a bend in the road and slowed. Dozens of cars lined the shoulder. A group of people knotted together in the field.

"Looks like they've almost got everything ready," Kaci said. "Maybe we'll be done before it gets started."

They passed by Summer's car, and Winter felt a pang of longing to stop. "Yeah, maybe."

They rounded a couple more turns and Kaci slowed. "We're here."

The old farmhouse, barn, and grain silo sagged with loneliness. Boards hung haphazardly across the windows and doors of the bottom floor. The tall, unkempt grass overtook nearly everything, and crows circled the silo.

Winter twisted in her seat and looked behind them. Tendrils of smoke curled into the air from the CLC bonfire, and she could see the tower of Olamel rising above the trees.

"It's closer than I thought," she said.

"I know. I should have thought of this place before."

Winter felt butterflies in her stomach. The premonition nagged at the back of her mind. "I'm not sure about this."

"It'll be okay," Kaci said with a warm smile. "It doesn't look like anyone is here anyway—none of the usual make-out crowd. Let's go."

They walked to the house first. The turn-of-the-century farmhouse had a tall second floor and a faded whitewashed exterior. Gaps left by missing shingles dotted the roof like a black and gray checkerboard. The steps leading up to the wraparound porch were old and splintered, and a few porch boards were black with rot. They stepped carefully to the door.

"People like to sneak in here sometimes," Kaci said, pulling the loose planks away from the unlocked door. "Come on."

Inside, high traffic routes appeared as worn paths in the faded wood floor. Dusty pictures hung crooked on the dingy walls. The back door could be seen straight ahead at the end of a long hallway. Just to the right, a set of stairs led to the second floor.

"Anything look familiar?" Kaci asked.

Winter panned the room again. "Not really, but…" Finally, the premonition started to work properly.

"But what?"

"A premonition. I've done this before."

Kaci nodded. "Good, that means we're making progress. Can you find the cellar?"

Winter crossed the room to a small door under the stairs. "Here, I think." She opened it to reveal old, shoddy steps dropping into a black hole.

"I knew it!" Kaci said over her shoulder. "Come on, let's go!"

"I don't know, Kaci."

"Stop it, Winter, I don't want to hear any more of that! We are doing this no matter what you think. We have to help Peter. Why can't you understand that?"

"Fine," Winter snapped. "Did you happen to bring a light?"

"As a matter of fact…" Kaci pulled a small flashlight out of her pocket.

"I'll go first." Winter grabbed the flashlight and gritted her teeth.

She clicked the light on and started her descent, and Kaci followed behind with one hand on Winter's shoulder. Near the bottom, she could see a door on the left. Winter paused one step above the door and listened.

"What?" Kaci whispered.

"Nothing." Winter took the final step to the door.

She shined the light into the dark cellar, panning old shelves and dusty mason jars. Winter recognized it immediately.

A rat squealed and Kaci jumped.

"Don't do that!" Winter said.

"Sorry. Is this the right place?"

"Yeah, this is it."

"Any visions or anything?"

"No."

"Then let's check it out, maybe we'll find something."

Winter moved her foot out and let it hover a moment above the step that she remembered Xaphan sitting on. Then, after a brief hesitation, she stepped into the room.

"It's colder than I remember," Winter said when she stood on the dirt floor.

"I'm not cold at all. Are you okay?"

Winter shivered and tried to rub the chill bumps from her arms. "Yeah, I'm okay."

Kaci crossed through the room to a shelf illuminated by the dim light. She rubbed her finger through the thick dust.

"Doesn't look like anyone's been here for a long time," Kaci said. "Do you see your locket?"

Winter walked to the center of the room and turned in a slow circle. "No. I think they used this place only for me. Maybe they were trying to throw me off track." She scanned the ground with the light, hoping for any glint of gold or silver as Kaci walked to her side. "At any rate, there's nothing here. And I'd really rather not stay, if you don't mind."

Kaci took a deep breath. "Okay, I understand. Let's go."

Winter turned and eased up the stairs.

"You know," Kaci said, as they reached the first floor. "If the cellar was here, that means that the silo may actually be…"

"I know." Winter tried to rub the chills away again. Why wouldn't they go away? "Let's hurry, just in case Xaphan shows up."

"Right."

They walked out onto the porch, and Kaci paused to replace the planks across the door. Then they started toward the right side of the house where the grain silo stood. The crows looked like gnats around the top of the old metal structure, and their cries echoed off the forest behind the farm. Against the cylindrical building, wild shrubs and brambles had grown thick.

Winter followed Kaci around the silo through the thick grass, peering into the undergrowth for the grain door. About a quarter of the way around the silo, they found it. It stood wide open, and the brush wasn't as thick there. Winter pushed past Kaci and went to the door first. She extracted the flashlight from her pocket and clicked it on.

"Be careful," Kaci whispered.

"Too late for that," Winter mumbled. Her stomach twisted into knots, and her teeth chattered from the cold.

Winter stepped in, and Kaci followed right behind. It took a moment for Winter's eyes to adjust. The dry grain covering the ground crunched beneath their feet. The silo smelled musty, and a faint shaft of light streamed in from somewhere near the top, illuminating the cloud of grain dust they had kicked up.

The premonition screamed.

"This isn't it," Winter said. The blood drained from her face. The chills turned to numbness. "We have to get out of here, now! This isn't right."

An engine roared outside. Gravel crunched.

"Someone's here!" Kaci said. "What do we do?"

Winter's mind spun. "Come on!" she said and turned for the door.

Crouching low, they exited to hide in the underbrush. Winter crawled around to where she could see the road through the tangled shrubs.

Five men dressed in black climbed out of an old van. Three of them carried knives, one a short length of chain, and the last one had a machete.

"We have to get to the car," Kaci whispered, "and get out of here!"

As the words came out of her mouth, one of the guys went to Kaci's car with a knife and began stabbing her tires. Kaci stifled an infuriated scream.

Cold numbness spread through Winter's chest and heart. "They're not here to capture us."

Kaci whimpered.

The men began to split up. Two walked toward the barn on their left, two to the house on the right, and one to the silo.

"What do we do?" Winter asked. Her premonition seemed to have fizzled out.

Kaci chewed her lip in thought. "The bonfire isn't far from here. Maybe we can make it there."

"And if they see us?"

"Then we'll just have to outrun them. It doesn't look like they brought guns, anyway."

"At least none we can see. Hey, maybe we can take their van."

Kaci looked at her and widened her eyes. "Good idea. Shh...here he comes."

Winter held her breath as the man with the chain walked by.

"Now!" Kaci said when the man ducked into the silo.

They made a horrible noise clambering through the brush, but were free within moments and rushing toward the van. As they sprinted through the high grass, the two men walking to the barn turned to intercept.

"Faster!" Winter said. The van closed in. Winter chanced a look around and saw their lead had widened.

When she turned back, the driver's door of the van opened. Winter dug in her heels and watched in horror as Xaphan stepped out.

"Hello, girls," he said. "I warned you, Winter, but you just wouldn't listen."

Four Years Ago

Winter sat at the lunch table, mortified. Claire sat beside her, and they clenched hands together beneath the table.

"Who is she?" Alison yelled. She leapt to her feet, and her chair banged to the floor. Her voice carried across the entire lunchroom. Phillip, who had just arrived, stood dumbfounded—like a man staring at a hungry lion.

Alison knocked the lunch tray from his hands, and the food splattered across the floor.

"What's wrong with you? I don't know what you're talking about!" Phillip said.

Alison's face twisted with rage. "Yes you do! I found lipstick in your car! In the BACK SEAT! Now you tell me what that slut's name is or I'm going to kill you!"

"I don't know anything about the lipstick. How do you know it's not yours? You've spent plenty of time in the back seat!"

"Are you completely stupid? Don't you think I know what brand of lipstick I buy? You're an idiot! How could you think you could get away with this?"

She slapped him, and his face flew sideways. Phillip lunged forward, leaned into her face, and cursed.

She slapped him again.

Phillip put a hand to his face and growled. "You're accusing me of cheating on you? You whore! How many guys have you slept with while we've been dating? It was so easy for me to get you in bed—why should other guys be different?"

Several teachers stood. A couple of the men started walking toward Phillip and Alison. Everyone in the cafeteria had quieted, watching.

"I knew it! Is that all I am to you? You're nothing but a walking hormone! I can't believe I've stayed with you this long. You don't understand me at all! You think I sleep with you just for the fun of it? Believe me, it's not much fun. I can't believe I ever did it!" Alison said.

"Well, that just proves how much of an idiot you really are!"

"Idiot?"

"You're just a dumb blonde like every other girl I know. If you would lay off all the mushy love stuff, maybe you could get to know the real me! Doesn't matter anymore, because now that I know how you really feel about me, I'm done!"

"DONE?"

He smirked. "Yeah, I'm done with you! Maybe that wasn't your lipstick."

She slapped him again. This time, he struck back with his fist. Alison fell to the floor with a hand over her mouth. But she jumped back to her feet and started swinging for Phillip in a wild blur.

The students in the cafeteria began to cheer and yell. The first two teachers reached them, and more rushed over. Phillip allowed himself to be walked away when the PE teacher grabbed him, but it took two teachers to pull Alison in the opposite direction. Ali's nose and lip bled, and Phillip had long, bloody scratches all over his face.

Stacy's mouth hung open. "Oh, my God! I can't believe it! How could something like this happen?"

Winter and Claire exchanged the same knowing look.

The spell had worked.

Present Day

Winter stared at Xaphan, her thoughts on getting a confession. She ignored the pounding of footsteps growing closer.

"Winter!" Kaci said.

Winter turned and saw a chain flying through the air. She ducked as Kaci jumped out of the way. The chain struck the ground, and Kaci bolted back toward the silo. With a second glance at Xaphan, Winter followed.

The two men from the barn blocked their escape. Kaci veered left toward the house. Winter pushed herself to catch up.

The two men who had entered house came around the back corner.

"We need to split up," Kaci said. "Meet at the bonfire."

"No! Stick together!" Winter said, but Kaci had already veered back toward the silo.

Winter stopped for a moment as she watched her friend run away. "Kaci!"

The two men from the barn turned to pursue Kaci. The men

from the house and the man with the chain were closing in on Winter.

Frustrated, Winter took off across the front of the house, angling toward the road.

She chanced a glance behind and found the men adjusting to intercept. Winter arced back to the right and ran down the far side of the house. She made it to the back corner of the house and turned again, momentarily alone. She needed to hide.

Winter vaulted over the back porch. Her left foot broke through the boards, and she fell to her knees. Splintered wood dug into her shin as she yanked her leg free. She gritted her teeth and grabbed the nearest windowsill, then launched herself through the open window.

The landing jarred her body and made her side ache. Ignoring the pain, she scrambled against the wall beneath the window and lay there panting. Her heart pounded for more oxygen, and she took deep controlled breaths, listening. Where her leg had fallen through the porch, her pants felt warm with blood. It throbbed with each heartbeat.

The room was a bedroom. It looked the same as much of the house, as if it had been abandoned instead of the inhabitants moving out. A moth-eaten quilt draped across the foot of an old iron bed. A thick layer of dust covered the floor.

The thumping of feet outside made her hold her breath. The feet stopped just outside.

"Go check the forest," one of them said. "And you go to the other side of the house back toward the silo." Two sets of feet pounded away.

The third person came up the stairs. She heard him jiggle the locked door and then slam his shoulder into it. The door splintered and crashed into the wall. Winter rolled across the floor to the bed and slid beneath it just as he entered the room.

She watched his black army boots slowly round the foot of the bed and stop in front of the window. The tip of a machete hung near her eye level. The man stopped just in front of a bright red blood smear, and Winter bit her lip. His legs bent, and one hand came into view. He touched the blood and then stood again.

With a loud cry, she reached out, grabbed him around the ankles, and pulled as hard as she could. His feet slid easily across the dusty floor and he fell face first. His head slammed against the windowsill with a dull crack, and he crumpled onto the floor.

Winter pushed herself out the other side of the bed and fled from the room. At first she turned left, exiting through the back door, but she stopped just outside when she saw one of the other men coming from the forest. He saw her and started running for the house. Winter turned and ran back inside, through the long hall, and toward the front door. She rounded the corner, saw stairs, and the premonition told her to go to the second floor. She took the steps three at a time.

The stairs? Are you crazy? There's no way out from up there!

At the top of the landing, she turned right and rushed to the room at the end of the corridor. She could hear footsteps coming up the stairs. She slammed the door behind her and locked it.

This room was another abandoned bedroom. She shoved her shoulder into a nearby dresser and pushed it in front of the door just as her pursuer hit it from the other side. Winter yelped and stepped back. But the door held.

The man pounded rhythmically with his shoulder, and the lock broke. Winter looked around the room, desperate for a solution. She ran to the window and found that it overlooked the roof above the wraparound porch. A loud crash made her look back to the door. The dresser and door had moved several inches. Long bony fingers wiggled through the narrow opening. She grabbed the window, shoved it up, and scrambled out.

Standing on the roof above the porch, she could see the entire farm. Just in front and to the left, stood the grain silo. Beyond that was the barn, and then a large overgrown field. Four figures were running through the tall grass...Kaci and three of the men.

"Come on, Kaci!" she whispered. "Run!"

Movement to the right caught her eye. Xaphan stood beside the van with his arms folded. Their eyes met, and the air temperature around her dropped. Chills crawled across her skin.

She looked around for an escape. Now what do I do?

The forest, said a voice. She heard it with her ears but felt equally sure it had come from her head...much more than a premonition.

She turned and ran the length of the porch roof. At the back of the house, she sat down and dropped to the ground ten feet below, rolling to absorb the impact.

Then she was running...running as fast as she could for the trees about fifty yards behind the house. It felt like over a mile. With each step, she half expected to hear shouts of pursuit...or the loud thunder of a gun.

Finally, she reached the cover of the trees, jumped behind a large oak, and peered around. No one followed and everything seemed eerily quiet. But Xaphan had seen her on the roof, and it would only be moments before he alerted the others.

She clutched the stitch in her side and turned to go deeper into the forest. Less than twenty yards in, Winter came to a dry creek bed. She crawled down into it and, despite the protesting of her body, turned to the right and ran.

After several minutes she stopped to catch her breath. Doubled over on her knees, it took her a long time to calm her breathing to a point where she could listen for signs of pursuit. She heard nothing, so she sat against an embankment and rested.

Dusk came and everything began to turn to shades of gray. Winter had to get up and get somewhere safe before nightfall. An evening breeze blew through the trees. That's when she smelled it.

Smoke.

Winter crawled out of the creek bed. A bonfire flickered through the trees in a field less than a hundred yards away.

"The CLC party! I'm such an idiot," she said.

Winter wandered into the party like a lost animal. Hundreds of people milled around laughing and enjoying snacks. The CLC praise team sang from a flatbed trailer nearby. A generator hummed underneath, providing power for the sound equipment and the three floodlights that had been erected for the party. The intense heat of the enormous fire forced a wide perimeter around the flames. A couple of smaller fires glowed nearby, where people roasted hot dogs and marshmallows.

"Have you seen Kaci?" she asked the first people she came to. They laughed at something in their conversation and then shook their heads no.

Winter scanned the shadowed faces around her. She found Summer serving behind the refreshment tables.

"Everybody's here!" Summer said. "They're all talking about the CLC opening. Isn't it awesome?"

"Have you seen Kaci?" Winter asked.

"No. Why? What's wrong?"

"Nothing." Winter pushed through the crowd, crisscrossing the party. If Kaci were here, she would have made herself easy to find for Winter's sake.

Unless she wasn't here.

Images of Kaci lying dead in a pool of blood surfaced in her mind. She pushed the thoughts away. No!

Summer grabbed her from behind. "Winter, wait. What's wrong? Where's Kaci?"

"I'm not sure," Winter said. "Just let me know if you see her, okay?"

"Okay," Summer said. She walked back to the refreshment table.

Winter circled the perimeter again, asking everyone she could stop about Kaci. No one had seen her. Her head spun. She could hear the blood rushing through her ears. The images in her mind became more persistent and more vivid. NO!

"Have you seen Kaci?" she repeated over and over. The answer was always the same. No.

Finally, she came back to the refreshment table. Summer took one look at her and ran off. Winter collapsed on the ground and put her head on her knees. Her mind pulsed with the bloody images. She felt sick.

"No...No!"

The images continued to flash like scenes from a horror film.

"NO!"

Summer returned with Davis. "What's wrong?" Summer asked. "Winter! What's wrong? Where's Kaci?"

Winter looked up from the ground, her cheeks wet with tears. "He has her."

"What do you mean he has her?" Davis asked. "Who has her?"

"Xaphan has her. We were at the old farm near here, and he showed up with his men. We split up and were supposed to meet here."

"How do you know he has her? Maybe she'll still come," Summer said.

Winter shook her head. "No. She ran this way to begin with. If she was going to make it, she would have been here first. He has her, and it's all my fault."

"Well, maybe she's still hiding at the farm," Summer said.

"Either way, we need to go look for her—just in case," said Davis. "If she's not there, we call the police."

Winter stood. "There's something else. We were looking for the room Jennifer was killed in."

"And?" asked Davis.

"And, the last time I dreamed about that room I saw Kaci there…dead. I can't get the images out of my head."

The other two stared at her, and their eyes widened.

"If we don't find her soon, they're going to kill her," said Winter. "She may be dead already."

Davis pursed his lips and clenched his fists. "Then let's go. Summer, where's your car?"

"This way," she said with a trembling voice. She sprinted away. Davis helped Winter to her feet, and they followed. The three of them clambered into the green Bug, and Summer spun her tires in the loose gravel.

"This way. It's not far, just around a couple of bends," Winter said.

A minute later they were there. Darkness had settled in. The only light came from the stars.

The old van was gone.

"Back up and point your headlights to the farm," Davis said. Summer did, and the bright halogens illuminated the silo and most of the barn and house.

"Come on," said Winter. She opened the passenger door and started to get out, but Davis reached up from the back seat and grabbed her arm.

"No, wait. If there's someone still there, then we need to stay near the car. If Kaci's hiding, she'll see the lights and hear us. Just call to her."

Winter nodded and stood with one foot on the ground and the other still inside.

"KACI!"

Her voice echoed from the trees behind the farm and came back to her hollow. She waited for several silent seconds. The purring of Summer's car drowned all other sounds out.

"KACI!"

She waited for several more painful seconds before flopping back into the car.

"She's not here…it's too late…" She buried her face in her hands and started crying. Summer leaned against her and cried into her shoulder. Winter put an arm around her. Davis sat silently in the back.

"It's all my fault…" Winter moaned. "I knew Kaci was in danger, and I knew something bad was going to happen, but we went anyway. We should have just come to the bonfire with you two."

"No, it's not your fault," Davis said. "Xaphan would have found you two no matter where you went. He had this planned. He's a murderer, Winter."

"God, please don't let Kaci die," Winter said. She lifted her face to the ceiling. "I'll do anything, just show me what to do."

"There may be something we can do," Davis said.

Winter released Summer and turned to look at him. "What?"

"Well, not something we can do; something you can do."

"I'm not sure I understand." She rubbed her eyes with the heels of her hands.

"You've seen the room, Winter. You've seen where Kaci dies."

Summer and Winter looked at him in silence, then Summer turned to her.

"He's right. You know where they're going to take her."

"But I don't know where the room is," Winter said. "I've only seen it from the inside."

"Then you need to have another vision," Davis said.

"I'M NOT A PROPHET! It's all been a game! Xaphan picked me to be his so-called enemy, and after he kills Kaci, he's going to kill me. He's done this before—the FBI said so. These visions haven't been real, just stupid dreams and nightmares of an overactive imagination. I can't do this!"

"That's not true," Davis said. "Why don't you tell that to Laurie Dunaway. Was it just an accident that you saved her? What about Peter? You pulled him out of the car! Dr. Streffield and the CLC…were those numbers fake? Xaphan may have picked you to be a pretend prophet, but God picked you first. And the sooner you accept that, the sooner we can find Kaci."

Winter stared at him. The whole year came crashing down on her. Who was she really? Davis had just echoed almost the exact words she had used to defend herself to the FBI. Did she mean it then? Did she really believe God had picked her? Could she really be an actual prophet?

"I can't," Winter said. "I don't know how. I can't be a prophet."

"I believe you can," Davis said. He leaned forward and put a hand on her shoulder.

Summer grabbed Winter's hand and squeezed. "Me too."

Winter took a deep breath and looked from Summer to Davis. "Why? How can you believe in someone like me? You don't know me."

"We're your friends, so it doesn't matter," said Summer.

"Who cares how screwed up your life's been. What matters is now. You are not alone anymore. We're here. Accept it," said Davis.

You have been chosen, Winter. I, the Lord, believe in you!

"Kaci's your friend too," said Summer. "She's probably believed in you more than anyone else."

As Winter thought of Kaci and the bond they had developed, she could not help but feel a stab of anger at what Kaci might be facing at that exact moment. She clenched her teeth.

"Okay, I'll try," Winter said. "But I only saw the room in dreams, and dreams come to me on their own. I've never been able to control those."

"But you've controlled your visions before, right?" Davis asked.

"Yes, I think. I need something."

"What do you need?"

"Last time I had an object I could touch. I had Jennifer's ID, and when I tried to have a vision, I always saw Jennifer. I had something connected to her. I need something connected to Kaci or the room."

"What about her car?" asked Summer.

Winter jerked her head forward and fixed her eyes on Kaci's car. She threw open the door and jumped out.

"Winter! What are you doing?" Summer said.

She ran to Kaci's car and grabbed the door handle. The soft gravel slid beneath her feet, almost making her fall.

Locked.

She searched the ground for something hard but found nothing. Then she rushed back to Summer's car.

"Pop your trunk!" she said.

"What?" Summer asked as she rolled down the window.

"The trunk, Summer!"

Winter ran to the back of the car and waited. There was a soft popping sound and the trunk rose an inch. Books and clothes layered the trunk floor, and she shoved them aside until she found the loop to the false floor covering the spare tire. She tugged it up and held it with one hand. With the other, she reached in and grabbed the tire iron.

She ran back to Kaci's car and smashed the passenger window before coming to a complete stop. The glass rained in the interior like crushed ice. She reached through the jagged opening, pressed the electronic lock button, and flung open the door. The dome light illuminated Winter's cell phone sitting on the passenger seat. In the cup holder was Kaci's. Winter grabbed both and ran back to Summer's car. She tossed the tire iron back in the trunk, slammed it shut, and jumped back into her seat.

"What was that about? Geez!" Davis said.

"Shh! Be quiet!" Winter closed her eyes and squeezed Kaci's phone in both hands.

"Winter, are you okay? Your hand is bleeding," Summer said.

"Do you want me to do this or not? Now SHUT UP!"

Summer and Davis sat back and stared.

Winter moved her lips in prayer as she tried to clear her mind, but her heart pounded too fast. She took a deep breath to calm herself. Summer put a hand on her shoulder. Winter slapped it away.

With another deep breath, her body relaxed enough. Colors

exploded in her mind, and images formed. A face. Kaci.

"Is it working?" Davis asked.

Kaci's face disappeared.

"It was," Winter said through clenched teeth, "until you opened your mouth!" *Easy. Getting angry won't help.* She took another deep, relaxing breath and tried to tune out everything around her again.

Kaci's face returned. She was frightened—she was screaming. Blood speckled her cheeks. The image enlarged, and Winter could see people standing around her—Xaphan and others dressed in black. They stood in the round room.

Bells were ringing. Winter started counting. 7…8…9.

"What time is it?" she asked, straining to hold on to the image.

"Ten after eight," Summer whispered.

Winter decided to try something she had never done. She forced her mind to grab the vision and take control. It worked. She could move around and see things from different angles. Where were they? Winter started moving toward one of the windows. Kaci screamed and pleaded behind her. Winter's throat constricted and her chest shook, but she didn't turn to look.

Winter reached a window and discovered she could pass through it like a ghost. She was high—very high. Flying. Winter hadn't felt this strange of a sensation since she had the dream about Peter's wreck. She floated out several feet, then turned to look back at the window. That's when she recognized it.

The Olamel bell tower.

Her heart thundered against her ribs and the vision pulled away. "No!"

But it was gone. She blinked and looked around. Summer and Davis watched with pale faces.

"Well?" Davis asked.

"The bell tower. We have to hurry! I heard the bells ringing nine o'clock in the vision…we have less than an hour."

Summer threw her car into reverse and spun her tires again on the gravel.

"Take me by the dorm first," Winter said as the car caught traction on the blacktop.

"Why?"

"I need to get something. I'll run to the chapel from there."

Summer slammed the pedal to the floor.

"We're coming with you," Davis said.

"No. This is something I have to do alone. Besides, I need you two to do something else."

The premonition had returned, and Winter embraced it.

Four Years Ago

That Friday, Winter slipped fifty dollars out of her dad's wallet. She took the bus to school, but as soon as she got off she went to the parking lot where Phillip and Claire waited.

"Ready?" Claire asked.

"Sure," Winter said.

The sat together in the back of Phillip's car, and he took them off campus.

"Can I read it now?" Winter asked.

Claire reached into her bag and pulled out the spell book. "Sure, go ahead."

Winter flipped to the bookmark for her spell and read.

"You mean, I have to do that?" she asked.

"Yeah. You want to save your mom, don't you?"

Winter put a hand over her mouth and nodded. "Why do I have to do everything myself?"

"Because, it'll make the spell more personal, and that'll make it more likely to work. I don't want to take any chances, do you?"

Winter shook her head. "No, it makes sense. I just can't believe I have to do that."

Claire laughed.

They went to a pet store first. Winter went to the back of the store and picked out a gerbil from one of the cages. She tried not to spend too much time picking one out and chose a generic gray one.

She rounded the corner to where Claire and Phillip waited. "Hey, I got it." She stopped. The little white box containing the gerbil swayed in her hand.

Claire was leaning against the shelves with Phillip pressed up against her, all but swallowing her face. Their hands wandered to places they shouldn't be in public. Winter felt sick in her stomach and walked away.

After the gerbil, Winter bought candles, more poster board, mint oil, myrrh, rose petals, and an herb called turmeric. They had to make several stops at various little shops to get everything they needed, but by lunchtime they had arrived back at Winter's house. Phillip helped them carry their things inside before he left.

Claire's face beamed when they were finally alone in Winter's room. "Are you ready?"

Winter felt strangely excited. "Yeah, let's get started."

"Okay, me first!" Claire said.

Claire sat on the floor and pulled a piece of poster board in front of her. She took the marker and carefully drew a pentagram. Winter watched and chewed her lip.

"I still can't believe we're doing this," Winter said.

"I know. But it's going to work, you'll see."

Claire took black candles and placed them at the points of the pentagram as she had done before. When she had lit them, she instructed Winter to turn out the lights. Winter did and returned to her place across from Claire.

Then Claire opened the spell book and flipped to a bookmarked page. She dumped out the remains of the shopping bag and started rummaging through the contents. Satisfied that she had everything she needed, Claire took a little ceramic salad bowl and set it in the center of the pentagram. Winter watched silently.

"First, a picture of the enemy," Claire said. She placed a picture of her dad in the bottom of the bowl. He looked like a kind man.

"Next, a piece of the enemy's body." She took a Ziploc bag and opened it. It contained a fine brown powder.

"What's that?" Winter asked.

"Clippings from my dad's electric razor." Claire crinkled her nose.

Winter grimaced. "You actually got that?"

"Hey, I'm desperate just like you, remember?" She shook the clippings over the top of the picture and reached for more ingredients. "Two cloves of garlic," she said, dropping them in. "Then salt." She took a salt shaker and shook some in. "And holy water." She emptied a small vial over everything.

"Where'd you get that?" Winter asked.

"From the Catholic church. I took it from that bowl thing by the door when no one was looking."

"I didn't think you were religious."

"I'm not. But I needed the water."

Claire took a pestle and ground the garlic and salt into the water on top of the picture.

"Now, the incantation," Claire said.

They held hands and Claire read from the book. "Spirit, spirit, powerful and strong. Protect me from mine enemy who does me wrong. Ward away the evil of this man and bring to me peace again.

"Okay, now we say it together ten more times." Claire squeezed Winter's hands and Winter squeezed back.

They chanted slowly and quietly at first, but their voices grew with each repetition. When they finished, they looked at each other in the flickering candlelight and giggled.

"Now what?" Winter asked.

"We burn away the enemy," Claire said with a grin.

She took a container of lighter fluid and squirted a little into the bowl. Then she struck a match and tossed it in. The contents erupted for a moment and then died low. It continued to burn for several minutes, and when it finally went out nothing was left but black ash.

"That's it," Claire said. "Now it's your turn."

"Can't you do it for me?" Winter asked. "I don't think I can go through with it."

"No, we've been over this already. If you don't do it, it might not work." She cleared away her bowl and candles and motioned for Winter to get started.

Winter sighed and took out her own white candles, placing them at each point of the pentagram. Then she set her own salad bowl in the middle. After Winter lit each candle, Claire opened the book and read the spell aloud.

"First a picture of the loved one."

"A picture." Winter placed a picture of her mom in the bottom of the bowl.

"Then a piece of the body of the loved one."

"My mom's hair," Winter said, "from the hairbrush I took from my old home. I never use it, it was hers." Claire gave her a sympathetic smile as Winter dropped the hair into the bowl.

"Rose petals and turmeric," Claire read.

Winter sprinkled the petals and the herb over her mom's picture.

"Mint oil and myrrh."

Winter poured the oils into the bowl.

"And the animal sacrifice."

"Are you sure we have to do that?" Winter asked.

"Of course. You need to provide something to take your mom's place. Death is at work and must be appeased. If you don't give a substitution, then the spell won't work."

"But I just don't feel comfortable about it. Couldn't you do this one part?"

"No, you have to do it all."

Claire reached behind Winter and grabbed the little box that held the gray gerbil. She took the rodent out and handed it to Winter. The gerbil wiggled its nose and looked around. It squirmed and squeaked.

"You have to," Claire said. She held out a knife. "It's the only way to heal your mom."

Winter closed her eyes and nodded. She took the terrified gerbil in one hand and the knife in the other. Holding the gerbil firmly in the bowl, she placed the knife along its neck. Winter held her breath and closed her eyes.

"I can't," she said.

"Do it!"

"I can't!" Winter screamed.

Claire reached over and grabbed Winter's wrist. She leaned in and the gerbil's neck snapped. "Now finish it!"

Sniffling, Winter dragged the knife across the neck of the lifeless rodent, spilling its blood.

"Now, repeat after me," Claire said. "Candle, body, oil, and blood hear this plea of pure love."

Tears rolled down Winter's cheeks, but she managed to repeat the words in a whisper.

"Bring us healing, both body and mind, and cure the sickness for all time."

"Bring us healing, both body and mind, and cure the sickness for all time," Winter said. A warm tear fell from her cheek and landed in the bowl.

"Now, hold hands, concentrate on your mom, and let's chant it together seven times this time."

The girls clasped their hands together and began to chant. Their shadows danced on the walls like a spiritual audience, nodding and cheering in approval.

66

Present Day

Winter ran all the way from Carmichael Hall, through the Meadow, and down the sidewalk that led to the Chapel Garden. She slowed as she neared the garden so she could enter undetected. Though the premonition told her no one was there, she still clung to the shadows.

She could barely see the chapel as a dark gray mass in the dim starlight. The lamp posts by the sidewalk had been turned off. She looked up to where she knew the bell tower should be and could see a noticeable gap in the stars …a silhouetted black hole against the dark sky. Faint light came from a window high in the tower.

Winter rushed to the left side of the chapel and searched the darkness for the side door. It didn't take her long to locate it, but when she twisted the handle it didn't move. She pushed her weight against the door to test its sturdiness. It wouldn't budge. Her face heated in frustration and she gritted her teeth.

She stepped back and took a deep breath, mumbling a prayer to God for guidance. The premonition had told her to come here, so why was the door locked? She grunted and slammed the palm of her hand against the door.

"Open!" she said.

Something clicked. Winter tried the handle again, and the door opened.

The darkness engulfed her the moment she set foot through the door. Following the premonition and her own memory of her last visit, she turned right and felt along the wall until she came to the sanctuary doors.

It took her several minutes to fumble her way along the altar rail, crossing the blackened sanctuary. At the other side, she let go and walked with measured steps through the darkness to where she remembered the balcony stairs.

Her toe slammed into something. She knelt and felt along the ground, and found the bottom stair. Leaning forward on her hands, she crawled up on all fours. At the top of the landing, she continued crawling straight ahead into the darkness, going to where she remembered the door to be. If her hunch was right, this would be the door into the bell tower.

The premonition agreed.

Her hand reached the wall, and she rose to her knees and felt until she found the wooden door. Twisting the handle, she smiled when the door opened with ease.

Light waited on the other side. Not much light, but enough that she had to squint after spending so much time in total darkness. To her left were old wooden stairs. They wandered to the right, following the outside wall of the tower. Small candles sat on the steps, spread out—only one every four or five steps. They oozed lifeless blood that pooled at their base and coagulated into white scabs.

Directly across from her stood a rough wooden door with an old iron handle, and she eased it open. Inside she found a large round room with slotted windows in the sides—just like in her dream. But there was no nasty mush on the floors and no blood on the walls. She looked up, and the candlelight cast just enough light to glint from massive bells hanging from the ceiling. Chains hung from them, and they went through the ceiling into a room above. Winter imagined there were many rooms like this—she just needed to find the right one. One thing was certain though—she had found the right place. She had been here before.

Winter went back to the old wooden stairs and began to ascend. With the first step they groaned, and she hesitated. She broke a candle free and continued her ascent, tilting it so it bled on the planks.

Darkness pressed in from beyond the candlelight. The shadows behind taunted her by name, while the shadows above beckoned with false hope. More than once, she thought she recognized a shape—a person or animal—in the shadows, only to have the light flicker and send the phantom away. Slotted windows perforated the outer wall every few feet, staring at her with cold, lidless eyes.

She passed a rough wooden door with an iron handle. It was not her destination, so she continued. On her journey she passed many doors the same as the first. The stairs dissolved into black eternity. Her feet hurt, her knees hurt, and her heart pounded with cold dread. Each footstep echoed in the empty stairwell, answered by moans from the wooden steps. She wanted to flee—to turn and go back. But she couldn't. She must continue. Sweat leaked from her body, matting her clothes to her skin. A bitter breeze drifted through a window and she shuddered.

Finally, the endless line of candles stopped before a door just like all the others she had passed. She reached out and brushed the handle with the tips of her fingers. It felt cold. Cold radiated from the door like heat from a furnace. Evil waited beyond this door…expecting her. She could feel it, and the instinct to flee seized her stronger than ever. Every hair on her body stood rigid, and she trembled with anticipation. Her arms and legs numbed, but she knew she must enter. She had to save Kaci. It was her destiny—her calling.

"This is it," she whispered to herself and God. She grabbed the handle, took a deep, desperate breath, and pushed.

Xaphan waited on the opposite side of the room. She locked eyes with him the moment she entered.

"You're late, prophet," he said. "Honestly, how do you expect to even have a chance of defeating me if you never show up on time?"

A cold wind tore across her body and clawed at her hair. The candlelight flickered and sputtered out. She flung the candle aside.

At least twenty other people wearing black robes filled the tiny round room, each holding their own candle. Xaphan wore red and held a bloodied knife.

To the right, the gears and sprockets of the clock purred like the engine of a car. As the minute hand advanced closer to nine o'clock, it boomed with each click. The bats chattered, and the room reeked with the foul stench of guano.

Xaphan stood behind a large pentagram. Tall pillar candles stood at each point, and iridescent blood pooled in the center.

Kaci was not there.

"Where is she?" Winter asked. "Where's Kaci?"

Her stomach twisted and froze, and her knees almost buckled. She fought to stand. Something like electricity rippled across her skin. The blood drained from her face and she blinked to see straight.

"What's the matter, Winter? You look pale. Is this the first time you've been in the presence of real evil?" Xaphan said.

Winter felt very dizzy. She swayed and grabbed the doorjamb with one hand. Xaphan laughed.

"Give me strength, Father," she whispered.

The cold wind stopped and warmth returned to her legs. Her vision became sharper than it had ever been, and she knew God had joined her. She planted her feet and stood straight.

"WHERE IS SHE?" Her voice reverberated from the bells hanging above. Bats scattered. The clocked ticked another minute.

Xaphan stopped laughing. A shadow of doubt crossed his face and was gone. The others shuffled their feet and looked at him.

"Oh, it's too late for her," he said. "I warned you someone might die, but you didn't believe me. Her blood is on your hands." He waved his hand to the pool of blood in the pentagram.

Winter swallowed hard. *But it isn't nine o'clock yet!*

"I don't believe you!" she said. "She's still alive. Now tell me where she is!"

"I don't think you're in any position to make demands," Xaphan said. He loomed forward and clenched his fists. "Do you think you could make it out of this tower alive unless I allowed you to? What did you expect to accomplish here with your foolish heroics? You're lucky I have other plans for you! Don't push your luck, or I may change my mind!"

"I won't cooperate with anything you want me to do."

"You don't have to, Winter. The only thing better than killing you and watching you suffer in death is watching you suffer in life. Kaci's body will eventually be found, but we won't be here when it is. You, however, will be."

"You're going to frame me?"

"Very good. And I thought you were slow."

"It will never work. I'll never do anything to give you evidence against me!" she said. "And no one will believe it—Kaci's my friend."

"Evidence is very compelling, girl. You've already given me everything I need to make you a convicted murderer. It was pathetically easy to collect your DNA and wrap your hand around the knife. And where, may I ask, is your locket?" His lip curled.

Winter took a quick breath.

Xaphan grinned. "Or have you forgotten that you've spent time unconscious with me?"

Winter balled her hands into fists. "So that's how you framed Peter."

"Yes." His smile deepened.

"But why? Why frame him? And why did you have to kill Jennifer? They didn't do anything to you!"

"Fear! Dear girl, FEAR! I couldn't have made half the progress I did this year without fear. I needed to make a sacrifice to create the atmosphere I most love to work in. Peter and Jennifer proved to be admirable candidates too. Nothing makes a Christian doubt faster than seeing one of their own fall from grace. It was poetic."

"Well, it didn't work. You couldn't fool me—I saw through everything. It's over, Xaphan."

"Yes, how unfortunate. In the last twelve hours, everything I've worked for this year has come unraveled."

Winter smirked. "You're welcome."

"Don't try my patience!"

"Why exactly are you here?" she asked. "What do you want with this school? What do you want with us?"

"You'll find out soon enough…if you live that long. My plans are too complex for you to understand now."

"Well, whatever it is, your reign of terror ends tonight. You may have gotten away with your plans in the past, but God has had enough of you! He will send me to stop you no matter where you go. The biggest mistake you could ever make is letting me live."

"Your god is not as powerful as me. I burned Heaven! I am Xaphan!" His voice thundered throughout the room. A few more bats fluttered and flew out of the narrow windows.

"You're a joke."

Xaphan barred his teeth. "Do not mock me, or I will put an end to you right now."

"Then what are you waiting for? DO IT!" she screamed. "KILL ME! Kill me just like you killed Jennifer and Kaci!"

"Do not tempt me!"

"Why not?" Winter's face burned. She couldn't believe what she was saying. But the premonition…"Or could you not kill them yourself? Did you need one of your lackeys to do it for you? You're pathetic. All you do is talk, but it's all just a show. You're the weakest person in this room."

Xaphan cursed and pointed the knife at her. The edge glinted red in the flickering candlelight.

"Don't dare insult me! You don't know who I am!"

"Another empty threat? I know exactly who you are. You're a crazy psycho who thinks he's a second-rate demon, when really you're just a washed up loser. And that's all I need to know. You didn't have the guts to kill the other two girls, and you certainly don't have the guts to kill me. You're a coward!"

"I'll show you just how much of a coward I am! Change of plans," he said to his followers. "It looks like we're going to have two sacrifices tonight." He stepped over the pentagram. "And I'm going to personally slit your throat—just like I did Jennifer's and just like I did Kaci's."

Winter shoved both hands into her pockets. With one, she withdrew her little digital recorder that she sometimes brought to classes. She held it in front of her and made a show of pressing the stop button. Then, she held her cell phone up with her other hand.

The hate-filled silence was so taut that the sound of the phone snapping a picture reached every ear.

"Thank you," she said with a small curtsy.

Four Years Ago

The next Monday, Winter arrived eager to school. She wanted to find Claire and ask if the spells were working yet. Even though she knew it might take a little while for her mother to completely heal, in Claire's situation results could be immediate.

But Claire didn't come to homeroom.

At lunch, only Ali and Stacy sat with her. Phillip had abandoned the table and avoided them as a group completely.

"Have either of you heard from Claire?" she asked.

"Not since yesterday," Stacy said.

"Hey, I heard you two were doing some sort of spells!" Ali said. "Did they work?"

Winter's face flushed. "One of them did, I think." She shuffled her food. Ali's eyes lit up.

"Tell me about it!"

"I'd rather not."

"What about the other spells? Did they work too?"

Winter shrugged. "I don't know yet. That's part of why I want to talk to Claire."

"Well, next time you do a spell, let me in on it. It sounds cool!" Ali said.

"It's not that great. I didn't like doing it." She looked around again, scanning the lunch line and the other tables. Where was Claire?

"Why not?" Stacy asked.

Winter looked at her and shrugged.

Winter's curiosity and fear gnawed at her stomach all day. That afternoon she climbed onto Claire's bus.

When the bus stopped at the far end of Claire's road, several students got off and rushed down the sidewalk. Winter waited until most of them had disappeared before moving on.

Winter clutched her books to her chest and began the short walk to Claire's house at the end of the street. She walked as slowly as she could, rehearsing all the different possibilities in her head.

Winter pushed open the gate in the middle of a white picket fence, and wandered up the sidewalk to the Victorian style home. Shouts came from inside, and she paused at the bottom of the steps. Then, setting her jaw, she went up.

Claire cracked open the door before Winter could knock. She looked at Winter with sad, bloodshot eyes. Angry red skin and green bruises covered her face. Her swollen lip had dried blood at one corner.

"I saw you coming from the window," she said, her voice flat.

"I was worried about you. I came to see how you're doing. I thought you might be sick or something."

"No, I'm not sick." More shouting from inside. Something crashed. Claire looked away and then back at Winter. Her eyes betrayed tremendous fear, but she kept her voice steady. "You should go now."

"No! I don't want to leave you, Claire. Come with me."

Claire's face softened and her eyes compressed with sadness. "I can't," she said. "I can't leave my mom."

"Then let me call the police."

"No! I told you before—no police!"

"Isn't there something I can do?"

Claire shrugged and eyed the ground. "I'm sorry, Winter, I have to go. You shouldn't have come. I'll be back at school in a day or two." She started to close the door.

Winter grabbed the door and held it open a crack. "Maybe the spell hasn't had time to work yet. Maybe it just needs more time."

"No, I don't think so," Claire said. "It's over."

"CLAIRE!" roared a man from within the house.

"You have to go!" Claire's voice wavered, and her eyes started watering. "Just leave, okay? Leave!"

"But, Claire—"

The door closed in Winter's face. Something crashed inside. Claire's dad shouted curse words. Winter heard a smacking sound followed by Claire crying out in pain.

She turned and ran away as fast as she could. By the time she reached the street, she could only sob between heavy breaths. After hurrying to the street corner where the school bus had dropped her off, she sat down beside a tree and hugged herself.

Winter decided to call her dad and tell him everything. She pulled out her prepaid phone, but before she could dial her dad's number, the phone started ringing.

"Hello," she said. Her voice cracked and trembled. She wiped the tears from her cheeks.

"Winter! Where are you? You weren't on your bus!"

"I rode the bus to Claire's. She wasn't at school and I wanted to check on her."

"What street is that?"

"Dad, there's something I need to tell you," she said.

"Now's not the time, Winter. Just tell me where you are."

She looked at the street sign. "I'm at the corner of Chestnut and Harris. I'm so sorry, Dad. Please don't be angry. I shouldn't have come here."

"I'm not angry, sweetheart. I'll be there to pick you up in a few minutes."

This time Winter heard the emotion in his voice. Her heart fluttered and she stood.

"Dad, is everything okay? What's wrong?" she asked.

Silence on the other end of the phone.

"Dad, tell me!" She heard a sniffle. Was he crying? "DAD!"

"It's your mom," he said with a trembling voice. *"They've taken her to the hospital."*

Present Day

Xaphan roared. All the bats scattered and swirled through the room like a cloud. The premonition told Winter to move and she jerked to one side. The bloody knife embedded in the doorframe, wobbling mere inches from her face. A crimson drop of blood fell from the edge…Kaci's blood.

"KILL HER!"

His followers moved as one in her direction. Winter grabbed the door handle, ran into the stairwell, and slammed the door closed.

Instinct said to go down, but her premonition told her that was wrong. So she turned and sprinted up instead. She took the steps in threes, getting enough around the bend to cling to the inner wall in the darkness and not be seen. Only seconds had passed. The door below burst open and banged against the mortar wall. The followers poured out like black water.

They went down. She held her breath until they were gone. Then she went a few steps further up to one of the slotted windows in the outer wall. She still clenched the phone in her hand and it took her only a moment to scroll through the phone book to find Summer's number. She pushed the dial button, then shoved the phone back in her pocket and let it ring.

Flashlights below winked on and off, and she smiled. Now to find Kaci.

Winter sprinted back down the stairs to the room. She rushed through the open door, and the premonition warned her too late. Xaphan stood just on the other side. Waiting. He took two quick steps as she entered and backhanded her across the face. The force of the impact knocked her to the ground several feet away.

"You'll learn your place, prophet!"

"I know my place!" Despite the pain in her jaw and the stars speckling her vision, she stood and faced him. "It's right here! Where's Kaci?"

Xaphan growled and took another quick step. Before Winter could move, he had an iron grip around her throat with one hand. He squeezed, and she felt her windpipe closing. She grabbed his wrist with both hands and tried to pull him away. With inhuman strength, he lifted her straight into the air. Her lungs burned. Her vision faded. She started thrashing her feet.

"Now, you're beginning to understand," Xaphan said. "I can see it in your eyes. You fear me now. No mortal can stop me—especially you."

He flung her across the room. Her body wrapped and whiplashed around one of the bell chains that passed through the floor. As she twisted to the ground, the bell tolled, compressing the air in the room.

Winter couldn't breathe. She tried to rise to her hands and knees, but the pain in her side made her gasp and cough. Her mouth had split against the floor, and she spat blood.

"Death is coming for you, Winter! I AM DEATH!"

Xaphan slammed his foot into her stomach with supernatural force. She flew through the air and crashed hard on her back. Blood soaked through her shirt and smeared across her arms. Winter whimpered and drew her knees to her chest. When she rolled to the side, she saw the pentagram and the pool of blood around her.

"Now we will end this," Xaphan said.

She turned to him and watched through watery eyes as he pulled the knife from the doorframe. He crossed the room in only a few steps. She tried to roll away, but her body wouldn't respond.

He knelt by her side and shoved her onto her back. His hand felt like a vice grip, and she cried out.

Raising the knife high above her chest, Xaphan said, "Tell your god I'm coming." With his entire body behind the knife, he plunged it down.

The premonition took control.

Winter rolled and the knife struck the floor. The premonition guided her hand to one of the candles, and she smashed it against Xaphan's side.

His robe ignited. Xaphan fell back with a shriek—writhing and clawing at the flames. The smell of burning flesh and polyester mixed with the acidic stench of bat droppings.

It took him only moments to wrestle the robe from his body. He tossed it aside and glared back at her with demonic hatred. His undershirt hung in black smoldering strands, fused to the bubbling skin on the left side of his body.

Xaphan's whole body trembled. He shook the knife and rushed forward, bellowing like a wild beast. Winter tried desperately to stand again, but her feet slipped in the blood, and she fell back to her knees. She clenched her eyes and held her arms in front of her face. Xaphan's feet thundered closer.

It was at that moment that the lights came on—spotlights from outside—bright ones. Light flooded the room from every window and every angle. Xaphan stopped only inches from her. She opened her eyes as Xaphan ran to look out of one of the windows. A voice floated up from below, aided by a megaphone.

"This is the FBI, we have the place surrounded. Come out peacefully, and no one will get hurt."

She heard a booming crash of splintered wood. Then gunshots. Xaphan cursed.

Winter found strength. Pushing through the pain, she stood and planted her feet. Xaphan turned back to face her. She narrowed her eyes and clenched her fists, blood dripping to the floor from between her fingers.

"You lose."

Xaphan yelled and rushed again, but this time voices in the stairwell made him stop. He bolted for the door instead.

As he stepped through the door, he paused and looked back. Extending the knife at her, he said, "This isn't over!" Then he went up the stairs to the top of the tower.

As soon as he had gone, Winter collapsed onto the floor. Her whole body seized like a giant cramp. She wept.

Men in black SWAT suits with helmets, shields, flashlights, and guns flooded in. The first man grabbed his radio and said, "We found her!" He came to her side and knelt while other men filed behind.

"Where are you hurt?" he asked.

"I'm not. Not really." she croaked. "It's not my blood. He went upstairs."

The officer turned to his men and motioned for them to go up. When they had left, Agent Gains came into the room, wearing a bulletproof vest and brandishing a handgun and flashlight. When he saw her, he holstered the gun and rushed over.

"My God, what did they do to you?"

"It's not mine. I think it's Kaci's. We have to find her."

A SWAT officer came running back into the room from upstairs. "He got away," the man said. "There's a cable attached to another building from the top of the tower. He must have slid down it."

"Then search the entire campus! Find him!" Gains turned back to Winter, then took her by the hand and helped her to her feet.

"We have to find Kaci right now!"

"Where is she?" he asked.

"Here somewhere, I think. I'm not sure." She looked at her watch. "But we have five minutes to find her or she'll be dead."

"I don't understand. What do you mean five minutes?"

"Just trust me, okay? Five minutes…we have to hurry!"

"Winter, all the rooms in the bell tower and chapel have been secured. Are you sure she's here?" Gains asked.

"We have to keep looking," she said. "Kaci is here somewhere, she has to be. You've missed something. Have your men search every room again!"

Gains nodded and grabbed his radio. "All units, we have a missing person within the chapel and bell tower. A quick recovery is critical to survival. Subject is about 5'6" with light brown hair. Check every room, cupboard, and hole. Find her! And bring in the dogs."

He looked back to Winter. "If she's here, they'll find her. But I can't guarantee it will be in five minutes."

"Then I'm going to look for her myself," Winter said. "She's my friend—I can't let her die."

"You need to see the paramedics."

"I NEED TO FIND HER!"

Gains frowned for a moment, then nodded. "I'll stay with you. Where do you want to start?"

Winter looked around at the room. Blood covered the walls, just like in her dreams. Was all of that Kaci's? Deep red stains could be seen in some places, and she wondered if that could have been Jennifer's blood. She panned the room, praying for some guidance— praying for a vision or for the premonition to come back. But all she had were the memories of her dreams.

"Okay," she said after turning a full circle. "Why are there windows on only two sides of the room?"

Gains looked around. "Well, the stairs are behind one side."

"But what about this other? There's nothing behind this wall but the outside. Why is there no window?"

Agent Gains and Winter walked over to the blank wall. Winter felt across it with her hands.

Gains knocked on it gently. "Here…it's hollow. Look, this panel is removable."

Winter and Gains both clawed at the cracks with their fingers until they were able to wrest the panel from the wall. Behind it they found an empty shaft, no more than three feet square. Two cables ran up and down inside the shaft.

"What is it?" Winter asked.

"A dumbwaiter, I think," Gains said. "They must have used it to bring food and supplies up to the upper levels during construction."

"But there's no car."

"It must be on another level. The stairs must wrap around the outside of the shaft."

"Look here!" Winter said. Bloody smears painted the insides of the wall. "Kaci!"

Winter turned and bolted out of the room. She stopped when she came to the door and stared at the outer wall of the stairs. There was a red arrow pointing down. It appeared to be drawn in blood.

"Where did that come from?" she asked.

"What are you talking about?"

"The arrow," she said pointing.

"What arrow?"

As Winter studied the arrow, a SWAT agent came by from the upper floor. When he passed, the arrow had vanished.

"That's it!"

"What's it?" Gains asked.

Without any further hesitation, Winter followed the arrow and took the stairs three at a time to the next landing. Her body protested with each jolt.

She burst through the door and ran across the room. A faint "X" in fading blood marked the wall, and she rushed to it. She and Gains grabbed at the panel almost simultaneously. It took them only a moment to pull it free.

They found nothing but cables.

"This is the wrong one!"

The bells began to ring. Nine o'clock.

"No! It's not time!"

The sound swallowed the last of her words whole. Winter and Gains both clutched their ears as they rushed out of the room. She saw another red arrow on the stair wall.

"Hurry!" Winter shouted but couldn't even hear herself in the drone of the bells.

She flew down to the next landing, pushing SWAT agents aside as she did so, and threw open the next door. Gains stayed right behind her, and she grabbed his flashlight. Shining it across the room, she saw another "X" on the wall.

Winter continued down the stairs. The bells rang their fifth chime. At the next landing—another "X". Winter grunted in frustration. The bells chimed seven.

Winter all but jumped the stairs to the next landing and nearly collapsed to the ground. She landed hard on her knees and screamed, but managed to throw open the door despite the pain.

On the far wall, written in fading red, was the word "Here."

The bells chimed nine. The sound felt like the nailing of a coffin.

She didn't remember crossing the room when she slammed into the dumbwaiter panel. Time seemed to slow. Tears made her almost blind. Her fingertips left bloody smears as she clawed the old wooden panel.

Not Kaci. She couldn't lose Kaci.

Agent Gains reached her side. He shouted something, but all Winter could hear was her own frantic breathing and the pounding of her heart. Together they pulled and finally the panel gave way. As it fell to the floor, the ninth chime faded to silence.

They found her, naked and covered in blood. She had been stuffed into the dumbwaiter like a rag doll.

"Kaci!"

She and Gains grabbed Kaci's bloody body and pulled her out. Gains spoke into his radio again, but Winter didn't listen.

Kaci's face looked like raw meat. Hundreds of slashes crisscrossed her body. Deep purple bruises covered her torso and, where there were no bruises or cuts, her skin was pasty white. Her left arm flopped at an unnatural angle. Bone protruded from her left thigh. A long ugly gash crossed her throat.

Winter's locket hung from her neck, the chain half embedded in the gash.

"NO!" Winter screamed. "No! Not her, please not her!"

Her screams turned to sobs, and Winter threw herself across Kaci's mangled body. She wept, and her body heaved with each painful breath.

"God, please! Please, not Kaci! Not Kaci!" She brushed at the matted hair covering Kaci's face.

One of Kaci's eyes fluttered and the eyelid parted.

Winter held her breath.

Kaci's lips moved.

"She's still alive! Hurry! She's still alive!"

"The paramedics are in the chapel now," Gains said. "They're coming, Winter."

She turned back to Kaci. "Hang on, okay? Just hang on. It's going to be all right, you'll see. They're coming to get you. Just stay with me."

Kaci's eye fluttered shut.

"Kaci! Come on! Open your eyes! Look at me, Kaci! Don't you do this, don't you leave me! Kaci!"

Gains tugged at her shoulders. "They're here, Winter. Move."

Winter allowed herself to be pulled away. A white-clad paramedic took her place and went to work.

Winter turned into the arms of Agent Gains and cried. Like a loving parent, he held her and whispered soothing words to the top of her head.

Another paramedic rushed into the room with a backboard. They moved Kaci and strapped her down.

"Is she still alive?" Agent Gains asked as the paramedics began to leave the room.

"Barely."

By the time Winter and Gains walked out the front doors, the ambulance carrying Kaci had gone. Meanwhile, Xaphan's followers were being loaded into a police van. Two black body bags lay nearby.

"It's all my fault," she said.

"No, it's not. Don't blame yourself," said Agent Gains. "Xaphan is a monster. You probably saved Kaci's life. You were there when I should have been."

"I want to believe you. But I don't know if I can right now."

Gains rubbed her back and motioned for paramedics. As Winter was led to a waiting ambulance, Summer and Davis ran up to her from the garden. They both looked frantic.

"Was that Kaci?" Summer asked. "In the other ambulance?"

Winter nodded, and Summer fell onto Davis's shoulder. Winter reached out to them, and they came over. All three were soon covered with the blood from Winter's clothes—Kaci's blood.

"Miss, we need to finish," said one of the paramedics.

"Okay," said Winter. She nodded to Summer and Davis, and they backed a couple of feet away.

Nearby, Agent Gains was talking with Detective Fox.

"Get them," Winter said to Davis.

Davis nodded and jogged away.

"How are you?" asked Agent Gains a moment later as he came over.

"Nothing serious," said a paramedic. "She's just a little banged up, but otherwise fine. The worst thing is a gash on her leg, but she says that happened earlier today."

"I have it," Winter said. She reached into her pocket and pulled out the digital recorder.

"Have what?" Detective Fox asked.

"A confession."

Detective Fox smiled.

Agent Gains shook his head and took the digital recorder from her outstretched hand. "You're no ordinary college girl, are you?"

Winter sighed. "You have no idea."

71

After being cleared by paramedics and interviewed by the FBI and the Cherithville Police Department, Winter sat with Summer and Davis in silence on a garden bench. A crowd of students had gathered along the police-tape perimeter, ogling the forensic specialists processing the scene. Winter even saw Dr. Streffield a couple of times. The first time he was talking with Agent Gains and the second time with Detective Fox. He looked over at them at one point, but never approached. Finally, Detective Fox broke away from the madness and came to see them.

"You three should get cleaned up," he said. "I'll send a couple of officers with you to your rooms. Then I'll personally give you a ride to the hospital."

"Thank you," Winter said.

Fox motioned for two people to come over. They wore street clothes, but police badges hung on lanyards around their necks. "This is Lieutenant Erica Darling and Lieutenant Joe Nockles. They'll be your escorts for the rest of the night in case Xaphan decides to return."

"Do you really think he may come back tonight?" Winter asked. Summer leaned against her.

"No, Winter. I don't think he will. Xaphan is smarter than that. He'll wait."

"That's not very comforting," said Davis.

Detective Fox shook his head. "No it isn't." To the two officers, he said, "Take them to their rooms, and radio me when they've cleaned up."

Winter, Summer, and Davis were ushered to a sedan. Lieutenant Darling drove the car out of the garden by way of the pathway that led away from the Meadow. A uniformed officer held up the police tape to let them pass. After dropping off Davis and Lieutenant Nockles, Lieutenant Darling took the girls to Carmichael Hall.

Lieutenant Darling followed them to their hallway. "I'll wait for you here."

Winter and Summer entered their room without speaking and gathered their toiletries and clean clothes.

Winter stared as soapy water and blood swirled about her feet and into the drain. If she had more tears, she might have cried again.

Thirty minutes later, they were both clean and dressed. Lieutenant Darling radioed in, and Detective Fox met them beneath the awning in front of the lobby. After Fox dismissed Darling, the girls climbed into the back of Fox's car, and they went to pick up Davis.

Detective Fox seemed neither willing nor able to speak to them about what had happened as they drove to the hospital. Winter sat in the middle and clung to both Summer's and Davis's hands. The mournful silence pressed against her chest.

They entered the hospital through the emergency room doors. Scattered people sat in the waiting area, reading magazines. Nurses in navy blue scrubs walked by holding clipboards. The air smelled clean and sterile.

Walking into the hospital brought a flood of horrible memories to Winter. The nostalgia stabbed her, and she grabbed at Summer for support. Almost four years to the day.

Fox walked to the blonde receptionist and spoke with her for several minutes. When he returned, his face was grim.

"She's in surgery," he said. "Wait here." He turned and followed a nurse further in.

After sitting and staring at each other with nothing to say, Summer managed to find a comfortable enough position to sleep, and Davis took to wandering around. Winter tried closing her eyes and getting some rest, but images of Kaci's mangled body would not go away.

Kaci's parents arrived at one o'clock in the morning. Beverly found Winter immediately, and Winter rushed to her. From somewhere, Winter found more tears, and she wept as Beverly held her and cried with her.

Chris led them to the receptionist.

"Um, our daughter is here," he said. His voiced wavered. "Kaci Williams."

The receptionist nodded. "Through the door; I'll lead you."

As they walked to the door, the receptionist glanced at Winter. "I'm sorry," she said, "but family only."

Beverly locked her jaw. "She is family."

The receptionist looked from Beverly to Chris and nodded. Winter turned to tell Summer, but she was still sleeping.

The receptionist led them through a set of double doors to an elevator. "Go to the second floor," she said. "Take a right. You'll find the surgery waiting area there."

"Surgery?" Chris asked.

"They'll be able to answer all your questions there," she said.

They followed the directions and came to the appropriate waiting area. Chris told the new receptionist they were there to see Kaci, and the woman got up and walked through double doors posted with the words "Do Not Enter, Surgical Area." A few minutes later, a doctor in green scrubs and surgical cap came out. His brow furrowed.

"Mr. and Mrs. Williams?" he asked.

"Yes?" Chris said.

"My name is Dr. Freeman. I would like to speak with you in private," he said with a quick look at Winter.

"Whatever you have to say, you can say in front of her," Chris said.

Dr. Freeman nodded. "First, let me tell you your daughter is alive. But her condition is not good."

Winter grabbed Beverly's hand and squeezed it tight. Tears were already coming back to Winter's eyes.

Dr. Freeman hesitated. "Perhaps we should sit down." He led them to some chairs nearby.

"She has several broken bones," he said, "including her cheekbones, nose, collarbone, four cracked ribs, and left arm and leg. There is also some internal bleeding, which we are operating on now, in addition to setting the bones. One of her broken ribs had punctured a lung and caused it to collapse."

Beverly covered her mouth. Winter trembled.

"She also received more than a hundred lacerations over her entire body. The deepest cut being across her throat. Thankfully, it appears that was done in haste and was not deep enough to sever either of her carotid arteries. The hastiness of the cut may have saved her life. Victims don't usually survive Satanic rituals."

Beverly stifled a cry. Chris put an arm around her, and they held each other tight.

"There is something else," Dr. Freeman said. He pursed his lips and looked at the ground. "There is evidence of multiple rapes. We've collected DNA samples for forensics, but based on her injuries I would estimate no less than five attackers...maybe more."

Beverly wailed into Chris's shoulder. Chris's face contorted with controlled rage.

"I'm sorry," said Dr. Freeman. "I really am. In all my years of medicine, I've never seen anything like this. I'll make sure you're updated on her surgery." He got up and left.

Winter had not known about the last part. She leaned over gagging and coughing, heaving with dry sobs. Her body shook, her stomach muscles so tight she could barely breathe.

Beverly put an arm around her and pulled her in, like she was part of the family. Somewhere in her mind, Winter spared a thought for that. The three of them wept on each other for a very long time.

Four Years Ago

Winter's dad picked her up and drove ninety-five miles per hour going to the city. Neither of them talked. Winter felt cold on the inside, like her life was being sucked away. Memories of her mom flashed through her mind the entire trip. Her throat ached from the bottled emotion.

Even at the speed they traveled, it took them forty-five minutes before they pulled into the parking lot of St. Mark's Hospital. Her dad jammed the truck into park before it completely stopped, and the vehicle lurched in protest. He looked at her, his face tight and red.

"Are you ready?"

Winter blinked back tears. Her dad's shoulders slumped, and he hung his head. He climbed out and opened her door. Winter fell out of the truck and into his waiting arms, clinging to him for the first time since she was a child.

They walked with their arms around each other into the front doors of the hospital, through the white sterilized halls to the ICU waiting room.

"We're here to see Marie Maessen," her dad told the receptionist.

"Good, you're here," said a voice from behind them. They turned to see a doctor with glasses and a long white coat. "I'm Dr. Lewis."

"How is she, Doc?"

Dr. Lewis looked at them both with a grim face. "Not good," he said. "In fact, it's a miracle she's still here. She's not exactly lucid. She's done nothing but ask for winter. Do you know what that means?"

"I'm Winter," she whispered.

"Ahh. Now it makes sense. Well, she wants to see you. In fact, waiting to see you is probably the only thing that's kept her alive. But let me warn you, she doesn't look good, and she could go at any moment."

Her dad held her close. "Do you want me to come with you?"

"No. I can do it."

"Are you sure?"

She nodded.

"Follow me, then," Dr. Lewis said.

"I'll wait for you here," her dad said.

Dr. Lewis led her through a set of double doors to a large room with a built-in nurses' station in one corner. The rest of the walls were made of glass, and behind the glass were the ICU rooms. A few of them had blinds drawn. Dr. Lewis led her to one.

"I'll be here at the nurses' station," he said.

Winter stood at the door several moments before she finally entered. Monitors beeped along the back wall, and a respirator hissed. Her mom lay on the bed, slightly inclined. An oxygen mask covered her face, and plastic tubing led to a taped-over needle in her arm. Bags of saline hung on a rack behind her head. She seemed to be asleep. Winter took a tentative step toward the bed.

Present Day

Dr. Freeman came back to them two hours later looking tired and frustrated. The three of them stood as he approached. Dr. Freeman took a seat, and they sat with him.

"We've had a complication," he said. "We've been unable to isolate the source of the internal bleeding, and her vital signs began to drop."

Beverly shook.

Dr. Freeman wrinkled his brow. "It's touch and go right now, but we've moved her into a surgical recovery room until we can stabilize her. Then we'll have to go back into the operating room. But if she doesn't stabilize, and we can't find the source of the bleeding…well…things don't look good."

"What are her chances, Doctor?" whispered Chris.

Dr. Freeman sighed, pulled off his surgical cap, and rubbed his hand through his gray hair. He shook his head. Beverly started to cry.

"I've arranged for you to see her, if you would like. But there isn't much time," said Dr. Freeman.

"Then let's go," Chris said.

Dr. Freeman led them down the corridor and through a set of double doors. He took a right and went through another set of doors marked "Authorized Personnel Only." A moment later, he brought them into a small surgical preparation room, with lockers and large stainless-steel sinks.

An olive green operating room lay on the other side of a plate glass window directly ahead. To the left was a separate set of glass windows and a smaller white room beyond.

Kaci lay on a gurney in the white room. Gauze wrapped her entire face, and a giant breathing tube was taped to her mouth. A white sheet covered the rest of her body. Two nurses attended the machines and monitors behind Kaci. Two bags of blood and two bags of plasma hung from the rack beside where Kaci lay. Tubes ran from each bag and into the one arm that draped on top of the sheet.

Chris, Beverly, and Winter crept to the window. Beverly laid one hand on the glass and the other over her heart.

"Can we go in?" she asked.

"I'm afraid not," Dr. Freeman said. "It's a sterile environment, and we didn't close all of the incisions when we moved her. It's against hospital protocol for me to even allow you this far."

"Chris…my baby…" she moaned.

Something stirred inside of Winter. Her chest and face burned, and the tears that came at that moment scalded her face. She hugged herself as the quiet fire inside roared to life.

"There is one good thing I failed to mention," Dr. Freeman said. "Her blood work revealed she was taking birth control."

"Yes," Chris said, his voice strained but controlled. "She took it for medical reasons."

Dr. Freeman nodded. "In any case, if she survives you won't have to worry about pregnancy."

Hearing Dr. Freeman say those words poured fuel on the fire. It raged within and spread to Winter's arms and legs.

Xaphan had taken so much from Kaci—so much that was sacred. She couldn't even fathom the horrors Kaci would have to live with after this was over.

If she lived.

She stared at Kaci, wanting to look away but unable to. The pain in her heart and the fire in her body made her sob almost to the point of hyperventilation. But she no longer cried from sorrow.

She cried from anger.

Deep in her soul, she no longer felt alone. And she knew her anger did not come from herself, but from God. With the anger came a deep swell of agony and compassion that threatened to overwhelm her own feeble human emotions.

A rumble like thunder filled her ears. The heat and tears in her eyes blurred everything. The palms of her hands throbbed and tingled. In that moment, she remembered the stories of Elijah. And she realized what God wanted her to do.

"I need to touch her," she said as calmly as she could.

She felt their eyes turn to her. But Winter couldn't see them. All she could see was Kaci's broken body, the only thing that remained focused through the tears. The rumble grew louder in her ears—it was God screaming. Soon the scream would burst from her own mouth too.

"I'm sorry, that's impossible," said Dr. Freeman.

"You don't understand! You have to let me see her!"

"Open the door," said Chris. Winter heard renewed strength in his voice. "Let her in."

"I can't. It's against surgical protocols."

"You have to let me in!" The thunder…the screaming. "You don't understand; if you don't let me in she's going to die!"

"We're giving her the best medical treatment possible. There's nothing you can do."

"Let me in NOW!"

Winter rushed to the door before Dr. Freeman could move to

stop her. It was locked. She had dealt with locked doors before. God would not let this stop her. A second try found the door unlocked.

"No! You can't! You'll contaminate her!"

"What's going on?" Beverly cried.

Dr. Freeman grabbed Winter's arm. She turned to push him away.

But Chris pulled him back. "Let her do this!"

Winter invaded the sterile room and stood by Kaci's side. The startled nurses backed away.

Four Years Ago

She knelt beside her mom and grabbed her hand.

"I'm here, Mom," Winter said.

Her mom turned her head with obvious effort. Winter had not expected her to look so bad. She gasped.

Her mom smiled in that sweet way Winter loved so much. The sunken cheeks and pale face could not hide it.

"Hey, Winter," she said. She reached a shaking hand up and pulled the oxygen mask from her face. A single tear rolled down her cheek and landed on the white sheets.

"Don't cry, Mom. Please, don't cry…"

"I'm sorry, Winter," her mom said. "I'm sorry this had to happen. I'm sorry you have to go through this. A young girl should never have to lose her mother." She spoke slowly, with little movement of her mouth. Her words came out slurred.

Winter heaved a deep breath and let the tears flow freely down her face. "Why, Mom? Why does this have to happen? You said there was a reason before, but I can't see it. Mom, I don't want you to die."

"I don't know what the reason is, dear. Maybe God will use this so you can help someone in the future. Maybe God wants you to know what it feels like to lose someone you love. One day, you may have to comfort somebody else."

"But who's going to comfort me? You were always the one there for me, and now you're going to leave. I can't depend on Dad. He doesn't understand."

Her mom reached out with a trembling arm and brushed Winter's cheek. Her fingers felt like ice. "God will comfort you."

"NO! God did this to me. Can't you see that? If God loved me, you wouldn't die."

"That's not true," her mom said. "God does lots of things that we don't understand. This is not our home, Heaven is. Death is nothing to be sad over—you should be happy for me. I'm going somewhere where I'll never feel pain or be sick again."

"But you're going somewhere I can't go." Winter laid her head down on the edge of the bed and wept.

Her mom put a hand on Winter's head. "You can go there too…someday you'll understand that, sweetheart. You just have to trust God."

The minutes ticked by, and Winter couldn't bring herself to look up again. Her tears created a dark spot on the sheets. Nothing could have prepared her for the mixture of fire and ice that stabbed her chest. Her body trembled and her skin felt clammy. She sweated almost as much as she cried. Her heart seemed to have collapsed.

She didn't even notice when her mom had stopped touching her. When she finally realized it, she looked up.

"Mom?"

Her mom stared at the ceiling with her eyes open and a smile on her face.

"Oh, I wish you could see this, Winter."

The machines began to beep faster.

"Mom! No! Mom, don't go!" Fire…ice…her breaths came in

rapid gusts.

"I love you," her mom whispered.

"I love you too, Mom! Please don't die! Please, God please! Don't die!"

Her mom took a deep shuddering breath. Then the machine stopped beeping, and the sound was replaced by a long steady tone. Dr. Lewis rushed into the room, followed by a nurse.

"MOM!" Winter screamed. "MOM! NO! MOM! COME BACK!"

Her dad came in and wrapped his arms around her. She fought him, kicking and clawing, but he held her firm. The nurse turned off the monitor, and Dr. Lewis pulled the sheet over her mom's head.

"MOM!" The skin of her neck stretched beneath the strain of her grinding voice. After screaming, she sucked in air with the sound of fingernails on a chalkboard. Then she roared again.

Her dad picked her up like a small child and carried her from the room. Winter reached back in desperation. Her whole body shook with each agonizing breath. "MOM!"

75

Present Day

Winter knelt beside Kaci, images of her mother flashing through her thoughts.

Not this time.

Winter placed her tingling hands on Kaci's arm.

"You can't die!" she said. "Not yet! Not while I'm here!"

Her face burned and stretched as if the power of God were about to burst through. She leaned over and wept hot tears over Kaci's arm. The tears sizzled when they struck her skin.

"God, please! Even if it takes my life, let her live. I'll do whatever you want me to do. Just spare her life, please! You can heal her if you choose. Please! I plead for her life!"

Where her hands touched Kaci, strength left her body like flowing water. Her heart pounded and her body sagged. She opened her eyes but couldn't see. Dizziness washed over her, and she teetered backward. Her lungs burned. A sharp pain stabbed one side of her chest. Winter screamed.

Even if it takes my life. Winter held tighter, allowing everything in her to pass to Kaci.

Kaci gasped.

The machines and monitors went crazy, and then settled into steady rhythms. Dr. Freeman jerked away from Chris and grabbed Winter by the shoulders.

"What did you do?"

"Doctor, she's stabilized!" one of the nurses said. Dr. Freeman released Winter and ran to check the monitors.

Winter stumbled to her feet, then fell backward. Chris caught her by the shoulders and led her from the room. She couldn't see. She could barely breathe.

"She's breathing on her own," Dr. Freeman said, his voice filled with wonder.

Winter collapsed in Chris's arms and passed out.

An hour later, Dr. Freeman came back out and took a long look at Winter.

"Young lady, I don't know what you did," he said. "But the internal bleeding has stopped and the collapsed lung...well...fixed itself. And the bones! It's as if they were never broken. If I hadn't seen it for myself...What did you do?"

"I didn't do anything," she said. "God did."

"Does this mean..." Beverly said.

"That she'll make it? She already has. There was nothing left for us to do but close her up, and now she's being moved to the ICU for continued monitoring. But...I've never seen anything like it...it looks like she's going to make a complete recovery."

Winter, Beverly, and Chris embraced each other, and Chris led them in a prayer of thankfulness.

Dr. Freeman was still there watching when they finished.

"Do you actually believe God healed your daughter?" he asked.

"Yes we do," Chris said. "Can you think of any other explanation? It's nothing short of a miracle."

"But I don't understand," Dr. Freeman said. "If God is real, why do bad things happen in the first place?"

"This is a broken world," Winter said. "But it's not what God wants. It hurts him when we have to suffer. When my mom died, I thought God was punishing me. Now I realize that's not true, and now I understand he never really abandoned me at all."

"How can you say that? How can you have so much...hope?"

Winter looked at Chris for support.

He smiled. "Jesus is our hope. Would you like me to tell you more about him?"

Dr. Freeman checked his watch and glanced around. "I suppose I have time."

Winter followed Beverly, Chris and Dr. Freeman to the ICU, where they found a small waiting room beside a long nurses' station. One lone receptionist sat behind the counter, and a doctor stood nearby looking over a chart. Dr. Freeman approached the other doctor, and they spoke in hushed tones for several seconds. The new doctor grinned and gave Dr. Freeman a pat on the shoulder. Then both of them came over.

"I want to introduce you to Dr. Winston," Dr. Freeman said. "He'll be overseeing Kaci's treatment for the rest of her stay here."

"Nice to meet you," said Chris. He shook Dr. Winston's hand.

"I'll be checking in from time to time to see how's she's doing," said Dr. Freeman. "It really was a pleasure to meet all of you."

"Thank you, Dr. Freeman," Chris said.

"No, thank you." They shook hands and Dr. Freeman left.

Dr. Winston smiled. "I just want you three to know, I've been praying for Dr. Freeman for a very long time. I'm a man of faith, and I believe in miracles, but I never thought anything could break that man's shell." He rubbed his hand through his hair. "Your daughter has a long way to go, but I think she'll be just fine."

"I thought she was healed," said Winter.

"Major trauma, yes. But she's been through a lot, physically and mentally. The kind of healing she needs now is different. It may take some time. When she's settled in, I'll make sure you can visit her."

"Thank you, Doctor," Chris said.

Dr. Winston left, and the three of them found comfortable chairs where they could watch the TV mounted on the wall. As they waited, Summer and Davis came around the corner.

"You disappeared!" Summer said. "We've been looking all over for you!"

"Sorry," Winter said. "I didn't want to wake you."

Summer and Davis sat in chairs beside them.

"So," Davis said. "How's she doing?"

Chris, Beverly, and Winter all shared a warm smile.

"You tell them," Chris said.

Dr. Winston didn't come back until six-thirty in the morning.

"Okay, I'll let you see her now, but only a couple at a time," he said. "Chris, Beverly, would you like to come with me? Winter, you can see her after they come back."

Winter nodded, and Kaci's parents stood to follow Dr. Winston.

Summer and Davis tried to talk with Winter, but she couldn't focus through the exhaustion. The conversation felt weak and awkward at best.

Ten minutes after Kaci's parents had gone into the ICU, the double doors at the end of the hall opened. Detective Fox smiled at them and gave a wave. Peter Strong walked beside him with a small bounce to his step. Winter stood as they approached and took a deep breath. Peter came straight for her.

"Hi, I'm Peter," he said holding out his hand. He stood half a head taller than she—taller than she remembered. His brown hair was neatly trimmed now, and he had a small goatee and long sideburns. His blue eyes seemed to be measuring her…bright blue, just like hers.

"I'm Winter." She shook his hand.

"Listen, I just want to thank you for everything you've done. Detective Fox told me what happened while I was out." He smiled.

"It was nothing anyone else wouldn't have done," she said.

He furrowed his brow. "No, I think you're wrong. We don't even know each other. I don't think I've even seen you before. Why go to so much trouble for someone you don't know?"

"I guess I never considered knowing you to be a factor. I just did what God wanted me to do."

"Even so, not many people would go to those lengths, whether God told them to or not."

Winter shrugged. "I didn't really have a choice. To do what God tells me is a given. The consequences don't matter."

Peter smiled again. "You're an extraordinary person, Winter. Thank you. You've saved my life and, from what I've been told, the lives of others."

"So," Winter asked, "are you completely free now?"

"Not completely," Detective Fox said. "We still have to get his statement and some paperwork taken care of, but all that's really just a formality. Based on Kaci's ordeal and the confession you got, the DA dropped all charges."

"Congratulations," Winter said.

"I owe it to you."

"No," she said. "Owe it to God."

Peter shuffled his feet and shoved his hands in his pockets. "So, are you coming back to Tishbe next fall?"

"Yeah."

"Good. Maybe we can get to know each other better then. Looks like I've got to repeat junior year...maybe we'll share a few classes."

"But I'll only be a sophomore," she said.

He shrugged. "You never know."

"Let's go, Peter. I'd like to get everything done today so you can go home," Detective Fox said.

Peter hesitated, then took a step closer and hugged her. "Thank you again."

She smiled and closed her eyes.

He let her go and backpedaled a few steps. "See ya 'round," he said with a grin.

"Yeah, see ya."

Peter turned and followed Detective Fox away. Winter sighed and went back to her seat.

77

Four Years Ago

"Would the family like to view the body one final time?" the minister asked.

Winter stood between her dad and Claire. She suspected Claire had run away to be here...but today she really didn't care. Though the sun shone and birds twittered nearby, it couldn't warm the iciness inside of her.

Winter stepped to the casket, her dad by her side. Her mom wore a blue sundress. Her last smile still graced her face.

Winter ground her teeth, wondering what kind of god could allow this to happen and still be the same god that had given her mom that smile. She didn't understand—she didn't want to understand. In less than a year, her life had been ruined.

She felt hollow inside...dead like her mom. It was as if someone had scooped out her heart and soul, leaving a black hole. She could no longer feel sorrow or pain, only emptiness.

Winter went back. Claire reached over and grabbed Winter's hand, but Winter left her fingers limp.

Men removed the flowers from the white casket and closed the lid. One of them walked to the side and stepped on a switch. The casket began to lower into the ground.

"And now," the minister said. "A reading from the book of Isaiah, chapter fifty-one.

"Look up to the skies above,
and gaze down on the earth below.
For the skies will disappear like smoke,
and the earth will wear out like a piece of clothing.
The people of the earth will die like flies,
but my salvation lasts forever.
My righteous rule will never end!
Listen to me, you who know right from wrong
you who cherish my law in your hearts.
Do not be afraid of people's scorn,
nor fear their insults.
For the moth will devour them as it devours clothing.
The worm will eat at them as it eats wool.
But my righteousness will last forever.
My salvation will continue from generation to generation.
Wake up, wake up, O Lord! Clothe yourself with strength!
Flex your mighty right arm!
Rouse yourself as in the days of old
when you slew Egypt, the dragon of the Nile.
Are you not the same today,
the one who dried up the sea,
making a path of escape through the depths
so that your people could cross over?
Those who have been ransomed by the Lord will return.
They will enter Jerusalem singing,
crowned with everlasting joy.

Sorrow and mourning will disappear,
and they will be filled with joy and gladness.
I, yes I, am the one who comforts you."

Winter crossed her arms and scoffed. The minister was an idiot.

Present Day

As soon as Peter and Detective Fox had left, Winter's dad came in. He ran to her and snatched her from the chair, giving her a crushing hug.

"Are you all right?" he asked.

"I'm fine, Dad."

"And Kaci?"

"She'll be fine too."

He let her go and they both sat down by Summer and Davis.

"I'm sorry we have to leave so soon, sweetheart."

"It's okay, Dad. I understand. There's not much for me to do here anymore anyway. Thanks for not completely freaking out when I called."

"When do you want to go, then?" he asked.

"I want to see Kaci one last time," she said.

He nodded.

Chris and Beverly came back through the doors as if on cue.

"Okay, Winter. Your turn," said Chris. "But she's not awake."

Beverly grabbed Winter's hand. "They let us have this." She pressed Winter's locket into her palm.

Winter looked at it a moment, her eyes tracing the rust-colored blood stains. "Thank you," she said, as she squeezed Beverly's hand.

Winter set her jaw and stood, placing the locket in her pocket. Her dad reached out to her and touched her arm. She smiled at him and walked to the double doors.

This ICU was different than the one her mom had stayed in. The nurses' station stood in the center, and glass rooms surrounded it on all sides. Dr. Winston waited behind the station and motioned for her to come closer.

"This way," he said. He led her across the room to ICU room number six. He opened the door for her and left.

Winter walked to Kaci's side. She grabbed a chair and pulled it close. Gauze still wrapped most of Kaci's face and neck, her swollen eyes barely visible through a small gap. The tube in Kaci's mouth had been removed, replaced by an oxygen tube to her nose. The monitors beeped with a steady rhythm, and the oxygen machine hissed softly.

Kaci's bandaged right arm lay on top of the sheets, an IV taped to her wrist. Winter reached out and took Kaci's hand.

"When my mom died," Winter said, "the minister read a passage from Isaiah. I've read it hundreds of times since then, and even memorized parts of it. Only in the last year have I begun to understand what it means, and even now I think I understand a little bit more. It says:

"Listen to me, you who know right from wrong, you who cherish my law in your hearts.

"That means you, Kaci.

"Do not be afraid of people's scorn, nor fear their insults. For the moth will devour them as it devours clothing. The worm will eat at them as it eats wool. But my righteousness will last forever.

"It means that when bad things happen, don't be afraid. The people who did this will get what's coming to them. God won't forget. This life is only temporary, and there will be judgment for all evil people. They'll pass away, but God and his righteousness will last forever. Cling to that righteousness, Kaci, and you'll be okay.

"And I know it's going to be hard." Winter put her other hand to her mouth and stifled a sob. "But I know you can do it. You're a strong person, and you shouldn't let this get you down. Don't let Satan defeat you. Come back stronger than ever, do you hear me?"

Winter paused and looked at the floor.

"I'm sorry this happened to you. I should have been there faster, Kaci—I'm so sorry. I knew something bad was going to happen, and I could have stopped this. But I didn't. I didn't because I was afraid you wouldn't understand—I was afraid you wouldn't listen. If I could change anything, I would trade places with you. Godly people like you should never have to go through something like this. It's people like me that deserve this kind of pain." She sniffed back a tear, and one quiet cry escaped.

"I promise I'll come see you this summer. I'll see you as much as I can, and I'll call you so much you'll get sick of me. You're my best friend. I haven't had a friend like you in a very long time, not since my mother died. I can't come back to school without you—I need you and your strength. Without you, I wouldn't be as close to God as I am, and I wouldn't know how to use this gift he's given me. With you, I'm the person I've always wanted to be—I'm the person I should be. And I don't think I could do it without you. So you see, you must get better. Besides, you've already committed to being my roommate next year, and you can't back out now. Summer's going to be an RA and, well, I don't like meeting new people. So you've got to come be my roommate, okay?"

Winter felt her throat tighten. Somehow, her body managed to produce more tears. "I love you, Kaci. Don't go away from me, okay? You can get past this, and I'll be there to help. I love you—remember that!" She squeezed Kaci's hand.

Kaci squeezed back.

Winter walked back through the doors into the waiting room, rubbing the tears out of her eyes with the heels of her hands.

"Is everything okay?" asked her dad.

"She squeezed my hand," she said with a small smile.

"What?" said Beverly. Kaci's parents leaped out of their seats and rushed back into the ICU.

"We need to go soon," her dad said.

Winter nodded. "Let me just say goodbye."

"Okay. I'll wait for you in the truck. Summer, it was good to see you again and, Davis, it was good to finally meet you."

Summer and Davis stood. Her dad gave Summer a quick hug and shook hands with Davis. Then he turned to leave.

Winter gave Summer and Davis both warm hugs, but as much as she wanted to, she could not concentrate on saying goodbye. Her mind was elsewhere.

On Xaphan.

"What's the matter?" Summer asked.

Hot anger rose within Winter again. She pulled the locket out and studied it. She pried it open and looked at the picture inside, remembering her mother and the unwavering faith she showed just before dying. Winter read the inscription again, like she had done hundreds of times. Never forget. Never forget her mom. Never forget to be happy. Never forget to love. Never forget about God.

She closed the locket and studied the dark stains on the outside. Kaci's blood. Never forget.

"Xaphan got away," she said through clenched teeth. She closed her fist around the locket.

"There's nothing you could have done," Davis said.

"But I can do something now," she said. "I can find him and stop him. I can't let him get away with what he's done to Kaci."

"But, Winter, what can you do?" Summer asked. "You barely made it away from him alive yourself."

"That was before I realized who I am," she said, "before I realized what God wants me to be."

"And what is that?" asked Davis.

"You were right before, Davis. Xaphan may have chosen me to be his so-called prophet, but God chose me first."

"Winter," Davis said. "I think you misunderstood me—I meant that you have the gift of prophecy, and you needed that to find Kaci. But having the gift of prophecy and being a prophet are two completely different things. Just because you have visions, that doesn't make you a prophet. You know that...you told me that yourself."

"God's not done with me yet," Winter said, "and the correct term is prophetess."

"Winter, don't fool yourself. You're not a prophet. If you go after him, he's going to kill you!" Davis said. "Besides, there's nothing a prophet can do that will do any good against someone like Xaphan. It's useless."

Winter squeezed her eyes shut and said a prayer for guidance. It came as a mighty rush of God's power and anger. When she opened her eyes they burned like coals, but she felt no pain. Her skin seemed to stretch tight, and the rumble of thunder returned to her ears.

"You obviously don't know much about the prophets." Her voice sounded strange to her, like the thunder in her ears had come out of her throat.

She gripped the two ends of the locket's chain and wrapped it around her neck.

Summer took a step back and a look of fear crossed her face. "Winter ...your eyes. They're...they're..."

"Glowing," Davis said. He stepped back with Summer.

"If God wants me to be a prophetess..." Winter said.

Her hair began to ruffle in a phantom wind. The wind swirled around her body, making the sleeves of her shirt flap.

Summer and Davis seemed to have stopped breathing, and the blood drained from their faces. They took several more trembling steps away from her.

"...then I will be the greatest there has ever been!"

She spun and started walking toward the double doors. The fire in her eyes raged, and she could see things more clearly than ever. Through the rumbling, she heard the very heartbeats of every person in the room. The wind accelerated and blew her hair wild. As she passed by the nurses' station, papers scattered and flew around in a supernatural cyclone. The lights overhead flickered with her passing—one fluorescent bulb exploded, sending a shower of sparks and glass down to the floor.

And as she approached the double doors, they burst open before she even touched them.

Then God said,
"Behold, I am going to make a covenant.
Before all your people I will perform miracles which
have not been produced in all the earth nor among
any of the nations;
and all the people among whom you live
will see the working of the LORD,
for it is a fearful thing
that I am going to perform with you."
Exodus 34:10 (NAS)

Winter's story continues in

Prophetess
Winter Book 2
ISBN: 978-0-9989596-2-7

By Keven Newsome

One act of violence is not enough to fulfill Xaphan's plans. One near escape does not justify Winter's growing gift.

There is more. She can feel it. The warnings swell within her. He's searching for someone. A person of promise...a person of prophecy.

And Winter must find her first.

ABOUT THE AUTHOR

Keven Newsome began his writing career at the young age of ten by creating fanfiction of his favorite video game. He only wrote four pages, though, painstakingly in King James English since that's how they spoke in the game. It was horrible and he promptly abandoned his writing career forever. Thankfully, some years later, fourteen-year-old Keven disagreed with that hasty decision and discovered writing could actually be fun. Since then he has authored five novels, published four of those, and written and published several short stories. He has also recently returned to his favorite video game and become an award-winning fanfiction author on Wattpad. The four books of his Winter series, *Winter, Prophetess, Acolyte,* and *Mantle,* have together been finalists for seven awards and winners of three of those. Originally from south Mississippi, he and his wife live a nomadic ministry life, followed relentlessly by the collective cries of his fans to finish writing his next book already.

http://kevennewsome.com
https://linktr.ee/knewsome.author

www.ingramcontent.com/pod-product-compliance
Lightning Source LLC
Chambersburg PA
CBHW051210120726
47905CB00004B/1065